The heliplane lowered itself down through the gassy lights, swaying past knots of people spectating from behind the glass mantles.

Mhairi studied the fifth module and glimpsed a woman's lonely silhouette on an upper floor. Then dirt and snow blown up by the rotors blotted everything out and the heliplane grounded. Mhairi remained seated, reluctant to move. A ground blizzard reduced the complex to a fluorescent blur and shivered the craft on its undercarriage.

'I suggest you wrap up,' Grippe told her. 'It's rather raw outside.'

Despite the warning, she was unprepared for the savagery of the wind. It punched the breath back down her throat and buffeted her sideways.

'My God,' she shouted, 'how can you bear to live in such a godforsaken place?'

Grippe's horse teeth glistened.

'What?' Mhairi shouted.

Grippe gulped for breath and cupped his mouth against the gale. 'I said, up here Zygote stands in for God.'

Windsor Chorlton was born in the north of England and worked for an international publisher before taking up full-time writing. A wilderness expedition to study a Tibetan Buddhist community in the Himalayas inspired his first acclaimed novel *Rites of Sacrifice*. *Cold Fusion* is his fifth thriller, and he has also written a book on ice ages. Windsor Chorlton lives in Dorset with his wife and daughter.

By the same author

Rites of Sacrifice
Canceleer
Blind Junction
Latitude Zero

COLD
FUSION

WINDSOR
CHORLTON

ORION

An Orion paperback
First published in Great Britain by Orion in 1999
This paperback edition published in 1999 by Orion Books Ltd,
Orion House, 5 Upper St Martin's Lane, London WC2H 9EA

'The End of the World' from *Poems of Thirty Years* by
Gordon Bottomley, 1925. Reproduced by kind permission of
Constable Ltd.
Grateful acknowledgement is made for permission to quote from
'Personality' by Harold Logan and Lloyd Price. Copyright © 1959
MCA Music Ltd.

A CIP catalogue record for this book is available from the
British Library.

ISBN: 0 75282 619 0

Typeset at The Spartan Press Ltd, Lymington, Hants
Printed and bound in Great Britain by Clays Ltd, St Ives plc.

The snow had fallen many nights and days;
The sky was come upon the world at last,
Sifting thinly down as endlessly
As though within the system of blind planets
Something had been forgot or overdriven.

Gordon Bottomley, *The End of the World*

ACKNOWLEDGMENTS

I would like to thank the following for their help.

Dr Dan Thompson, Dr Jenny Thompson and Dr Toby Thompson gave me invaluable information on coma, neuroprostheses and retroviruses.

Pippa Falstrup and Sam, Andrew and James Thompson helped boost my enthusiasm for the story during the early stages of writing.

Jane Wood and Robyn Karney spared me a lot of blushes by their astute editing.

Most of all, I'm indebted to Deborah and Lily Chorlton for their encouragement and support.

PROLOGUE

The pickup was shot to hell, its tailgate a colander and the windshield shattered. Masked against the icy slipstream, the driver kept the throttle pressed to the floor. The juggernaut chasing them had run him off the dirt track and now he was bucking across frozen tundra.

He squinted into the rearview. 'They still with us?'

The Vag beside him swung her head in a response that could have meant anything. A drift of snow exploded over the hood.

'Hang on!'

The Vag's head whiplashed as the truck leapt a crest and landed with a shock that drove a grunt from her belly. She pitched again, smacking her chin on the dash as the truck nose-dived to a stop.

Below them, a fence drew a taut line across the barrens.

The driver unlocked his hands from the wheel and pulled his mask down. He was about forty, dark-haired with a lean, tensile face and the kind of eyes that made most men step quietly around him.

'Figure out where we are.'

He dropped to the shale and scrambled up to the ridge. The land to the north ran away in grey and silver planes. He cupped his numb hands to his mouth and stood listening.

Stark silence. Desolation. Nothing stirring.

He gave it five minutes, alternately blowing into his hands and holding his breath. At last he turned and slithered back to the truck.

'Lost or quit.'

The Vag had got the map out, but didn't look like she'd moved a muscle. She was only a girl, pale skin pulled tight over her cheekbones, eyes shocked to points.

'What happened back there?' she murmured.

'Got themselves killed, like I said they would.'

She nodded in meek acceptance.

The man looked at her quickly. 'Were they kin to you?'

'Friends. They took me in when my parents died. One of them was my boyfriend.'

The man stared away, his jaw set, thinking of the six lost lives he'd pledged himself to saving. In the last eighteen months he'd got more than thirty Vags out of the permafrost belt. This run, he'd started out twelve days ago from Spokane with two families and this girl, the only survivor.

He looked into the sun without blinking. They'd stayed clear of trouble until they reached Blitzen, fifty miles from the Nevada border, where a True North militia roadblock had forced them east on a diversion that used up most of their food and gas. That morning they'd passed a turnoff to a backroads township, and the Vags had insisted on going in to barter for fuel. When he'd told them not to be crazy, they'd put it to a vote, for chrissakes, and the upshot was that six of them, armed and feeling secure in numbers, had driven down to the settlement in the second vehicle. After waiting fifteen minutes, the driver had got out, softly cursing, and told the girl that if he wasn't back in an hour, she should drive south and hand herself over to the first troopers she met.

She didn't have to wait that long. Forty minutes later, she heard gunfire and saw him come running up the track, weaponless and pursued by a funnel of dust with an armoured wagon at its core.

Now she surveyed the fence tapering away in both directions. 'Is that the Line?'

The driver absently plucked a sliver of glass from his cheek. This territory was strange to him; usually he made the crossing fifty miles further west.

'Reckon not. Maybe some kind of military installation.'

He took the map and tried to work out their position. Eventually his finger sighted on a reef of mountains running in strange corrugations towards the south.

'Must be the Pine Forest Range. Nothing but lake and desert for the next hundred miles.'

Blood squeezed back into his frost-bitten fingers. Pulp filled with splinters. He clamped his hands under his armpits and hissed. The girl cast an anxious glance back up their tracks.

He gave her a watery smile. 'You're right. Best get moving.'

He slipped the truck into gear and idled down the grade, aiming for one of the signs posted at intervals along the fence. He rolled to a halt just close enough to read the warning.

DANGER OF DEATH
TOTAL EXCLUSION ZONE. DO NOT CROSS PERIMETER.
ARMED RANGERS PATROLLING. ALL TRESPASSERS WILL BE SHOT
Genesis Ranching Corporation

'What would they be ranching up here?' the girl said, her voice just audible above the dawdling engine. 'There's nothing to eat except moss and lichens.'

The man killed the motor and surveyed the basin fading into dirty oblivion. 'Tundra species. Caribou, musk oxen. Or maybe the techies have engineered cows that can live in the arctic.'

He examined the structure. It was about fifteen feet high, topped by two cables insulated from the heavy-gauge mesh. He couldn't see any sensors or cameras. He shouldered his door open.

'Wait here.'

Twenty yards short of the perimeter, the air came alive, zinging with electricity.

He had set off the alarm.

Grimacing, the man eased up to the fence. Behind it was a ditch about five feet deep and ten wide, with a four-strand electrified fence on the far bank. The placement of the strands was eccentric – a bottom pair about one foot and three feet off the ground, the third strand three or four feet higher, then a five-foot gap to the top wire.

'Stock fence, activated by body heat or infra-red.'

The girl had climbed out. She turned as if alerted to some impending upheaval. 'I don't like this place.'

Neither did the man. He tracked the fence to dwindling point in both directions. 'We'll drive around it.'

3

They covered two miles before running up against a dry creek too deep to cross. The fissure zigzagged up to the ridge and there were more wash-outs on the other side. The end of the fence still wasn't in sight.

'Maybe we should go back,' the girl said. 'Hide up till evening, then cut back to the road.'

'If we follow the road, we'll get picked up as soon as we hit the Line. That means prison for me and Vag camp for you. *That's* if we're lucky. Catch a bad break and we could end up . . .'

The girl's eyes had widened.

The man turned and his scalp lifted. 'Hellfire.'

Silhouetted on the skyline where they'd halted was the squat black shape of the wagon.

The man's eyes skittered. He looked hard at the creek bed where flash floods had undermined the fence, exposing the bottom strand.

'Grab the gear. We're going under.'

'But the warning.'

'To hell with that.'

The man dropped into the gulch and fell to his knees, hands clawed in dread of electrocution. He screwed up his eyes and grabbed.

'Dead!'

He began digging.

'They're coming!'

The wagon was slip-sliding towards them on a steep traverse. The girl's attention switched back and forth, measuring the vehicle's progress against the slowly widening gap.

'They're halfway.'

The man cursed his useless hands. He unsheathed a knife and hacked at the compacted surface. His hair flopped over his eyes.

The wagon was close enough now for the girl to make out the slit in the armour plated over the windshield.

'Hurry,' she whimpered. 'Hurry, hurry!'

'Get down here! Help me!'

With a last terrified glance, she scrambled into the gully and began clawing at the hardpan. The gap was still no more than

4

seven or eight inches high and not much wider. The man rose to his knees and saw the wagon now less than half a mile away. He pushed the girl flat.

'Go!'

She squeezed her head and one shoulder through before jamming, kicking like a swimmer trapped in a net. The man hauled on the straining wire. One more squirm and she was through. As she rose to all fours, one of the backpacks sailed over the fence and landed with a thump. The second one caught the top and slid back, bridging the live cables with an explosive flash.

The man left it. He threw himself on to his belly and forced his arms through the hole. The girl grabbed his wrist, but he shook her off. He was much bigger than her, bulked out by layers of clothing. Watching him struggle, she knew it was a physical impossibility, and when he realised it too, he stopped fighting and arched his face up.

'Get going,' he told her calmly. 'Head south.'

'No,' she sobbed, and seized hold of his hands. She dropped back on her heels and heaved until her shoulders were on the point of popping. Slowly, like a cork being drawn from a bottle, she felt the man coming through. Another heave and she was flat on her back, the man trampling her, trying to find his feet. He hauled her upright, grabbed the remaining backpack with one hand and pushed her up the ditch. She ran in a crouching stumble, vaguely aware of bullets smacking off the shale and plucking at the fence.

She ran until she couldn't run any more and collapsed against the side of the ditch. Breath whooping, she saw two figures toiling over the broken ground on the other side of the fence.

The man pushed her into motion again. 'Keep going. They won't catch us unless they come through.'

Half a mile further on, he jammed the pack under the bottom strand of the stock fence, lifted the girl around the thighs and boosted her under. As he followed, his arm dislodged the pack and the live wire twanged across his shoulders. The current cut

5

in with a wallop that almost stopped his heart. He took another surge before he rolled clear.

'Jesus!'

Dizzied by the shocks, he staggered away. The girl trotted after him until her legs slurred and she sprawled.

'It's no good,' she gasped.

The man began to yank her up, then relaxed, slowly straightening. 'Easy now, easy. They ain't following.'

She rolled over, broken-winded, and saw the figures that had been chasing them static behind the fence, four or five others clumped by the wagon.

The man shrugged off her unspoken question and looked into the ill-omened light to the south.

'I guess we're in someone else's territory now.'

They walked until the fence was gone from sight and cold desert pressed all around them. There the man halted to take account. The pack they'd salvaged contained a sleeping bag, a few cans of food, some rock-hard bread and a propane stove. He walked up a rise and scouted across a mosaic of snow and gravel flats and petrified thickets of sagebrush. Dead, everything leached of colour, like a sepia negative viewed through dull light. He consulted the map again, converting the few inches of contours into journey time. Even if they managed to breach the fence on the southern side, it would take them at least two days to reach the next two-laner.

The girl was watching him, silently dependent. He smiled falsely. 'Nothing to stop us walking clear through to Mexico.' He hoisted the pack. 'Ready?'

He led her across the vast and hushed bowl. Above them, the sun was a black blister ringed by a halo of ice, and in its impoverished light they cast no shadows. The sagebrush parted before them with dry shivers. Several times in that solitude they came upon the chalky skeletons of cattle, but apart from a couple of ravens quarrelling over a bone, they saw no sign of any living thing.

6

'Maybe Genesis pulled out,' the girl said.

'Leaving the juice switched on?'

They trudged on, retreating into their own thoughts. The emptiness bore on their spirits. A breeze sprang up and fretted at the scrub. Down the wind came a distant moaning that made the man stop and search the horizon behind.

Their feet grew heavy and senseless. At dusk, the soft lights of the aurora swirled overhead. Almost sightless in the weird twilight, they barged together in fright as something started up with a snort and lumbered invisibly away. After a moment, the man detached himself from the girl's grip.

In the pale green and rose glow of the aurora, he could just make out where a patch of mosses had been raked away. To one side of the scrape was a circular shadow. Feeling it, his hand traced a depression as large as a dinner plate. There was another about six feet away. His eyes followed the spoor into the dark. A musty odour spiced the cold air.

'I'll be damned!'

Twenty yards away, the girl's face shone pale as a paper lantern. 'What was it?'

'Musk ox,' he lied.

'Can we stop?'

He scanned the dark without moving his head. 'Not here.'

He located a swale where they wouldn't be skylined. Not risking a fire, he heated a can of beans on the stove. They ate under the shared sleeping bag, and when they'd finished, they lay close to conserve heat.

The girl watched the boreal lights. They were as beguiling as spirits, one moment leading her gaze into space, the next streaming back into a gauzy curtain that hung in folds, its hem apparently so close that she reached out to touch it. The Rapture, people called it – the Rapture that would sweep them up from a world doomed to extinction.

'Where are we aiming?' she asked.

'Black Rock Desert, near the Argo launch site. You know about the space probe?'

The girl hadn't heard a radio or TV broadcast for three years.

7

Any news that filtered above the Line arrived as distorted as Chinese whispers. 'Have they really found an inhabitable planet?'

'So they say – Virginia Nova, ten light years away, about the same size as Earth, with oxygen and water and living organisms. Argo's heading out there next fall. You'll be able to watch the launch.'

She was quiet for a while. 'I don't know what I'm going to do. I haven't got any relatives south of the Line.'

The man thought of his own dear, dead daughter. 'You stay with me as long as you like. I'll find you work.'

'I'd like to go back to college. I've missed three years' schooling.'

'You can catch up.' He rolled over. 'Get some rest now. We start early. I want to be clear of this place by dawn.'

She tried to let the lights lull her to rest, but the cold soaked into her kidneys, reducing sleep to fleeting interludes between bouts of shivering.

In one span of wakefulness, she levered herself up at the sound of an eerie cry, pitched between laughter and moaning, drifting from a distance and direction hard to gauge. From the tension in the man's body, she could tell that he'd heard it too.

'Are those wolves?' she whispered.

He didn't answer.

She tugged at his arm. 'Those aren't wolves!'

'Hush.'

They held their breath. In the dark the man looked half wolf himself. The chorus rose to a demented yodelling that stopped abruptly. In the silence, the girl could feel fear bumping against the walls of her heart.

'They're after us.'

The man thought about the odd spacing of the stock fence and the tracks of the animal they'd spooked. Genesis. He threw aside the sleeping bag.

The girl scrambled after him. 'Don't leave me.'

The man slashed at the sagebrush. 'Quick, build a fire.'

The girl ferried the brush as fast as he could gather it. She'd

8

built a stack waist-high and had hurried back for another load when he checked her. He slowly turned his head.

'They're close.'

'What are?' She beat at his chest. 'What are?' Suddenly she was crying.

'Ssh.' He placed a finger to her lips.

Her stare followed his. Somewhere off to the right, gravel trickled. The girl's eyes opened as wide as lamps. She thought she heard a clinking behind her and swung with a gasp. Every direction harboured danger.

'Light the fire! Light the fire!'

'That brush is dry as a bone. Don't want to waste it.'

She seized his arm. She felt his muscles tighten and gripped harder.

He aimed with his knife. 'There they are.'

'Where? I can't see anything. Damn it, why are you frightening me like . . . ?'

A sob of tragic laughter froze her tongue to the roof of her mouth. In one move she pressed up against the man.

'See? Up on the rise. About a dozen of them.'

At first she couldn't make out anything real, and her imagination transformed clumps of brush into monsters. But when she did see them, they were as hideous as anything conjured by nightmare. They configured out of the dark in a loose line, dog-like but alien, high humped shoulders caped in midnight fur. Everything went loose inside her.

'Oh my God!'

The glow of the Rapture painted highlights on their manes and struck sparks from their eyes. They closed in until she could see their primitive details – bat-faces with noses like holes, massive forequarters sloping down to rumps like an afterthought.

'They're going to eat us!'

The man separated some scrub from the pile and flicked the lighter. The fuel was ten years dead and flared up in tarry flames. Arrested by the firelight, the beasts lolloped off, shoulders hunched and tails curled under their bellies.

9

The girl searched the darkness. A minute passed, then the baleful eyes floated back. She breathed in sharp gasps.

The man picked out a burning brand and ran at the pack.

'Don't leave me!' the girl screamed.

Four times the man made sorties against the beasts. After each scattering they regrouped a little closer. He recognised some kind of hierarchy and pack strategy at work. The fourth time they held their ground until he was right up to them. He swung his boot at the nearest beast, but it skipped out of range, and suddenly he was sweating, panicking under the weight of numbers. He went back to the fire and cudgelled his brain for some effective defence. A few hours ago he'd possessed an arsenal; now, he'd give anything for a club or spear.

The girl watched him feed the fire another branch and looked at the diminishing stack and thought of all the hours until daylight. She began to weep.

The man turned to her and the hardness left his eyes. He hugged her to his chest as if he was trying to squeeze her inside him.

The beasts had gone quiet. They were patient. One of them flopped on its rump and scratched energetically. Half-grown pups romped behind the adults.

Piece by piece the man doled out the fuel. The time came when he laid the last branch. It spluttered and burned and the flames died. The girl watched the coals glow hot and then dwindle to grey.

All they could do was wait.

It wasn't long. One of the beasts trotted out and bared its teeth. The man eyed it, primitive rage rising in him like a drug. Bellowing obscenities, he sprang up and charged. The beast skittered sideways, losing its footing, and for a moment he thought he'd got it, but as his knife slashed down it recovered its balance and darted away. The man's momentum carried him too far and he knew he'd been outwitted when he saw out of the corner of his eye shadows glide between him and the girl. It had been a feint. He pivoted desperately but jaws clamped on to his left leg. Blindly he stabbed and felt the knife turn on bone. Still the beast hung on, wrenching. Reversing his hold, the man drove the blade up between its legs. It released him and fled, doubled up and pursued by some of its ravenous associates. He saw the girl beleaguered, took a step towards her and his leg buckled under him.

Ten feet away, the girl stared mesmerised into the gargoyle face of the beast that had appeared confidingly at her knees. Its eyes looked into hers as if it wanted to explain, then its head exploded forward and its jaws met in her thigh. After the first excruciating shock, she suffered no pain. The beast shifted its grip, its black eyes still fixed on her, then they closed and with one violent shake it pulled her to the ground.

Other muzzles bored in. She felt a ragged upheaval in her belly and then, completely anaesthetised, she watched one of the beasts backing away, unravelling her intestines. Another was tugging at her splintered arm. She was dimly aware of the man yelling, but the sound had no volume and her vision was closing down, spinning slow and dark around a light that reduced to a tiny dot.

And then, not even that.

Trapped as in an underwater nightmare, the man crawled towards her. The beasts were butchering her before his eyes, worrying away jawfuls of her flesh. He lurched to his feet and struck out like a madman. Around him the sagebrush was frosted with silver and the beasts had grown so distinct that he could see their dripping muzzles and the scars on their hoary hides. His shadow cavorted among them, and then they vanished.

He staggered, and raised his hand against a burst of diamond brightness. Blinking stupidly, he swayed back and toppled over the backpack. He fell on his side, put his hand to his leg and felt a hole where the beast had torn a piece out of his calf.

He hooked the pack over one arm and began to crawl away. Brute instinct impelled him. A hole, he thought. Find a hole. The beam followed him. When it swung off, the darkness was as much sanctuary as he wanted. He pulled himself back against a clump of sage and stuck out his injured leg. Bone gleamed in the oozing crater.

The beam stopped at the remains of the girl. He saw two figures cross it. He tried to spit the foul taste out of his mouth. He grew colder and his teeth began to chatter. The sound of the vehicle starting up stirred him from a semi-swoon. The axis of light zeroed in on him again. It wheeled a full circle around him before halting fifty yards off. An electric motor spun to rest. Two figures walked down the beam and stopped ten yards away. The light was too harsh to see the men's faces behind it.

'Got yourself a nasty nip there,' one said.

The man made no response.

'Can't you read? We've been watching you since you crossed the perimeter.'

Masking his eyes with a hand, the man made out a hard-bitten face crevassed by weather lines. 'Why didn't you pick us up?'

'Knew you weren't armed. The guys who bred those brutes wanted to see how you'd make out.' The ranger glanced over his shoulder. 'Who's the other happy camper?'

'She was just a girl.'

'A Vag,' said the ranger. He hunkered down and pushed back his hat, frowning. 'You ain't no Vag, though. You're a tracer, ain't you?'

'Just quit your yapping and shoot me.'

'Hell, no. Those creatures ain't through feeding yet.'

'You'd best shoot me, mister.'

The ranger looked down with a musical sigh, then placed both hands on his knees and pushed himself up. He cupped a radio to his mouth. 'Echo North to base, do you copy? Yeah, we found 'em – one code seven. A Vag. Nothing much left. And a tracer. No, he's still alive. Just about to make his last run.'

ONE

1

Time is short. Right now, the world is in the final countdown. Right now, my friends, right now. But John the redeemer is coming. He's coming to save you. He's travelling back to Earth through the cold vacuum of space. My friends, he's coming right now!

Cope's eyes darted under their lids and flicked open.

Bands of coloured vapours drifted past with dreamy slowness. He stared into them with the fixity of a dead man, listening to the blood pumping through his heart, the hiss of filtered oxygen, the remote hum of engines. Shadows swam out of the haze, hardened into objects that were recognisable without being familiar. He was in a glass capsule, looking out through clouds of interstellar gas.

So he was in space, he thought vacantly. Nothing out there but the unearthly lights.

God-like detachment gave way to an awareness of mild discomfort, one hand numb, his face pushed out of shape against his shoulder. Too drowsy to move, he found himself beginning to roll over with no effort on his part and, as he turned, his body came in sight, stretched out like an unfamiliar island on a silvery sea, naked except for a pair of shorts, planted all over with electrodes and tubes and wires that snaked out of sight.

Life support systems for his intergalactic journey.

His cabin was only a tiny part of the spacecraft. Behind the glass wall on this side was a semi-dark chamber filled with phantom shapes. His gaze wandered across them and came to rest on one that seemed more significant than the rest. He studied it, trying to isolate it from the reflections in the curved glass, and after a while it dawned on him that he was looking at another human. He had the impression it was a scated woman.

A companion on his voyage through the universe, he

assumed, and wondered with idle curiosity who she was. He had no idea how long he'd been inside the bubble. The sense of floating dislocation suggested that he'd been asleep for a long time — so long that it felt more like a place than a state, somewhere far away and strange.

He waited for the woman to look his way. His attention began to meander and he caught himself just before he dropped off. 'Hey,' he called — or would have if his mouth had obeyed his brain. He tried to speak and no words came. It was like one of those dreams where wish won't translate into action — at first frustrating, almost comical, then frightening. But this wasn't a dream.

Help!

Her face turned, a pale blur. Very slowly, she levered herself up, sending something crashing to the floor. She trance-walked out of the shadows — mousy with a thin, blanched face, gawking at something above and behind him. She blinked and gave her head a little shake before lowering her gaze to his.

'John?' she whispered, as if addressing a presence only suspected. 'John?'

That jolted him. Was John his name? He didn't know. And then in a rush he realised he didn't know anything except that he was somewhere in space. He didn't know who he was or where he had come from or what he was doing in this glass bubble. Straining to remember, he had the sensation of spiralling down a brilliantly lit shaft with only white light at the bottom. His fear grew to a flame.

'John, you can't see them, but behind you are a dozen monitors. They indicate that you're conscious. I need to know if you can hear me.'

No matter how he struggled, he couldn't break loose from the smothering muteness.

'John,' the woman said, and gave a broken laugh. 'I'm sorry, I don't know if that's your real name. It's what we call you. *My* name is Dr Scritti — Monica. I'm a scientist. I'm one of the team who . . .' She stifled a sob with her hand.

Cope watched her with frightened incomprehension.

'John, speak if you can hear me. Make a sound.'

Again, the message from Cope's brain never reached his throat. He clung to the woman's stare, scared she would lose interest in him and go away.

'Try to move your right hand.'

Cope could see it on the periphery of his vision. He watched his fingers clench and slacken, but the movement was all in his mind. The flame died, leaving him chilled. I'm paralysed, he thought.

'Oh, your eyes moved! John, if you can hear me, blink your eyes.'

This might be his last chance. If he failed, the woman would turn away, leaving him sealed inside the cave of his own mind. He pictured his eyes. He imagined his brain. He mapped the pathway between them. Only when he'd got everything worked out did he try to make the connection. He felt the soft scrape of lashes against skin.

The woman clapped her hands. 'Again!'

Madly he blinked away.

'Oh my God!' The woman was as white as her tunic. 'John, I know you're frightened, but you're perfectly safe. You're in a clinic. You've been in a coma. I have to tell my colleagues you've regained consciousness. I won't be long,' She bit her knuckles. 'Oh, John!'

She backed out of sight and a door gulped shut behind her. Left in the quasi-silence, Cope made another effort to sift something solid from the mental soup. He couldn't remember anything and his eyes were the only part of his body he could move at will, but if he was paralysed, why could he feel pins and needles in his left hand? How come he could feel muscles tensing rhythmically in his abdomen, in his calves?

Again without volition on his part, he turned over until he was facing the lights once more. He stared into them, hypnotised by the emptiness in his head.

Urgent footsteps entered the room. In some defensive reflex, Cope shut his eyes. The footsteps halted.

'Good grief,' a male voice said, faint with wonderment.

'What were you doing in here?' a harsher voice demanded. 'What the hell is that mess on the floor? Who installed the TV? For Christ's sake, Dr Scritti, this isn't a cafeteria.'

'I visit John every evening. I wash him, analyse the readouts, take samples, check the prosthetic implants.'

'We employ technicians to take care of that. You're a molecular biologist, Dr Scritti, not a nurse.'

'I enjoy looking after John. It gives me a chance to catch up with myself. I talk to him. I discuss my work.'

'Your work? And what does John have to say about that?'

The woman didn't answer.

'Were you talking to him when his brain activity increased?' the gentler voice asked.

'No, I'd been watching the news – a report about that cult leader who's causing trouble up at the Argo launch site. I had that crawly sensation you get when you sense someone behind you, and I turned and saw the monitors. Then I realised John was staring at me. I mean, consciously staring.'

'But he didn't speak or gesture.'

'I asked him to blink if he could hear me. He did.'

'He often blinks,' the harsh voice said, 'It's only primitive reflex, decorticate posturing.'

'No, he repeated the response on command.'

'He's not responding now,' the harsh voice said. 'Are you sure you didn't imagine it?'

'The brain traces don't lie,' the soft voice said.

There was a lengthy pause.

'It's a miracle,' the woman sighed.

'All right, Dr Scritti,' the harsh voice said, 'would you mind waiting outside?'

'But John needs me.'

'Outside, please. And keep this to yourself.'

Cope heard the door shut, then the harsh voice uttered a bitter laugh. 'You hear that, Grover? She thinks he needs her. Now I know why she hasn't taken any leave all year. She can't bear to be parted from her sleeping beauty.'

'Emotional attachments aren't unusual in a situation like this.'

18

'Her contract's up for review, so I've been reading her psychological evaluation. She has no sexual partners; she never uses the CybErotic facilities. Instead, she spends her free time communing with a coma victim.' The voice moved around the bubble. 'Look at him, Grover. Young, good-looking, virile – and utterly helpless. The answer to a sexually-repressed maiden's prayer, wouldn't you say?'

Grover gave an embarrassed laugh. 'I'm sure that Dr Scritti doesn't . . . hasn't . . .' His defence trailed off into a cough.

'I think she could be a problem. I think we're going to have to transfer her. Until then, better tell Paige to keep an eye on her.'

'But John's her life's work, Warren. She made the break-through. She practically created him.'

'John is Zygote's baby, damn it! Christ, Grover, the billions we've got riding on him.'

Cope had worked out that the harsh voice belonged to the man called Warren.

'Well, she's right about one thing,' the man called Grover said. 'It's a miracle.'

'It's a fucking disaster. We should have let the Agency take him while they were still hot.' Warren exploded with anger. 'Why now? Why now?'

Grover cleared his throat delicately.

'Let me think,' Warren said. He began to pace.

Cope tracked his footsteps moving back and forth.

'Okay, every test confirms that the treatment works. You've successfully duplicated it on apes. You said yourself that there's no reason why we shouldn't go to full trials. John's given us as much as we need. We'll never be able to parade him before the public.' The pacing stopped. 'Is it possible to put him back into coma by psychosurgery?'

'Destroy a part of his brain? Christ, Warren!'

'Yes or no, damn it.'

'Theoretically, yes, there are a variety of techniques we could use. But there's no guarantee any of them would restore him to the same stable condition.'

'That wouldn't be our problem.'

'I don't follow. Are you saying . . . ?'

'That's right. Wipe his mind clean and sell him to the Agency.'

When Grover spoke again, his voice was shaky. 'Warren, the Agency's next evaluation isn't due for three weeks. I urge you to wait and see how John progresses. Maybe he'll relapse. Maybe this is as far as he's going to get.'

'Maybe isn't good enough. Suppose he regains full consciousness? Suppose he remembers who he is?'

'After all these years, the likelihood of that is remote. At best, his memory will be fragmented.'

'And suppose one of those fragments tells him he's got a wife or a sweetheart or a brother living in Phoenix or Talahoosa. What if he can remember the name of his fucking lawyer?'

'Please, Warren, before we decide anything, let's get a professional prognosis.'

'Call in a neurologist? Are you kidding?'

'The experiment still has years to run. So far, all the data's been positive, but some of the Agency scientists suggest the results have been distorted by the fact that John's a coma victim who's been kept in an artificial environment. Here's our chance to prove them wrong. Here's an opportunity to demonstrate that John isn't some test-tube wonder. Don't you want to see if he can walk and talk? Aren't you curious to meet the man of the future?'

'The only reason John's here is because he *had* no future.'

'I know that.'

'No you don't! We gave him a life he didn't deserve. We gave him time to which he isn't entitled.'

Grover's voice became sullen. 'All I'm saying is, let's assess his cognitive status before taking irreversible measures. An examination could tell us a lot. Almost certainly it's our treatment that's regenerated the neural pathways.'

'And how do we explain what a biotechnology company is doing with a coma victim?'

'We show them the spin-off technology. There isn't the remotest possibility of anyone working out the main programme. And the person I've got in mind won't go running to the media or ethics committee. She's an immigrant – got family above the Line.'

Warren breathed heavily. 'Name?'

'Dr Mhairi Magnusson, a neurophysiologist specialising in memory retrieval and consolidation. She escaped to America from Canada four years ago. We were colleagues at Stanford. She's at the University Medical Center now.'

Warren began to pace again. 'Okay, send me her record. But remember, we're not dealing with a fruit fly or a laboratory rat or one of your chimpanzees. John's a man, and that makes him unpredictable. I'm not taking any risks. Once this neurologist's finished with him, I want him put back the way he was. In the meantime, not a word to anyone. Close access to everyone except Dr Scritti, and make damn sure Paige monitors her visits.'

Grover hesitated. 'Understood.'

'Okay, let's get back to the party.'

Cope heard their feet move away.

'Wait.'

Cope waited, heart thumping against his ribs.

'The traces indicate excitement. You think he can hear us?'

'No, he's dreaming. He's in what's called paradoxical sleep. If he could . . .'

'Wake up!'

Cope flinched internally.

'Dead to the world. If he does come back on line – boy what a shock he's in for.'

After they'd gone, it was a long time before Cope opened his eyes. A lot of what the men had said had surfed over him, but the bits that had lodged confirmed what he'd known on waking. He *was* in space, speeding through galaxies at unimaginable velocity, but he must have been intercepted, captured and held prisoner by enemies who didn't want him to complete his mission.

2

Mhairi Magnusson was growing fretful. The last session of the conference had run late, and by the time Professor Yrigoyen rose to deliver his closing address, it was past six, with what remained of the August daylight absorbed by the icebergs floating in cloudbanks beyond the Golden Gate. Looking down at the ghostly squadron made Mhairi's head swim. From inside the observatory, the seventy-metre spokes suspending it from the Science Tower were invisible, giving her the giddy sensation of being seated in thin air nearly a third of a kilometre above the glittering city matrix.

'Progress is shock.'

Mhairi gave a little shiver, drew in her feet, and stared at Yrigoyen.

'The greater the shock, the faster the rate of progress. And . . .' Yrigoyen paused for effect, '. . . ten years ago, our planet suffered the most catastrophic shock since the cosmic impact that wiped out the dinosaurs.'

Mhairi was unable to resist the tide of memory. Like everyone else in the audience, she could recall exactly where she was and what she'd been doing on the night of the Big Bang. Alone at sunset outside the family cottage in Sutherland, the soft lapping of waves on the lochside and the liquid song of curlews attuned to her mood of sweet melancholy at the prospect of leaving Scotland for a new life in Canada.

A lot of people claimed to have had some premonition of the disaster. Not Mhairi – not unless the sense of the world sunk in stillness had been a portent. When the skies of the north caught fire and the loch turned to blood, she assumed in the first stunned moments that she was witnessing a nuclear conflagration. But the radio and TV were dead even before the shockwaves hit two hours later. Several days of wild rumour passed before she learned that what she'd seen had been the fireball thrown up by a meteor hurtling into the Greenland ice

22

cap, with an impact equivalent to the simultaneous explosion of five thousand strategic warheads.

'It could have been worse,' Yrigoyen was saying. 'That's what we told ourselves. If that meteor had struck closer to the main population centres . . .' He let a silence hang. 'You don't need me to tell you how much worse it turned out to be. The explosion threw billions of tons of debris into the stratosphere, blocking 70 per cent of solar radiation. The atmosphere cooled, then the oceans. The world has been plunged into a new ice age. The temperate zones, with their massive concentrations of population, industry and agriculture, have been reduced to sub-arctic barrens. Some of you – Canadians, Scandinavians, Russians – are immigrants from countries that exist only on paper. Famine, disease and conflict have claimed more than half a billion lives, and twice as many people have been displaced. One third of the United States is in the permafrost zone. More than a hundred million Americans are refugees in their own country.'

Mhairi's concentration strayed again. The observatory had revolved through 180 degrees and she was now facing the East Bay, looking down into blacked-out sectors of Oakland. The knot in her stomach tightened. Even in daylight those neighbourhoods were virtually no-go areas, and with every passing minute the chances of finding a cab willing to take her downtown grew more remote.

A discreet departure wasn't possible. The observatory was a huge glass-and-carbon ellipse, all its exits arranged around the axis right under the stage where Yrigoyen was holding forth. Mhairi winced at the idea of walking out under his eyes. He was an important man – not only the genius behind the space programme, but also chairman of the President's Science Council and, it was rumoured, a contender for presidential office himself.

Mhairi tried to bring her concentration back to bear on him. He'd finished cataloguing the shock and was starting on the progress.

'When I was a small boy, my parents took me around

23

Washington's Space Museum and the Smithsonian.' He chuckled. 'Apparently, I came away with the idea that it was the Pharaohs who'd made the first moon landing.' His voice swelled. 'A generation after NASA's lunar achievements, that's how remote the space programme had become – a few artefacts in a museum.' His voice fell away. 'But that meteor made us realise what a small and fragile place our planet is. It forced us to search for new and distant horizons. It lifted our eyes to the heavens.'

Yrigoyen slowly lowered his arms. 'Within three years of the impact, we had mounted the first manned mission to Mars. A year later we installed an infra-red telescope on the dark side of the moon to search for a planet capable of sustaining human life.' Again he paused, a frail figure backlit by a computer image of a blue and green planet spinning in inky ether. 'And we found one – Virginia Nova, a new world, a new beginning.'

Even Mhairi's attention had been reclaimed.

'Ladies and gentlemen, in three weeks the inter-stellar probe Argo will leave earth on the greatest odyssey ever undertaken by humanity. It will take sixty years for Argo to complete its mission, and despite the assurances of my medical colleagues, I doubt that I'll live long enough to see it arrive. But my grandchildren will, and I wouldn't be surprised if *their* children go there themselves.'

The words 'mission' and 'children' reawakened Mhairi's anxiety. Glancing around for an alternative line of escape, she caught the eye of a Berkeley rival, who then nudged her neighbour and whispered something from the corner of her mouth – probably wondering why Mhairi had gone to all that trouble redesigning her face and figure and done nothing about that blunt, ski-jump nose.

Mhairi hitched one haughty eyebrow and looked pointedly back at Yrigoyen.

'How did we achieve such prodigious progress?' he demanded. 'How were we able to mount a project whose benefits will not be reaped for perhaps another century?' He milked the silence. 'Because that meteor has marginalised professional

24

politicians with their short-term aims and electoral quick fixes. For the first time in history, the people who've done the serious thinking for everybody else are in charge. Esteemed colleagues, I salute the founding members of the world's first scientocracy.'

The applause the delegates awarded themselves was all the opportunity Mhairi needed to cut and run. But she had a lot of legs to negotiate, and as she extricated herself from the last pair, her purse caught and slid off her shoulder, spilling half its contents into the aisle.

'Shit!'

She stooped to shovel her belongings away and had half-risen when she realised that Yrigoyen's silence had extended beyond rhetorical bounds. She met his glare with a sickly smile. Other people in the audience picked up his cue and began turning, one after the other, until it seemed that every one of the seven hundred delegates was staring at her, whispering and clicking their tongues. Shouldering her purse, she set off on the long march to the exit. At moments like this, she wished she wasn't so tall, so bloody *conspicuous*.

'I'm aware that not everyone shares my optimism,' the professor said, waving a dismissive hand. 'I know there are some among you who fear we are creating a scientific oligarchy dominated by a handful of corporations who wield their power like medieval barons.'

Mhairi was walking straight towards him as he said this. She was within fifteen yards of him, her eyes fixed on the exit sign right in front of her. She passed under the stage, out of Yrigoyen's sight. The door gaped.

'The truth is that every great age . . .'

The door hissed shut on whatever platitude he was about to utter. Mhairi leaned against it, crucified by the knowledge that tomorrow every scientist between Boulder and San Diego would know about her botched departure.

After a few seconds she gave a rueful laugh, but as she headed towards the elevator her embarrassment quickened into anger. The truth *is*, she muttered to herself, that within a couple of miles of this temple in the sky, people are living at subsistence level, without access to medical care or proper education. The truth *is* . . .

'Mhairi.'

Her hand flew to her heart. Clumsily she turned, Yrigoyen, her mission downtown – everything – eclipsed by the sight of the golden-haired man framed in the door she'd just left.

'Grover,' she said feebly. 'Where did you spring from?'

'From a few rows back. Been spying on you all afternoon.'

As his features came into focus, she felt her legs go hollow. It was ridiculous. She hadn't seen Grover Byron for three years, yet her treacherous body was reacting as if it had been primed for this moment.

'I didn't see your name on the list of delegates.'

'You checked, then?'

Mhairi covered her blunder with a laugh. 'Sure, I always check. You used to be such a conference animal. Where have you *been*?'

'In lover's exile.'

As Mhairi tried to ride that, he kissed her and stepped back. She wished the lighting wasn't so unsparing. Her hair had almost been a fetish with Byron, but now there were one or two threads of grey among the dark red waves. She tossed her head.

'You haven't changed one bit,' she told him. She wasn't being flattering. Byron's eyes were still as blue as a Florida swimming pool, his hair golden yellow.

'Nor you.' He laughed and shook his head in fond reproof. 'Impulsive as ever.'

'What? Oh, that. I wasn't making a gesture. I have to be somewhere else, and Yrigoyen's such a windbag.' She giggled. 'Boy, the look he gave me.'

Byron winced. 'Timing was never your strong suit. He's a man who never forgets a snub. I bet the moment he gets off stage he'll be asking who the tall redhead is.'

Mhairi tried to make light of it. 'Oh well, bang goes my tenure.'

Byron laid a hand on her wrist. 'Hey, don't worry. Next time

I see him, I'll tell him you were taken ill. I'll tell him you're one of his greatest admirers.'

Her brow crinkled. 'You know Yrigoyen personally?'

'In his capacity as chairman of the Advanced Research Projects Agency. Zygote has several contracts with them.'

Mhairi digested this as she started for the elevator again. 'So what are you doing at Zygote? Are you still working on language evolution in primates?'

'Why don't you come and see for yourself?'

She looked at him sharply, searching for the catch.

'Zygote wants to hire you for a few days' consultation.' They had reached the elevator. 'Let's go somewhere private to discuss it.' He made a hands-off gesture. 'Business only, Mhairi. I promise I'm not here to rake through the ashes.'

Her heart beat painfully. So much had been left unsaid, so much poison spilt.

'Grover, I can't spare the time right now. I've got an urgent appointment.'

'Hospital call?'

Mhairi knew the truth would only scrape open old wounds. 'No, it's personal.' She saw Byron's arched eyebrow and laughed like a silly girl. 'Not that kind of personal. There isn't anyone else in my life.' The words flew out of her mouth.

'Nor me. Seems we still have something in common.'

She tried to make a joke of it. 'Grover Byron without a love interest? I don't believe it.'

He locked eyes with her. 'I never said I didn't have a love interest.'

She broke contact and stared at the elevator doors. Her face smarted. Unable to trust her tongue, she kept it still. When the doors yawned open, she reached gratefully for the controls.

Byron's hand got there first. 'Whatever you've got lined up, cancel it. Believe me, this is more important.'

That dismissal was a sharp antidote. She'd let Byron override her personal interests once before. Her own fault, but she wasn't going to make the same mistake again.

'Grover,' she said, 'I'm delighted to see you and I'd love to

27

catch up with your life, but you couldn't have picked a worse moment.' She prised his hand away and stepped into the elevator. 'Call me at UMC.'

'Too late. I'm flying back tonight.'

The doors were closing and Mhairi had only an instant to make her mind up. 'All right. At home. After ten.'

The elevator dropped with swooning swiftness. When she opened her eyes, her flushed reflection confronted her in the mirrored wall. The knowledge that Byron had been watching her all afternoon made her feel naked. Her flesh shrunk as she imagined what he must have been thinking.

That woman is only sitting here because of me. I saved her life; I rescued her career; I sacrificed my marriage for her. That bitch took everything I had to offer, and then she dumped me.

3

Outside was cold and clammy, the vapour lights dimmed by fog creeping up from the bay. When Mhairi told the autobubble driver where she wanted to go, he turned right round and looked her up and down from fur-capped head to tightly-nipped waist.

'It's a bar,' she explained, 'near the old container port.'

'I know what it is, lady. I was raised in that part of Oakland, and you wouldn't catch me within four blocks of the place. Even the cops stay out.' He tapped keys on the control console. 'But don't take *my* word.'

The destination you have selected is in a hazard zone, a sticky-sweet female voice said. *Entry into this area will invalidate your insurance. Please redirect.*

The driver glanced off across the street. 'Listen, if you're the adventurous sort, I know this joint off Broadway.'

Mhairi was slow on the uptake. She'd been truthful when she told Byron that she hadn't had any sexual partners since the break-up – not real flesh-and-blood ones. Most professional women used the interactive Loveloop agencies, but she knew some who, bored with perfect simulations but reluctant to get into potentially messy relationships, sought anonymous one-on-one encounters in the discreet establishments called Aphrodite Lounges.

The suggestion that she was one of them winded Mhairi.

'I am not looking for action. I am searching for a man who . . .' She broke off, aware that what she was planning was illegal. '. . . a man who traces missing persons.'

Understanding softened the driver's expression. 'A tracer, huh? Thought you were foreign. Don't make no difference, though. If I take you down there, chances are that's two more he'll have to come looking for.'

Mhairi bit her lip. What she'd told Byron about having an appointment was untrue. All she had was the name of a man, Pilkinghorn, and a place where he might be found – the Valhalla.

'What will it take?'

The driver pursed his mouth. 'How about one-fifty?'

Mhairi was in no position to negotiate. 'Okay.'

The driver grunted and programmed the autoguide. DRIVE appeared on the head-up display. With an electrical whine, the autobubble glided into motion. The driver began filling in his work sheet, letting the car find its own route. Though it was still early evening, there were few other vehicles on the boulevard, and no one walked any more. Mhairi watched the green blip sliding down the screen. When it reached Van Ness, she slumped back and released an involuntary sigh.

Her affair with Byron had lasted only six months. She'd met him at a conference in San Diego, on her first trip abroad in years. After her grindingly drab existence in Montreal she'd been dazzled by the opulence of life below the Line – the extravagant lighting, lavish food, couture clothes. Back in Quebec, the infrastructure had completely broken down. Rationing and power cuts had been in force for two years, and under emergency legislation Mhairi had been transferred from the neurological institute at McGill to a general hospital filled with the victims of malnutrition and diseases that had once been historical footnotes even in her med school text books.

At the post-conference reception, shabbily conspicuous in her home-made clothes and improvised make-up, she'd felt like an oversize Cinderella stranded at the ball after the clock had struck twelve. Then, just like a real-life Prince Charming, Byron had sauntered out of the crowd, flashing his incendiary smile, dousing her in charm, sweeping her away.

Literally. When she'd told him she was flying back to Montreal next morning, he'd given her a look that had melted her to the soles of her feet and said, 'then let's make the most of our time'. As they departed, pockets of envious silence had opened among the other female guests.

They hadn't slept that night. It wasn't just the sex, though there had been plenty of that. Afterwards, Byron had spent hours pleading with her to stay in the US. If she returned to Canada, he insisted, she'd be risking her life and certainly chucking away all hope of making it back into the academic fastlane.

It wasn't until days later that Byron confessed he was six years into a seven-year marriage contract with a patents lawyer. And by then it was too late to go back to her family. The US had sealed off the Canadian border.

'Wanna catch the news?'

Mhairi straightened to find they were being borne along in a river of fog-smeared headlights. The guidance system showed they were on the New Oakland Bridge approach. The driver had switched on the dashboard TV.

Top story as usual was the Argo countdown. On screen the rocket looked so fragile, needling up into a basalt-coloured sky. Only the service vehicles crawling around its base, mere grains of motion, conveyed its colossal scale – seven hundred metres tall, twelve thousand tonnes mass, fuelled with enough anti-matter to melt half of Nevada.

There was a glitch in the genetic software that controlled the reaction chamber, the reporter said. Debugging was well in hand.

Second lead was linked; Mhairi could see the upper stages of the probe above the desert horizon behind the correspondent.

'I'm standing fifteen miles west of the Argo launch pad,' he said, 'on the edge of the exclusion zone.' The camera panned across a ruined settlement that looked like a Western movie set. 'This is Mustang, the ghost town occupied by the mysterious cult leader Sun Dog and his followers. We still don't know who he is, but so far more than two thousand people have responded to his prophecy that on the night of the Argo launch, a messiah will appear to transport them to a paradise on the other side of the universe. Earlier, I spoke to one of them, retired civil engineer Earl Karras, from Brownwood, Texas.'

The camera cut to a dignified old boy. 'Sir, you've travelled a long way, given up everything you own. Why?'

'It's written in Revelations, the Hindu scriptures, Nostradamus. They all foretell the world will end the very same night Argo blasts off. The White House knows it, too. Why else would they spend five trillion dollars on a space ship that ain't gonna reach anywhere until long after we're in our graves? They say nobody's gonna be on board. Bullshit there ain't. It's a life vessel for the President and a bunch of Zionist bankers.'

The correspondent took it in his stride. 'But you hope to travel a lot further and faster for free.'

'Yes, sir. The soul has no speed limits.'

Cut to the reporter. 'We've been here before – other cults, other places. To date, not one of their predictions has come to pass, and Nevada governor William Pliny is worried about what might happen if there's another no-show. Too many times, we've seen cults self-destruct rather than admit they got their dates wrong. Governor Pliny has personal reasons for hoping there's a happy outcome; his own daughter is one of Sun Dog's disciples. Maybe that's why he hasn't ordered the troops in.'

Mhairi shook her head at the folly of humanity.

'And he isn't the only one with a headache,' the reporter

continued. 'NASA's concerned by how close these people are to the launch pad. An official who declined to be named admitted that if anything goes wrong when Argo lights up, Sun Dog and his followers could end up in paradise sooner than they expect.'

The driver's eyes swiped back at Mhairi. 'Think there's anything in it?'

'It's bollocks.'

Hardly a day went by without another false prophet appearing on the televangelism network, spouting some fresh doomsday scenario. End-of-the-world hysteria was a superbug, constantly mutating into some wacky new form: The world was running out of oxygen; the meteor had been a softening-up exercise devised by little green men; the President had evacuated Washington for the Happy Isles, leaving robot lookalikes in charge of the administration.

'Yeah, well,' the driver said, 'wife's cousin's family's gone up there. Mind, they're Rosicrucians.'

He flicked off the TV and took the wheel for the first time, overriding the autoguide. It only worked on the arterials, but his manner had become more vigilant than road conditions demanded. They had crossed the bridge and were descending from the interchange, slipping past mangled freight yards into one of the blacked-out tracts Mhairi had seen from the tower. The fog had condensed into drizzle, activating the wipers.

'First trip downtown?'

Mhairi nodded, fascinated and appalled by her surroundings. It wasn't completely dark; generators and lanterns and bonfires provided a medieval level of lighting that illuminated gaping store fronts, trashed parking lots, and graffiti-daubed walls pasted with flyers advertising a new life in South America or Africa. This part of town had been hit hard by the quakes that followed the meteor strike. Half the properties were spoil heaps and riots and looting had cleared out what remained of traditional commerce.

So Mhairi was startled to see how crowded the streets were. Men and women clustered around barter stalls and food vendors, mooched in the doorways of flop houses and hock shops, touted outside front parlours and Cyberporn booths, congregated under the evangelical eyes of wayside gospellers. Child beggars ran along beside the autobubble with outstretched arms and sores on their gums. Mhairi was ashamed. This was the closest she'd got to the new underclass.

The driver swore as he swung to avoid a group of youngsters scattering like rats. They went scrabbling up a mountain of rubble, pursued by a squad of paramilitaries. At the next intersection, troopers rigged out in masks and armour furiously waved them past a street where blue spinners freeze-framed more soldiers herding people into the back of a wagon.

'Vags,' the driver said.

'You mean refugees?'

The driver made an indifferent shrug. 'Refugees, tailgaters, scooters – Vags. Don't matter what you call them. We don't want 'em.'

'But most of them are Americans.'

'They ain't Californians, though, and that's what counts. Ain't enough food and work to go around the natives.'

Mhairi had the sense to let it ride. As an immigrant herself, she'd experienced hostility from both sides of the American divide – the refugees from the north who'd lost their homes and livelihoods; the residents of the south who resented the influx of Yankee metropolitans competing for precious jobs. The exodus had started only weeks after she'd come south. People in the north had panicked when they heard the government was planning to cut aid to the freeze zone. They took off, loaded what they could into their autos and stampeded south, fifty million in one week, backed up solid from Buffalo to North Carolina. Florida was now the most populous state in the Union. Boston and Chicago and Detroit were virtually ghost cities, Washington a frontier capital.

Mhairi wiped the strobe tracks from her eyes. 'Will they be sent to a transients' camp?'

'Vag camps are full. Me, I think they just dump them back over the Line.'

33

Mhairi tried to sound casual. 'Do you know if people are still getting across?'

'If they ain't got out by now, they ain't ever gonna make it.' The driver's seen-it-all eyes engaged Mhairi's in the mirror. 'Lady, I'd say this is a wasted ride.'

She dug her nails into her palms.

'Yep,' the driver said, 'if the military don't pick them up, the militias get them. And those boys don't bother about camps.'

Mhairi sank back. She had no way of establishing how much of what the driver said was true. Radio and telephone communications above the Line had broken down – contamination by meteor fall-out was the official explanation, though most people believed the government was jamming transmissions. Whatever the reason, the world's richest and most technically advanced region had become a terra incognita, a place of rumour and speculation. Mhairi had heard that a Mafia boss had crowned himself King of New York and was exacting tribute in the form of canned foods and gasoline. Wiggier elements claimed that aliens had colonised the Big Apple.

Mhairi was too wrapped up in her worries to notice the crowds thinning out. When she surfaced, the autobubble was creeping down a dereliction row strewn with the contents of commercial properties. Up ahead a fire twisted in a brazier improvised from a trash can. Three down-and-outs sat around it on seats ripped from a gutted car, spooning food from a hubcap. They stopped eating to watch the autobubble go by. Under their serfish stares, Mhairi shrank into her furs.

'Deadheads,' the driver said, as if he was naming some scavenger species in a safari park.

Not much more than a hundred metres further on, he pulled over and nudged his chin at a faulty neon sign.

'Cocktail heaven.'

Mhairi eyed the stuttering letters. She scanned back up the darkly shining street. 'Would you mind waiting?'

'Five minutes in this neighbourhood and this bug'll be ready to go back on the assembly line. Me, too.' He sighed heavily as another bill appeared in Mhairi's gloved hand and reached for his security baton. 'Make it quick.'

She descended on to the greasy sidewalk. Rain-laced wind sent garbage skirmishing towards her. She looked up to where the stars should have been and shivered, hating this perpetual darkness. The bar was set below street level and she could feel the thumping of a generator through her feet. The driver was watching her, solemn as an owl. She gave him a queasy smile, went side-footed down the steps, drew breath hard and pushed open the door.

All the energy contained within hit her in a raucous wave.

4

Mhairi had expected a dingy drinking hole. Instead she found herself on the sidelines of a subterranean hangar crowded with men and women in unbuttoned social mode. Through the smoke-coiled lights, lowlife vignettes imprinted themselves – three pairs of hairy hands squabbling over junk; a troupe of strippers high-kicking to the archaic tempo of a Hoochie Coochie band.

The set ended. As her presence registered, a testosterone-rich silence spread, pierced by a single, hungry whistle. With as much indifference as she could muster, she set off on the long walk to the bar. Never had she been so conscious of the soft, rolling articulation of her hips.

'Hey, Bobo, this the new act, or have the aliens finally hit the beach?'

Bobo was one of the bartenders, a tattooed giant with the features of a vandalised war totem who lowered his eyelids in disapproval until, by the time Mhairi reached the counter, they were sealed.

'Coffee, please.'

'Liquor only.'

'Liquor up front,' someone cackled, 'poker in the rear.'

Mhairi pretended lofty disdain. 'An Arctos.'

Down on to the counter came a frosted bottle etched with a jolly polar bear. After a grudging interval, Bobo followed up with a glass. Mhairi ducked her head to sip.

'Do you know where I can find a man called Pilkinghorn?'

Even the barman's eyelids were tattooed. He unhooded them, recording the bill folded in her glove. He closed his mitt around it and rapped on the counter.

'Ask,' he told Mhairi. 'It's a free country.'

She was handicapped by a voice incapable of raising itself to a shout. 'I'm looking for a man called Pilkinghorn.'

A few people shook their heads with exaggerated blankness, then a young-old man in a patched coat down to his ankles got up, scratching his lank hair. 'Pilkinghorn,' he lisped through a section of missing teeth. 'Yeah, I know where he hangs out.'

'The fuck you do,' the barman told him. His eyes targeted Mhairi and drooped in warning. 'You come to the wrong place. You got wheels?'

'Outside.'

'Use 'em. No yellow cabs down here.'

But Mhairi had staked too much on this slim chance to back off. Shrugging, the barman went back to his TV.

'Why do you want to visit the moon?' a woman's voice asked.

'Well, I hear the sex is pretty good,' another woman said. 'Like, you know, on the moon you weigh only one-sixth what you weigh on earth.'

Fretting over what options were left to her, Mhairi found her own gaze drawn vacantly to the flatscreen.

An eyelash-perfect hostess smirked at her. 'You mean weighing less will improve your romantic life?'

The guest looked down sheepishly. 'Well, I guess I could lose a few pounds, and my husband ain't exactly petite. But it ain't that. I figure it'll, like, you know, slow him down some.'

The gale of synthetic laughter mocked Mhairi's own futile mission. She surveyed the room with the gut-sinking realisation that even if Pilkinghorn had been among that company, she wouldn't want anything to do with him. The bartender said

36

something she didn't catch. She shook her head. Slowly, like a figure vacating a bad dream, she walked out.

She was back up on the sidewalk before a gust of rain slapped her to her senses. The cab was gone. Refusing to be panicked, she inspected the dead end to the left, then searched right, past the bums' wrecked car. No fire now, no light at all except, high above the dreary canyon and miles away, the science observatory presiding over the city like the half-closed eye of a watchful reptile.

Behind her the door opened with a splash of sound. She found her stride in an instant. Feet padded wetly behind her. Rain needled her face.

'Walking into trouble that way. My word on it.' A slack laugh for emphasis.

Through the slanting rain, Mhairi saw a shape separate from the gutted car, then two more. They flitted across the street and one of them stooped and picked up something that rang metallic. The strength drained out of her legs. As her pace faltered, her stalkers drew level. One was the ageing boy with ruined teeth, the other an older man, bloated with muscle run to fat, eyes like pools of glue with hot coals embedded.

'This here's Brusher,' the kid told her. His remaining teeth shone in the dark. 'I'm Gash.'

Mhairi clenched her fists and sidled to keep them both in front. 'What do you want?' she demanded lamely.

Gash pointed with his chin towards the blank end of the street. 'Guy you're after lives down yonder. It ain't far.'

'I don't believe you.'

Gash widened his eyes, mock affronted. The fat man called Brusher went on staring at her as if he was wondering which piece to eat first. Absent-mindedly he wiped rain from his nose.

'Keep your hands off me,' Mhairi snapped.

Shadows stretched his face, thrown by a pair of headlights prowling out from the dead end of town. Mhairi's feeble hope of rescue died when it drew level and she saw through the clapping wipers a bald man hunched over the wheel in sozzled concentration. It crawled past, a gas-driven dinosaur, tyres swishing on the wet tarmac, and angled erratically in, wheel rims scraping the kerb. The driver poked his head out.

'Aiming for the bridge,' he slurred.

Gash stepped in front of Mhairi. 'You're aiming straight, mister.'

The drunk peered up the street for enlightenment. 'No,' he decided, 'I just come from there. Been going round and round, round and . . .'

The door jerked open and flapped against its hinges. On the second try, the drunk heaved himself out, fighting for control of a street map. Gash sucked air through the gap in his teeth and reached inside his coat.

Oblivious to his peril, the drunk staggered closer, holding his street plan over his skull. He smiled like a sodden cherubim. 'Hey, fellas, just show me where I am.'

Even Mhairi was infuriated by such imbecile disregard of life and limb.

Gash pulled a cleaver from beneath his coat and ran at him. 'Wide-open city, and you're . . .'

'. . . the keeper of the fucking keys,' the drunk told him, aiming a rock-steady pistol into Gash's open mouth.

Mhairi lunged then, but Brusher had anticipated the move and pulled her in tight. She screamed a puny tin whistle scream and lashed back with feet and elbows, saw metal arc past her face and went slack just before the knife reached her throat.

The bald man ignored her. 'Drop it,' he told Gash. 'Okay, face flat, hands on the back of your head.'

'It's wet, man.'

A sideswipe across the mouth dropped him on to his hands and knees. He remained there, spitting blood flecked with porcelain until the bald man put one foot on the small of his back and pressed him into the required position. Then the bald man backed off a step and redirected the pistol so that Mhairi was looking into the muzzle from a range of no more than five metres.

'No way out but one.'

Brusher ratcheted up the pressure on Mhairi's windpipe. 'Fuck you. I'd sooner cut her throat.'

'Then I shoot you in the balls, then I put two more through freak's eyes.'

'The woman's still dead.'

'The kicker is, she don't mean nothing to me. Guy calls, says this broad walked in, looks like queen of planet Zog. Maybe she is. Who cares?' The bald man jerked the pistol.

Gash, down on the ground, risked a glance in Brusher's direction. 'Do like he says. He ain't new to this.'

'Fuck you,' Brusher said, 'Fuck him.'

And me, Mhairi thought, gauging the desperate limitations of Brusher's behavioural repertoire by the tremor in his knife hand and the tightening of his stranglehold. Stars began to cluster in her vision.

'Here's the deal,' the bald man said, glancing behind at the trio skulking for leftovers. 'You let the lady go, I hand your asses back. You don't, the vultures get to pick them. The lady's big, but you're bigger. You're sticking out all over.' The bald man widened his stance. 'Ten seconds. One . . . two . . .'

Even if Brusher had been the reasoning type, his shallow panting told Mhairi he was in no state to weigh pros against cons. On the count of four, she raised her right hand and tapped his elbow. 'There's nearly a thousand dollars in my purse,' she gargled. 'Take it.'

'Huh?' the bald man said.

'I'm giving it to him,' Mhairi croaked. 'It's a gift.'

The bald man uttered a laugh and kicked the sidewalk. Then his eyes went as hard as stones.

'Five,' he said, 'and six.' He consolidated his aim. 'Seven . . . eight . . .'

Mhairi knew that Brusher wouldn't wait for the count to reach ten. 'Stop!'

For an indeterminable period the entire planetary system seemed to reconsider its path, then Brusher gulped as if he'd swallowed a hard-boiled egg and his left hand began to creep towards Mhairi's purse.

'Only the money,' she warned him.

'Take the lot,' the bald man snarled. 'Piss me off.'

Brusher fumbled among the bric-a-brac, cursing his clumsiness and the situation in general. The veins on his forehead were standing out like snakes. Mhairi sensed that at any moment some piece of his mental wiring was going to snap.

'Why don't you let me?' she said, reaching for the bag.

Her hand touched his and she glimpsed on his face the glassy terror of a bayed animal. Fighting for steadiness herself, she located her wallet, emptied the cash out and shoved it into his hand. 'Go on. He won't shoot.'

'Any move but back and you can bet your fucking life I will.'

'Don't do nothing crazy,' Gash moaned. 'Just split, man.'

Suddenly the pressure lifted off Mhairi's neck. Knowing the crisis wasn't over, she forced herself into stillness, tensed for the knife thrust that part of Brusher's brain was lusting to inflict. She tried to interpret what was happening from the bald man's expression, but he was just an aiming device. The seconds stretched out and the pistol began to track left and then, far behind her, she heard feet splashing away. Bile scalded her throat. She lurched for the wall.

'Terrific,' the bald man marvelled, harrowing his brow with the pistol. 'I backed the wrong fucking side.'

Gash spat more blood. 'Hey, captain, cut me a break, huh?'

It was a bad moment to draw attention to himself. Without so much as a glance, the bald man buried a foot in his kidneys.

'Stop that!' Mhairi cried.

The bald man hiked his pants up and glowered at her. 'In the car.'

She stumbled forward, fumbled the door open, slammed it behind her and wrapped her arms around herself. Scowling like an ape, the driver dumped himself behind the wheel and wrenched the shift, drawing a chirp from the tyres and sending Mhairi sprawling against the rear pillar. By the time she'd righted herself, they were around a corner. She stared blindly ahead, massaging her bruised throat.

'You know how close you came to getting croaked?' the driver demanded. He took a hand off the wheel and made an invisible gap between thumb and finger tip. 'That fucking close.'

Mhairi exploded. 'What do you care? You practically told him to do it.'

The driver met her fury face on. 'Hey, if I'd known that swamp rat was gonna walk with a thousand bucks, I might have clipped you myself. Here!'

Mhairi stared dazedly at the pack of cigarettes. 'I don't smoke.'

'It's for *me*.' The car veered under the force of his indignation. 'Take it,' he mimicked in a corny falsetto. 'It's a gift. Jesus, you must have rocks for brains! What are you – Swedish?'

'I am Scottish,' Mhairi said with icy clarity, and snatched the cigarettes. Grimacing with distaste, she got one started and thrust it back at arm's length.

The driver sucked greedily. Light from a gas lantern slid across his wet pate and pitted jowls. Mhairi's lips rippled in disgust as she became aware that she was sitting on something soft and squashy.

'It's okay, dump it on the floor.'

With the tips of her fingers, Mhairi extracted a half-eaten krillburger and dropped it in the opposite footwell. She wiped her hands on the seat and eyed her saviour with revulsion.

'Listen,' he growled, head sunk between his shoulders, 'you might be the princess of the north, but if that makes me a fucking frog . . .' He aimed a fat kiss at her reflection.

Mhairi averted her eyes and breathed deeply through her nose. 'Are you Mr Pilkinghorn?'

'Harry Fender, Sam's partner. So what's the juice?'

Mhairi had difficulty stringing words together. 'I . . . work at the University Medical Center. A nurse there . . . she's from Michigan . . . She told me that Mr Pilkinghorn had arranged . . .' Mhairi paused to get command of her emotions. 'She said he smuggles Vags across the Line.'

Fender's glance was noncommittal. 'A doctor, huh? I get these chest pains. I got them now. Stress-related. Think you could fix me up?'

'Not that kind of doctor. I'm a neurologist.'

41

'Too bad.'

Fender wheeled right and stayed quiet. The rain streamed so heavily over the screen that he had to press his nose almost to the glass to read the potholed surface. Shock combined with the suffocating atmosphere was making Mhairi nauseous. She rolled down her window a few inches and saw waterfront architecture loom by – gothic warehouses zig-zagged by fire escapes pouring like cataracts.

Without warning, the car pitched to a stop. The rain beat against a peeling facade bearing an illegible name. Down the wharf, abandoned lifting gear craned against the sky. When Fender doused the lamps, all was darkness.

'Mr Pilkinghorn works *here*?'

'This is it.' Again using his map as an umbrella, Fender let her out and towed her at a scamper up an alley and into a recessed doorway. Squeezed against her, he grinned up from the level of her breasts.

'So tell me what's on my mind?'

She shuddered.

Fender got the lock to yield and ushered her into pitch blackness. His lighter rasped and he held a stub of candle to it.

'Say hi to the future.'

It smelt of the past – cardboard and machine oil and Indian cotton. Mhairi followed Fender's strenuous breathing up a flight of wooden steps and along a passage. The flame preceded her, briefly animating portraits from a bygone age. At the end of the corridor Fender opened a glass-panelled door with Grand Barbary Shipping Co. stencilled on it. Beyond was a room so cavernous that Mhairi drew back as if confronted by a drop. Fender's prompting hand sent her groping over bare boards, and when a big office desk loomed out of the dark, she clutched it for support. Fender took up a hurricane lamp and got it going. The crocus flame grew, throwing primeval shadows from a pair of horns mounted on the wall behind the desk. On one side of it, photographs shaded out into gloom. Fender placed the lamp on the desk and went wheezing doorwards.

'Sam will be right down.'

Mhairi sat still, hands in her lap, listening to a metal casement banging in another part of the building. Gradually the stillness of the room drowned external noises and her hand crept towards the photo frame on the desk. It was a family portrait – three handsome young men, two in jeans and Stetsons, the other wearing army uniform, flanking proud parents in front of a ranch house beneath a towering blue-white sky. The domesticity of the scene reassured her and stung her with a dart of grief.

Carefully she replaced the photo. The wind blew an eerie glissando and she held her breath, her eyes patrolling stiffly. The lamplight made no impression on the corners of the room and the sensation of being centred in darkness insinuated itself unpleasantly. To ward it off, she stood and examined the trophy horns. A tarnished plaque said they belonged to the last buffalo shot in Steadfast County, April 1883.

The photos drew her towards the dark corner, through generations of Pilkinghorns – formal in frock-coats and crinolines, on horseback among columns of cattle straggling into dusty infinity; grinning over a bag of sage grouse, mugging for the camera at some ranchers' beanfeast. The family album stopped at a picture of the rangy soldier, wearing a different uniform with a star pinned on his shirt, lounging against a Jeep outside the Sheriff's Office, Steadfast County, North Dakota.

Next to it was an embroidery sampler. In the creaking stillness, Mhairi read the faded lettering.

> Our days run thoughtlessly along,
> Without a moment's stay;
> Just like a story or a song
> We pass our lives away.
> Amy Elizabeth Pilkinghorn, December, 1855

'That range was always a cow killer.'

Mhairi gasped and wheeled round.

Pilkinghorn condensed out of the dark. He was very tall, his widow's peak sharper than in the photos, his face all lean V's, made even more saturnine by the light striking up from below. He walked round the desk, one leg dragging stiffly, and beckoned her to sit. As he took his place opposite, she glimpsed a holstered pistol slung beneath his sheepskin jacket. He pushed a glass towards her.

'Whisky. Guess you could use it.'

Mhairi hadn't touched alcohol for years and she shuddered at the taste of the harsh spirit. She cradled the glass in both hands.

'Harry says you're Scottish.'

Mhairi decided that a smile wouldn't go amiss. 'From Sutherland, but my father's family is from Iceland.'

Pilkinghorn wasn't interested. 'How long have you been in America?'

'Since the beginning. One month after the impact, I took up a research fellowship at Montreal Neurological Institute. When it became clear that the cooling was permanent, my parents and younger brother came out to join me. Like most Scots, we have relatives in Canada.'

She paused, assuming that Pilkinghorn would apply some oil to the conversational wheels. When he didn't, she tried another airy touch. 'Out of the fridge, into the deep freeze.'

'I meant, when did you cross the Line?'

His lack of empathy made Mhairi's voice wobble. 'Four years ago, when I was invited to a conference in San Diego. By then the situation in Canada had become desperate. Rationing had broken down and most of the French population had left. At the conference, I met someone who warned me that the US was unable to cope with its own refugees and that this was my last chance to gain entry.' Mhairi bit her lip, shamefaced. 'I was very lucky. That was only a few days before they closed the border.'

'You left your family in Canada.'

Guilt fastened claws inside Mhairi. 'You make it sound like I deliberately abandoned them.'

'I didn't make it sound like anything.'

44

Mhairi's throat gave a slow pulse. 'I only stayed because the man – the person who helped me – told me it would be easier to get my family out if I had resident status. That turned out to be wrong. I went to a tracing agency. They took my money and I never heard from them again. I tried others without any success. The last one I hired told me that my parents were dead.' Mhairi dipped into her purse. 'But last week a man brought me this letter. My parents are still alive. Not in Quebec, but in Winnipeg.'

Pilkinghorn's face bent closer to the light and Mhairi saw he was younger than she'd first thought, not more than six or seven years older than herself. Everything was relative, though. Since his last photo had been taken, events harsher than the passage of time had revised his features.

He handed the letter back and stropped a finger down his jawbone. 'That message was written nearly a year ago. Your parents must be over sixty and last winter was the cruellest yet.'

'Cold winters aren't a novelty to us Scots.' Deciding that only money would thaw him, Mhairi set down her drink and placed both hands on the desk. 'I want you – I'll pay you – to rescue them.'

Pilkinghorn's mouth relaxed. 'Harry's a romantic, or he would have told you I've quit the tracing business. Even if I hadn't, I'd still tell you no. I never took on illegals. There are still more than three million American citizens across the Line.'

'Three *million*? But the government says there are only a few thousand.' Despite Pilkinghorn's withering response, the news ignited a spark of hope. 'Surely that must mean there are communities, some form of government?'

Pilkinghorn looked at her deadpan. 'The people left up there are the one-per-centers. Cons, lunatics, the dirt-poor, stupid and downright wicked. Society's remnants.'

Anger collected under Mhairi's sternum. 'My parents are not remnants. My father's a professor of linguistics. My mother's a music teacher.'

'That ain't a highly sought-after skill-set in today's world.'

Mhairi snatched up the drink and swallowed her anger as if it were a pill. 'Mr Pilkinghorn, this isn't the first time my country has suffered climatic disaster. Millions of Scots have emigrated to the New World. People like them built America.'

'The Chinese laid the railroads, but that doesn't mean we should resettle the population of Beijing.'

Mhairi sat tall. 'I'm prepared to pay whatever you ask. Whatever I'm capable of raising.'

Pilkinghorn shook his head as if she was slow-witted. 'You're too late. The only way to reach the Line is with an armed convoy. It's the end of August and the last convoys will be ready to roll.' He gestured at the window. 'Five hundred miles north of here, that rain is falling as snow. In less than a month the roads will be blocked.'

'But there must be a way.'

Pilkinghorn was still for a while. 'I can put you in touch with some people. They ain't cheap and I'd say you'd be wasting your money.'

Mhairi thought of the money she'd already thrown to the winds. Pilkinghorn was one of the least sympathetic characters she'd met, but his very implacability suggested that if he ever did give his word, he wouldn't break it lightly. Her hands fidgeted on the desk.

'Mr Pilkinghorn,' she said, barely audible to herself, 'I don't want to try anyone else. I believe I can trust you. How can I persuade you? Tell me. Anything.'

He regarded her steadily. 'Anything?'

She'd had drugs in mind, medicines virtually unavailable downtown at any price. When she saw what interpretation Pilkinghorn had made, she stiffened in anger, only to discover that her outrage was token. If sex was what it took, it wasn't much of a price to pay.

She raised her eyes straight to Pilkinghorn's. 'Whatever you say.'

For several seconds he gave her the full weight of his stare, then he canted his head and rubbed the nape of his neck. 'I can't help you.' He scraped his seat back. 'In a few weeks, I'm cutting out.'

'I'm sorry, I don't . . .'

'Leaving. Going overseas.'

What was left of Mhairi's composure crumbled. She set down her drink and the glass chattered on the desk. She covered her face with her hands. When she felt able to look up, her mind had blanked. She stared around.

'How will I get home?'

Fender came downcast out of the shadows. He took Mhairi's arm and led her to the door.

'Dr Magnusson.'

She stopped.

'Harry tells me you're a brain surgeon.'

'A neurophysiologist,' she said woodenly.

Pilkinghorn was still seated in the circle of lamplight. 'But when the surgeons have to decide whether a patient's life is worth saving, it's you they ask.'

Anger filled Mhairi's sails. 'Don't try to compare what I do with what you do.'

'I'm saying we're both experts. In my opinion your parents are dead.' Pilkinghorn stood, without any change of expression. 'Don't be too hard on yourself. If you'd stayed, you'd be dead too.'

On the drive down to Palo Alto, Mhairi concentrated on the runnels of water creeping across the side windows. She brushed back her own fugitive tears.

Fender lit another cigarette, his eyes attentive in the mirror.

'I guess you think Sam's a cold case.'

What Mhairi thought of Pilkinghorn was irrelevant, but in some way she felt his refusal had been a fitting indictment on her vanity and selfishness. Why should a stranger risk his life trying to save the family she'd abandoned for a smart lifestyle. Oh, she'd believed Grover Byron's assurances that he could swing things to get her family out, but only because she'd wanted to.

Fender formed a circle with his lips and vented smoke. 'Sam lost his own family up there. Hung on long after things were past saving. Reckoned because he was sheriff, because his family ploughed the first furrow in Steadfast, he owed it to the community not to quit. Wife and daughter died of diphtheria two winters ago. Guess he still carries a conscience.'

Mhairi remembered Pilkinghorn's parting words and a cold hand seemed to touch her spine. 'Then why has he stopped?'

'Went into Oregon on a Vag run last spring. Didn't show again for six weeks. By then I'd closed out his account. Then one day he's back. Only, you know, it's like part of him's not back – and I'm not talking about his leg. Never said how he got hurt. Never said what happened to the Vags. Guess he lost them.'

Mhairi watched traffic sliding by like ghosts.

'He told me he's leaving America.'

'Yeah, heading south to Ecuador. Going where the living's soft and easy.'

'Are you going with him?' Mhairi's voice shook.

'Would if I could raise the dough.' Fender flicked his stub out of the window. 'But a living's hard to find.'

For some reason, the idea of this tough, ugly little man abandoning America left Mhairi feeling confused and anxious – like a child lost knee-high in a room full of adults. And if she felt like that, no wonder so many people with none of her privileges clutched at the straws proffered by phony visionaries. In a world where the stars had been extinguished, you didn't believe in nothing: you grabbed at anything.

She tried to rally. 'I know things look bleak now, but a great future lies ahead. Every day, scientists are achieving the most incredible breakthroughs.'

'A scientist is someone who finds out more and more about less and less until he knows everything about nothing. That's what I was taught – someone who knows a lot about fuck-all.' Fender gave a cigarette-stoked laugh. 'Remember global warming? All those experts swearing the planet was gonna go up in smoke next century but who couldn't say if it was gonna rain for tomorrow's Raiders game.' He shook another cigarette out of his pack. 'Predicting's easy,' he said, 'except where tomorrow's concerned.'

Mhairi's eyes narrowed. 'One thing I can guarantee. Keep puffing those things and you'll be dead in ten years.' Her voice rose. 'Apart from the fact that they're illegal, they're so outdated. For the same money you could get mood tuners, drop-out drops, clever candy. Far more pleasure without the risk.'

'Risk,' Fender informed her, 'is the ketchup on your burger.'

Mhairi folded her arms in resignation. 'What was your work?'

'City cop. Detroit PD, homicide section.'

She tried to envisage Detroit as it might be now – miles of untenanted blocks and frost-buckled canyons scoured by arctic winds. 'Have you been back?'

'You kidding? Detroit was never sun city even before the rock hit.'

'I meant across the Line – with Mr Pilkinghorn.'

'Me? No. I only function on asphalt. Mostly I track down people from families that got split up in the stampede.'

'But he must have told you what it's like. All the stories. Are they true? Is it as bad as they say?'

'Bad as it gets. Sam says it's a fairytale world up there.'

'What!'

'That's what *I* said, and Sam said, yeah, fairytales without the happy ending. Above the Line, the big bad wolf gobbles up the little piggie-wiggies and Hansel and Gretel never come out of the gingerbread house.'

Mhairi's voice was faint with horror. 'You mean people up there are *eating* each other!'

'There ain't a lot else on the slate.'

Mhairi crammed her knuckles between her teeth.

Fender shifted uncomfortably. 'Hell, what do I know?'

Mhairi's imagination free-ranged over every conceivable kind of atrocity until a half-registered landmark prompted her attention back to the present. 'This exit here.'

A couple of miles off the freeway, she directed him into a road signed Rose Valley Community, Passholders Only. It wound up through carefully tended groves planted with discreet security lights and ran out on to a pleasantly landscaped plaza. Fender slowed to an idle, prospecting a wall wreathed in razor wire and sensors. Behind it was a test-tube monoculture – nearly 400 scientists. Seeing it through Fender's eyes made Mhairi uncomfortable.

'I'd go nuts living in one of them gated communities,' he said. 'Don't you get lonesome?'

'Lonely?' Mhairi said, touched in an undefended spot. 'Of course not. It's very comfortable.'

'Comfortable ain't enough.'

Out of a gatehouse stepped a laser-armed security guard, pointing a blinding strobe.

'Schmuck,' Fender said, shielding his eyes. 'Hey,' he shouted, 'get that fucking light out of my face.'

'It's all right, Frank,' Mhairi said quickly. 'Mr Fender's a policeman. A real policeman,' she couldn't resist adding, because Frank was a lecherous jerk.

Frank could hardly tear his eyes from Fender and his heap of junk, but finally his gaze settled on Mhairi. His mouth tightened. 'Dr Magnusson, you have two visitors – a Dr Byron and a gentleman who declined to give his name.' His face flicked towards a car on the other side of the plaza. 'Without prior notification, I was unable to offer them access to the reception lounge. Please observe the proper protocol in future.'

The evening's events had driven Byron from Mhairi's mind. Her heart foundered when she saw the two overcoated men walking towards her. She was damp and distraught, unable to cope with any more demands. In her confusion, she forgot about Fender until she was out of the car. She fumbled at her bag. 'You saved my life. At least let me . . .' She remembered she'd handed over every last cent to the man with the knife. 'Oh, my God. What can I say?'

'Yeah, I know,' Fender said, massaging his nose with the heel of his hand. 'Knight in rusting armour.' His cop's eyes were trained on the two men as if they represented a type familiar to him. 'You know those guys?'

'The fair-haired man. Not the dark one.'

50

'Looks like a hellfire preacher. Bet he's a lawyer. Want me to stick around?'

'That's all right.' Mhairi bent down. 'Thank you.'

'Wait,' he said, raking through the flotsam on the dash. He came up with a card. *Private and Criminal Investigations Undertaken with Discretion.*

Mhairi couldn't contain a smile at the thought of Fender being discreet. 'Really,' she said, 'I don't need . . .'

'Wouldn't have told me that a couple hours ago.'

6

Grover Byron watched Fender's heap of obsolete iron depart, then frowned and sniffed, offended by the cop's odour trail.

'Forgive my astonishment, but don't tell me *that* was your urgent appointment.'

Fatigue made Mhairi careless. 'He works for a man I asked to smuggle my parents out of Canada.' In a far-off, light-headed way, she remembered that not more than an hour ago she'd offered to prostitute herself to that man.

'Not so loud,' Byron muttered, checking on the guard. 'If the immigration people find out, you could lose your resident status.'

'Don't worry, Grover. He wasn't interested.'

'Better a flat refusal than have your hopes raised. False promises are what those people trade in.'

Memory of his own empty pledges fanned embers of resentment. Sheer tiredness doused them. Mhairi stroked the skin on her cheek. 'I've had an awful day. Can this wait until tomorrow?'

The dark stranger stepped forward, peeling off his glove. 'Warren Grippe. I apologise for intruding at an inconvenient moment, but we're on a very short schedule.'

He didn't seem remotely sorry, Mhairi decided, looking into the bulbous stare of one of the most forbidding faces she'd ever

51

seen. Grippe's head was massive, his mouth a tight, wide slash over a projecting chin.

'Warren is a vice-president of Zygote Investments,' Byron told her. 'He oversees our R & D projects. I did tell you the matter was important.'

Mhairi's decision to turn them away fizzled out in resignation. 'You'd better come in.'

Rose Valley was straight off the architect's computer – eight four-storey residencies, an octahedral community centre and a mini-mall laid out campus-style, surrounded by neat fake-grass lawns and walkways. The rulebook governing tenancy ran to 132 pages and was constantly being updated. Mhairi had a second-floor balcony apartment offering theoretical hill views. Inside, the decor was pared-down Twenties retro – beech-effect floors, a suite of knitted titanium chairs and chrome units, some paintings she'd bought to fill the empty walls. A violin stood propped in the corner. Everything she owned had been purchased since she'd left Canada.

She took off her coat and made a small sound of exasperation when she saw the pelt matted with ketchup from Fender's burger. She looked into the mirror for more signs of damage and fingered her bruised throat. 'Can I offer you anything?'

Both men murmured that they would join her in a Halcyon. She gave them their drinks, poured herself one, swallowed half in one gulp and closed her eyes, waiting for the drug to take. When the tension began to uncoil, she opened her eyes to meet Grippe's Old Testament reflection.

'Tonight,' she told it, 'a man told me to accept that my parents are dead.'

Byron murmured something solicitous. Grippe went on examining her in a way she found unsettling.

'Do you?'

'What I believe doesn't matter,' Mhairi said, slumping in one of the chairs. The knitted cradle immediately adjusted to the correct ergonomic posture. 'There's nothing I can do for them.'

Grippe glanced at Byron, then leaned forward, clasping a

small case to his knees. 'Let me start by saying this conversation is confidential.'

Mhairi smothered a yawn. All the big-ticket research organisations were obsessed by secrecy, but Zygote was notorious for the zealous methods it deployed to guard its patents. Aware that her own research had commercial applications, she didn't know whether to feel threatened or hopeful. She struck a neutral tone.

'Of course.'

Grippe swirled his drink and admired the cloudy blue whorls. 'I was privileged to work with Zygote's founder, the late Donald Paradise, when the company was a single make-shift laboratory on an industrial park out by San Francisco airport. Among the first to recognise Donald's genius was Adrian Thorne, the robotics pioneer. Five years ago, Thorne's teenage son was brain-damaged in an auto smash and remained on life support for five months.' Grippe raised his head. 'Grover told me your brother was the victim of a similar mishap. I understand that's one of the reasons why you chose a career in neurology.'

A band tightened around Mhairi's chest. 'My brother was brain-damaged in a climbing accident. He died in Montreal three years ago, a few months after I left.'

Byron fiercely studied his drink. Grippe nodded, and continued.

'Then you'll understand Thorne's distress. In his desperation he sought advice from people outside mainstream medical circles, including a pair of Jungian snake doctors who claimed they were in communication with the boy. Partly as a result of their intervention, Thorne never fully accepted the hospital's decision to withdraw life support. When he set up a fund to research brain damage, he by-passed the neurological centres and gave the money to Zygote.'

Unease began to disperse the veils of tiredness. Mhairi looked at Byron, superimposing on his face the bone-white anger he'd displayed the night she'd broken off the relationship.

'It wasn't an irrational decision,' Grippe continued. 'As a pioneer of thinking machines, Thorne believed that advances would be made by non-clinical means, including synthetic neural implants. In some respects, he's been proved right.'

Mhairi's head cleared then. 'Grover, that's a line you followed when you were working on chimp language.'

Byron laughed vigorously. 'Way off the mark. Zygote isn't in the business of messing with human brains.'

'Quite right,' Grippe agreed. 'To be candid, if Thorne hadn't been a personal friend of Donald's, Zygote wouldn't have accepted his grant. As it was, we debated long and hard how to target the funds, and finally decided to honour our benefactor's wishes by developing radical neuroprosthetic devices that would keep coma patients not just alive, but physically fit.'

Mhairi frowned. 'Neurostimulator implants?'

'Of a type far more advanced than anything currently available.' Grippe half-raised his glass to his mouth, then decided against. 'A little over three years ago,' he said, 'we heard about a young man in a persistent vegetative state in a Salt Lake City hospital. John, as we call him, had been found frozen in a snow-drift. Fortunately, he received the correct head injury protocol before any secondary damage could occur. In addition, he was given a transplant of neuroepithelial stem cells that apparently regenerated the damaged brain sites without, alas, restoring consciousness. John carried no identification, and police enquiries failed to establish who he was. I assume he was a Vag. DNA profiling indicated that he was a healthy young male, aged about 25, of Caucasian and Native American extraction.'

Mhairi tried to smile. 'You removed a patient from a hospital.'

Grippe smiled back – like a wound opening. 'You make us sound like body snatchers. By the time we found John, the country had degenerated into chaos. Medical facilities were stretched beyond limits, and since there was no realistic prospect of John recovering, the hospital had no choice but to switch off his respirator. Or would have done if Zygote hadn't stepped in.'

Mhairi dispensed with her smile. 'If you couldn't trace his relatives, who gave you permission?'

'We have the necessary federal licences.'

'Licences?' Mhairi repeated. She stood up. 'I find this very disturbing.'

Byron sighed with restraint. 'John would be three years in the ground if Zygote hadn't taken him.'

'Zygote wouldn't invest huge resources to prolong the life of some vagrant. You took this man because he had no one to protect him.'

'From what?' Byron asked softly.

Mhairi's response jammed in her throat. She went to the window and crossed her arms. 'I can only assume that Zygote is using this man as a guinea pig. For what, I don't know. I don't *want* to know. I think you'd better leave.'

Neither man spoke for a few seconds. In the darkened glass, Mhairi saw Grippe open his case and produce a sheet of paper.

'Take a look at this, Dr Magnusson.'

Mhairi turned slowly.

'Please. You'll find it interesting.'

Mhairi reached for the sheet as if it were a small bomb. It was an EEG trace, two weeks old, showing high-amplitude, low-frequency brain waves.

'Typical coma reading?' Byron asked.

Mhairi shrugged. 'I couldn't draw any conclusion from a single trace.'

'Okay, how about this one?'

Mhairi's cursory glance stuck wide open. She flicked back to the first trace, comparing its lazy pattern with the jagged, high-frequency rhythms on the second sheet. She checked the date again. Only four days old.

'It's the same patient,' Byron said quietly. 'It's John.'

Mhairi felt for the back of her chair. 'My God, what did you do?'

'Apart from keeping John alive – nothing. He's emerged from coma spontaneously.'

Mhairi's eyes switched from one to the other. 'I can't accept that. I've studied dozens of coma patients and none of them has shown this degree of . . .'

Grippe cut her off. 'If Zygote had found a way of repairing brain damage, we wouldn't be announcing it to you over a drink. By now we'd have a dozen patents filed and a media conference lined up.'

'It's true,' Byron assured her. 'It's uncanny. It's like a switch has been thrown, a contact re-established.'

Grippe nodded in sombre agreement.

Mhairi tried to marshal her thoughts. 'Can he speak? Does he follow commands?'

'He's uttered inarticulate sounds,' Grippe told her, 'and there are indications that he hears voices and understands some of what is said to him. He's somnolent, drifting in and out of consciousness, but his responses grow more positive each day. When we left him, his eyes had begun tracking movements. By the time we get back, I wouldn't be surprised to find him sitting up and watching the late flick.'

Mhairi sought some kind of firm ground. 'Who's in charge of the case?'

'John's day-to-day welfare is handled by a Dr Monica Scritti,' Byron replied.

'Never heard of her.'

Byron hesitated. 'Dr Scritti's a brilliant biologist who devotes a great deal of time to him.'

'But she's not a neurologist,' Grippe admitted, 'and that's why we're here.' He put down the glass of Halcyon which he'd never intended drinking. 'Dr Magnusson, we want you to conduct a thorough assessment of John's cognitive state.'

It would be ethical suicide, Mhairi knew. She shook her head. 'That's something I could only consider if John were admitted to hospital.' It was the first time she'd used his name.

'It was a hospital that decided to end his life,' Byron reminded her.

'But you've admitted that you haven't got the staff or facilities to treat post-PVS patients. If John does make a partial recovery, he'll need intensive therapy.' Mhairi fluttered the brain traces. 'Don't be deluded by these. After three years in coma, John's cognitive processes will be permanently impaired. He will have suffered chronic memory loss. He will probably be paranoid, possibly psychotic.'

'Until we know the level of his impairment,' Grippe pointed out, 'we can't decide on the appropriate clinical treatment.'

Mhairi stared at him with dubious hope. 'Are you saying that after I've examined him, you'll transfer him to a neurological clinic?'

'Dr Magnusson, I'm responsible for the smooth running of a research establishment with a multi-billion-dollar budget. The last thing I want is a convalescent coma patient on the premises.'

Mhairi felt as if she was being compressed into a small space. She swayed and put a hand to her forehead. 'I'm sorry,' she said faintly, 'this isn't a good time to be asking me about such a complicated matter.'

Byron was suddenly in front of her. 'Mhairi, I know that you've had a lousy evening, and that right now your parents are uppermost in your mind.' He led her to her seat and when he had settled her in it, he crouched at her knee, one hand on her wrist. 'No expense has been spared in safeguarding John's physical well-being. He's tended around the clock. I know it's painful, but contrast his situation with your parents' predicament – stranded in a lawless wilderness, another winter coming on, no food, medical care or any chance of getting out.'

Mhairi struggled against the lump in her throat. 'Don't.'

'Except one,' Grippe said.

Byron squeezed her hand and nodded.

Grippe cleared his throat. 'We're a rather old-fashioned organisation, Mhairi – some might say paternalistic. We believe that our employees focus better, give more of themselves, if their personal lives are contented. Grover has already told you that Zygote has important contracts with various government departments, including the Advanced Research Projects Agency. When he told me about your family's situation, I called a couple of influential people in Washington. I told them that we hoped you would be doing some service for us and explained your personal anguish.'

57

Byron backed him up gravely. 'They've promised to do their level best to find your parents and bring them to safety.'

Mhairi hardly dared to believe what they were saying. 'Can they do that?'

'Sure they can,' Byron said. 'They've still got a military presence up there.'

'If your parents are alive,' Grippe added, 'we'll find them.'

Mhairi passed one hand across her eyes. 'What equipment do you have?'

'We have the latest PET scanner.'

Mhairi shook her head feebly. 'I'd need a neurologic topographer.'

Byron waggled his eyebrows at Grippe and received some message in return. 'We can acquire one. It'll take a week to source and set up.'

'That will give you time to make your own preparations,' Grippe told her. 'Can you make yourself available for five days starting next Wednesday?'

An anxious little voice was still warning Mhairi not to go anywhere near Zygote. 'I have so many commitments – patients, lectures, a review to finish. My department head will never agree.'

'Leave her to me,' Grippe said. 'Zygote carries a lot of weight.'

Looking into his brimstone eyes, Mhairi had no doubt of it. And in that moment she intuited that she was in the grip of forces it would be dangerous to resist.

She looked into space. 'I'll need John's case notes.'

'All here,' Grippe said, patting his case. His hand went inside and brought out a disc. 'Shall I?'

As Mhairi accepted, she had a sense of dark waters closing over her head.

Grippe gently slapped his knees and rose to his feet. 'Good. A car will call for you at four. I look forward to escorting you to the Wellspring Institute myself.'

Mhairi's gaze implored Byron. *You* go with me. Convince me that I'm doing the right thing.

Grippe intercepted the look. 'Unfortunately, Grover has urgent commitments. He's flying back up to Wellspring to-night.'

'Up?' Mhairi said, bemused all over again. 'I thought your facilities were in southern California and New Mexico.'

'Wellspring is in Oregon, Dr Magnusson. We sited it there at the beginning of the freeze as a cold-climate agricultural research station, but we hadn't anticipated just what a chill wind was coming. When we decided it was unviable, it was the resident scientific team that persuaded us to keep it going. They're a very dedicated group of people, and in recognition of that, Zygote has dedicated Wellspring to our most challenging projects.'

'But it's on the other side of the Line.'

Grippe smiled his alligator smile. 'Don't worry about that. We cross back and forth all the time.'

7

The monster's great big bug eye descended out of a luminous haze.

'Don't be frightened,' an electronic voice said. 'It's me, Monica. I'm wearing this suit for your protection. You're in a sterile environment and your immune system has broken down. You have no defence against germs.'

Dr Scritti's hazel eyes came into focus behind her mask. The same instant Cope recognised her, the memory of the two men he'd heard but not seen rushed back. Warren and Grover, Warren and Grover. His eyes darted behind Dr Scritti. The chamber was empty.

'It's evening,' she told him. 'I just finished work and I stopped by to see how you are and give you a body bath.' She held up a flannel and basin. 'There are still some chores people handle better than robots.'

She stared at his face. She wasn't pretty, he decided – too

thin, eaten up by nerves. Her hands moved down his body, and as he succumbed to the sensation, he closed his eyes. His belly warmed under the rhythm. Her movements grew less brisk, then brisker, then slower until they stopped altogether. She uttered a breathy laugh.

'My goodness. You *are* responsive today. Nothing paralysed about *that*.' She began to hum under her breath.

Opening his eyes a crack, Cope saw hot spots on her pale cheeks. He studied her, calculating how far he could trust her. He wasn't going to get out without help, and there was no one else he could turn to. She had him completely at her mercy, yet from the way she looked anywhere but at his eyes, he sensed he wasn't powerless.

She completed her grooming in silence. 'What are you looking at?' she asked eventually. She followed his stare and jumped up. 'Oh yes, the lights. Aren't they beautiful? I can watch them for hours. They're produced by electrical storms in the magnetosphere.' She smiled sadly over her shoulder. 'Poor John, there's so much you've missed. So many terrible, wonderful things.'

She picked up the basin. 'I can't stay. I'll stop by before bedtime.'

Cope saw her press an illuminated panel he hadn't noticed before. A door in the capsule opened with the hiss of a vacuum puncturing.

'Time is short.'

His voice seemed to come from nowhere. He recognised it only by its proximity to himself.

Dr Scritti dropped the basin. 'You spoke! My God,' she squealed, 'you spoke!' She hurried back. 'Say it again.'

This time the words had to be wrung out. 'Time . . . is . . . short.'

Dr Scritti moaned in rapture. Then her eyes snapped open. 'Do you know who you are?'

Cope's tongue lolled. 'John.'

'John who?'

'John.'

Words began to spill over him – names, dates, places. All meaningless. At last the torrent stopped.

'Can't you remember anything? Family, friends, where you were raised, what work you did? Anything at all. You see, John, we're all in the dark. Nobody knows who you are, and we won't be able to find out unless you give us a clue.'

Cope stared up past her. Since he'd first woken, hours or days ago, changes had taken place in his head. His mindscape was no longer a void. Now it lay spread all around like the ruins of a city, every building razed to mounds of rubble, with here and there a section of wall or facade that looked tantalisingly familiar. As soon as he started to explore this shattered landscape, he lost his bearings. His mental footsteps led back only as far as the voice in his dream. He couldn't put a face to it.

'Wait,' Dr Scritti said, fumbling in her suit.

Light flashed above him and he was looking at a young man, shaven-headed, with clear blue eyes. He blinked and the unfamiliar eyes blinked in unison. With nerve-crawling slowness, he realised he was looking into his own face, and for the first time he realised how lost he was. While he had been unable to see himself, he'd been able to take his sense of self for granted, his individuality reinforced by every thought, every internalised sensation. But now his own reflection confronted him with terrifying proof that this blue-eyed face and the consciousness that inhabited it were strangers to each other.

Dr Scritti sensed his dismay. 'It'll come back, John.'

His gaze floated to the window. 'How far are we from earth?'

'From earth? This *is* earth.'

'So what are we doing in this space ship?'

She laughed weakly and her shoulders slumped. 'John, you're in a clinic. A brain clinic in Oregon.'

He tried to find the lie in her eyes. 'So I made it,' he whispered.

She squeezed his hand. 'Yes, you made it.' She gave a joyous laugh. 'You're back, thank God.'

He lay quietly, thinking about it. They must have caught him when he'd landed. He couldn't remember landing. 'What city?' he asked.

A shutter seemed to fall across her face. 'This isn't a city. We're a long way from any city.' Her laugh rang false. 'We're way out in the boonies.'

'Where?'

Her expression grew even more defensive. 'You're in a private ward, an isolation chamber. As I told you, you're not able . . .'

Her lies made Cope impatient. 'I gotta go.'

She was all anxious concern again. 'When you're well. You've been very ill.'

'They're waiting for me.'

She smiled down at him as if he was a child. 'Who is?'

'Sun Dog.'

Dr Scritti's condescending smile froze, then formed again, very tentative. 'Where on earth did you hear that name? How do you know about him?'

Cope was sure he'd be able to explain if he put his mind to it, but it would take too long. It would take years.

'Oh, I get it,' Dr Scritti said. 'You must have heard his name on the news bulletins when you were semi-conscious.' She rocked back with a sigh. 'Imagine, all those hours I've sat out there watching TV, unaware you were listening in. You've probably heard of the Argo probe, too.' She cocked her head. 'Argo? The space rocket? That man Sun Dog's set up his cult next to the launch site.' She waited, her smile dwindling into sadness. 'Well, never mind. All in good time.'

If she knew about Sun Dog, why did she keep pretending there was no hurry? 'No, I gotta go.'

'And I've told you, you're too ill to leave. We don't know if you'll be able to walk. Even if you regain the use of your limbs, you'll need months of rehabilitation. You must be patient.'

Her complacency left him awash with agitation. 'Gotta,' he gasped.

'Ssh,' she whispered, soothing his forehead. 'You'll make

yourself ill.' Tears formed behind the faceplate. She made a futile attempt to brush them away.

'They're gonna kill me.'

Her expression grew infuriatingly tender. 'Now, now. Nobody's going to hurt you. You're far too precious.'

'Heard them.'

'Heard who?'

'Warren. Grover.'

Her hand jumped away. 'That's not true. You're suffering from delusions.'

'Said they ain't ever gonna let me go. Said they're gonna put me back to sleep.'

She swallowed and stole a glance behind her. 'John, you mustn't say things like that. It's very upsetting.'

'You, too.'

She sat bolt upright. 'Me? Good gracious, whatever are you talking about?'

'Said you had to go.'

What was left of her smile degraded into a rictus. 'John, I know you can't help it, but I don't like to hear you talking like that.'

'Said they were gonna get rid of you.'

'Me?' she repeated stupidly. 'But why?'

John suddenly realised where his power lay. 'Because you love me.'

Shock blackened her pupils. 'No, that's not true. How dare you . . . they . . . It's simply . . .'

'You love me.'

'No,' she said again, this time in a whisper, her head dropping.

'You love me,' Cope said for the third time.

Her face stayed downcast. 'Is that a crime?' she said at last.

Cope studied the red tip of her nose, the tired mouth. 'You gotta help me. We'll get out together.'

Her mouth began to tremble. 'Did they really say those things – about getting rid of me?'

'I ain't got anything to lie about.'

She tilted her head back and tears pooled in her eyes. 'I've given everything to Zygote.' Her hands balled into fists. 'Everything.'

'You gonna do it?'

She looked at him as if he wasn't there, then rose heavily. 'Nobody's getting out. Even if we found some way of escaping from Wellspring, there's nowhere to go.' She gestured at the lights. 'You asked if we were in space. Well, we might as well be. There's nothing out there but wilderness. We're more than a hundred miles north of the Line.'

'What line?'

'You see, you have no idea.'

'You can figure a way.'

She began striding about the capsule. 'Firing me. After all I've achieved, all I've given. How dare they? How fucking dare they?' She struck the glass and looked at him, real mean.

'What's that?'

She shook her head, following some train of thought into the distance. 'There's only one thing I can do, but I daren't tell you what. If Grippe found out . . .' Her voice died, then came back firmly. 'First we have to get you moved out of isolation. We can only do that when we've built up your immune system. We have to take it one step at a time.'

'Time is short,' he said again.

'How many times do I have to tell you . . . ?' She passed a hand over her face mask, regained control. 'Forgive me. I'm acting as if you're a rational person.' She dragged in a breath. 'John, even if you could walk out right this minute, I wouldn't let you. You have no defence against the world. You've been isolated so long that the bugs you're used to have probably mutated half a dozen times. One touch from a stranger could make you sick. A kiss could kill you.'

'Even yours?'

'Even mine.'

'Try it.'

She gave a foolish laugh. 'Whatever do you mean?'

'Kiss me.'

Her cheeks burned. 'Don't be silly.'

'Take that helmet off.'

She backed away. 'Out of the question. It would be completely irresponsible. Now stop it.'

Now he was in touch with his thoughts and the long-buried words began to flow. 'If I'm gonna have to face the world, I might as well start with you.' Cope made his voice gentle. 'Please. I want you to.'

He'd got her pinned like a deer in headlights. A long, frozen minute later, she sighed as if some part of her soul was taking flight and her hand moved to the mask. She lifted it and gave her head a quick shake, letting her hair come free. She stood there blushing as if she'd just removed every stitch of clothing. 'God,' she murmured, 'why am I doing this?'

'Because you want to.'

She shuddered. 'Yes,' she whispered, and shuddered again. Her face came closer. Her eyes grew heavy and her lips parted. Her breath came in feathery gusts.

He felt her lips on his – a soft dryness, an elusive scent. When she drew back, her face was bloodless, as if she was on the verge of fainting.

Her discarded mask slipped to the floor. She snatched it up and crammed it back on. Then she set about furiously mopping up the spilt basin. When she'd finished, she was calmer. She sat beside him and took his hand, fanned out his fingers and traced his palm as if both their futures were laid out there. 'In two day's time,' she said, 'a doctor is coming to examine you. She'll give you tests and ask you lots of questions. You mustn't tell her about people threatening to kill you. If you do, you'll get us both into trouble. It has to be a secret between us. Do you understand?'

'I ain't stupid. If I tell anyone, they'll kill me.' He paused. 'Both of us.'

Her throat bobbed. 'And who am *I*?'

Details like that didn't come easily. 'Monica?'

She turned away as if some sound had captured her attention. 'It's your memory they're scared of. If you don't have one, you're no more of a threat than a new-born child. That gives me a better chance of finding a way out.' Her eyes narrowed. 'There's a famous case history – a young man called Henry who was brain-damaged by surgery. When he regained consciousness, he couldn't remember any of the events leading up to the accident, and he was unable to form new ones. He was trapped in a perpetual present. Everybody he met was a stranger, no matter how many times he'd seen them before. That's how you must be. No matter what you do remember or what you're told, you must pretend that you can't hold a thought for more than a few minutes. Do you think you could do that?'

Cope thought about it. 'Reckon it ain't so different from the way I am.'

She managed a wan smile. 'All right, what's my name?'

'Dr Scritti.'

She jumped up and faced in a direction Cope couldn't see. 'Oh, Paige,' she gasped, 'you gave me a fright.'

'Dr Scritti, would you accompany me to my office, please?'

She backed away, her face telegraphing last urgent messages.

Cope lost sight of her, then picked up two underwater shapes outside the chamber. The word 'Exit' lit up green above them and the wall slid open, revealing a section of white corridor. Dr Scritti passed through the door in the company of a tall, broad-shouldered silhouette. The door slid shut and a second later the Exit sign turned red.

Cope had a flash, an intuition, that he'd been here before. He kept watching the space where the door had been, and all the while he waited, the feeling grew that when it opened again, someone he knew would enter and tell him it was time to take a walk down the white corridor.

But when the light turned green again, the man who crossed through the shadows was a stranger – a well-dressed guy with chiselled features who looked like he'd stepped out of a billboard. He seemed not to spot Cope for a moment, but once he'd located him, he entered the capsule without hesitation, not bothering to put on a protective suit. Cope shrank from his cheesy smile.

'Good evening, John. My name's Paige. I understand you've found your voice. Did you have a pleasant conversation with Monica?'

Something about the man wasn't quite right. Cope decided to stay quiet.

Paige's attention tacked about the room as if he was trying to locate a fly. 'In a few days, a doctor is coming to examine you. Before she does, I have a few questions of my own.'

'I ain't got a thing to say to you.'

Paige made himself comfortable at his bedside. 'Look at me.'

Now Cope saw what it was about the man that bothered him. His eyes were like bottles with something moving at the bottom.

Paige took hold of both Cope's hands. ' "There's no art to find the mind's construction in the face." William Shakespeare, a man who knew a thing or two about human nature, wrote that. But hands – that's another matter. Now then, do you believe me when I say I'll know if you're telling the truth?'

Cope stared back like a mouse entranced by a snake. He unstuck his tongue from his palate. 'Yes.'

'Good. Do you know who you are?'

'No.'

'Do you know how you came to be in a coma?'

'No.'

'Has Dr Scritti told you why you're here?'

'No.'

Paige released him and stood. 'Excellent. Don't tell Dr Scritti you've been talking to me.' He stared at Cope as if memorising the contents of his soul. 'I'll know if you do.'

8

Zygote had cloned a human brain.

The possibility was like a loose tooth that Mhairi couldn't stop probing. It wasn't beyond the bounds of science. If the last decade had taught her anything, it was that if something was imaginable, it would happen – and sooner than you thought. Biologists had already pharmed cures for cancers and AIDS and most hereditary diseases. The brain itself was no longer a closed frontier. Mhairi herself had helped unravel the hard wiring, map the neural pathways, develop scanning techniques that could pinpoint faults anywhere in the system.

She roamed her apartment. Suppose Zygote had genetically engineered brain components and implanted them into John, then found that they'd malfunctioned.

Mhairi's train of reasoning hit buffers at this point. Scientists capable of synthesising brain tissue wouldn't need to ask *her* where they'd gone wrong. Besides, Grippe had admitted Wellspring didn't even possess the state-of-the-art equipment essential for delving into the deepest workings of the brain. They didn't employ any neuroscientists, for heaven's sake.

Byron's glib assertion that Zygote wasn't in the business of messing with people's minds began to look credible. Which left Mhairi with only one conclusion. Zygote had selected John precisely because his brain *didn't* function. They'd chosen him because he was completely passive. They could mess with his body any way they liked.

But now he'd woken up.

On some work-related pretext she called a colleague and found that Grippe's story about Thorne, his brain-damaged son and his personal association with Zygote's founder, checked out. The corroboration reassured her, but only for a while. She got up, sat down, got up, sat down. In the end, reproaching herself for her cowardice, she went round to a neighbour, a neurotherapist called Cusack.

'Listen, I heard a rumour that Zygote's entered the neurostimulator implant field.'

Cusack pulled a face. 'News to me. Zygote's into blue-sky research, whereas neuroprosthetic technology's as old as the heart pacemaker. Besides, the market's been cornered by NCT in Dusseldorf. Where did you hear that?'

'Oh, someone at the conference mentioned it. I found it hard to swallow, too.'

More indigestible still was the idea that any company would use a coma patient – a single coma patient – to testbed new technology. If you wanted to develop devices that restored locomotor functions, you'd select a trial cohort of paraplegics – people with spinal cord injuries, car-crash victims.

Unless, Mhairi thought, Zygote's techniques were so invasive, so high-risk, that no conscious individual or their relatives would consent to them. Even a quadriplegic could still think, still make choices, still say no.

The implications were still plaguing her when she arrived at work on Monday morning. Her ten o'clock appointment shunted them aside. Ron and Amerila Gloss were the parents of a nine-year-old girl, Kit, who'd been in a coma since contracting meningitis six months earlier.

She found the parents at the child's bedside in a private ward. Unable to breathe unaided, she was on a ventilator – an angel in a breathing mask, surrounded by soft toys. A tape compiled by family and friends played on an endless loop; the room was scented with flowers and the little girl's favourite perfume.

The mother greeted Mhairi with a wasted smile. 'Just before you came in, I'm sure she moved.' She leaned across Kit and wiped saliva from a corner of her mouth.

'We've completed our analysis of the latest tests,' Mhairi said. 'Shall we go to my office?'

The father checked his wife. 'What's wrong with telling us here?'

Mhairi composed herself at the foot of the bed. 'The tests confirm our previous diagnosis. Kit's condition is irreversible. I'm very sorry.'

The father gave a snuffle of laughter. 'They can clone people and animals. They can send an interstellar probe ten light years into space. They can build a telescope on the dark side of the moon. Hilton and Marriott are planning a joint-venture lunar hotel.' An ugly laugh bubbled out. 'They can do all that, and yet you can't wake my daughter up.'

'Dr Magnusson,' the mother said, 'even scientists can't predict where we'll be in five years. Who's to say that in two or three years time you won't make a breakthrough? Imagine if that happened and we'd let our daughter go.'

For a moment, Mhairi saw the jagged profiles of John's EEG traces superimposed on Kit's sluggish contours. 'Never is a word I hate to use, but if by some miracle Kit did regain consciousness, she wouldn't be the daughter you knew. Part of her has gone and won't return. Believe me, I understand how you must be feeling.'

The father's jaw clenched. 'Do you have children, doctor?'

The skin around Mhairi's mouth tightened. 'No I don't.'

'Then don't talk to me about what we're feeling.'

Mhairi rose. 'I have to go away for a few days. Use the time to discuss it. Talk to your counsellor. Let's meet again the same time next week.' She hesitated. 'You know, I've seen the emotional toll this has taken on you. It must be affecting your other children, too.'

Mrs Gloss's sobs followed Mhairi out of the door. She stood in the corridor, heart palpitating, and found herself back in her office with no idea how she'd got there.

Chantal, her assistant, poked out her bottom lip and told her that her department head wanted to see her. Mhairi knew what the summons meant. She didn't hesitate.

'Come in.'

Professor Lena Newman was at the window, the angle of the light accentuating the ambiguous sexuality of her features. 'You *are* in the spotlight,' she said, deceptively friendly. 'First, I hear you made a fool of yourself during the IAAS conference. Then yesterday, at home, I receive a videocall from a man called Warren Grippe telling me you've agreed to act as a consultant to Zygote.'

'I would have told you, but he insisted on approaching you himself.'

Newman turned and lowered herself into her chair with menacing slowness. 'Tell me, Dr Magnusson, what one of my consultants is doing moonlighting for a bio–engineering company with connections to the military-space complex.'

Mhairi knew how dependent she was on Newman's good will. Her contract expired in January, and if it wasn't renewed, her Category One residency status would be automatically downgraded. At the same time, she had to balance the risk posed by a resentful boss against Zygote's actions if she reneged on her agreement.

'I'm very sorry, Lena. I'm not at liberty to say.'

Professor Newman's lips compressed in anger. 'You're employed by this hospital; your loyalty is pledged to this institution.'

'There's no conflict of interest.'

Professor Newman settled back, examining Mhairi's expression. 'That man you were involved with – Grover Byron. He works for Zygote, doesn't he? You were seen leaving the conference together.'

Mhairi's blush was more eloquent than words. 'It's got nothing to do with him.'

'You don't need me to tell you what I think of him.'

But you're going to anyway, Mhairi thought. 'I know you disapprove of his research on primate language.'

Professor Newman snorted. 'Teaching chimpanzees to talk – the idea's ridiculous. You know what Wittgenstein said about giving an animal the power of speech, don't you?'

Mhairi answered as if by rote. 'It inhabits such a different consciousness, you wouldn't be able to understand what it was talking about.'

Even during her affair with Byron, she'd never been able to summon up enthusiasm for his undertaking to get apes to speak. It stemmed from his theory that human intelligence had evolved through the acquisition of language, primate grunts developing into words which, by a process of positive feedback, produced more words and generated new meanings that fed into the brain and produced thought.

Mhairi looked down at her boss. 'Do I have your permission to go?'

'Under duress.'

'Thank you.'

Mhairi was at the door before Newman delivered her parting shot 'You weren't the only one, you know.' She spoke in the dead voice of a thwarted lover with nothing to lose. 'A lot of moths have been burnt on that flame, but you were the only one to get away. If you go back to him, I shall consider our friendship at an end.'

A nasty taste flooded Mhairi's mouth. Vindictive bitch, she thought.

The exchange pulled her spirits down for the rest of the day. She was still in the doldrums that evening when Frank the obnoxious security man called.

'Got a federal official in reception to see you. From the Department of Immigration.' His voice burbled with malign pleasure. 'Hope you aren't in any kind of trouble.'

Mhairi's first palm-tingling reaction was that the autobubble driver must have reported her visit to the Valhalla. The penalties for conspiring to smuggle Vags were severe – imprisonment followed, in her case, by deportation.

'Send him over, would you?'

It wasn't a him. Five minutes and one large Halcyon later, she opened her door to admit a young woman with an infectious smile. Her badge, which she insisted on showing, identified her as Karen E. Trivers, a special investigator who'd be co-ordinating what she called the search-and-rescue mission. Her own family were from Duluth, Minnesota, and were of Norwegian stock, so she knew just what kind of misery Mhairi must be going through.

'If your parents are alive,' she said, 'we'll find them and bring them out. On that, you have my word.' She smiled. 'I'll need photographs to distribute to our field agents.'

'I've only got one. It's years out of date I'm afraid.' Mhairi unearthed her wallet and offered a snap.

'Is that your brother? Wow!'

Mhairi gave the best smile she could manage. 'I'm afraid Charlie's dead. He died three years ago. He'd been ill for a long time.'

Trivers reddened to the roots of her hair. 'Oh, I am so sorry. They never said . . .'

Her mortification was so intense that Mhairi never got round to wondering how the Immigration people could be so slipshod. She began to copy the photo. After a minute, Trivers brushed impatiently at her watch.

'Look, I need a couple of dozen copies and I've got to catch the ten-thirty shuttle. Why don't I take the original and mail it back soon as I've finished?'

Mhairi looked at the dog-eared snap. 'You'll take good care of it, won't you? It's the only keepsake I've got.'

At the door, Trivers held it up and winked.

When she'd gone, Mhairi felt the weariness of someone who has laid down an impossibly heavy load. Her eye fell on the disc containing John's medical file. Until now she hadn't dared examine it, scared of what it would reveal. Well, she thought with relief, too late to back out now.

There were no nasty shocks. The medical record was startling only because it seemed to confirm Grippe's story that John had recovered consciousness with no outward intervention. Mhairi ran a search on the traces, looking for any anomalous patterns that might provide a clue to his recovery. But apart from some random blips – no more significant than a mayfly breaking the surface film of a pond – the profiles had the characteristic laziness of coma.

For day after day, month after month, year after year, John had lain in suspended animation. It was as if his mind had vacated his body and then suddenly returned. Mhairi looked up from the monitor and stared into limbo.

She put music on and resumed her task.

The first significant changes had occurred a month ago, in mid-July, when the blunt peaks had grown sharper, suggesting a state between deep sleep and semi-coma. They'd fluctuated at that level until three days before John regained consciousness, when they began to show indications of dreaming activity. The timing was interesting – always in the evening, the excitation starting soon after nine, then slowly dying back. Mhairi assumed it had something to do with the circadian rhythm.

When she'd finished, she found that the anxiety that had caged her had fallen away. In its place, the gem-like flame of curiosity burned.

TWO

9

Wednesday arrived wind-driven and sleety. At San Jose airport Grippe, wearing black hat and Ulster, was waiting to escort Mhairi to a heliplane. She'd tried to soften him in her memory, but his lantern jaw and bullfrog eyes were as intimidating as she remembered. She smiled secretly at the image of him ranting from the pulpit of some fiercely Calvinist church.

'Major development,' he told her brusquely. 'John's regained the power of speech.'

'But that's marvellous! Has he said anything coherent?'

'Not really. He appears to be totally amnesiac. No idea who he is, no idea what happened to him. Doesn't even remember the meteor.'

It didn't sound hopeful. Because long-term memory was laid down over days and weeks, brain-trauma victims usually lost recollection of events leading up to the accident. But memories that had already been stored were encoded in different neural networks throughout the cortex and were rarely completely erased by localised injuries. To lose *all* recall of the past suggested damage to the entire brain. Yet if John could talk . . .

Mhairi smiled, not wanting to be drawn. 'These are early days.'

'Indeed.'

Through the rain-beaded windows she saw the spangled navigation lights sink away. She had no idea what course they were following – didn't even know where in Oregon Wellspring was located. Grippe, ignoring the empty seats, settled himself next to her. For some reason that had nothing to do with sex, sitting knee to knee with him made her acutely aware of her gender.

'Why you.'

'What?'

'You're wondering why we chose you.'

The possibility that Grover had an ulterior motive had certainly played on Mhairi's mind. 'Well,' she conceded, 'there are plenty of neurophysiologists better qualified than I.'

'You're too modest. I approved Grover's recommendation because you're the leader in the field of memory retrieval. Your personal life's of no concern to me – provided it doesn't interfere with your work.'

So he knew about the affair. Of course he would. 'Then let me set your mind at rest. I'm not here to rekindle an old flame.'

'Old flames leave scars.'

Mhairi kept her tone light. 'Do you see scars?'

Grippe ran his eyes over her as if she was a piece of livestock he was vaguely considering buying. 'In fact, it was Grover I was thinking of. I understand you broke off the relationship the day he terminated his nuptial contract.'

It was a low blow. 'Did he also tell you,' she said shakily, 'that that was only a few days after I heard my brother had died?'

'No,' Grippe said, 'he didn't mention that.'

'He'd died three weeks earlier. After that, I couldn't . . .' Mhairi pulled herself together. 'As you said, my private life isn't any of your business.'

Grippe was unabashed. 'Before we get off personal matters, I'd better warn you that Dr Scritti has developed an infatuation for John. You might find she resents your presence. If she tries to interfere, let me know and I'll take appropriate action.'

Mhairi gave a tight-lipped nod. 'Excuse me,' she said, gathering her things, 'it seems a pity to waste all this space.'

She went and sat across the aisle and ran through the programme she'd devised for John's examination. Five days wasn't nearly enough. Ordinarily, she could have counted on the assistance of a neurologist, an organic psychiatrist and a neuro-therapist. She stole a look at Grippe. It seemed that he wanted news of John's recovery to be kept to as few people as possible.

A shift in the atmosphere distracted her. The light at the window had brightened enough to sting her eyelids. They broke into clear sky and she saw the heliplane's shadow racing them across the clouds. She clapped her hands like a child at a magic show.

'The sun!'

Grippe looked up indulgently. 'The skies are a lot clearer inland. At Zygote we get gorgeous sunsets – all the dust in the atmosphere.'

The sun wasn't much of a spectacle now – an orange blur, smouldering like a coal dimmed with the ash of its own burning. Mhairi peered down at leaden hills rising from a sea of dull mercury.

'Have we crossed the Line?' she asked quietly.

'About fifteen minutes ago.' Grippe leaned forward and flicked on the intercom. 'Grady, is it safe to take us lower?' He smiled at Mhairi with half his mouth. 'Sometimes people take pot-shots at us.'

The heliplane raced above slopes strewn with fallen trees. A road coiled out of the hills and set off across flatland. The blacktop was frost-crazed and littered with slewed cars and other wreckage. This had been desert a few years ago. Now ice-contoured lakes and braided streams flooded the depressions, and a green-grey scum of mosses had colonised the playa flats. Across one of the lakes rippled a white rectangle, the movement beginning at one side and undulating in a slow wave towards the other – a flock of snow geese passaging south from their Montana breeding grounds.

A smudge at the road's vanishing point hardened into a few houses and trailers strung out beside a cement-block gas station still flying a sign that was the only blip of colour between horizons. Mhairi held her breath, expecting to see a figure break cover, but the settlement had been emptied of movement.

The town fell back and they flew on over a high wilderness chilled down to tundra striped like a bar-code. To the north, four or five separate snow squalls drifted earthwards in dark tendrils. Night was beginning to fill the hollows of the land when Mhairi spotted a shadow curving like smoke across the barrens. She rubbed her eyes.

'I can see a herd of animals – thousands of them.'

Grippe came across and straddled her seat with his hands. 'Caribou,' he said. 'We get musk oxen, too, and even the occasional polar bear in winter. No megafauna, though. They're further west, near Massacre Lake.' He glanced down. 'You know about the Genesis project – cloning Pleistocene mammals as a new food source?'

'I know we imported mammoths from Russia.'

'Not only mammoths. Genesis has replicated giant ground sloths, sabre-tooth cats and dire wolves from La Brea tar pit specimens.'

'Dire wolves?'

'Nasty brutes, like a hybrid of hyena and timber wolf, larger than either and powerful enough to crack open a mammoth's shin bone. Scavengers. They used to lurk around the tar pits waiting for other creatures to get trapped, but a lot of them got mired themselves.' Grippe bared his teeth. 'Life in Los Angeles hasn't changed much in 20,000 years.'

'Why would anyone want to recreate such a creature, let alone release it into the wild?'

Grippe dropped into the seat beside her. 'Genesis are studying predator-prey dynamics among the megafauna in the hope of shedding light on their mass extinction. Did you know, Dr Magnusson, that at the end of the last ice age, in the very dawn of the modern era, 70 per cent of all the large mammals in North America vanished in the space of a few thousand years? Wiped out in a geological eye-blink.'

'I assume the warming climate killed them.'

'They'd survived several previous interglacials, and there was nothing significantly different about the last one.'

'Except the presence of man.'

'Mammoths eleven feet tall and bears twice as large as an Alaskan grizzly exterminated by a few thousand savages armed with bows and spears? No, the clue to what happened is preserved in the mammoths recovered from the Siberian permafrost. Although they were deep-frozen, their stomach contents included birch leaves and flowers, indicating they'd died in the summer. Now what does that suggest to you?'

Across Mhairi's mind flickered newsreel sequences filmed in the months after the meteor strike – a herd of cattle standing flash-frozen in a New Hampshire pasture; the corpses of shoppers sheathed in ice outside a Beijing hypermarket; European forests flailed to poles by hailstones as big as baseballs.

'Another cosmic impact,' she said.

'God may not play dice, as Einstein remarked, but he does seem to shoot pool.'

After Grippe had returned to his seat, Mhairi kept watch until twilight had drowned every feature except a cape of mountains rooted in the west. She was about to abandon her vigil when she spotted something that made her stiffen.

'A light,' she said. 'There's some kind of light.'

Grippe didn't stir. 'We see a few.'

Mhairi glanced back at the winking pinpoint. 'Shouldn't we investigate?'

He looked up. 'Dr Magnusson, that could be anyone down there.'

'But it may be someone in distress.'

'Or it could be someone trying to attract us within range. There isn't much food above the Line, but there are still plenty of weapons and some very nasty people prepared to use them.'

When Mhairi turned back, the light was gone. Night had fallen like an axe. She stared into it through her own reflection. That could have been anyone, she thought. That could have been me.

She jerked out of a doze to find Grippe leaning over her. The sensation of having lost her bearings produced a tight, trapped feeling in her throat. She blinked aimlessly. 'Where are we?' she demanded in a sleep-thickened voice.

'Nearly home,' he murmured, pointing at a grounded star pulsing in the darkness. He lowered himself once more into the seat beside her, speaking with a reverent tone. 'To me it's more than home. I think of Wellspring as our ancestors must have regarded monasteries in the ninth century – beacons of enlightenment in an age of barbarism.'

From a distance the guiding light shone warm yellow, but as it drew them in its colour values shifted to the cold end of the spectrum.

'How many people down there?' Mhairi murmured.

'Nearly four hundred. We have no difficulty attracting applicants; the problem is finding candidates who pass Zygote's screening process. Our technical support staff are easier to match than scientists; most are ex-military with spotless service records, people used to the discipline of confinement.'

'In that case, I doubt if I'd pass through the eye of Wellspring's needle.'

Grippe's mood was almost jocular. 'I suspect you wouldn't. Not that you'll find Wellspring monastic. We have three restaurants, a sports complex, multiplex cinema, a tropical arboretum, several musical and dramatic groups – and, of course, the full range of personal facilities.'

'How do you stay in touch with the south?'

'Ah, the rumours about government jamming radio transmissions. Well, they're wrong; the electromagnetic disturbance created by the meteor has played havoc with conventional satellite systems. All the signals we send and receive have to be cleaned up. We've had to make special arrangements with the military.'

That was the second mention of a connection between Zygote and the military. Mhairi didn't follow it up. 'Do you recruit couples?'

'As a rule, no. Obviously, in a closed environment like Wellspring, sexual liaisons can't be entirely suppressed, but the moment they become too obsessive, we separate the couples.'

Sounds like an entrancing place to live, Mhairi thought. 'Are your employees allowed back into civilisation?'

Grippe laughed. 'Wellspring isn't a labour camp. All our staffers have one month's annual leave. Most spend it at one of our resort centres in Guatemala or Hawaii. On their return they're subject to a random security debriefing. Which reminds me,' he said, handing her a document. 'Sign this, please.'

It was a non-disclosure agreement. Mhairi eyed the blue constellation. 'Mr Grippe, you know my responsibility to John takes precedence over everything else.'

'Of course, but our work on neurostimulators is only one project among many. Although your movements at Wellspring will be restricted, it's inevitable that you'll glimpse aspects of other areas of research. Whatever you see or hear or surmise, you must keep to yourself.'

'Such as the human brains you're cloning?'

Grippe's expression returned to default mode. 'Joking comes under speculation.' He tapped her gently on the wrist. 'Six years ago, when Zygote operated a much laxer regime, our genetics team developed a strain of wheat that would ripen in low light levels and sub-zero temperatures. Two years and half a billion dollars later, a rival company filed patents on our invention a few days before we completed trials. One of the team had been passing on details of each breakthrough as fast as we made it.'

Mhairi wondered at the back of her mind what had happened to the traitor. She took the paper, scribbled her signature without reading the small print, and handed it back. 'Do any of your employees choose not to return?'

'Yes, it has happened. We follow them up. We do our best to ensure they don't prosper. So far, our best has always been good enough.'

This is going to be the most entertaining five days of my life, Mhairi thought.

About a mile from Wellspring, the heliplane's rotors extended with a shudder. Now Mhairi could see that the complex was pentagonal, the buildings laid out like a molecule consisting of a nucleus bonded by arms to five smaller units. The heliplane slowed, the complex rotating around them. All the buildings were perfect ovoids, the nucleus about twelve storeys high, double-skinned in glass and elevated on legs above the snowy compound.

'Administration and accommodation,' Grippe explained,

motioning to the central building. 'Clockwise from left, genetics, molecular biology, AI, and recreation modules. The streamlined design isn't an architectural whim. We sometimes get hit by winds in excess of a hundred mph.'

The heliplane lowered itself down through the gassy lights, swaying past knots of people spectating from behind the glass mantles.

'Where do you keep John?'

'Module 5 – special projects.'

'With Grover's apes?'

Grippe's head seemed to slide round on bearings. 'Dr Magnusson, we're on Zygote territory now, so I suggest this is the moment to put frivolous conjectures behind you.'

Abandon hope all ye who enter here, Mhairi thought. She studied the fifth spheroid and glimpsed a woman's lonely silhouette on an upper floor. Then dirt and snow blown up by the rotors blotted everything out and the heliplane grounded. Mhairi remained seated, heavy-legged, reluctant to move. A ground blizzard reduced the complex to a fluorescent blur and shivered the craft on its undercarriage.

'I suggest you wrap up,' Grippe told her. 'It's rather raw outside.'

Despite the warning, she was unprepared for the savagery of the wind. It punched the breath back down her throat and buffeted her sideways.

'My God,' she shouted, 'how can you bear to live in such a godforsaken place?'

Grippe's horse teeth glistened.

'What?' Mhairi shouted.

Grippe gulped for breath and cupped his mouth against the gale. 'I said, up here Zygote stands in for God.'

He made a run for it, heading crabwise towards an access ramp angled into the belly of the building. Mhairi struggled after him, hands splayed against the stinging grit. Through streaming eyes, she registered that the arms connecting the modules to the centre were glassed-in bridges elevated about fifty feet above ground. She caught up with Grippe at the base of the ramp. Two sets of doors insulated the entrance. As the inner one shut behind them, the white din of the storm was replaced by a jarring hush. Mhairi shook her head as if she'd just dropped thousands of feet through an air pocket.

'Phew!' she gasped. 'I'd hate to be outside and find I'd forgotten my keys.'

'Don't joke about it.'

'You mean people have been lost?'

Grippe brought a mournful gaze to bear. 'We did have a tragic accident a couple of years ago.'

Mhairi followed him on to the escalator with the wary solemnity of a pilgrim entering a holy place. Holograms celebrating Zygote's achievements in agriculture, medicine and robotics climbed the curved walls. Grippe had begun humming some ditty from a time before Mhairi was born. He broke off to point out a motto scribed in lights above the top of the stairway.

ZYGOTE
WORKING FOR POSTERITY

'One of our artificial intelligence researchers, Louis Dart, a genius in irrational numbers, got high one night and tacked a sign underneath saying: "What did posterity ever do for me?"' Grippe chuckled. 'Of course, he was off the compound within the hour. Dr Dart will be lucky if he's riding a garbage truck now.'

'You've made your point. No peeking, no negative thoughts, no levity.'

Grippe softened like a teacher who's finally got a simple lesson through the skull of an awkward pupil. 'Good,' he said, giving Mhairi an affectionate prod. 'There's no place for cynicism at Zygote. We take an optimistic view at all times.'

The escalator slid them out into a domed atrium so vast that the white-coated employees commuting across the hall behind the reception party were little more than stick figures. Mhairi's heart did a quick one-two at the sight of Byron. Standing a

85

measured distance behind him were two security guards, one male and one female, both wearing smiles that seemed to have been handed out with their ultramarine uniforms and holstered sidearms.

But after the first take, it was the man beside Byron who captured Mhairi's attention. Tall and dark, with features honed to matinee idol perfection, he stepped forward with an obsequious simper.

'Good evening, Mr Grippe,' he intoned fruitily. 'Delighted to have you back with us. How was your foray into the metropolis?'

'Productive, Paige,' Grippe said, curiously offhand. 'This is Dr Mhairi Magnusson, the neurologist who'll be examining John.'

Paige's hand savoured hers as if he'd been waiting for the opportunity all his life. 'Beautiful,' he breathed. 'Fire and ice, sunlight and boreal mists.'

'Well thanks,' Mhairi said, taken aback. 'You're kind of, er, impressive yourself.'

He smiled at her as if her skull was transparent. Under the exaggerated intensity of his attention, her own smile bent out of shape. She broke contact to see Byron grinning. Something clicked in her mind then. Cautiously, side-on, she examined Paige's expression and saw his irises alter size – an oddly primitive movement that reminded her of a fish's eye reacting to a change of light. She slowly raised one hand and passed it across his face. The eyes followed it with limpid curiosity. She jerked her hand away and his gaze lost it for a second, before zooming back into focus. Her hand dropped limply.

'My God, he's a robot.'

'Smart girl,' Byron said, clapping softly. 'The eyes are the give-away, but most people don't get it.'

Now Mhairi saw that Paige's eyes were tiny cameras that latched on to every movement. Everything else, including skin and hair, appeared organic.

'Unsettling, isn't he?' Byron said. 'He can see, hear, respond appropriately to emotions. Not bad for a few DNA parallel processors harnessed to the latest silicon and gallium arsenide technology.'

Paige winced theatrically. 'If you prick us, do we not bleed? If you tickle us, do we not laugh? If you poison us, do we not die? And if you wring us, shall we not revenge?'

'*Wrong*,' Byron told him. 'If you *wrong* us.'

'Not according to the quarto edition of 1600. Both wring and wrong derive from the Old English wrang and were used interchangeably until the . . .'

'All right!' Byron cried. 'You win.' He rolled his eyes at Mhairi. 'He can recite every word written by Shakespeare, Goethe, Dante, Confucius, Newton, Einstein – in twelve languages. Given the slightest encouragement, he will.'

'Yes,' Mhairi whispered, 'but what's he for?' She glanced at Grippe. 'If that isn't a breach of security'

'I *am* security,' Paige announced. 'None who enter here shall evade my scrutiny.'

'He handles the personnel debriefings,' Grippe explained.

Paige bowed slightly. 'Mr Grippe, I'm afraid I must ask you a few questions about your trip.'

Grippe made the best of it. 'You see,' he told Mhairi, 'even I'm not exempt.' He glanced at his watch. 'Grover, after Dr Magnusson has been logged and cleared, would you show her to her rooms. We'll meet in my office in forty minutes.' He looked at Paige and his shoulders drooped. 'All right, let's get it over with.'

Mhairi watched Paige's smoothly co-ordinated departure. 'But what if I go for a vacation?' she heard him ask. 'Who will examine the examiner?'

'You aren't going anywhere.'

Laughter bubbled in Mhairi throat. 'He's incredible.'

Byron's expression soured. 'He's a pain in the ass. Whatever you do, don't ask him a question of fact. His shortest answer will run on for hours. It turns out that the world's most intelligent being is also the biggest bore. And the creepiest. Paige is the only employee given unrestricted access to every part of the complex. Turn a corridor and you'll find him waiting. Look over your shoulder, and there he is, smirking.'

Mhairi was amused by the rancour in Byron's voice. 'Don't tell me you're jealous of his looks.'

'It's weird, but sometimes I get the feeling that Paige can think for himself, and that one of the things he's thinking is that he doesn't like me. The feeling's mutual. The day he's decommissioned, I'm going to throw a party – next spring, when the new model comes on line. Now *that* is going to be one . . .' His mobile bleeped. He grabbed it, half-turned away and frowned. 'She's with me now.' He listened, his expression closing down. When he put the phone away, his expression remained shut. 'That was Dr Scritti. Something's come up.' He turned to the female security guard. 'Sergeant Murray, could you process Dr Magnusson and then show her to her quarters?'

10

'She's here. A big redhead. One of Grover Byron's trollops. Jesus, you'd think he'd be more discreet.'

Dr Scritti's voice rousted Cope out from a strange country between dreams and wakefulness. He felt worn out and boneless, like something half-chewed up and regurgitated. In his throat was a sharp pain he couldn't swallow. Dr Scritti's words seemed to reach him through layers of hot muslin.

'We'd better get you smartened up,' she said, applying a flannel to his forehead. 'They'll be over soon.'

Cope welcomed the cool poultice, but there was nothing arousing about her touch today. She scrubbed his chest, taking out her anxieties on him.

'All the years you were unconscious, I was the only one who cared for you. Now they're all lining up to take credit.' She stepped back. 'You know what to do?'

He looked at her through sticky eyes. 'Sure. Remember to forget. Only I got nothing to forget.'

'Yes you have.'

Cope listlessly examined the ceiling. 'Heard any more from Sun Dog?'

Scritti stopped in mid-rub. 'I hoped you'd forgotten that nonsense.' She sat down at his side. 'Look, John, you're not the saviour come to carry off the faithful in a burning chariot. Sun Dog's just another cheap fraud preying on the anxious and gullible. He makes all his followers hand over their worldy possessions. I tell you, the only person he's interested in saving is himself.'

Cope's throat gave a wet rattle. 'How do you know I'm not the one? You don't know *who* I am.'

Scritti looked a bit baffled. 'Well, I must admit it's strange. You being called John and waking up when you did and having Indian blood. If I was a superstitious soul . . .' Her face got caught in an odd smile. 'No,' she said, and laughed emphatically. 'Absolutely not.'

She went back to work on him.

'You got things worked out yet?'

'I asked to have you moved and they turned me down cold.'

'So I'm fixed here for keeps.'

She didn't appear to hear him.

Cope used the only lever he possessed. 'I thought you loved me.'

She threw down the cloth. 'John, please, I'm already under suspicion. The night Paige caught us . . .' She shuddered.

'Who is he?'

'An animatron, a lie-detecting robot. You can't hide anything from him. If he'd interrogated me, that would have been the end of it.'

'It's the end for me if you don't get me out.'

Scritti groaned. 'I'm working on it.'

'How?'

She made sure the coast was clear and bent close. 'Remember I said how important you are? Well, there are other companies that would give anything to get their hands on you. As soon as this neuro is through, I'm going away to negotiate a deal. My knowledge for your freedom.'

In Cope's ear, it sounded as though she was proposing to trade one glass cell for another. 'Why don't you leave today – right now?'

Scritti's expression grew arch. She reached out and traced her finger across Cope's lips. 'And leave you all alone with that woman?'

Cope sweated in helplesss fury.

Scritti finished her rub-down and appraised the result. 'Now then, are you ready to face her?'

Cope was almost too weak to speak. 'I don't want to see anyone.'

Scritti clasped his hand in a way he found infuriating. 'Oh, John, I'd keep her away if I could. I'd keep everyone away. If I had my way, it would be just you and me. One day, it will be.'

Cope sneezed against her faceplate. The recoil threw him back on the pillow.

'Bless you,' Dr Scritti said. She felt his brow and frowned. Her eyes went up to the monitors and the back of her hand floated to her mouth. 'That kiss,' she whispered. 'I knew I should never have . . .' Her voice tailed off and, all at once she was in frantic motion, patting her suit, searching for her phone. 'Can I speak to Mr Grippe? Byron then. I don't care *who* he's with. It's a crisis.'

Cope watched her patrolling his capsule, her lips rehearsing soundlessly.

'Grover!' she cried, 'John's running a slight fever – less than two degrees above normal.' Blood rushed to her cheeks. 'Well, how should I know? He was perfectly well when . . .'

Cut off, she made an abject figure. A muscle fired in her throat and her pupils got big and floaty. 'Don't be sad, my darling, but I think this could be the last time you and I will be together for a while.'

Three men spilled into Cope's ante-chamber. He recognised Grover Byron and, alongside him, a doctor called Coombs. Both assholes basically, who spoke heartily and never looked at him face to face.

The third man approached. Dark-complexioned and heavy-set, he had the familiarity of a figure who'd walked many times through Cope's dreams. Even before he heard him speak, he knew it was the man called Warren Grippe.

The trio arranged themselves outside the glass wall and studied him with varying shades of feeling.

'It's probably only a slight cold,' Dr Scritti said in the background.

'Only a cold,' Grippe repeated, wrapping the words in sarcasm. 'About the only disease we haven't been able to cure.'

'There's a risk of it developing into pneumonia,' the doctor said. 'I'll give him an anti-pathogen shot and arrange to have a ventilator on stand-by.'

'I want to know how this happened,' Grippe said. 'In all the years John's been in our care, we've never had a contamination incident. Then within days of him regaining consciousness, his capsule is swarming with germs. *Your* germs.'

'I don't know,' Dr Scritti said, trying to unscrew her fingertips. 'Maybe on the night he woke I left the doors open for a moment.'

'You entered his capsule without protection?'

'I might have. I was excited, overwhelmed.'

'So am I,' Grippe snarled. 'Your recklessness has endangered John's life and jeopardised Zygote's most important project. If you were an orderly, I'd fire you on the spot.'

Dr Scritti's shoulders quaked.

Byron drew a line up and down his brow. 'Warren, this hasn't been an easy time for Monica. She's long overdue a break. How about she takes some of that leave she's accumulated?'

'Good idea,' Grippe agreed crisply. 'Monica?'

Dr Scritti recovered a semblance of composure. 'Yes, a week's vacation would do me a power of good.'

Grippe waved a hand as if she was already gone. 'Personnel will make the arrangements.'

She skulked up to him. 'I don't want to go to one of the resorts. I've got a girlfriend in Albuquerque I haven't seen for years.' An over-bright smile. 'Truth to tell, I'd like to forget Zygote for a while.'

Grippe's tongue explored his cheek. 'Very well. You can leave tomorrow.'

Scritti recoiled. 'Tomorrow! No, not so soon.'

'You'll brief Dr Magnusson. After that, you'll take no further part in her examination.'

Scritti grabbed Grippe's sleeve. 'Please!'

'Control yourself,' he said, unhooking her hand. 'The last thing Dr Magnusson needs is your hysterical presence.'

Scritti stumbled back. 'She told you to get rid of me, didn't she?'

'Dr Scritti!'

Grippe's shout stunned the room into silence. He resumed in a normal voice. 'You'll leave Wellspring tomorrow and return at the end of next week. That's my last word.'

Scritti looked disbelievingly at everyone before exiting at a wailing run.

'What do you make of that?' Grippe asked.

'We'll have to postpone the examination. Dr Magnusson's going to love that.'

'I was talking about Dr Scritti.'

'You think she's having a breakdown?'

Grippe's gaze bore down on Cope and narrowed in dark surmise.

'Maybe.'

11

After logging Mhairi's voice and iris prints, Sergeant Murray escorted her to Level 10 in a glass elevator that rose like a bubble in a capillary. All the surfaces were boron or synthetic mica that seemed to emanate their own pearly light. The effect was of floating up through caverns of ice.

At Level 10, Sergeant Murray led her along a deserted

curving corridor. Listening to her cushioned footfalls on the slightly clingy floor, Mhairi had the sensation that at any second she would meet herself coming the other way.

Her journey ended outside room 7221. Murray pointed to the pocket-sized scanner at eye-level. 'Step within a metre before speaking.'

Mhairi did as she was told and said 'Access'. The door obeyed. Expecting a sleep pod with soporific walls, she found herself instead on the threshold of an apartment warmly furnished with rugs, paintings and antiques. At the far end, a full-length window opened onto an enclosed balcony garden.

She orbited the room, studying the paintings, picking out books and sliding them back. All her favourites were there. Knowing who was responsible, she entered the bedroom with mixed feelings to find it anonymous. Lethargy overcame her. She stretched out on the bed and let her mind empty.

When consciousness returned, her hand had crept out as if to caress someone lying beside her. She snatched her hand back, saw that nearly half an hour had disappeared, and swung off the bed. Quickly she unpacked. She flung open the closet and broke into a rash of embarrassment at the sight of a CybErotic headset and harness. Banging the door shut, she wondered if that had been another one of Byron's welcoming touches.

Back in the sitting room, she let herself into the balcony garden. Directly opposite, Modules 4 and 5 glowed like irradiated polyps. The ground blizzard was still seething, but on this side of the glass the atmosphere was motionless down to the smallest molecule.

A buzzing at the door made her jump. With no background noise, every sound – even the catch of her own breath – startled her. She opened up to find Paige waiting.

'Mr Grippe requests your company.'

Mhairi stepped out and looked both ways down the corridor. She seemed to have the entire floor to herself. The walk to the elevator teased her nerves. No matter how covertly she looked at Paige, his eyes always caught her out, making progress a continuous collision of glances and strained smiles. Training her gaze straight ahead made her feel as if she was marking time while the walls slid past.

'You're uncomfortable,' Paige said. 'Perfectly understandable. Your intellect tells you I'm a mindless machine, yet every other intuition tells you I'm a sentient being with whom you should strike up a pleasant conversation.'

'Er, in my opinion . . .'

Paige held up an admonishing hand. 'I have no time for opinions. As Galileo observed, the authority embodied in the opinions of thousands is not worth a spark of reason in one man.'

'You said I was beautiful. That's an opinion.'

'Not to me. I'm programmed to recognise the aesthetics of spatial symmetry. Also, I flatter within reason.'

'So you don't think I'm beautiful?'

'To be truthful, you should have had your nose remodelled when you did the rest of your face.'

Mhairi braked. 'Not you, too. Let's get this straight. See this,' she said, touching her nose, her eyes, her mouth. 'This is the face I was born with, and I'm keeping it that way.'

'Suit yourself.'

His droll expression made Mhairi laugh. 'Grover said you respond appropriately to people's moods. Does that mean you experience emotions yourself?'

'The undisciplined squads of emotions are a waste of microprocessor space.'

'Grover's got it into his head that you don't like him.'

'I am not allowed to comment on my fellow employees.'

'Would you if you could?'

'No comment.'

'The security debriefings – how do you conduct them?'

'I ask the subjects to be seated, and then we talk.'

'You analyse micromodulations in their speech patterns?'

'Language was invented so that men could conceal their thoughts from each other. I go deeper. I get behind the words.'

'Then we're both in the mind-reading business. What method do *you* use.'

'I'm just a crude lie detector. I analyse the electrochemical pulses on the subject's skin.'

'A polygraph? That *is* crude.'

'But effective.' Paige took both her hands in his and exerted an uncannily human pressure. 'And I have seen the eternal Footman hold my coat, and snicker. And in short I was afraid.'

Mhairi tried to wriggle out of the chill that settled between her shoulders. 'It's hard to be scared of someone who sounds as if they've swallowed a dictionary of quotations.'

Paige looked at her from far back in his skull. 'Your hands tell me otherwise, Dr Magnusson.'

Mhairi walked into an atmosphere thick with recrimination. Grippe was installed behind a kidney-shaped desk in a domed penthouse suite with a fish-eye view of the heavens. Behind him, Byron tried to convey a sense of remove. A third man dressed in surgical white was present. Grippe's displeasure was focused on a thin woman with a pale, wilted face and eyes inflamed by crying.

He flicked a hand. 'Dr Magnusson, Dr Scritti.' He made another gesture. 'Dr Coombs, our senior medical officer.'

'Delighted to meet you,' Mhairi said, taking Scritti's hand. It was as cold and moist as a frog. 'I know how devotedly you've been caring for John. I'm relying on you to help me win his confidence.'

Scritti regarded her with tight-pressed hostility.

'Dr Scritti is leaving on vacation tomorrow,' Grippe announced. 'At her own request.'

'Oh,' Mhairi said, nonplussed, 'what a shame.'

'John's picked up a viral infection,' Grippe told her, making it clear where the contagion had originated. 'We've taken precautionary measures, but obviously your examination will have to be delayed until his condition has stabilised. I apologise for this lapse. I assure you it's not typical.'

Mhairi frowned. 'John's notes didn't indicate he was being kept in a sterile environment.'

95

'We don't take chances at Zygote,' Grippe said, placing his knuckles on the desk. 'Right, let's pay a call on our Lazarus.'

They dropped down to Level 2 and set off in loose convoy towards Walkway 5. Mhairi fell in alongside Scritti.

'Monica – do you mind if I call you that? I'm really sorry I won't have your input. Could we get together later and talk?'

Scritti kept her eyes fixed ahead. 'I don't have time. I have to pack.'

'Not even half an hour?'

'No,' Scritti said, and began to accelerate.

Mhairi took her elbow. 'Just one question then. On the three evenings before John regained consciousness, the traces displayed characteristic dreaming activity. The timing was the same in each case. Were you with him on each occasion?'

Scritti shook herself loose. 'Yes.'

'Talking to him?'

'Of course. That's why he woke. I brought him back.'

'I'm sure your presence was an important factor,' Mhairi said. She smiled soothingly. 'So I'm surprised you didn't notice the changes.'

Spots of red broke through Scritti's pallor. 'My attention was on John, not the monitors.'

'He would have exhibited rapid eye movement and sexual arousal – an erection.'

Scritti's flush spread down her neck. 'Are you suggesting that my conversations with John were lewd?'

'Heavens, no! All I want to know is . . .'

But Scritti had shot ahead, leaving Mhairi standing.

Byron dropped back to her side. 'Touchy, huh? What wrong button did you press?'

'I was trying to find out what she was talking about when John woke. It's just conceivable that something she said penetrated his consciousness.'

Byron walked a few paces in silence. 'It wasn't her.'

'What?'

'She wasn't talking to John when he came round. She was

watching a TV programme about that cult leader in Nevada – Sun Dog. You heard about him?'

'The latest con man of the apocalypse.'

Byron laughed. 'You think some nut prophesying the end of days turned John back on?'

Mhairi gave him a look. 'Hardly.'

'Well, something got through to him. I'll ask Paige to check it out.'

Two security guards checked them on to the bridge to Module 5. It was a seventy-yard walk and there was another security barrier at the other end. An elevator carried them to Level 3. The first door Mhairi passed carried biohazard warnings and a notice limiting access to P3 Authorised Personnel.

'What goes on behind there?' she asked Byron.

He slipped her an amused glance. 'Grippe give you his three monkeys spiel?'

Mhairi coyly put a fingertip to her mouth. 'See nothing, hear nothing, say nothing.' Her voice dropped to a fierce whisper. 'Grover, how can you stand working in this place? It's a prison.'

'I wouldn't be anywhere else. Seriously, this is the nursery of the future.'

Ahead of them, Grippe stopped and straddled his legs.

'Access.'

Mhairi's palms had gone damp. Breathing high in her throat, she entered a semi-circular room housing a glass dome with a double-doored vestibule. Her hackles rose. This wasn't a hospital ward. This was a laboratory.

She stole forward. John's body was so densely covered with electronic devices that at first she couldn't make sense of it. Then she identified the vulnerable angles of a shoulderblade and a face in half profile. She stopped like a wader fearful of stepping out of their depth.

'What's wrong?' Byron asked.

Mhairi shook her head numbly. For a moment it had been her brother lying there. One sideways step revealed that the resemblance didn't go beyond gender and age.

'Handsome fellow,' Dr Coombs said. 'I bet he's broken a few hearts.'

He *was* very good-looking, Mhairi saw – like the image of a god immortalised on an ancient coin. She turned her attention to his body. An IV central line was strapped to his chest and a catheter ran away from his genital area. Multi-coloured electrodes colonised almost every inch of skin, from the top of his shaven head to the soles of his feet. Beneath all the paraphernalia, his physique was as well-defined as an athlete's.

'Admit it,' Byron said, 'we've kept him in terrific shape.'

Mhairi tracked the loom of wires converging on the monitors and terminals behind the bed. One of the screens displayed John as a virtual figure with nerves and muscles traced in blue and red lines that brightened rhythmically as different circuits energised. She spread her hands, inviting explanation.

'Okay,' Byron said, 'we've surgically implanted stimulators in all the sensor motor control pathways. The big challenge was maintaining lower limb function. Because of the concentration of motor pathways in the lumbar area, it's difficult to target individual nerve and muscle groups without extensive surgery. Our nanotechnologists solved the problem by designing miniature sensomotors – no larger than macromolecules – that operate selectively in a single surgical field. The signal processing and actuating system is also an in-house development governed by a telemetry network that monitors various physiological indicators – lactic acid build-up, oxygen depletion and so on.' Byron drew breath. 'What it boils down to is that, each day, John gets the equivalent of a one-hour workout.'

Grippe stepped in. 'It's a major contribution to the care of long-stay hospital patients, paraplegics – any situation where an individual is immobilised for a lengthy period.'

Byron grinned. 'I bet there'll even be a market for rich Americans who want to cultivate the body beautiful without leaving their beds.'

'I'm impressed,' Mhairi said, meaning it. Relieved, too. Though questions still outnumbered answers, Zygote's neuroprosthetic system was way in advance of any other she'd seen. The commercial potential was huge.

'Well,' Byron told her, 'we've supplied the healthy body. Now it's up to you.'

'Can John hear us?'

Byron pressed a panel in the door. 'He can now.'

'Would you introduce me?' Mhairi asked Scritti.

'He's asleep.'

Mhairi studied the traces. 'No he isn't.'

Scritti moved grudgingly up to the capsule. 'This is Doctor Magnusson,' she said in a stifled voice, 'the neurologist I told you about.'

Mhairi kept her tone honeyed. 'Thank you for those welcoming words.' She brushed past Scritti. 'Hello, John, I'm sorry you're not feeling well. My name's Mhairi. I'm a doctor who helps people who've lost their memory. When you're feeling better, I'd like to try and help you.'

John's eyes cracked open and moved from right to left and back to centre. Reacts to light, Mhairi thought, shows visuo-spatial awareness, distinguishes individuals, demonstrates emotion appropriate to situation.

'He's not very communicative with anyone except Monica,' Byron explained.

'Switch the sound off,' Mhairi ordered. She turned a circle. 'I'm not surprised. Look at this place. It's more like an operating theatre than a hospital ward.' She put her hands on her hips and glared vexedly at the brain topographer and its bank of instruments. Occupying nearly half of John's chamber, the machine was a claustrophobe's nightmare – a four-foot cube of unpolished metal reminiscent of an industry-standard washing machine.

'I've repeatedly asked for John to be moved,' Dr Scritti muttered.

Byron tugged at his ear and gave a loose laugh. 'We never thought we'd have to worry about the decor.'

'Put yourself in John's place,' Mhairi told him. 'Imagine waking up to find yourself pinned down on an operating table with strangers goggling at you through a glass wall.' She volleyed Grippe's glance. 'I can't conduct a clinical examination from out here, and I can't establish a bedside relationship dressed like an astronaut.'

Grippe tapped his teeth. 'Doctor?' he said to Coombs.

'I advise against transferring John until we're satisfied that his immune system can handle it.'

'There's your answer,' Grippe said. Ploughing across Mhairi's protests, he led the exodus. 'Dr Magnusson, I hope you'll join me for dinner.'

12

Grippe went at his meal like a machine. In went the food, round went the jaws, up and down went his Adam's apple. Mhairi and Byron were the only guests. A butler and a starched maid – both human so far as Mhairi could tell – attended them. Through the roof, a rind of moon hung in veils of arctic light.

'Explain your programme,' Grippe said between mouthfuls of farmed whale meat.

Mhairi flung up her hands in frustration. 'If you can call it that. I'd planned to spend three days giving John clinical and psychometric tests before carrying out the scan. There's no point trying to analyse his higher mental functions without knowing if he can concentrate or memorise.'

Grippe indicated that he'd like more meat. 'Tell us how the topographer works.'

Mhairi tried to wind down. 'It functions on the same principle as a magnetoencephalographer. MEG measures blood-flow changes in the brain by recording the radio waves given off by cells vibrating in a magnetic field. This model has extremely accurate time and space resolution, enabling us to pinpoint and measure neural surges in an area as small as a thousandth of a cubic millimetre. Specific sites of arousal are associated with particular feelings. By mapping the scan results against a database, we can record and quantify the subject's emotions – desire, hatred, fear, amusement, aggression. The topographer is even capable of distinguishing nuances of mood and conflicting emotions.' Mhairi watched Grippe sawing at his food. 'Hunger and revulsion, for example.'

'How do you elicit the responses?'

'I show the patient a ReelWorld film I devised with a team of psychologists.'

'Can he cheat?'

'Suppress or disguise his reactions? No.'

Grippe shook his head at Byron. 'So much for free will. So much for a mind of one's own. Just a series of switches and circuits.'

'Knowing what someone is feeling doesn't tell us what they're thinking – or how they might act on their feelings. Mathematically speaking, the brain is still a chaotic system, inherently unpredictable.'

'A system of crude kludges according to my AI team. Give them ten years, they tell me, and they'll be able to come up with a better one.'

Mhairi addressed her response to her plate. 'Is that what you meant about Zygote playing God?'

Grippe carried on chewing. 'My father was a Baptist minister,' he said. 'His dearest wish was that I follow him into the ministry, but I abandoned my vocation when I found I was trying to justify my beliefs.' He dabbed at his mouth. 'You can't reason God into existence, Dr Magnusson. You have faith, or you have nothing.'

'What was the stumbling block?'

'Evolution. Not the theory that we'd evolved from bacteria by way of reptiles and apes. If anything, the concept of life growing ever more complex over billions of years seemed compelling evidence for a shaping force, a divine creator. But then . . .' Grippe sipped his Mexican claret. 'You're familiar with the Lopez case, seven or eight years ago.'

Mhairi nodded. 'A couple whose two-year-old son was dying of an incurable, inherited disease illegally arranged to have a copy of the child cloned from one of his mature cells. As part of the same operation, they introduced a gene into the embryo to correct the genetic defect.'

'A new, improved version of the child,' Grippe said. 'At that point, I realised we'd become the makers of our own destiny. Rapid, purposeful evolution has overtaken the ponderous process of Darwinian trial and error. We're now capable of achieving in a single generation what would take natural selection millions of years. Remember the public outcry at the time of the Lopez case? Forgotten now. Every city has clinics offering parents the opportunity to design babies to their own specification. Fair hair and blue eyes, tallness, high intelligence, disease resistance – you name it, junior can have it.'

'For the tiny minority who can afford it.'

'Unfair, perhaps, but the wealthy have always given their offspring the best start in life. One way or another, there's always been an inherited elite.'

'But in the past it was hit-and-miss – arranged marriages, special schooling, expensive healthcare. At least the genetic playing field was reasonably level – or rather, equally uneven. Now, though . . .' Mhairi hardly knew where to begin. 'Insurance companies demand genetic print-outs from their customers. Lovers run DNA checks on their partners. A hereditary disposition towards a particular illness is accepted grounds for divorce. We've legitimised eugenics. At this rate it won't be long before we've separated into two different races.'

'Perhaps more. Personally, I envisage a not-too-distant future when we'll have engineered strains of musical geniuses, warriors, athletes. I'm only surprised it's taken us so long to apply to humans the selective breeding techniques we've been using on domestic animals since biblical times.'

'Mr Grippe, people aren't dogs or horses.'

'Most of the human race will remain mutts, of course. I had one when I was a boy – Buster.' Grippe's gaze drifted in fond recall. 'Yes,' he said, attacking his food again, 'there'll always be a place for mutts.' He darted a sly look between Mhairi and

Byron. 'Don't worry, Dr Magnusson, with or without genetic enhancement, you'll have the pick of the gene pool.'

She pushed aside her unfinished plateful. 'I guess I'll take my chances with the mongrels.'

Grippe chased the last morsel of whale meat around his dish. 'You're being hypocritical. Your own work on hard-wired emotions has become an everyday tool of social engineering. Employers routinely mind-scan job applicants to identify criminal or anti-social tendencies. Only last year, the defence lawyers in a murder trial used their client's brain scan to show that, since he was genetically disposed to violence, it would be wrong to punish him for his innate make-up.' He aimed his knife at Mhairi. 'You, Dr Magnusson, are responsible for the death of individual responsibility.'

She eyed her congealing plateful with a rage made all the more acute by the knowledge that Grippe's accusation was close to the truth.

He indicated the topic was closed by summoning the butler. 'When John's well enough for you to examine him, Grover and I will sit in.'

Mhairi bridled. 'No, absolutely not.'

Grippe looked at her from under his eyelids. 'It wasn't a request.'

'If I can't carry out the examination in my own way, then I won't carry it out at all.'

Byron came down on her side. 'Mhairi's right. Our presence would be a distraction. We can use the video link.'

Grippe patted his mouth with a napkin. Before he could pronounce judgement, Paige came in and handed him a note. He looked at it briefly and passed it on to Byron, who studied it for a while, then pulled an enigmatic face at Mhairi.

After Paige had left, Grippe chatted about the civil war in China, the greening of the Sahara and Hilton-Marriott's proposed lunar hotel in the Sea of Tranquillity. Mhairi found all these topics less disturbing than conversations about the extinction of God and the individual self.

*

Alone in her room, she couldn't put Grippe's dinner-table conversation out of her mind. Unease sat in her stomach like her half-digested meal. She decided to relax in a bath and had just started to run it when someone rapped on her door. The knock, furtive yet urgent, seemed projected by her own anxiety. She turned off the water and edged up to the screen to see Dr Scritti peering away down the corridor.

Immediately the door began opening, she slipped through the gap.

'Monica, are you all right. You look . . .'

Scritti barged past, her arms held as stiff as sticks. 'I hope you're satisfied.'

'Monica . . .' Mhairi drew herself up. 'Dr Scritti what are you talking about? Why are you so antagonistic?'

Scritti turned viciously. 'Don't pretend it wasn't you who told Grippe to get me out of the way.'

Mhairi got a rein on her anger. The woman was unhinged. 'The first I knew you were leaving was when Grippe told me. Frankly, I was astonished. I *want* you here. You're the only person John trusts. Anyone would think you don't want me to help him.'

'And how are your mind games going to do that?'

It was all Mhairi could do to keep from shaking her. 'By getting a picture of his mental state, I can plan an appropriate rehabilitation programme.'

Scritti swung her head pityingly. 'You really don't get it. Grover's blinded you.'

Mhairi's hand shot out. 'He's got nothing to do with this. Now if you've got something to tell me, spit it out.'

Scritti looked at the hand clenched on her arm. 'Grippe will never let John leave Wellspring.'

Blood withdrew from the surface of Mhairi's body. 'Why not?'

Scritti detached Mhairi's hand. 'Because he's the blueprint of the future.'

Mhairi's thoughts floundered. 'How? I don't understand.'

Scritti had started walking to the door. 'Ask yourself how a molecular biologist comes to be caring for a coma patient.'

Mhairi hurried after her. 'What have you done to him?' She ran down the corridor. 'Listen, if you've performed illegal experiments on John, I'm going to report it.'

'Who to? As far as the world's concerned, John doesn't exist.'

Mhairi stopped as if an abyss had opened across her path.

Scritti looked back with calm resolve. 'I'm the only one who can save him. If you really want to help, let him keep his thoughts to himself.'

Her footsteps grew fainter and fainter, and when they had passed right away, Mhairi turned and trudged back up the corridor as if she were climbing a hill.

'Mhairi, what are you doing out here?'

She looked up to see Byron smiling at her. 'I was saying goodnight to Monica,' she heard herself say. 'She stopped by to give me some advice on how to handle John.'

'Good,' Byron said. He held up a disc in each hand. 'Got something fascinating to show you.'

He breezed into her room, making straight for the Digistation. She followed, sat down and pulled her clothes tight about herself. As she observed Byron, her heart distilled poison. Shallow, vain, blinkered by ambition – oh, she was the perfect choice. Why you? Grippe had asked her. Because she wasn't a threat. Because whatever she discovered, she couldn't do anything about it. Not when her parents' lives were at stake.

'Have you heard Sun Dog's pitch?' Byron looked up with a frown. 'Mhairi?'

She gave an apathetic shrug.

Byron shoved himself up off his knees. 'Listen to this, then. It's the programme Monica was watching the night John woke up. I've synchronised it with his EEGs. It's uncanny.' He came and sat beside Mhairi. She shifted away. TV screen and computer monitor lit up.

My friends, I want to tell you the true story of an American pilgrim called John who lived in this land of America 16,000 years ago. Yes, 16,000 years ago, my friends.

Mhairi dully registered the contrived intimacy, the repetitions and inversions.

One day when John was hunting buffalo on the prairie, he saw a light blazing from out the heavens. My friends, that light was made by a spaceship arriving from a distant galaxy. In it were beings billions of years more advanced than us. And you know what? My friends, I tell you that these visitors had no physical form, but were the purified essence of reason and love.

Mhairi remembered her bath growing cold.

Those gentle aliens carried John away from earth, back to their own world. Five years passed on that journey, and when it ended John was 9,000 light years from earth. Yes, my friends, I said 9,000. That's more earth miles than there are raindrops in a thunderstorm or grains of sand in a desert. Scientists will tell you it's not possible to travel that far in five years or even in a thousand lifetimes.

'The traces,' Byron said.

Mhairi half-glanced at the fluid lines.

My friends, the scientists are wrong. They're wrong, my friends, and I will prove it right here and now.

'This bit's good.'

My friends, in my hand I'm holding a softball. I drop the ball. There! It falls to the ground, accelerating at a rate determined by the law of gravity, a law no scientist can dispute. Thirty-two feet per second per second. My friends, that's how fast the spaceship accelerated. No faster than a falling stone, no faster than an auto-bubble leaving the lights.

Sun Dog's voice sank into a lower register.

My friends, I want to tell you now about this world that John found himself in. It's a world hundreds of times larger than our own sick planet, a place of stunning beauty, richer and more fertile than I can describe. John lived in this paradise with its gentle beings for two years and he was happy. He was happy, my friends, except for one thing. He was lonely. He missed the family he'd left behind. He pined for the woman he loved. He wanted to share this blissful world with others.

'Keep watching the traces.'

So John went to the leader of this alien nation and he explained his heartache. The wise leader said he must return. He must return because a terrible disaster had befallen his world and only he could save humanity. He returned as he had gone, in the same way and at the same speed.

'He won't find his girlfriend,' Mhairi muttered. 'She'll have been dead for thousands of years.'

'Sun Dog's got it covered.'

But when John returns, his family and sweetheart and all he holds dear will be nowhere to be found in a world transformed beyond all his remembering. My friends, he's travelled so fast that he's left time itself behind. My friends, John is only ten years older than the day he left, but the earth has aged 16,000 years and it's sick.

Mhairi raised her head.

Yes, my friends, the time of John's coming is now. Time is short. Right now, the world is in the final countdown. Right now, *my friends, right* now. *But John our redeemer is coming. He's coming to save you. He's travelling back to earth through the cold vacuum of space. My friends, he's coming right* now.

Mhairi watched John's traces subside into a drowsy rhythm.

Byron flicked off. 'How about that?'

'Brain washing for idiots.'

'I don't know, it kind of grows on you. But the point is, he got John's attention. You can even see how his mind jumps when Sun Dog says "now". He's the guy who woke him up.'

A headache throbbed behind Mhairi's eyes. 'You're telling me the man in Module 5 is Sun Dog's redeemer.'

'I'm saying there could be a personal connection.'

'Then get Sun Dog to identify him.'

'He's sealed inside a military cordon. We still don't know who he is. We've got *two* mystery people.'

Mhairi climbed to her feet as if she was manoeuvring on a cliff ledge. 'Goodnight, Grover.'

Byron followed her to the bedroom. 'Sun Dog woke John from his coma. The evidence is overwhelming.'

'I've only got your word John was in a coma. I've only got your word for everything.'

Byron laughed into his palm and rubbed his top lip. 'Mhairi, why are you acting so cranky?'

She choked back Scritti's revelations. 'I've spent my day in the company of a megalomaniac, a robot and a woman on the edge of a breakdown. My patient is sick and is being kept in an isolation chamber.'

Byron came towards her. 'Poor Mhairi.'

She swayed back. 'Don't!'

'I only want to comfort you.'

She found herself rooted by a massive inertia. Byron's tongue probed against her teeth. His hand cupped her breast and his thumb stroked her nipple. So predictable, she thought, feeling the thickness in his pants.

'Mhairi,' he breathed, 'if only you knew how much I . . .'

She shoved him away. 'If I want that sort of comforting . . .' She stormed to the closet and flung it open, revealing the CybErotic harness dangling like a bondage fetishist's rig. 'We were incompatible at every level except the sexual, but that's one temptation I don't have to worry about any more.'

Byron's mouth turned white at the corners. He made a faint motion of revulsion at the stimulators and pressure pads. 'Do you use those things?'

'Of course I do. Don't you? Or are you going to pretend that you use the manual method. There hasn't been another woman since me, remember?'

Byron passed a hand across his eyes. 'Mhairi, on the few occasions when . . . it's you I'm with.'

'How flattering – electronically violated by a man whose last words were to the effect that he'd like to see me dead. Well, when I strap myself in, it's not you I'm screwing. It's a tall, dark stranger, and the wonderful thing is that after we've brought each other to multiple orgasm, I say goodnight and switch him off until I need him again. No fuss, no emotional fall-out. Just guaranteed satisfaction time after time.' Mhairi whirled away, eyes smarting.

Byron lowered himself on to the bed and picked at the cover. 'You speak as if you're the injured party. Yes, I said some bitter things when you dumped me. God damn it! I'd just signed away a marriage to be with the woman I loved.'

'The marriage you forgot to tell me about.'

'I was scared of losing you. And you were happy enough to string me along until you'd got back into the academic fast-lane.'

'Until I found out that you'd been cheating on me as well as your wife.'

'The others were meaningless. You were the only one who counted. With you it would have been for life.'

'No, you're not cut out for long-term relationships. Once I'd been pinned in the album, you'd have gone after another specimen.' Mhairi sighed as if expelling bad air. 'People like you can't change their nature.'

He came up off the bed. 'Nor can you.'

His phone chirruped. The fatuous sound stilled the churning in Mhairi's stomach. She massaged her arms. 'You'd better answer that.'

Still staring at her, Byron extracted the phone and slowly raised it to his ear. 'What!' he said, jerking erect. His eyes slid shut and he groaned in almost sexual agony as he tilted his head back. He remained in that attitude for several seconds, then emptied his lungs and made for the door.

'I have to go.'

Mhairi took a step towards him. 'Is it John?'

Byron batted her hand away.

'It's John, isn't it?'

Muscles rippled along Byron's jaw. 'The fool's broken out of his capsule.'

13

Cope watched his hand slide down his thigh as indifferently as if it was an animal sneaking about its own business. He was so used to his body doing what the hell it pleased that his brain was slow to catch up with what his eyes were telling him.

His hand was moving because he'd wanted it to.

The discovery paralysed him. He darted a feral glance around the chamber, then studied his hand, not sure what to do with it. Slowly he extended the fingers. He did the same with his other hand, then raised his head and peered down the long expanse of his body at his toes. He wiggled them.

Okay.

He tested his mobility joint by joint. Sometimes impulses outside his control competed with his intentions, so that he found himself trying to bend his arm while some other force insisted on straightening it.

He stretched round and saw for the first time the wires leading from his body to the screens racked behind him. Watching the pulses and waves and bars, he wasn't sure if he was only an extension of the machines.

Only one way to find out.

He felt for one of the electrodes on the back of his left hand and nervously, staring at the screens, peeled it away. Nothing happened. No pain, no short-circuited plunge into darkness. He swallowed the tart taste in his mouth, reached for the electrode on his left wrist and pulled it off in one movement. His hand gave a spastic contraction, but when he rolled his wrist, it still functioned and he grimaced at the screens in triumph. Another bug dead.

There were dozens of them, clamped on him like ticks. Once he'd started, he couldn't stop. He stripped them off randomly and they protested with insect noises – bleeps and squawks and a plaintive whistle.

When he'd cleared everything within reach, some of the screens were still active. His hands went to his head and he whimpered as they encountered more parasites. He tore at them. More screens went flat.

Fuck you.

He was sweating and sickly, but he hadn't cleared the swarm. Dozens of filaments ran into a fleshy pad stuck to the small of his back. It peeled off easily, but as it came free, hot needles stabbed down his thighs and his legs convulsed. The thing was a flaccid, flesh-coloured parasite. He held it at arm's length and dropped it with a grunt of disgust. It swung away and dangled, bobbing flabbily.

He sat up and the fluids in his body separated, blood siphoning into his head, water squeezing out through his skin. He hunched over his knees until the objects in his chamber floated back into their proper places and proportions.

He was still tethered by the tube strapped to his chest. Another one ran from under his shorts. Delicately exploring, he discovered it was plumbed into his penis. Breathing hard through his nose, he exerted a gentle pressure and felt the tube give. A moment of burning pain and it slid loose.

That left the plastic line taped to his chest. He prised up a corner of one of the tapes and gave a couple of exploratory tugs. It didn't want to budge. Screwing up his nerve, he ripped with both hands. It tore loose with the sensation of flames and the sound of tearing calico. He did the same to the other tapes.

After all that, he still wasn't free. The tube in his chest had been sutured in place.

He tracked it to the boom above his bed. He tested its strength and calculated its breaking strain was greater than the force he could muster. He lay back, jammed his teeth together, grasped the stump of tube where it vanished into his body and yanked as if pulling out a tap root.

When he came out of his faint, blood and serum were running from the wound and the free end of the tube. His hands were slick with the stuff. He turned to the screens and saw that none of them had anything left to say.

'Find someone else to suck on.'

He dangled one leg over the bed and felt for the floor. Contact established, he lowered his other leg until gravity took over and he slipped, almost collapsing under his unaccustomed weight. Spread-eagled against the bed, he pressed himself up to full height.

Once he'd got used to a world turned through 90 degrees, he cast off, but the moment he loosed his hold, he discovered his sense of balance had gone. He grabbed for the bed, missed by a

111

mile, and spectated helplessly as the room pinwheeled round him like a scene from a carnival ride.

He pitched broadside and stayed staring into the crook of his arm at his own little patch of universe. After the stars had cleared, he lifted his head like a beached seal, saw the illuminated door panel and dragged himself towards it on hip and forearms. Though it was only a few inches above his upstretched hand, it took several lunges to made contact. The airlock broke. He hauled himself towards the outer door of his capsule and repeated the process.

Cool air raised his clammy skin. Sharp odours pinched his sinuses. He crawled on until he reached the door to the corridor. He reversed and arched, feet on the floor and shoulders pressed against the door. Palms slapping for purchase, he made a slowly extending bridge. Sweat sprouted on his brow. He thought his heart would burst out of the hole in his chest. At last his legs locked straight. He fought for air, thinking the first breath would never come. His heart under his hand whomped like a rabbit in a sack.

When his breathing had stopped rioting, he let go of the door. He felt like a rootless tree at first, but eventually he got accustomed to standing on his own two feet. He backed off and addressed the Exit sign.

'Access.'

'Voice not registered. Access denied.'

His chin dropped to his chest. 'Let me out.'

The door didn't answer. Keeping to the walls, Cope towed himself hand by hand towards the window.

The view stilled him. First impression was of staring out from the surface of a moon at a giant planet enveloped in cold blue plasma. Monica had lied. This was not America. This was not Earth.

Then he saw larval figures trudging along bands of light that ringed the sphere. His gaze travelled out across a gap of darkness and stopped on an icy sheen of mountains.

Cold air feathered the back of his neck. The glass reflected two giant beetle shapes creeping up behind him. He sprawled

112

round and they stopped, light spilling off their facemasks and armour.

'Take it easy, pal,' a muffled voice said. 'No one's going to hurt you.'

Cope shuffled towards a corner, the guards matching him step by wary step.

'He's bleeding bad. You think we should take him?'

'Grippe said hold off until the doc gets here.'

Cope fetched up against the wall and the guards stopped, too. One of them made a cagey inspection of the chamber.

'Shit, look at this set-up. You know this guy was here?'

'I heard rumours.'

'You know who he is? They tell you what they're using him for?'

'I figure he's one of the Agency projects.' The guard's eyes rotated upwards. 'Him and Byron's apes.'

As the stand-off continued, Cope's overdrawn body called in the debt. He went cold and hot all in the same moment and an oily saliva filled his mouth. His knees began to knock and his eyes had to blink faster and faster to keep from blurring.

One of the guards peered out of the fast-falling fog. 'He don't look too good.'

Cope teetered on the rim of a black vortex.

'Grab him!'

Hands caught him before he hit the floor.

'Hang in, friend, help's coming.'

Vaguely he registered more people tumbling into the chamber. Fish-eye faces loomed in on him.

'Get away from him!' a woman's voice cried. 'Both of you. Now!'

'Be careful, Mhairi.'

'For Christ's sake, the man's been flat on his back for three years. Where's Dr Scritti?'

'She can't cope with this. She'll flip.'

A hand cradled his chin and his eyelids were pulled apart. He saw a woman's thick, ravenous lips, a fat snout and green eyes elongated around the curves of her cheeks. Another gargoyle crowded down and a voice faded in and out . . . '. . . subcutaneous bleeding . . . possible embolism . . . risk of gross infection . . . resuscitation unit . . .'

Something cold smothered him. He heard his breath rushing in his head and in one last lucid moment saw Grippe lowering above, cheeks sucked in, mouth puckered into a poisonous bud.

Then something stung his arm and everything thinned to a thread and snapped.

14

He was strapped down in a room with aspirin-white walls. Grippe and Byron and a whole lot of people without faces were seated in tiers on the other side of a glass screen. They were pointing at him and laughing uproariously.

'What's so funny?' he asked.

Coombs, dressed in beetle armour, entered and inserted a transparent tube into his arm. He looked down gravely.

'It's for your own good, John. We don't want you to hurt yourself.'

On the other side of the screen, the audience chuckled knowingly and looked up.

Cope saw that the tube snaked so high that its other end was lost among stars. A silvery bubble was sliding slowly down it, and he knew with cold certainty that when it reached him, he'd be dead. There was nothing he could do to prevent it. He waited, mesmerised by the drop of quicksilver coming nearer and nearer until, like a light extinguished by a tunnel, it vanished into his arm.

He yelled and bolted up in a spasm. His breath choked in a gasp. He fell back with a groan.

Only a dream, a recurring nightmare. There were no straps around his wrists and ankles, no tube in his arm. As his wits reformed, he realised that Coombs must have removed them while he slept. The first time he'd come round – yesterday? –

the doctor and the red-headed woman had been arguing over him, Coombs insisting the restraints were for his protection and the redhead shouting that if he didn't release him, she was taking the first plane out.

He pulled himself up against his pillows and looked round his cluttered new quarters – table, chairs, books, paintings and posters, a television. His inspection ended at the door and lingered. Sixth sense told him there was a guard outside it.

A buzzing drew his attention to the window. A fly that had somehow got into Wellspring was aimlessly batting against the glass. Watching it, Cope ran his hand over his head, striving against his own invisible barrier inside. Sometimes he seemed so tantalisingly close to breaking through as images rose like bubbles, only to vanish as they broke the surface.

In his frustration he grabbed the TV remote.

A slinky female with a shellac complexion popped on-screen. 'What would you like to watch?' she purred.

Cope eyed her with suspicion, wondering if she'd come off the same production line as Paige.

'Name your programme,' she said. 'Anything. Whatever your interest, we've got it covered. And don't be shy. This line is adult-rated.'

'Just tell me what's happening.'

Another glossy female appeared.

'Upcoming, NCDV newstime, giving you the world in ten minutes. But first, today's weather. Cold and windy, peaking at forty-five, with tonight's low twenty-nine and snow flurries as far south as Monterey.'

A commercial break followed. Watching brand-name pornography for products he'd never heard of heightened Cope's feeling of being in a world skewed out of true.

A male newscaster addressed him.

'Fifteen days before the Argo launch, speculation mounts that mission control will shortly announce a startling new development. Meanwhile, NASA and Nevada state authorities are preparing for the estimated ten million people expected to turn up for the launch. With half a million already gathered outside

115

the site, the authorities are under increasing pressure to end the standoff with cult leader Sun Dog and his five thousand followers. He's refused the latest offer of a negotiated withdrawal, and it's rumoured he's retreated into one of the old mine workings around his stronghold . . . In Khartoum, US trade secretary Dilys Dupree has concluded a seven-year . . .'

Cope hit the off button in guilty panic. Time was short, shortening all the time. Any hopes that Monica would get him out were fading as fast as her memory. If he was going to escape, he'd have to do it himself.

His attention returned to the window. The wall clock said it was late morning, but whatever hour of day it showed, the light outside always seemed to be mingled with darkness. The desire to get a fix on where he was grew until it became the only idea in his head.

Sitting up left him so frail he had to rest for a minute. He set off, his feet scuffing beneath him like exhausted animals. He reached the window and grasped the ledge for support. The building he'd mistaken for a planet bulged against a dirty sky lit by a sun that shone no brighter than a flop-house bulb behind frosted glass. At ground level, a fence stitched across the near distance separated the Zygote compound from a great span of snow-streaked plain. The view wore him out just looking at it.

'John, are you awake? Can I come in?'

He estimated his chances of making it back to bed and decided he wasn't up to it.

A creamy face framed by a torrent of dark red hair poked round the door and stopped in surprise. 'Oh, you're up.'

She walked in, set down a case and advanced with a faint silken swish. He resisted the urge to give ground. She was tall, her green eyes nearly on the same level as his own. He could see himself reflected in them.

'You look anxious. Don't you know who I am?'

He remembered waking to find her asleep at his bedside, sitting so close he could make out the delicate veining under her eyelids and the faint bridge of childhood freckles across her nose. She'd murmured from somewhere in her dreams.

116

He shook his head. Remember to forget.

'Mhairi Magnusson.' A cool sound in the stuffy room.

She stepped away, giving him room to let his breath go.

'I hope you like your room. We don't know your tastes or hobbies, so we threw in a bit of everything. I don't know if you prefer baseball to football.'

He realised the interrogation had started and decided not to speak unless asked a direct question.

She stepped to the window and he couldn't help noticing the way her body moved inside her clothes. Her grin ambushed him and she drew up her shoulders in a mock shiver.

'Pretty bleak for August.'

He shrugged.

'Mind you, the sun's a lot brighter than it was three years ago. The last time you saw it, it was just a red hole in the dark. We groped around like lost souls.' Her eyes quizzed him.

Cope relaxed a little. 'People keep telling me about some meteor.'

'And you don't know what they're talking about.'

He shook his head.

She appraised him thoughtfully, then recited some names.

He had no difficulty looking vacant.

'They're the last three Presidents of the United States. Any of them strike you as unusual?'

Cope walked all round the question, not sure where to draw the baseline of his ignorance. 'One of them's a woman.'

'America's first female president. Ring any bells?'

'News to me.'

Mhairi came closer. 'Is there *anything* you remember from before your accident?'

He looked her in the eye. 'Not a thing.'

She put her head on one side. 'You don't sound too bothered.'

He smiled bitterly. 'Seems to me it's one damn thing less to worry about.'

She frowned. 'What *does* worry you?'

He could see the going beginning to get uncertain. 'Not knowing what comes next.'

'Do you think about leaving here?'

'I think . . .' He stopped, his tongue thick in his mouth.

She backed off. 'It's not fair me asking all the questions. There must be heaps of things you want to know.' She parked herself on the window ledge and hooked her thumbs into her tunic pockets. 'Fire away.'

Dozens of questions crowded forward.

'What's that singing?'

Tucks formed in the centre of her forehead. She eased herself off the ledge. 'Singing?'

'Coming from up there.'

She scanned the ceiling as if searching for a leak. 'What sort of singing?'

'Lousy singing. Comes all times.'

'Right,' she said, very slowly. 'Anything else?'

He hesitated. 'Not really.'

'Aren't you curious about anything?'

He stared at her.

'Do you dream?'

'I guess so.'

'Tell me what you dream about.'

He looked at the window. The fly had landed on the glass and was walking about. Cope noticed a spider's web in the top right-hand corner. A lump swam into his throat.

'It ain't much different from being awake.'

Mhairi seemed to nod inwardly. 'We'd better get on. We've got a lot of ground to cover before lunch.'

Without thinking, Cope checked the clock. Twenty after eleven. His heart sank. Nearly two hours to get through.

His dismay must have shown. 'How much time does that give us?' Mhairi asked.

'I . . . it's . . . I dunno.'

'But you know where to look.'

The dryness in her voice warned Cope to sharpen up his act. He mounted a diversion. 'How come I know some things and not others? Like I know you're a woman and that's a clock and that's a TV and that's snow out there.'

118

Her expression settled into medical seriousness. 'We have different kinds of memory. For example, you know when you're driving a car and come to a stop light and you downshift and brake?'

Cope nodded automatically.

'You see, you don't need to think about it, even though those are complex activities that take a lot of learning. But imagine crossing town to a place you've only visited a couple of times. Remembering what turns to make requires conscious effort. Same with facts like telephone numbers and people's names. Those are the sort of memories you've mislaid. My job is to help you get them back.'

Cope was wearied by the thought of trying to learn a whole world from scratch.

Mhairi noticed. 'John, you're still very weak. Come and sit down.'

He let her lead him to the table. She sat opposite and took writing materials from a case.

'What's that for?'

'Some simple tests. Here.'

Before he could stop himself, he'd caught the object she'd lobbed at him. A ballpoint.

'Co-ordination excellent,' she said, and wrote something down. 'You're right-handed, I see. But you seem a little stiff on that side.'

Cope, looking ahead for her next trick, answered sullenly. 'It ain't nothing.'

'Close your eyes.'

'What for?'

She reached out, giving him a glimpse of cleavage, and slid his eyelids down. He flinched at the contact of her fingers.

'How many places did I touch you?'

'Two.' He had to act dumb, but not that dumb.

'Open your eyes.' She was displaying three fingers. 'Now how many?'

'I . . .'

She pulled one down. 'Leaves . . . ?'

119

He'd begun to sweat. 'Two.'

'And one more is . . . ?'

'Three. But only because I don't have to think about it.'

'Let's try something harder then. How old do you think I am? Don't flatter me.'

Thirty-three, thirty-four, he guessed. 'Forty,' he muttered. 'Fifty.'

Mhairi laughed like someone to whom laughter came easy and often.

To his dismay, Cope found himself warming to her. 'What's so funny?'

'John, never believe a woman who tells you she doesn't want flattery. I'm thirty-five. How old would you say you were?'

He felt he was being corralled. 'How would I know?'

'I'd say twenty-five. What's left if you take that from thirty-five?'

'I never had no head for figures.'

'There you are! You *do* remember something.' She cradled her chin in her hands and wrinkled her nose at him. 'Go on, make a guess.'

'What's the point? Either I know or I don't.'

She didn't push it. 'What's my name?'

'I forgot.'

'You remember Monica's.'

'I've known her . . .' He was going to say 'longer', then realised Monica's name hadn't been mentioned since Mhairi had been in the room.

'A minute ago, I told you where I have to go tomorrow.'

'I didn't hear you.'

'Yes you did.'

'Los Angeles,' he said wildly.

'Well done.'

Her mistake drew an involuntary glance. She caught it with narrowed eyes.

'Right, let's get started.'

120

15

Acting dumb wasn't as simple as Cope had thought it would be. It was hard to be consistently stupid and Mhairi kept setting little traps, so that after a while he felt he was tangled in knots of his own half-assed deceit.

She slid another piece of paper across. 'On this sheet are twenty-five numbered circles arranged in no particular order. I want you to draw a line connecting them in the correct sequence – 1,2,3 and so on.'

Not sure whether to go for wild randomness or plodding uncertainty, Cope ended up doing a bit of each. He shoved the paper back.

'No more games.'

Mhairi's breasts lifted as she sighed. 'These aren't games – at least, not to me.' She mused for a while, then fished out a fresh set of cards. 'Last test. On each card is a simple pattern. I'll show you it for ten seconds, then I want you to copy it from memory.'

'We already . . .'

'This time I'm going to add a design of my own.' She scribbled something he couldn't see and held out the card. 'First one.'

Cope sank into a delinquent slouch. 'I can't see it properly.'

She tapped her index finger. 'Look closer.'

Cope leaned forward with ill grace.

Why are you pretending?

His glance jarred against hers. Her eyes quivered a warning. She put the card away face down and cupped a hand over it.

'Your turn.'

Cope stared at his card. The room had turned stifling. Cold circles formed under his arms.

'Take your time.'

The blank card stared back, mocking him. His gaze worked round the room and settled on the window. While he'd been preoccupied with Mhairi's tests, the fly had blundered into the web and now the spider was trussing it.

He looked back at Mhairi torn and anguished. He remembered how fiercely she'd fought to get his limbs untied. He recalled how vulnerable she'd looked asleep by his bed. An obstruction worked in his throat and his eyes smarted.

'I know how difficult it is,' she murmured.

He picked up his pen. Shielding the card with his hand, he sketched the pattern she'd shown him. He moved the pen to the bottom of the card. *Scared* was the word burning on his mind.

The point of the pen went through the paper as he recalled that Mhairi was one of Byron's women. He couldn't trust her. Oh, she acted kind, but they wouldn't have chosen her unless she could play the part.

His pen skidded and he spun the card across the table.

Mhairi pretended to study it, one hand fiddling with the top button of her tunic. 'You missed some detail.'

'That's all I saw.'

She reached for another card. 'We'll try again.'

His hand trapped hers. 'No, that's it.'

She sucked in her cheeks and nodded reluctantly. Then suddenly she smiled and stood up in one movement. 'Now for the enjoyable part. You're going to watch a movie.'

'What kind of movie?' Cope asked, slowly rising.

She slipped her arm through his. 'A very special kind that could provide clues about your past.'

Too confused to resist, he let her lead him to the door. On the other side stood a guard with a wheelchair. He broke away. 'Fuck the past! What about my future?'

She seized him by both arms. 'John, the key to that is in your past. If we can find out who you are, we can trace your relatives.' She drew him so close that her hair brushed his face. 'I know you're frightened,' she whispered, 'but I'm on your side. I promise I won't let anything bad happen to you.'

Caught up by terrifying inevitability, he let the guard settle him into the chair. The walls began to move and his breathing grew fast and shallow. Mhairi moved ahead and opened a flush-fitted door on an empty room as bland as a departure lounge. Then she moved aside and he saw a metal booth with a circular hole in one side and a padded trolley sticking out, next to a panel of controls and screens.

His mouth filled with the taste of bad dreams. He fought to rise, but the guard sank his fingers into pressure points and forced him back.

'Hideous object,' Mhairi said, giving the kiosk a slap. 'Hideous name, too – neurologic topographer.' She pivoted. 'It's a kind of time travel machine that takes you . . .'

Her eyes snapped past him. 'What the hell do you think you're doing?'

Grippe and Byron had issued through the door. 'I told you we'd sit in for this session.'

'Excuse me,' Mhairi said, bearing down on them. Big as Grippe was, she scooped him into the corridor as if he weighed next to nothing.

Byron wandered past and winked at Cope. 'Viking blood. You don't want to get her mad at you.' He popped up on the couch and hoisted one leg over the other. He smiled. 'Worked out how you're going to make your date with destiny?'

Cope felt the air grow congested.

Byron raised a dial. 'Got it all on here – you and Sun Dog.' He laughed and slid off the trolley, wagging his finger. 'You know, I reckon there's a lot more going on in your head than meets . . .'

He broke off as Mhairi stormed back in. She paused to stare a hole in him, then came and crouched in front of Cope. 'I'm sorry,' she murmured, 'they insist on being present. But you won't see them and they've promised not to interfere.'

Cope flipped her hand away. 'No, I ain't doing it. Take me back.'

'Please, John, you'll enjoy it.'

Terror broke down his defences. 'You're full of shit! I'm just a rat on a wheel. You think I don't know what you're fixing to do.'

Her skin turned waxy and a pulse beat in her throat. 'Tell me, John.'

123

His hand shot out. 'Ask *him*.'

Mhairi pushed herself up. 'Grover?'

Byron laughed defensively. 'Hell, I was just asking him about Sun Dog.'

Cope thought she was going to hit him. 'John is *my* patient,' she said, her voice quivering with rage. 'If you want to play at being a psychologist, go talk to your apes.'

Byron's country club languor deserted him. 'I was trying to help, damn it.'

Mhairi grabbed him and hustled him towards the booth. 'In that case, you can do a dummy run.'

He dug in on his heels. 'Hey, now look.'

'Grover!' Grippe barked. 'Just get yourself in there.'

Lips trembling, Byron stalked to the trolley. Mhairi, still sizzling with anger, went over and slid a headset on him, then turned to the control centre and punched a button. Byron slid into the booth like a body being consigned to the furnace. Mhairi's hands performed rapid passes and five screens lit up with thousands of dancing lights.

As soon as his head was inside, Byron changed his tune, sounding like an enthusiastic father coaxing a timid child into some theme park experience. 'Hey, oh wow! John, this is great. You'll love it. It's so real.' His arms came up as if they were on strings.

'It *is* real,' Mhairi said. 'I'm looking into your mind, Grover. How does that feel?'

Byron's arms dropped. 'Er, depends what you see.'

'You said you loved me.'

A sigh emerged. 'Yes, and if this machine tells you different, you must have bought it on Times Square.'

'When we met, you promised to save my family. Leave it to me, you said.'

One of Byron's legs kicked and went still. 'Lay off, Mhairi.'

'True or false?'

'Dr Magnusson!' Grippe roared. 'I told you to leave your emotional baggage at home. Now get him out and get on with your programme.'

124

Byron's face emerged as red as a tomato. He snatched off the headset and scrabbled at the console controls. 'Give me that disc.'

'Scared what it'll tell me?'

Grippe snapped his fingers. 'Give it to him.'

Smiling acidly, Mhairi ejected it and tossed it at Byron. 'I don't need a machine to tell me what goes on in your head.'

Byron shoved the disc in his pocket and brushed his hair back. He uttered a weak laugh. 'Just like a woman, huh John? Just like a fucking woman.'

Cope was utterly baffled. Mhairi knelt down and made a contrite face. 'Sorry about that. I got carried away.'

He looked at the metal cube and a bead of sweat ran cold down his ribs. He looked back at Mhairi and knew that he'd made a mistake about her. She *was* on his side. He filled his lungs.

'Let's get it over with.'

The guard wheeled him forward. Mhairi helped him on to the trolley and put the headset on him. He clutched her hand.

'Relax. In a moment you'll be in another world.'

He lay back, his stomach corded with tension. Underneath him, the trolley began to move and he squeezed Mhairi's hand so tight she cried out.

The next second he was in a sun-dappled wood. Birds trilled in the canopy, and a brook tinkled over to his left. Searching for it, he saw it sliding down an emerald run of mossy boulders into a pool hazed by insects. The scene was so three-dimensional that he reached out to touch a tree. He wasn't aware of Mhairi's hand slipping from his.

Her voice spoke in his head. 'If you recognise anything, shout. You can stop the film any time you want. I'll speak occasionally, but you don't have to answer unless I ask a question. Ready?'

He nodded.

'Enjoy the ride.'

The wood dissolved into a night sky filled with whorls of stars. One of them glowed red and moved against the tide with

125

sinister speed. Suddenly it burst into violet flame and hurtled on down, forcing the darkness aside. It plunged beneath the horizon and its yellow tail was still streaked on the night when the sky flashed into searing brilliance that bulged high into space and then, like a film thrown into reverse, rushed back, crouching into a molten core. From the white-hot centre sprouted a red stalk that rose slowly, obscenely – an apocalyptic hard-on, its engorged head swelling in spasms, mushrooming until its phallic shape was lost and it began to bud and branch like the organs of a monstrous foetus.

The fireball spread until it filled the sky. Within the flames Cope saw faces, castles, dragons.

'That was the meteor strike filmed from Dundas air base in north-west Greenland.'

Cope didn't answer. He was in Earth orbit, watching a bronze stain creeping around the planet. The mantle enveloped the globe and brightened to dazzling white. Within it, three soft bursts of red blossomed and died.

'That was the Russians trying to melt the ice shield with thermonuclear devices.'

Cars crawled down a city street through a rain of wet ashes, their tyres squirting slurry, bleary headlights sliding across a billboard showing three laughing teenagers drinking Coca-Cola. A fishing boat cartwheeled across a coastal town dismantled to bricks and matchwood. Icebergs floated regally past the Statue of Liberty. A blizzard streamed over suburban roofs and a stump of flagpole flying tattered remnants of the Stars and Stripes.

The skies cleared and he was on a meadow dotted with flowers. Seagulls flapped across a sun squatting on the horizon like an orange buddha.

Now lightning forked out of bruised overcast. Scene after scene flashed before Cope's eyes. A woman breast-feeding her baby; another mother shaking her bawling kid fit to kill it. A young man shouting at a woman in a subway; the same couple locked in a lover's clinch. A mob beating a man to death . . .

The vignettes crowded into each other until his head began to spin.

'Stop!'

A rocket silhouetted against a dark sky, rearing so tall that its mid-section was wreathed in mist.

'That's Argo, the space probe. You've probably seen it on TV.'

'Earlier. Something earlier.'

'Any idea what?'

Something glimpsed and gone like the flitter of a bat's wings at dusk.

The film began to track backwards. 'Tell me when.'

An image so fleeting he wasn't sure if he'd recognise it again.

'There!'

He was standing on a city street crowded with people going about their workaday business.

'That's Sacramento. Do you know the city? Have you lived there?'

Cope didn't hear. His concentration was fixed on a cluster of people waiting to cross the street. 'There's a woman. She's . . . a . . .' Her significance slipped away the moment he tried to grasp it.

'Describe her.'

'About to step off the curb. Black, middle-aged, grey hair.'

'Let's take a closer look. There. Is that her?'

The woman was half-turned away, oblivious to everything except the traffic. Cope felt he was skimming the surface of a dream. 'I think so.'

'Do you know who she is? She looks kind of serious, doesn't she?'

'She's just a face in the crowd. Let's move on.' Grippe's voice.

'Mr Grippe,' Mhairi said in a terse voice. 'Now then, John, any thoughts?'

The more he tried to tease it out, the deeper it backed away. He slapped his hand in frustration. 'Lost it.'

'Are you sure?'

'He said he doesn't know.'

'For the last time, Mr Grippe, keep your comments to yourself. John?'

Cope gave a little gasp. 'No, it's gone.'

'Never mind. We'll come back later if you want.'

His failure to pin the woman down left him feeling null. He watched the rest of the film without comment and ended up back in the forest. He hung in a mindless hover, mesmerised by the play of light in the leaves.

Mhairi laughed. 'Hey, don't fall asleep. I've got a sound clip I want to play you.'

Cope looked for her in the trees, unsure where he was.

Time is short. Right now, the world is in the final countdown. Right now . . .

Cope's rectum drew tight and his fingers curled into claws.

'Have you heard that voice before? Do you know who's speaking?'

'Why should I?'

'He calls himself Sun Dog. John, do you think you're the person he's talking about?'

'No. Let me out of here.' He beat at the trolley.

'All right, John. Take it easy.'

The rack jerked and he began to move. His headset was removed and he blinked in the bleached light.

Mhairi smiled. 'Welcome back.'

Byron grinned over her shoulder. 'Show's over, John.'

16

Midnight was long past by the time Mhairi finished collating the scan data. She played it through against the ReelWorld film, seeing exactly what John had seen, matching each image to his reactions. The printout resembled an orchestral score, each emotion precisely assigned, graded and weighted.

On a scale of one to ten, Grippe scored ten for loathing and fear, Byron not much less. Scritti evoked a more ambivalent response – hope and aversion simultaneously. When Mhairi assessed John's reaction to herself, she was startled to find that affection outweighed distrust. The finding troubled her.

Three times she went over the sequence of the Sacramento street scene. Whoever the woman was, the sight of her had uncorked a welter of feelings – hope, dread, grief.

Mhairi fast-forwarded and analysed John's reaction to Sun Dog's speech. Byron was right. John did believe the cult leader was speaking directly to him. From Mhairi's experience with other brain-damaged patients, she wasn't surprised.

Her eyes itched with fatigue. She locked her hands behind her neck and gave a large yawn. Time to call it a night. She stood, kneading her eyes, and was about to head for bed when she heard someone walking down the corridor.

She'd heard that tireless tread before, patrolling at all times of the day and night, the footsteps making a sucking sound on the floor as they passed, fading out as they started another circuit.

Paige doing his rounds.

She opened her case and took out the card she'd written on. *Why are you pretending?* Slowly she shredded it and dropped it piece by piece into the bin, then wandered into her hermetic garden. She rested her forehead against the cool glass and watched snow-devils spiral lazily over the tundra.

'What are you going to do about John?' she breathed.

The moon looked down with a frigid squint. She turned for bed, leaving the question misted on the glass to fade away without an answer.

Her alarm woke her at six. She pulled on a tracksuit, hiked the empty corridors and descended to Level I in Module 4 – Recreation. Inside, tropical fog smoked above a turquoise swimming pool landscaped into simulated rain forest. She dived in and swam five laps. She was towelling the ends of her hair when she saw Paige standing, knee-deep in humid vapours, at the opposite end – a surreal apparition tailored and coiffed like an afternoon soap star.

'Good morning,' he called across the echoing hall, 'I trust you slept well.'

Mhairi checked to see if she was alone. 'Don't you ever go off duty?'

'Service is freedom,' he said, and went off through the mist as if he were mounted on castors. Mhairi found she was clutching the towel to her throat.

By seven, she was back at her work-station, dictating her summary findings. She was still at it when Paige arrived.

'They're waiting.'

Eleven already. 'On my way.'

The conference room was on Level 12. Grippe was seated at one end of a table big enough to park a heliplane. Byron was positioned down one side. Mhairi took her place opposite Grippe. The butler offered her coffee from a silver jug. As he poured, she began explaining the difficulties of reaching a definitive diagnosis.

Grippe cut through the preamble. 'Grover and I have been called to a meeting with the Advanced Research Projects Agency. We don't have much time, so just give us what you've got.'

Mhairi's cheeks tingled. The man acted like a tribal patriarch. 'Did you watch my initial examination?'

Grippe waited for the door to close behind the retreating butler. 'Yes.'

'Then you'll have seen that John was unco-operative, truculent and evasive.'

'Clinically paranoid,' Byron said.

His casual assumption irritated Mhairi. 'I disagree. Despite John's belligerent behaviour, nothing in the neuropathological evidence points to functional psychosis.'

Grippe threaded his fingers together. 'Layman's terms, please.'

Mhairi arranged three photographs upright in front of her. 'These are scan images of John's brain, with the damaged areas shaded red.'

Both men peered hard. 'I don't see any red,' Byron said finally.

'Because there *isn't* any damage – no lesions or neurological degeneration of any kind.'

Byron thrust back from the table. 'The guy's been in a coma. How can he not have brain damage?'

'I'm as mystified as you are,' Mhairi said. She looked at each man in turn. 'Or perhaps you know something I don't.'

Grippe's mouth set like a trap. 'As I told you, John was given a brain-cell transplant immediately he reached hospital.' He waved at her to proceed.

She looked back at her notes. 'The scan did pick up a minor malfunctioning of the pre-frontal cortex. That's the part of the brain that acts as a buffer of everyday experiences. In John's case, the constraints are relatively weak, making everything more vivid and loaded with significance – like in a dream.'

'Adds up to schizophrenia,' Byron said. 'Delusions of persecution coupled with the belief that he's Sun Dog's chosen one.'

'He didn't imagine Sun Dog's voice,' Mhairi pointed out. 'When he heard him, he was in a mixed state of consciousness, neither asleep nor awake. I think he confabulated – displaced Sun Dog's speech to some experience in his own past or latched on to it in the absence of any other meaningful reality. Such delusions often set in among amnesiacs as clouding of the consciousness recedes. They can be hard to dissolve.'

Grippe made a bridge with his hands and rested his chin on it. 'Tell us about John's memory – or lack of one.'

'Antegrade memory good and immediate memory span normal. I'd need much longer to assess his ability to consolidate new learning, but I suspect we'll find it's unimpaired.'

'And retrograde memory?' Byron said. 'Recall of events before his coma.'

This was the issue over which Mhairi had burned most of the midnight oil. 'The scan reveals some weak responses from scenes and events correlating to childhood and adolescence. But after that, nothing. On the face of it, John's a classic case of chronic amnesic syndrome. He appears to have suffered total loss of personal identity.'

Grippe sipped from his porcelain cup. 'Gone for good?'

Mhairi hesitated. 'Not necessarily.'

Grippe glanced at Byron and set down his cup.

Mhairi kept it as simple as she could. 'Organically-based amnesias of this severity don't occur unless the brain damage is serious enough to disrupt cognitive functions generally. Since John has no detectable brain damage and his intellectual faculties are sound, I have to conclude that his amnesia is non-organic in origin.'

Byron leaned forward, his eyes screwed up. 'Are you telling us it's all in the mind?'

'Where else? The area of the brain associated with long-term memory storage is also part of the emotional circuit. In states of profound psychological shock, the circuit sometimes overloads and trips, cutting off the mechanisms of recall. But the memories remain intact and are usually recoverable. I had a case last year, a middle-aged amnesiac whose original diagnosis of pre-senile dementia wasn't supported by the scans. Under mild sedation, we stimulated the hippocampus and temporal lobes and extracted episodes of the patient's life, including the event that caused the emotional trauma.'

'Which was?'

'Three years earlier, he'd killed two children in a hit-and-run. He told no one. Burying the memories was his way of dealing with the tragedy.'

'Extracted episodes of his life?' Grippe repeated. 'How?'

Mhairi gave him a crimped smile. 'Switches and circuits. Last century, Wilder Penfield found that stimulating the memory zones with electrodes could transport the patient back to previous episodes of existence. We've refined the retrieval techniques enormously since then. We can go much deeper into the brain and we have an infinitely more detailed map of the neuronal networks.'

Grippe's eyebrows gathered. 'And you think that by probing around in John's brain, you could do the same for him.'

'It's a more complex case. We don't have any starting pieces of the mental jigsaw. But yes, there's a possibility I could recover at least parts of his memory.'

Grippe stared as if he was in thrall to her. 'Extraordinary,' he said at last, and grasped the table edge in preparation for rising. 'Well, you've given us a lot to think about.'

'I haven't finished.'

Grippe sank back.

'A group of us at UMC have developed a programme that uses the topographer readouts to construct a biographical profile of the subject. The results aren't what you'd call scientific, but they've proved surprisingly accurate. I ran it on John's scan.'

Grippe's eyes narrowed. 'What did you come up with?'

'A few stepping stones in a lot of empty ocean.'

Grippe rotated his hand. 'Give it to us.'

Mhairi consulted her notes. 'Okay, John's from an economically disadvantaged family. Father either absent or disappears during early childhood. Mother loving but not exactly a parental role model, and she also vanishes from John's life while he's still a child. I think John grew up in institutional homes. He's bright, but was never going to be an academic achiever. Probably dropped out of high school and worked in manual jobs, mostly outdoors – fishing, agriculture or as a mechanic. He's led an unsettled life, spent time on the road, moving between jobs. He has anti-social tendencies and is resentful of authority.'

'A criminal?' Byron asked.

'There's a good chance he's been in trouble with the law.'

Grippe rocked forward like a judge interrupting a flawed submission. 'That isn't borne out by our investigations. If John had a police record, we would have identified him from fingerprints or DNA samples.'

'A lot of records have been lost,' Byron pointed out. 'John's probably a Vag, so if he . . .'

'Let's stick with the facts,' Grippe told him. 'The so-called facts.'

'Is he a violent man?' Byron asked.

'Capable of violence – like most young men. Actually, the scan indicates he has a well-defined sense of right and wrong. Where he did show aggression, it was directed at the bad guys.' Mhairi caught the tail end of Grippe's sneer. 'Did I say something amusing?'

His mouth clammed and he looked away. 'Carry on.'

'John's heterosexual with a healthy libido.' Mhairi saw Byron's smirk. 'Attracted to slim, dark, feminine types.'

'Anything else?' Grippe demanded.

'Non-addictive personality, though drinks alcohol in moderation and has used drugs.' Mhairi had run out of stepping stones. 'That's about it.'

Grippe broke the silence with a sound like an engine being turned on a weak battery. Laughter, of a sort. 'Now I *really* know the machines have taken over. Grover, when we decommission Paige, I think we'll replace him with one of Dr Magnusson's excellent devices.'

'Maybe we ought to wait until we've tested her claims.'

'It sounds more impressive than it is,' she admitted. 'Analyse the entire male population under thirty and a high percentage would have a similar profile.' She began to gather in her notes.

'We'll keep those,' Grippe told her.

'Why? They're meaningless to you.'

'All materials gathered by you remain the exclusive property of Zygote.'

'But I'll need to refer to them when John's transferred to my clinic.' Mhairi stood as Grippe scraped back in his seat. 'We need to discuss the arrangements.'

'I have to get some papers in order. Grover will tell you our plans.' Grippe advanced down the length of the table. 'It's been a pleasure having you at Wellspring. We'd hoped to give you a farewell lunch, but when Washington calls . . .' He bowed slightly. 'However, before you leave us, I believe Grover has a surprise for you.'

17

'The hit-and-and-run amnesiac,' Byron said. 'What became of him?'

Mhairi ran her finger-tip over the grain of the table, vaguely wondering whether the wood was real or simulated. 'He's in jail. He gave himself up once the psychiatrists had helped him come to terms with what he'd done.'

'Maybe you should have let sleeping dogs lie.'

'They weren't sleeping. They were eating him up.'

Byron leaned back. 'If you're right about John's amnesia being psychogenic – and personally, I don't buy it – it must have been one hell of a trauma.'

Mhairi shrugged. She was tired and depressed and her neck ached. 'So what's the big surprise?'

Byron linked hands behind his head and looked at her down his nose. 'I'm not sure you deserve it. At the conference, you asked if I was still working on ape language. You haven't mentioned it since. Not one word. You're like all those other snotty Stanford types who think I'm nothing but an animal trainer.'

Mhairi shut her eyes. 'Grover, I've had hardly any sleep for the last two days. If you want to show me, fine. If not, I'm going to catch a nap.'

Byron tilted up onto his feet. 'Come on then.'

Mhairi only began to pay attention when she realised that Byron was taking her to Module 5. The elevator swept past the floor where John was housed and stopped at the level above. The doors opened on a hall lined with offices.

Out of them stepped half a dozen young men and women with bright cerebral faces. They all looked thrilled to see Byron and pressed forward, competing to be noticed. Acolytes and hand-maidens, Mhairi thought. When he made the introductions, she sensed a catty arching of backs among the females.

'How's the gang today?' he asked.

'Genghis is acting up again,' one of the men answered. 'I don't know, boss. He's more trouble than he's worth. I know he's the most intelligent, but he's such a disruptive influence.'

'He won't be with us much longer,' Byron assured him.

A parade fell in behind him as he led the way through a large door. Mhairi caught a pungent reek she'd hoped never to smell again. It filtered out from an acrylic glass enclosure about forty feet high. Inside, distributed around a high-tech adventure playground, lounged eight or nine chimpanzees.

'Today we have a visitor,' Byron called. 'She's a good friend of mine. Her name's Mhairi. Say hello.'

'Hello, Mhairi,' the apes said in desultory chorus.

The hairs on her neck bristled.

'You think he fucks her?' a voice said high up in the cage.

'He fucks everybody else.'

Byron betrayed no embarrassment. 'Don't take what they say literally. Their world view is pretty basic. They see everything in terms of eating, excreting, copulation, grooming, childcare.' He raised his voice. 'I've told you not to use the F word in the presence of visitors.' He clapped his hands. 'Let's sing our special song.'

'What's in it for us?' the voice from on high demanded.

'Bananas.'

There was a whoop of derision.

'Okay, chocolate cookies.'

Genghis peered over his platform. Whatever signal he gave was non-verbal, but it was enough to make the other apes straggle towards the wall where Byron and retinue had gathered. Genghis descended last, looping lazily down through the system of bars and ropes. He ran at the wall, performed a casual back-flip and then bared his gums and gibbered. The thought came to Mhairi, immediate and horrible, that if she went into the enclosure, Genghis would kill her.

Byron marshalled his simian choir with the flustered energy of an entertainer at a children's party. 'That's good. No Madonna, you stand at the back – back! – between Babs and Kim. That's right. That's good. Okay, gang, hold it. Right, after three. One and two and three . . .'

The apes launched into singing so ragged that at first Mhairi hardly recognised it as music, then she identified it as the tune she'd heard Grippe whistling the night they arrived. Words emerged.

'Cos you've got . . .
                . . . personality.
        Walk . . .
                . . . with personality.
        Talk . . .
                . . . with personality.

A chill started at Mhairi's feet and slowly moved up her body. By the time the chimpanzees had finished their chorus and the stragglers had crossed the line, she felt as if she was immersed in ice water.

Byron, a sheen of moisture on his face, applauded like a man possessed. 'C'mon,' he growled at Mhairi, 'show your appreciation.'

She feebly put her hands together. 'Thank you. That was . . . extraordinary.'

'Up your ass.'

Byron lunged forward. 'I've told you, Genghis. Now what do you say? What do you say?'

'He's an ape,' Mhairi muttered. 'What do you expect him to say?'

Genghis rummaged in his hide and inspected his horny fingernails. 'Sorry.'

'Apology accepted,' Mhairi said. Looking into his tawny eyes, she felt like a governess addressing the inmates of a lunatic asylum.

Genghis muttered something. The male apes laughed and Genghis swaggered in front of them, chest puffed out, arms trailing loosely behind him.

'What was that?' Byron demanded.

'Never mind,' Mhairi murmured sweetly. 'Just get me out of here.'

He rounded on her in astonishment 'We've only just started. We've got a half-hour programme.'

'No, really, I've seen enough. Honest.'

'She wants him to fuck her.'

'Right,' Byron said, transferring his fury to Genghis. He

137

lashed at the glass. 'You know the rules. Three strikes and out.' He turned to one of his assistants. 'Isolation for twenty-four hours. No food, just water.'

'For Christ's sake,' Mhairi said, stepping forward.

'Shut up,' Byron shouted. 'This is my show.'

Mhairi hardly recognised him. His face was swollen and inflamed. 'You've lost it,' she said, and pivoted on her heel.

Byron's disciples watched in shocked silence as she walked out. In the corridor, she ventilated her lungs.

'I should have known,' Byron hissed behind her.

'What did you expect me to do? Call for an encore? Request the Anvil Chorus, ask them to perform a tango?'

'You think I was trying to impress a talent scout? You think I was auditioning for La Scala? Of course they're lousy singers. That's not the point. Didn't you see how they grouped to order, changed position when I asked them? They did it all by verbal command. Don't you see? They understand and use simple language, and because they understand language, they can do things no animal but man has ever done.'

'They don't seem to enjoy it.'

'Because fucking Genghis has got an authority problem.'

In some way she couldn't rationalise, Mhairi felt violated. It was as if her exclusive claim to humanity had been invaded. She began walking. 'You know, Grover, I can't help thinking of Doctor Johnson's comment about dogs standing on their hind legs. It's not done well, but the surprise is that it's done at all.'

Byron ran to cut her off. 'Johnson's comparison was with a woman preaching,' he snarled. 'What is it with you? Why can't you recognise my achievement?'

'It's not lost on me. You'll get a Nobel. There'll be a slew of books and films. Your all-singing, all-dancing apes will star in a musical.'

'Haw! You're the one with the fucking tent show. All that crystal-ball shit about John's life.' He placed his arms against the wall and buried his head in them. He gave a muffled laugh. 'I've realised what's wrong with you. You're not a proper scientist.

Emotion governs everything you do. You're a walking, talking mood ring.'

'Just like a woman, you mean. A sack of feelings – not a single thought in my featherbrained head.'

Byron raised smouldering eyes. 'Those kids back there are the best and brightest of their generation. And they respect me. They recognise my achievement. But when I demonstrate it to the person whose opinion I value most . . .' He punched the wall.

Mhairi breathed in slowly. 'Grover, what's the connection between John and your talking apes?'

Byron straightened, regaining control. 'None whatsoever.'

'The only way you got those apes to talk was by tampering with their brains. My bet is you implanted a synthetic Wernicke's area.'

Byron smirked. 'Read November's *Nature*. It's nothing to do with John. He's not even my project.'

'Then why are you so closely involved with him?'

'Because I'm the sap who recommended calling you in. And the way things have gone, I wish I'd kept my mouth shut.'

Mhairi set off down the corridor. Byron fell in beside. Their feet slapped in rapid cadences.

'I want to take John back with me.'

'He's too weak to travel.'

'Not on the same flight, but let me make the arrangements to transfer him.'

'He can't go anywhere until his recovery is complete. That could take months.'

Mhairi heard the whine in her voice. 'But you don't need him any more. He's given you what you wanted. You've got your neurostimulators.'

'There are still some important tests to complete.'

Mhairi pulled up ten yards short of the elevator. 'Cut the crap, Grover. You're not going to let me have him. You never were.'

Byron peered up the corridor as if he was looking for a cab. 'Suppose you took him. What sort of future could you offer?

Forty per cent of the population are unemployed. Who's going to give any kind of a job to a man with no memory?'

'I can cure him. I'm sure of it.'

'Wishful thinking. This is a guilt trip, Mhairi. I saw how you reacted when you set eyes on him. He's a surrogate for your brother.'

Mhairi stamped her foot. 'Memory isn't the issue. Consciousness is. You have no right to keep John. It's unethical, immoral and illegal!'

Byron winced. 'Mhairi, I know how impulsive you can be, so as someone who cares deeply for you, let me give you some advice. Tell anyone about John and Grippe will destroy your career. I don't mean he'll push you a rung or two down the ladder. I mean, *destroy*.'

'End up riding a garbage truck.'

'Remember your parents. Don't jeopardise that.'

'You promised to deliver John into my care. If you won't honour that, how can I believe anything you tell me?' Tears spilled into Mhairi's eyes. 'Four years ago you persuaded me to stay by convincing me you'd rescue my parents. That came to nothing, and now once again I'm leaving empty-handed.'

'Four years ago I didn't work for Zygote. Now, I can even ask favours of government. You've spoken to their agents.' Byron took both her hands. 'Mhairi, don't blow it.'

Her throat bulged with conflict.

Byron moved in. 'I love you, Mhairi. I want to marry you. I want us to have children.'

She turned her head away. 'How very 20th century.'

Byron moved eagerly. 'No. Yrigoyen's right. In a few generations we'll colonise another planet. Our genes should be out there.'

'I'm sure yours will be. There'll be no shortage of receptors.'

Byron pulled her close. 'Our genes. You and me. The future.'

She smelt the essence of ape on him. It was not an aphrodisiac. She looked into those blue eyes that had made her think of summer seas when she'd first met him.

'If you love me, give me John.'

140

Regret or annoyance flitted across his face. 'It's not my decision. It's not Grippe's either.' He took a look behind him and lowered his voice. 'Look, I shouldn't be telling you this, but John's no longer our baby. The Agency is taking him off our hands.'

'Why? What makes him so important? It's not the neuro-stimulators. You've done something to him. Tell me!'

'I can't. One day you'll understand.'

Mhairi stepped out of his embrace. 'You can tell Grippe I'll keep Zygote's secret.' She began walking to the elevator. 'For my parents' sake.'

THREE

18

Back at her Rose Valley apartment, the first thing Mhairi did was go through her e-mail and post. No word from Karen Trivers, and since it was Sunday, there wasn't any point calling her at Immigration.

Mhairi was left hanging. In her empty apartment, she haunted herself. Her brain resisted the Halcyon she took in order to sleep. She tossed and turned, her mood flipping from gut-twisting hopes about her parents to shameful anxiety about John.

She hadn't been able to summon the nerve to say goodbye to him. What could she have said? Everything's going to be fine, John? I lied to you, John?

Giving up on sleep, she rose at five, feeling as if her skin had been turned inside out. It was still dark when she reached her office in a UMC outstation sited in Golden Gate Park. She watched the clock hands pull themselves towards nine Washington time, then gave Trivers another half-hour to organise herself.

All Mhairi's emotional investment was wasted. Trivers was on assignment in Dallas, her personal assistant said, and wouldn't be back at her desk till Wednesday. No, there was no news, no messages.

Mhairi politely pointed out that the photo she'd lent Trivers hadn't been returned. The assistant said she knew nothing about that either.

Mhairi hadn't moved when Professor Newman looked in and swept her eyes over her as if she was a heap of soiled laundry.

'I hope your jaunt hasn't left you too tired to catch up on your work.'

Mhairi didn't know whether to laugh or cry as she realised

that her boss assumed her frayed appearance was the result of fucking Byron for four days straight.

Optimism had been crushed into one last redoubt by the time Wednesday came round. Mhairi picked up the phone. Her knuckles whitened.

'Please,' she murmured. 'Oh please.'

Trivers answered immediately. 'Hi, Mhairi, how you doing?' She sounded as if she was finishing a mouthful of food.

'Have you . . . ?' Mhairi couldn't get the words out.

'Your parents are alive.'

Mhairi sagged against the desk. 'Oh thank you. Thank you!'

'Unfortunately, we haven't made contact with them yet. Apparently they moved to British Columbia around April. No positive news since then, but I've got a good feeling about this one. Hang in till the end of the week.'

'I will,' Mhairi said. 'I will.'

'Okay, speak to you Friday.'

'Oh, the photograph. I still don't have it.'

'Are you sure? Because I certainly remember telling my assistant to return it.'

'She told me she knew nothing about it.'

Trivers breathed audibly, but didn't speak.

Mhairi was smiling desperately without being aware of it. 'That was the only photograph I have. I'd really . . .'

'I know,' Trivers said. She sighed as if Mhairi had laid an imposition on her. 'Okay, I'll chase it. But hey, why worry about a picture when you'll soon have the real thing?'

Mhairi laid down the phone and ran her finger along her eyelids, peeling away tears. She sighed from the bottom of her soul, expelling all her frustrations and doubts. Chantal, the only person she'd told about her parents, approached in nervous expectation.

'They're alive.'

'Oh, honey,' Chantal said, hugging her. 'I'm so thrilled.' She

146

stepped back with an apologetic grimace. 'I hate to spoil the mood, but your ten o'clock appointment's waiting.'

'Oh my gosh!' Mhairi said, the world rushing in on her.

She just had time to go to the cloakroom and dash water over her face before running downstairs on a cloud of joy to see if Kit's parents had decided to switch their daughter off.

Ron Gloss, red-eyed and haggard, was standing by the window. In Mhairi's experience, it was usually the father who held out against withdrawing life support for a child. She went to Amerila Gloss and took her hands.

'We've decided to let her go.'

A vision of John undercut Mhairi's relief. 'I think that's the only realistic decision.'

'Tell us what happens. I don't want Kit . . . I don't want her to suffer.'

Kit had been beyond pain or any other experience for months, but logic had little place in this situation.

'We'll give her a sedative before removing the respirator. She'll go quickly and peacefully.'

'When?'

'When you're ready.'

The father shifted guiltily. 'It's taken us a lot of tears to get here. I don't think we can bear to wait much longer. If it's going to be done, we'd prefer it to be . . .'

'I understand. The clinical evidence isn't in doubt. I need to fetch two colleagues as witnesses.'

The parents looked at each other. 'You mean . . . right now?'

'When you've said goodbye.'

At 11.13 Kit Gloss breathed her last sigh – a long intake of breath, as though she'd been struck by a thought so exciting, she couldn't get it out. Her heart continued beating for a minute longer, the ECG trace flattening and growing erratic until, at 11.15, it ceased to register any cardiac activity. At 11.17, Mhairi and two consultant physicians agreed that the girl displayed no vital signs and switched off the monitors. At 11.20 Mhairi signed the death certificate.

'Is it okay if we sit with her a while?' Amerila Gloss asked.

'Of course. As long as you like. Would you like me to stay with you?'

They shook their heads.

On the way back to her office, Mhairi pondered how cruelly fate worked, giving and taking away without favour or fairness.

'Mhairi?'

Chantal must have been standing in front of her for several seconds.

'Sorry, miles away.'

'There's a Harry Fender wants to talk to you, said he'd called on you at home, but the gateman wouldn't let him in. Says it's important.'

'Put him through.' Waiting for the connection, Mhairi felt light breaking through the clouds. 'Harry, how are you?'

'Okay, yeah. You?'

'Oh, up and down. It's good to hear you.'

'Right, same here. Look, Doc . . . Mhairi . . . I got something to tell you.'

'I've got some news, too.' Mhairi paused, still smiling. 'You first.'

'Not on the phone. I thought maybe I could stop by after work.'

'I won't be finished here till past seven. I've been away and I'm catching up on the backlog.' She pictured herself moping away the evening at home. 'Why don't we exchange our news over supper?' She waited. 'Harry?'

'Nice thought, but maybe not tonight.'

Worried about the expense, Mhairi decided. 'It's on me, Harry. The least I can do.'

Another cavernous pause. 'What the hell? In the worst of times you gotta eat. I'll pick you up quarter after seven.'

She felt strangely buoyed by the thought of seeing Fender, and when she emerged into reception she wasn't disappointed. He was chatting up a nurse – a double-breasted goblin in

148

elevator shoes, the scant remains of his hair noodled over his pate. His mood sobered when he saw Mhairi.

'So where are we eating?'

'You choose,' she told him. 'All the restaurants I know are used by colleagues, and right now the last thing I want to see is another scientist.'

'You like seafood?'

'So long as it isn't krill.'

'Then you're definitely paying, because my pockets don't go deeper than plankton.'

Out in the visitors' parking lot, Mhairi balked at the sight of his car.

'It's okay,' he told her. 'I got it valeted.'

On the drive he made stilted small-talk. 'So what took you out of town?'

'A consultancy – a coma case in Santa Fe.'

'Uh huh. What's the weather like down there?'

'Pretty good. Better than here. Actually, I'm not sure. I was indoors the whole time.' She skipped over the subject. 'Where do you live, Harry?'

'Hunter's Point,' he said without inflexion.

It didn't need any. The Point was the very worst district in the entire Bay Area. It was a post-industrial sore, a human cesspit, a reproach to civilisation. Mhairi had never ventured into it.

'We're not eating there, are we?'

'Hell no. Going to a place in Montara.'

Conversation dwindled. Fender took the Southern Freeway, shoehorning between commuters cruising half-asleep on their programmed rat runs. They hit the coast south of Daly City and Mhairi saw the toothy gleam of bergs out to sea. A mile or two further on, fog rolled across the road, slowing them to a crawl. Fender was giving off worrying vibrations. Unease wormed between Mhairi's ribs. After all, she knew nothing about him except that he had a low flashpoint.

She gave a nervous laugh. 'Maybe this was a mistake,' she said, gesturing at the fog but really meaning the whole outing.

A wail cut through Fender's response. 'What the . . . !' he exclaimed, swerving to avoid a pair of glaring button eyes.

A truck blared past, buffeting them with its wake.

'Prick,' Fender said, too late to carry conviction.

Mhairi opened her eyes. 'You were on the wrong side of the road.'

She spent the rest of the journey braced for the next head-on. By the time the restaurant lights appeared, she was worn out. Once inside, though, her spirits revived. It was four-fifths empty, respectable in a faded, pre-catastrophe style. The management was Italian and an aura of the Adriatic still clung to the place. Fender ordered whisky and Mhairi played safe with white wine.

'You look tired,' he told her.

'We took one of my patients off life support this morning. She was only nine.'

Fender began rearranging his table setting. 'Maybe dinner wasn't such a good idea. What I got to tell you isn't going to make your day any brighter.'

The word 'blackmail' sprang unbidden into Mhairi's mind. 'Oh dear.'

Fender levelled his eyes. 'Your parents are dead.'

It sailed right past Mhairi. 'Whatever gives you that idea?'

Fender was still bothered by the cutlery placement 'Sam went up to the Vag camp at Altamont. Asking around. He found this Norwegian couple – Arne and Christina Larsen? They knew your parents. Knew your brother, too. Charlie?' Fender moved a knife fractionally. 'Your parents died last January. Pneumonia.'

Mhairi felt like the calm eye of a storm. 'My parents are in British Columbia. They moved there this April. That's two months after you say they died.'

Fender went still. 'Where did you get that?'

A waiter hovered, eager for their order. Mhairi scanned the menu. 'The mesquite-grilled sea bass sounds good.'

Fender touched her wrist. 'Hey.'

Mhairi smiled at the waiter. 'Give us another minute.' She

watched him retreat. 'After Mr Pilkinghorn refused to help, I employed another tracer.'

Fender toyed with his glass. 'Mind telling me who?'

'They wouldn't want me to say.'

'I bet they fucking wouldn't.' Fender's shirt front crackled as he pulled in a breath. 'Whoever they are, they're screwing you.'

Mhairi couldn't get rid of her smile. 'I don't think so.'

Fender glowered at the other diners as if he suspected one of them was responsible. His voice dropped. 'Okay, let's say these people are on the level. I'm telling you they made a mistake, mixed your parents up with someone else.'

Mhairi felt very calm. 'These people don't make mistakes.'

'Nor does Sam.' Sweat beaded on Fender's forehead. He yanked his fingers around the inside of his collar. 'Jesus!'

Mhairi hunched forward. 'Pilkinghorn couldn't care less about me or my parents. As far as he's concerned, they're dead. So why would he drive all the way up to this camp to find out what he already knows?'

Fender lowered his head like a bull. 'You want to know why Sam did it? Okay, I'll tell you. I asked him how he'd feel not knowing if *his* family were dead or alive. I said it wouldn't hurt to use his contacts.'

Relief gusted through Mhairi. It was a scam. Fender needed money to start out in another country. With Pilkinghorn's connivance . . . No, she doubted if he'd be a part of it. Fender had seen how she'd thrown money at a man who was ready to kill her and decided she was easy pickings. Her relief turned to nausea.

Fender snapped a breadstick and crammed half in his mouth. 'I bet it was Turpin.'

'Who?'

The breadstick waggled obscenely. 'The guy who fed you this bullshit. I bet it was that fuck Turpin up in Eureka.'

'I don't know any Turpin. I've never been to Eureka.'

The breadstick disappeared. 'Whoever it was, give me their name and I'll go talk with them.'

'I'm not telling you. That's flat.'

Fender parked his mouthful. 'Mhairi, it won't hurt to make sure. I mean, did these people give you evidence – letters, tapes, photos?'

'They've given me all the assurance I need. They're not the kind of people who'd lie.'

Fender's chair screeched back. He watched his drink slop, dipped a fingertip into the dregs and sucked it. 'Then we got a problem.'

'Even if I told you, they wouldn't speak to you.'

Fender shot forward. 'If I want the truth, I'll fucking get it. I'll fucking burn their eyeballs if that's what it takes.'

Nearby diners were muttering and the staff shuffled, deterred from intervening by Fender's blatant toughness.

'I'm not listening to any more of this,' Mhairi said, and beckoned one of the waiters over.

'Ready to order?' he asked, grimacing askance at Fender.

'I'm afraid we've changed our mind. The check, please. And call me a cab.'

Fender crumpled in his seat like a virulent troll. He didn't speak while she was settling up, but the moment she rose, he was at her elbow.

'Harry,' she pleaded, 'leave me in peace.'

The manager stepped into their path. 'Excuse me, sir, I think . . .'

Fender bounced him against the wall without breaking stride. 'Okay, so this tracer's turned up your parents. He tell you how he's gonna transport them to California?'

'That's not a problem.'

'Not a problem,' he repeated. 'Not a fucking problem.' He reeled her in. 'How much they charging for this magic carpet?'

Mhairi twisted in rage. 'Get your hands off me!'

Fender yanked her so close she could smell the liquor on his breath. 'How fucking much?'

Mhairi's breathing was ragged. Getting away was the only thought in her mind. 'Twenty thousand,' she blurted. 'There! Satisfied?'

Fender tossed her arm away. 'Twenty thousand wouldn't buy

152

you a fucking week's meals above the Line. A gallon of gas costs two hundred.'

Mhairi broke for the door.

'They're playing you for a sucker,' Fender shouted after her.

She burst into the open and gulped draughts of damp air. Slow billows of fog wafted across the lot. No cab lights showed on any of the vehicle shapes. She turned and saw Fender coming and held out her hands. 'Harry, if it's money you're after, all you have to do is ask. You don't have to torture me like this.'

Fender laughed. 'That's what hiding behind walls does – makes you think everyone outside is looking to rob you.' He shoved his hands in his pockets and hiked his shoulders. 'Okay, play it your way. Give me the money and I'll get out of your life.'

A lump rose in Mhairi's throat. 'It's at home.'

He walked with squat gait to his car and flung open the door. 'I know the way.'

19

'You know what's funny?'

Five miles inland the fog cleared. By now most commuters were tucked away at home and they had the freeway almost to themselves. On the flyway, the LA-bound Maglev train rifled past on its magnetic cushion at 170 mph – a streak of gold, gone in a flash.

'You being a brain scientist,' Fender said, jabbing his forehead. 'That's what I call funny. You looking inside people's heads and not being able to read what's printed on their faces.'

Her parents were alive, Mhairi told herself. Nothing could shake that conviction. Her parents were alive. It was the only fact that mattered.

At Rose Valley, Frank stepped out of his booth and greeted them with malevolent courtesy.

153

'This gentleman's visiting,' Mhairi told him. 'He's not staying long.'

Frank pointed to a far corner of the plaza. 'Park that thing over there. We don't want to give offence to our other residents.'

Fender lobbed his keys at him. 'That'd be your job, flunky.'

Mhairi's nerves snapped. 'Harry!' she screamed. 'I have to *live* here!'

'No you don't.'

But he picked up the keys and got back into the car. Mhairi signed him in and went on, leaving him to follow. He was breathing unhealthily when he caught up. She threw open her apartment door and marched full-pace towards the bedroom.

'You got some booze?' he called. 'Not that chemical piss that makes you think the world's a fucking flower garden.'

'Over there. Don't even think of smoking.'

She rooted under her bed and pulled out the box where she kept her emergency fund. After the big walkout, everybody stashed some liquidity – cash, gold, jewellery, drugs. Nobody knew when the next panic might erupt. She counted out three thousand dollars and then sat down on the bedside, nailed by dread. When she summoned the will to return to the lounge, Fender hadn't moved from the doorway.

'I don't get it,' he said, screwing a knuckle into his temple. 'Less than ten days ago, you were begging Sam for help. Because you could trust him.'

'Just take the money and go, Harry.'

He swatted it out of her hand and bellied up to her. 'Whaddya think I am? If I wanted to put the bite on you, I wouldn't tell you the worst thing you wanted to hear. I'd have spun the same tale these jerk-offs told and hit you for a quarter million.'

Mhairi looked at the scattered bills and a hand seemed to squeeze her heart. She backed away and fell into a chair. She couldn't stop crying. Fender thrust a glass at her. She bawled all the louder. Fender forced it to her lips. The whisky gagged her. She coughed and spluttered and dashed the tears from her eyes. Fender shook a cigarette out.

She gave a little mew of laughter. 'Big girls don't cry, right?'

'Babe, you got reason.'

Mhairi took another jolt of whisky. After it had burned down, she didn't think she'd cry again. She wiped her nose and sniffed. The room had gone quiet, confessional.

'It was the Immigration Department. They told me this morning.' She snuffled. 'That was supposed to be my good news.'

Fender's eyebrows squeezed into each other. 'Immigration keeps Vags out.'

Mhairi gave a booze-fuelled laugh. 'I'm a special case.'

Fender sat down opposite, carefully easing his pants over his knees. 'This got anything to do with your trip to Santa Fe?'

'Don't ask, Harry.'

Fender clicked his fingers softly, as if summoning genies. 'Golden boy and preacher man – the guys hanging around the night I brought you home. They're tied up in this, aren't they?'

Spiders ran down Mhairi's spine as she recalled that night, Byron kneeling in front of her, telling her how they were going to get her parents out. He hated her. The thought knocked her cold. He hated her, and this was his revenge.

Fender rotated his glass as if searching for flaws. 'Mhairi, you got to decide who's telling the truth. You want, Sam will take you up to Altamont to speak to these Norwegians yourself.'

But Mhairi's illusions had collapsed. She remembered how Trivers hadn't known that her brother was dead. She thought of the agent's put-upon attitude when she'd asked for the return of her photo. Betrayal hit her with a seismic shock.

'How could they?' she whispered. 'How could anyone be so cruel?'

Fender squinted through a lungful of smoke. 'Tell me how you're mixed up with a federal agency, and maybe I'll come up with a theory that fits.'

Mhairi rocked her head violently.

'You mind?' Fender said, raising his empty glass. More whisky glugged into it. He examined it. 'Let's see if this floats. Some federal types need a brain doctor to do something for them. Don't ask me what, but something not on the level,

155

something no respectable medic would touch. So they look for a doc they can squeeze – an immigrant with family stuck above the Line. They put it to her: do this job for us down in Santa Fe and it's happy family time again. Maybe they mean it. Only when they follow up, they find your folks are dead. These people think, wait a while before breaking the bad news, make it look like we tried.'

Fender took a beady-eyed sip.

Mhairi squeezed out a tear-smudged smile. 'You should have been a cop, Harry.'

'So spill it. You got nothing to lose now.'

'Only my job, my resident status, my . . .' She pressed her eyes tight shut, making a cave in her head.

'Life? Jesus, what are these people into?'

Her parents were dead. It hit her like a thunderclap. Her parents had been dead for months and she hadn't known. Her family was gone, every one of them. The enormity of her loss filled her with hollowness, then into the vacuum rose a rage so intense it drove her to her feet. Blood throbbed in her temples and fogged her vision and drowned out Fender's cry. She gripped her shirt with both hands and ripped.

The first thing she heard when the mist receded was her own voice screaming. Fender had her in a clinch. She sagged in his arms and he brought her back up. His expression was shocked and awed.

'Jeez, when you lose it, you lose it big. I'd hate to be on the wrong side of that temper.'

'They even took my photo,' she wailed.

'Tell Harry and I'll kill them for you.'

The distant thundering turned out to be someone hammering on the door.

'Dr Magnusson? Are you okay? What's going on in there. Open up.'

'Everything's fine,' Fender called. 'Beat it.'

'We know you have a man in there. An uncouth individual. Now open this door or I'll ask Frank to use the master pass. You'd better tell your visitor he's armed.'

Mhairi stared dull-eyed at the floor. 'Go away.'

The door flew open. Frank's stun gun poked in, followed cautiously by his head. Behind him stood the supervisor and a couple of tenants craning on tiptoes. Their eyes rounded as they assessed the details – dollar bills scattered like confetti, Mhairi's shirt torn open, her breasts exposed, her cheeks tear-stained and her hair a riot. Frank goggled in lust and delight.

'You've been smoking and drinking,' the supervisor said in faint awe, 'and God knows what else.'

'You heard the lady,' Fender told him. 'Fuck off.'

The supervisor tugged his neck straight. 'I'm going to have to ask your gentleman friend to leave.'

'I'll leave when Mhairi asks me to. Now haul your ass through that door or watch it fly out in front of you.'

'Frank,' the supervisor quavered, 'eject this man.'

'Pleasure,' Frank said, levelling his stun gun.

Fender puffed himself up and pushed his chest against the barrel. 'You'd better have the fucking dial turned to roast, because if it ain't, I'm gonna put a load through that plastic badge.'

'Right,' Frank said.

The gun discharged with a scorching crack and Mhairi shouted and grabbed for Fender, only to find that in some interval of time she'd missed, he'd removed the gun from Frank's grasp and was using his ears as handles to ram his head through the wall.

'Call the police,' the supervisor shouted, falling back into the other panic-stricken spectators.

'This man is the police,' Mhairi yelled.

Frank's head made a dull sound as it collided with the wall. Fender stepped back, shooting his cuffs. The supervisor and the neighbours had gathered in a frightened tangle on the other side of the hall.

'He came here to tell me that my parents are dead,' Mhairi shouted. 'Now get out of my apartment. The lot of you!'

Frank, bleeding from the nose, groggily retrieved his gun and looked at it as if it was a sagging erection. The supervisor's eyes wobbled.

'Whoever this man is and whatever the purpose of his visit, I'm going to have to report this . . . this fracas . . . to the tenants' council. The result is a foregone conclusion. I suggest you start looking for alternative accommodation as from the end of the month.'

'Yeah, sure,' Fender said, assisting Frank's departure with a foot in his ass. He kicked the door shut.

Silence crept out from the walls. The fires inside Mhairi had gone out, leaving a hole burnt in her guts.

Fender used his index finger to bore a hole into the bridge of his nose. 'Now look what I done.'

'It wasn't your fault.'

Fender clicked his tongue in remorse. He bent with the grunt of the spectacularly unfit and gathered up the money. He riffled the stack, knocked the edges straight and placed it on the table.

'Keep it,' Mhairi told him. 'Split it with Sam. Thank him for me, would you.'

Fender looked wistfully at the bundle. 'Nah, Sam wouldn't like that.'

'You respect him a lot, don't you.'

'There's a lot to respect when you know him.'

She nodded. 'You'd better go.'

'I don't like to leave you like this. I can stay if you like. Camp on your couch. I won't smoke.'

'I'll be fine,' she said, hearing her voice coming from far off.

'Well, you know where I am if you want to talk.'

'I appreciate that. I appreciate everything.'

'Right,' Fender said after a moment.

Mhairi watched him head for the door as if he was walking towards a precipice.

'There *is* something you could do for me.'

Fender stopped gratefully. 'Shoot.'

'A missing person case, a young man called John who's lost his memory. We can't identify him, but I've got a picture of a woman who might know who he is. I'd like you to try and find her.'

Fender clamped one hand on the top of his skull and wiggled the taut skin. 'Have we hopped channels?'

158

Mhairi picked up the money. 'How much do you charge?'

'Most jobs, three-fifty a day plus expenses, but for you . . .'

'No discounts,' Mhairi said, peeling off two thousand and pressing it into Fender's hand. 'I'll get the picture. Help yourself to another drink.'

She went into her study and ran a spare copy of the disc she'd played to John. She skipped to the scene in the Sacramento street and printed two copies each of the whole frame, the woman stepping off the kerb and her face in close-up.

Fender examined them. 'How about a shot of your patient?'

'I haven't got one. He isn't in my hospital.'

Fender nodded reflectively. 'He's the guy they took you to examine – the one in Santa Fe.'

'It doesn't matter where he is.'

Fender made a tube with his lips. 'Mhairi, I'll take the job whatever the score, but I gotta know if I'm walking asshole deep into trouble.'

He was right. Quickly she weighed the risks. Zygote had John's scan results and any competent neuro would confirm that the woman in Sacramento had pulled a memory string. Grippe already knew it. That's why he'd tried to hustle her on when she'd pressed John about the woman. But he had no reason to suspect that she'd go looking for her. In any case, it was the skinniest of chances that John actually knew her. Probably she reminded him of a teacher or social worker. She might even be a total stranger. The mind was a strange hoarder of trifles. A face glimpsed in a crowd sometimes lingered more meaningfully than the image of a life-long workmate; a cloudscape on a day when nothing happened could spring new-minted to mind years afterwards.

'No risk, Harry. For now, just take my word.'

Fender slapped the wad of bills against his palm and tucked it into his suit. 'Sacramento's not a big place and this lady looks like a pillar of the community. Even if she's left town, my bet is someone will recognise her. I'll drive up tomorrow. I should wrap it up in three days, max.' He stowed the photos away. 'If I connect, what do you want me to do?'

159

Mhairi hadn't thought beyond this moment. 'Call me and we'll take it from there.'

Fender's gaze toured the room and stopped on the phone. 'If it's all the same with you, I'll call you at the hospital.'

Mhairi looked at the phone, too, and the first misgivings pricked her. She heard Grippe's voice. *Whatever you see or hear, you must keep to yourself.* She converted a shiver into forward motion.

'I'll walk you to your car. I don't want you getting into more trouble.'

Outside, a slow rain settled from the tidal blackness. At the gateway, Mhairi looked back at the lights of the compound.

'You're right, Harry. Comfortable isn't enough. If you hear of an apartment going vacant, let me know, would you?'

'I'll ask around,' he said, settling behind the wheel. He looked up at her like a concerned dog. 'Sure you're gonna be okay?'

Her hand touched his cheek. 'Go on now.'

She crossed her arms and watched his tail lights get smaller. His brake lights blinked at the turn and disappeared. She stood there until the rain had soaked through her clothes, then she turned and walked back, indifferent to Frank's murderous stare.

Behind closed doors, the aftershock hit, throwing her body chemistry into violent rejection. She only just made it to the bathroom before throwing up. She retched until her stomach was empty and sore. Weak and purged, she returned to the sitting room, tidied up, dimmed the lights and sat with her back to the wall, hands clasped over her head, her head on her knees, rocking quietly.

20

Activity was all that was keeping Mhairi together. She knew that the moment she stopped moving, she'd fall apart. Thursday, she spent her lunch break inspecting rental properties. She was about to get back to work when Fender called. From a bar judging by the background noise.

'How you doing?' he asked above the hubbub.

Mhairi made her voice strong. 'Staying busy. I've just viewed a dozen apartments.'

'In your lunch break?'

'Virtually visited. Saves a lot of time and effort. None of them was worth a proper look. I hope your enquiries proceed better than mine.'

'They're finished.'

It sounded so bleak. 'Oh.'

'And bingo!'

All the vertebrae in Mhairi's spine fused. 'You found her?'

'Easiest trace I ever handled.' Fender gave a bronchial chuckle. 'Okay, I hit town about ten and went straight to City Plaza. First guy I see, a street cleaner, I show him the suspect. Yeah, he says, looks familiar, try Bronsky, runs the coffee shop on the corner of Eighth, knows everybody. Yeah, Bronsky says, I seen her around, tip of my tongue.'

Mhairi danced from foot to foot. 'Harry, just tell me who . . .'

'So then I ask a beat cop. He looks at me like I'm a retard and points to the courthouse. Barbara Lovelock, he says, and you'd better not be late.' Fender paused. 'Know why?'

'Because she's a lawyer.'

Fender choked on his cigarette. 'Shit, if you already knew, why send me on a fishing trip?'

'I guessed. The woman has a legal appearance.'

Fender was only part-mollified. 'Anyway, you're out of date. Lovelock's a state judge. A big deal. Where does that leave us?'

Flummoxed. 'God, let me think,' Mhairi said. 'I never expected you to get a result so quickly.' As her mind slalomed, she heard the trademark rasp of Fender's lighter. 'Okay, start by finding what Lovelock was doing three years ago.'

'I've got her vitals right here. She was appointed judge two years ago. Before that she was a defence attorney. Took all the nasty cases. Won a lot, too. Does that narrow things down?'

'It suggests John was one of her clients. I can't imagine how else he'd know her.'

'Then get me a photograph and I'll wrap it up before dark.'

'If only it was that simple. Just believe me when I say it's not possible.'

'So we're dead-ending already.'

Mhairi racked her brains, but all paths led to the same door. 'I'm going to have to speak to her, see if a verbal description rings any bells.'

'Lovelock's been a lawyer for thirty years. All human life passes before her eyes. She's seen more men than a Third Street whore.'

'Got a better idea?'

'I might have if you tell me where the feds fit into the picture.'

'Let's see what Lovelock has to say first. I'll call her right now and get back to you.'

Ten minutes later, Mhairi was still eyeing the phone like an animal suspecting a baited trap. Misgivings had ganged up on her. Up till now it had been a token effort, a feeble up-you gesture of revenge. But suppose Lovelock did know John? Then what? Fragments of Grippe's speech followed her. *He'll be lucky to be riding a garbage truck now. We follow them up. We make sure they don't prosper.*

She stopped her circling and went to a public phone down on the ward. Before dialling she checked that nobody was in earshot. An intermediary answered.

'Can I speak to Judge Lovelock?'

'Please state your name and business.'

'Dr Mhairi Magnusson. I'm a consultant neurologist at UMC in San Francisco. I've recently examined an amnesiac, a young man who we can't identify. It appears that the name Lovelock means something to him. I believe he was in Sacramento about four years ago, and it's possible he was one of Judge Lovelock's clients.'

162

'Let me have your request in writing with the appropriate documentation.'

Mhairi eyed a distant figure down the corridor. 'My patient is gravely ill, in intensive care. He could die at any moment, and then the chances of identifying him will be next to nil. Couldn't I speak to her honor in person?'

'She's in court all day. Give me your number and I'll pass on your request. If she does call you back, it won't be until tomorrow at the earliest – more likely next week.'

Mhairi did as ordered and then got back to Fender.

He was thoughtful. 'First the feds, now a judge. The ante's being upped, and all my money's on a hand I haven't seen. Mhairi, I hope you're holding aces.'

Judge Lovelock called that evening, as Mhairi was putting on her coat to leave. She was calling videolink, and Mhairi quickly changed back into medical whites and seated herself so that Lovelock would see what was manifestly a hospital office. Her face came on screen, calm and friendly, but with an edge of judicial shrewdness that cautioned Mhairi not to take chances.

'It's very good of you to find the time.'

'It sounds like a tragic case. Tell me about it.'

Mhairi crossed her toes and tried to steer a course between truth and lies. When she reached the end, Lovelock weighed up what she'd heard.

'Do you want me to visit this patient?'

'That would be too much to ask. He's in Santa Fe.'

'Oh, I don't want to go to New Mexico. Have you got a photo there? We might be able to clear it up right now.'

Though Mhairi had been expecting the request, she balked. 'Not to hand. At the time he mentioned your name, it didn't strike me as significant. It was only when I returned home that I discovered you actually do exist.'

'Then ask your colleagues in Santa Fe to send me visuals.'

Mhairi launched into extemporisation. 'Judge, there's a difference of opinion between my colleagues and me. A clinical falling out. I won't bore you with the details, but rather than involve the Santa Fe doctors unnecessarily, I thought that if I gave you a physical description.'

'Either your patient would have to have some extremely distinctive feature or . . .'

'Twenty-five-year-old white male,' Mhairi said quickly, 'a little over six feet, dark hair, blue eyes, slim, good-looking.'

'He sounds,' Judge Lovelock said dryly, 'unforgettable. Are you sure the name he gave wasn't Gala Lovelock. That's my younger daughter.'

'I'm fairly sure he was one of your clients.'

'Oh, how so?'

'Because my brain scan suggested he'd been in trouble with the law.'

Lovelock's mouth kinked. 'Ah, yes, I'd forgotten that technology has made the justice system obsolete. Well, Dr Magnusson, imagine our positions were reversed, and I'd asked if you could recollect a patient you may or may not have treated several years ago.'

'John's part native American,' Mhairi said, kicking herself for overlooking his most distinctive features. 'His eyes have a slight epicanthic fold, his nose is slightly aquiline, his complexion is smooth and sallow.' She held her breath. 'Judge? Your honor?'

Lovelock's eyes had assumed an interior focus. 'You say this man's name is John.'

'That's what we call him. We don't know his real name.'

'Four years ago,' Lovelock said, frowning into the past.

There was such a distended moment that Mhairi was sure it must yield a result.

Lovelock's attention switched. 'No. I'm good at faces, and I believe I would have remembered someone of that description.' Her voice turned brisk. 'But this guessing game is unnecessary. Get me photos and I promise I'll give it my attention.'

'I'll do that. Thank you.'

When the screen faded, Mhairi swore and called Fender.

'Whaddya expect,' he said. 'I admit you had me going for a while, but then I thought: so John recognises a high-profile judge. Big deal. Doesn't mean she knows him.' He lit up. 'I'm through here. I'd head home tonight, but the Chevvy's alternator's fucked and they don't make 'em any more.'

'Why don't you take the Maglev like everybody else?'

'A cop using public transport? Anyway, I should be able to pick up a spare in a breaker's yard. I'll be back tomorrow evening. It's okay, I switched the meter off.'

Mhairi looked at the wall. 'Switch it back on.'

'What for?'

'Forget your alternator or whatever it is. You're still on the case. Go back through Lovelock's cases involving White or Hispanic clients below the age of, say, thirty.'

'A clip search?' Fender groaned. 'Mhairi, you got more chance of drawing the winning Lotto ticket.'

'Just pull photographs to start with. If you come up with something before I finish work, use the videolink.'

'Okay,' Fender said despondently.

A thought struck Mhairi out of the blue. 'That cult leader in Nevada – Sun Dog.'

'The guy offering tickets to the happy hunting grounds beyond the stars? What's he got to do with this?'

'Probably nothing, but it's possible he and John are acquainted. Have they identified him yet?'

'Not that I heard. Any more wild cards?'

21

When Fender called in about four next day, it was Mhairi who was bursting with news.

'I found somewhere to live – an old two-floor on Russian Hill. It's a settlement case, not a right-angle in sight. I love it. It's got a balcony and you can see right across the Bay to Marin County. I'm moving in tomorrow. You must come over.'

Fender's face was jowly and rumpled. 'That's great. Me, I've been dicking around in the *Sacramento Bee* archive all day.'

Mhairi sobered. 'No luck?'

'I wish. Busy lady, Lovelock. Sticking to your parameters, I turned up about eighty possibles.' He raised a sheaf of printouts. 'I got all sorts – murderers, armed robbers, grand larcenists, rapists. You got an hour to spare?'

'All set,' Mhairi said, shuffling on her seat like a quiz show contender.

'Take your pick,' Fender said, holding the first shot to his chest.

Though the man in the photo didn't remotely resemble John, Mhairi examined it with care, taking no chances. 'No,' she said.

Fender dealt the next one.

Again Mhairi took her time. 'No.'

It was trickier than she'd expected. Many of the faces were partly obscured or badly lit. 'No. No. My God, *no*,' she said, shuddering at a mugshot that radiated brute menace.

Fender glanced at the back. 'Cute. Chopped up his girlfriend and her lover.' He slid another possible centre screen.

'No. No. Wait. No.'

'Hold it,' Fender said. He flicked a cigarette out of his pack, lit up and blew smoke at the camera. He palmed another photo.

Mhairi folded her arms and leaned back resignedly. 'No.'

'Mind if I ask you something personal?'

'What?'

'Anyone significant in your life?'

'No.'

'A knockout woman like you – brains, and looks to match.'

'I meant "no", that's not him either. Just keep them coming, Harry, and we'll have a good laugh about my personal life when you get back.'

As optimism faded, her concentration wandered. The faces began to blur into each other and she feared that even if John turned up, she might fail to recognise him. Perhaps he'd already slipped through.

'Let me have another look at the one before last.' She examined it. 'No-o,' she said slowly, and puffed out her cheeks. 'How many more?'

Fender fingered the stack. 'About thirty.'

Mhairi found herself looking forward to reaching the end. Her thoughts drifted towards her new apartment and the matter of furnishings. She stopped calling out and simply shook her head as each stranger passed by. Sensing her indifference, Fender speeded up.

'Whoa! Stop!'

Fender was already slinging the photo onto the rejects and his clumsy attempt to retrieve it sent the pile cascading to the floor. 'Shit!' he blurted, diving out of sight. A few seconds later his hand came groping up 'This the guy?'

'Not that one. The one you just showed me!'

She tried to reconstruct what she'd glimpsed while Fender foraged beneath the table. Finally he rose, mottled and mournful, holding an untidy stack in both hands. 'Guess we'll have to start from scratch.' He raised a photo. 'Here.'

'No.'

It had only been a passing resemblance, Mhairi decided, going through the dreary line-up again. A waste of time, the whole exercise nothing more than a pathetic attempt to salve her conscience.

Then suddenly she wasn't thinking of anything. All her attention was riveted on the picture Fender was displaying.

'Harry.'

'Yeah?'

She felt a sick excitement so intense she couldn't speak.

'Mhairi?'

'It's him,' she breathed.

She slipped out of her seat, took a turn round the room to calm herself and crept back. She put her face ten inches from the screen and felt a fierce thrill.

'Got you,' she whispered. She threw back her head and laughed. 'That's him. That's John!'

Fender, cigarette pasted to the corner of his mouth, examined the pic. 'Sure? It's not the clearest of shots.'

'One hundred per cent positive.'

Fender reversed the photo. 'Name fits. Your blind date is

167

John sure enough. John Cope. And you know what?' Fender snickered and wiggled his brows. 'He's a murderer.'

Mhairi's grin fell off her face. 'You mean he was convicted?'

'Can't say.'

'Harry!'

'Hey, you told me to pull mugs. On top of that, I added the crime for which they were indicted and the date of the paper.' He spread his hands. 'Mhairi, if I'd given the full rap on all of them, I'd have been in that office a week.'

'But you must remember something about the case.'

Fender studied the picture from various angles. 'Nope. Doesn't matter though. Now we got a match, it'll only take a minute to get the whole story. I'll be back first thing tomorrow.'

Mhairi experienced the hunter's selfishness to be in at the kill. 'I want to see for myself. I'm coming up straight after work. Where are you staying?'

'The Excelsior, cheapo joint.'

'Book me in.'

The Maglev train took only twenty minutes to reach Sacramento. A sleet-storm had just swept over, leaving water sluicing down the gutters and the city lights splintered in black puddles. The Excelsior sign bled red on the forecourt. Fender was right. It was a crummy way-station of the night. The manager obviously assumed she was a whore or *femme fatale*. Fender was on the first floor, he confided from behind a cupped hand. Room 114.

She mounted the stairs in a buzz of excitement. The corridor was cold and frugally lit. At the door she steadied her heart with her hand before knocking.

She recoiled from a tall, dark shape that filled the frame. 'What are *you* doing here?'

Pilkinghorn shrugged laconically. 'Harry wanted someone to hold his hand.'

His cryptic comment passed her by. Her attention had

already darted to Fender, who was standing by the curtained window with his hand on a sheaf of cuttings. She hurried over.

'Are those John's details?'

He patted them without enthusiasm. 'The whole sorry story. Only there's no point you reading it.' He spread his hands. 'Mhairi, you got the wrong guy.'

'Don't be daft.'

'Could happen to anyone. You saw only one photo. By the way, it was a thousand to one it made the cut. It was a library pic they used for a feature on Lovelock's appointment to the chair. I had to go back a long way to find the case. Anyway, to save your blushes, here's another shot of Cope.'

He produced a photograph of a dazed-looking, shaven-headed young man manacled between two policemen. 'Not your patient, is it?'

Mhairi's brow knitted. 'Yes it is.'

Fender pulled the photo down and did a double take. 'What do you mean, yes?'

'What I mean,' Mhairi said tartly, 'is that's another picture of John.'

Fender shot a baffled look at Pilkinghorn. 'And this one?'

Mhairi clamped her teeth together. 'That one, too.'

Fender threw the photo down. 'Damn it, Mhairi, what are you playing at?'

'Me? You've shown me three photographs and I've positively identified all of them as John Cope.'

'Boy,' Fender said disgustedly, 'pray God I'm never stuck in a line-up with you the other side of the glass.'

Mhairi bridled. 'I spent four days with this man.' She stooped to bring her face down to Fender's. 'I was *this* close to him.'

'Ah, hell,' Fender said, squeezing the roll of flesh on the back of his neck. 'You tell her, Sam. I haven't got the fucking heart.'

Pilkinghorn peeled a sheet from the pile. 'The man you treated ain't John Cope. Not unless you found how to make a dead man walk.' He put his finger on an article, and spread it across his chest.

It wasn't a splashy story and Mhairi couldn't make out the print. She took a step closer and the headline sprang at her.

Triple Slayer First to Die in Death Row Catch-up

Her mind emptied of all thought. 'Let me see that.'

Convicted murderer John Cope last night became California's first death row inmate to be executed in the bid to short-cut the appellate system that is costing the state $300 million each year.

Shock stunned every molecule in her body into a new alignment. She looked up in a daze. Fender was rubbing an imaginary stain from his cuff. Pilkinghorn wore an expression of odd solicitude. She lowered her eyes and tried to make sense of what was manifestly impossible.

Cope was convicted by a majority verdict for the murder of Vosper and Katharine Earle and their 19-year-old daughter Margot, raped, shot, stabbed and burned at their Lake Tahoe vacation cabin four years ago.

Mhairi skated over the lines, searching for some statement that would demolish this nonsense.

Two appeals against conviction failed, and the third was refused last week after Congress passed the MacMahon bill, giving California the green light to clear the backlog of death row inmates, which until last night stood at 224.

After the execution by lethal injection, Barbara Lovelock, Cope's lawyer, made a brief emotional statement. 'What we have seen today is utterly barbaric – a procedural quick fix that has sacrificed the life of a man I firmly believe to be innocent.'

Cope himself appeared unmoved by the drama unfolding around him. According to prison spokeswoman Alexis Dahlia, he played chess only an hour before the appointed execution time. He waived his right to select witnesses and entered the execution chamber unassisted. In his final statement he showed no remorse. He said 'this world was shit' and he was glad to be moving on to 'a better one'.

According to Susan Brooke, sister of victim Katharine, 'he stared at me with a real piercing look' as he was strapped to the gurney. Afterwards she claimed that Cope's death was too humane. 'What he suffered was nothing worse than a visit to the dentist. He deserved to fry. I hope he burns in hell.'

Outside the prison gates, opponents of the death penalty were outnumbered by supporters who cheered as the black hearse drove up to the compound.

With thirty-six more executions scheduled before month's end, they'll have plenty more to cheer about in the days to come.

Fender and Pilkinghorn had moved to the far side of the room, as if whatever madness Mhairi was suffering from was contagious.

'One time,' Fender said to the air, 'I went after a hold-up artist described by the victim as tall, fair and male. When I caught the perp, he was dark, short and female. And you know what my witness said? He said, "yeah, that's the one." '

There was a curious reverberation in Mhairi's ears. She felt hot and cramped. She'd made a mistake. It was as simple as that. Just own up to it, apologise for wasting everyone's time and go throw herself into the bay. She opened her mouth to repent and produced only a sucking noise. She looked at her hands. They didn't seem to belong to her.

'I'm sorry,' she said in a voice that barely carried. 'I know you think I'm crazy, but the man I examined is John Cope.'

Fender smacked his forehead with his palm. Pilkinghorn quelled him with a touch, took the paper from Mhairi's fingers and flicked the article.

'It's there in black and white. Tried, convicted and executed in the sight of a dozen witnesses.'

Mhairi found she had sat down. 'I know what it says. I know it goes against every grain of reason.' She breathed heavily at the ceiling. 'The man in the clinic and the man in these pictures are one and the same.'

Her words seemed to travel very slowly across the room. Several seconds elapsed before Fender reacted. 'Maybe Cope had a twin,' he said brightly.

Pilkinghorn didn't dignify the speculation with comment. 'Like Harry said, the first photo was archive material. Check the date of the paper. Cope was executed ten years ago, but your man has been in a coma for only three years.'

Mhairi felt like a rat in a maze, stupidly twitching its snout down every blind alley. 'I've only got Zygote's word he's been in a coma for three years.'

'We're talking a seven-year discrepancy.'

'People have emerged from comas lasting longer than that.'

'Your guy in the clinic may be Rip Van Winkle,' Fender told her, 'but he sure as hell isn't John Cope. Cope was 24 when he got the needle, which would make him mid-thirties now – ten years older than your patient.'

Mhairi was manoeuvring in a cage that was getting smaller by the moment. 'Maybe coma slows the ageing process.'

'Not as much as death,' Fender said, and laughed.

Mhairi stiffened. 'Lazarus,' she said. 'The man who took me to see John said, "Let's go call on our Lazarus."'

Fender frowned. 'Who's Lazarus?'

'Guy Jesus brought back to life,' Pilkinghorn said, not taking his attention off Mhairi.

Fender's grin faded. 'Hell, are you telling us that the people in this clinic can raise the dead?'

'Of course not.' Even as Mhairi said it, she found herself unsure.

Pilkinghorn made a fork with two fingers and massaged his eyes. 'Mhairi, Harry's told me what grief you're going through. You've lost your family, been lied to, had one of your patients die. I'm no mind doctor, but I figure you're badly stressed out.'

Mhairi nodded. It was as rational an explanation as any she could offer.

'Be glad it ain't Cope,' Pilkinghorn told her. 'The world's a better place without him.'

After a few seconds, Mhairi peeked out from behind her fingers. 'You know his background?'

'Enough to know he ain't anyone's loss.' Pilkinghorn offered her the newspaper. 'Read that.'

172

'I don't need to,' Mhairi said. She struggled to her feet, hands half-raised like a medium trying to descry shapes through a dark glass. 'John Cope was the only child of a woman who worked as a dancer. He never knew his father. He dropped out of high school and worked in various jobs around the north-west, probably in forestry and fishing. He had one or two minor convictions, probably for auto offences.' She stopped.

Pilkinghorn frowned at Fender. 'You tell her all that?'

Fender made a mouth like a fish and slowly shook his head.

Pilkinghorn transferred his frown to Mhairi.

'I've been inside John's mind,' she explained.

Fender's cheeks ballooned, then slowly deflated. 'Anyone object if we continue this discussion over a drink?'

22

Sacramento's streets were deserted, its buildings hunched up in the mizzling rain. The bar Fender led them to hadn't seen a face-lift since the turn of the century. The only other customers were a couple of aged nighthawks staring off into some parallel universe. The bartender was absorbed in the television, watching another update on the Argo mission. With the launch only nine days away, national interest was reaching fever pitch.

'We're hearing the most amazing rumours,' a correspondent said excitedly. 'NASA will neither confirm nor deny that Argo will blast off carrying a volunteer crew of three astronauts.'

'Mind turning that thing down,' Pilkinghorn said.

'Hell, aren't you interested in the future?'

'It'll come soon enough.'

The barman gauged Pilkinghorn's response if he refused and reduced the volume to a murmur. Fender ordered three beers and brought them to a corner booth. Mhairi moved her glass in circles.

Pilkinghorn stopped her. 'Pick up from the night Harry drove you home and found those men waiting.'

Mhairi's thoughts spooled back. 'The dark one's Warren Grippe, a senior executive with Zygote Investments, the biotech corporation.' She searched Pilkinghorn's face for a reaction, but he wasn't the kind of man to let his thoughts show. 'The fair-haired man is Grover Byron.' She hesitated, not sure how much detail to give. 'We used to be lovers.'

Fender and Pilkinghorn looked at each other and reached for their drinks at the same time.

'Go on.'

'I told Harry that John's in a Santa Fe clinic. That's not true. He's being kept at one of Zygote's research centres in Oregon.'

Fender spluttered into his drink. Pilkinghorn settled into greater stillness.

'You went across the Line?'

'To a facility called Wellspring. I'm not sure where it is exactly – in the middle of a desert.'

'Wellspring,' Fender said, wiping his mouth with the back of his hand. 'Sounds like the fount of life.'

'Let Mhairi tell it.'

She pared down her account to the essentials. When she was done, she slaked her throat while Pilkinghorn mulled over what he'd heard and Fender screwed out another cigarette in the crematorium of butts.

Pilkinghorn spoke first. 'What makes you think Zygote's lying about using John as a guinea pig for these paraplegic aids?'

'The aids are genuine, but I'm sure they've been developed to keep John healthy while they perform long-term experiments on him. Monica Scritti's a molecular biologist. She said John was a blueprint of the future. That suggests interference at the cellular or genetic level.'

Pilkinghorn sipped pensively. 'Let's say Zygote got hold of John Cope's body after he was executed. Now this may sound stupid, but is it possible they could have cloned a look-alike?'

It didn't sound stupid to Mhairi. Germ cells taken from an individual, even one who was clinically dead, could be cultured to replicate the donor organism. In theory, there could be a thousand John Copes walking around.

174

'No, you can't clone memory. A John Cope replicant wouldn't have known who Lovelock was. Most of his explicit memory may have been obliterated, but he's a man with a past.'

'So we're none the wiser about what Zygote's done to him.'

'Since they're handing him over to the Advanced Research Projects Agency, my guess is it's something related to the military or space programmes.'

Pilkinghorn didn't answer. He knew how to wield a silence.

A slow burn started on Mhairi's face. 'What's the matter?'

'Does Zygote know John's history?'

Mhairi remembered how Grippe had shot Byron down when he raised the possibility of John having a criminal record. 'I'm pretty sure Grippe does.'

'So there's a good chance he recognised Lovelock.'

Mhairi recalled how Grippe had tried to hurry her on. 'Yes, I can't rule . . .'

'And he noticed your interest in her.'

Mhairi's flush spread as she saw where this was leading. 'It was pure coincidence that she featured in the film. Grippe would never have imagined that I'd follow it up.'

'But you did, and all he has to do is pick up the phone to find you've been in touch with her.'

'She'd tell them I drew a blank.'

'You think he'd leave it at that?'

Mhairi cast her face down. 'No.'

'And when he finds out you've uncovered John's identity, what do you reckon he'd do?'

Mhairi squirmed. 'That's my problem. They don't know about you. I told Byron I went to a tracer, but I didn't say who.'

Fender turned mournful eyes on Pilkinghorn. 'That gateman's got my name and plates. He knows about her parents.'

Pilkinghorn sighed very softly.

Fender banged his glass on the table. 'Everybody stop there. We're getting paranoid. Whoever the guy up in Oregon is, he can't be John Cope, because John Cope's dead and buried. John Cope's future-proof.' He quit smiling. 'Hell, Sam, don't tell me you've been converted.'

'Get us another drink,' Pilkinghorn said, staring at Mhairi.

He waited until Fender was at the bar before speaking. 'You shouldn't have sent Harry off to play leapfrog in the dark.'

Mhairi couldn't bring herself to meet his eyes. 'I never thought it would lead anywhere. And then . . .'

Pilkinghorn turned to watch a customer who'd come in out of the rain and was covertly studying them from the bar. When he met Pilkinghorn's gaze, he quickly found someplace else to look at.

'Have you noticed anything unusual – anyone following you, strangers calling, new neighbours?'

'No.'

Pilkinghorn nodded slightly. 'Okay, I reckon we haven't tripped any alarms yet, but now's the time to quit.'

Mhairi was frightened of provoking the anger she suspected lay beneath Pilkinghorn's exterior. 'Where does that leave John?'

'I don't give a damn. He's a triple murderer and rapist who's been tried and convicted by due process. If he did cheat the grave, as far as I'm concerned, Zygote can do what they want with him.'

'That's a terrible thing to say.'

'Worse things happen to better people than him. At least he's alive.'

'I gave my word I'd get him out of there.'

'You're not in any position to keep it. Go to the cops, they'll laugh in your face. They'll put you in a room with rubber walls.'

'I could tell Barbara Lovelock.'

'She'll love you for it.' Pilkinghorn's eyes trained on her like gun barrels. 'I'm telling you to give it up.'

'I couldn't live with myself if I did that.'

Pilkinghorn leaned closer. 'Mhairi, take this any further and you're going to land up in a mess of trouble.'

Mhairi ran a knuckle across her teeth. 'I'm sorry if I've put you and Harry in danger.'

'It's not us I'm worried about. In a couple of weeks, we'll be out of here.'

176

The news dropped like a stone into Mhairi's stomach. 'Harry's leaving, too?'

'Look at him.'

Fender noticed her stare, winked and said something to the barman, who nodded approvingly.

'He's a coronary waiting to happen,' Pilkinghorn said. 'Maybe next year, maybe next month. I'd like him to have a last look at the sun before he keels over.'

Mhairi felt desolate. She smiled. 'I'm glad you're taking him.'

'That leaves you.'

She thought about her family gone, eight months of winter to get through. She arched her shoulders under the crushing prospect. 'Oh, you needn't bother about me.'

'We'll look out for you until we leave. If nobody's come after you by then, I guess you're in the clear.' Pilkinghorn scribbled on a beer mat. 'Anything comes up, call me. If you can't get through, go to the Valhalla. Bobo will put you in touch.'

As Mhairi reached for the mat, his hand covered hers. The unexpected contact tingled like an electric shock. She saw that he wore a wedding band.

'Mr Pilkinghorn . . .'

'Call me Sam.'

'Sam. Harry told me about your own family. I'm truly sorry.'

'Most people are carrying grief.'

'Shit,' Fender grumbled. 'I turn my back for a minute, and when I look round, my partner's canoodling with the love of my life.'

Mhairi, blushing, took her hand from Pilkinghorn's and raised her glass ceremonially.

'Harry, Sam – here's to your places in the sun.'

Consternation showed on Fender's face. 'Sam, I asked you not to tell her.'

Pilkinghorn grinned and the years fell off him. 'That's Harry for you. Love 'em and leave 'em. Of course I told her. What were you going to do? Send a postcard.'

'Yeah, well,' Fender said, swilling his drink around. Suddenly his face lit up. 'Hey, why don't you come with us?'

177

Mhairi treated it as the joke it was surely intended to be. 'Sounds enticing, but I burn in the sun. I thrive in northern wastes.'

There was a silence that neither man knew how to break. Mhairi faked a yawn. 'Bed for me.' She gathered the cuttings. 'I'll take these if you don't mind.'

23

At the time of his arrest, Cope was nineteen years old and working in a timber yard about five miles from Lake Tahoe, where his victims had a vacation cabin. Vosper and Katharine Earle were a wealthy realtor and a socialite from Pasadena. Margot, their daughter, was the same age as Cope – a pretty and vivacious first-year student at the University of California in Los Angeles. Dark and slim, Mhairi saw. She'd got that much right.

After shooting the parents and shooting, stabbing and strangling Margot, the murderers had torched the cabin. But by chance a fire-fighting crew on exercise spotted the smoke and arrived in time to recover the partly-charred body of the girl. The parents were so badly burnt they could only be identified from dental records. Forensic found semen from three men in the girl. What they had done to the parents before they killed them was anyone's guess – though the prosecution invited the court to let their imagination run free.

Within hours, the police had a lead. A filling station attendant told them he'd seen a young man – 'a blue-eyed Indian kind of fellow' – in the vicinity of the cabin on two occasions. The police swept the area and picked up John Cope in his bed less than twelve hours after the firecrew had raised the alert. The attendant identified him as the Indian kind of fellow. It was enough to get an arrest warrant and authorisation for a DNA sample, which matched one of the semen samples.

Cope at first denied knowing the girl. Under questioning he

178

changed his story, admitting he'd been having a sexual relationship with her for the last two weeks. He claimed he'd met her at the roadside trying to fix a flat. Nobody came forward to verify this story. He told the police and subsequently the court that all his meetings with Margot had taken place in the woods. On the day she was murdered, they had met about three-thirty, made love and then, around five, he'd left her quarter of a mile from the cabin.

Asked who his accomplices were, Cope insisted he didn't have any. He claimed that on that last day, he and Margot had run into three strangers in the woods and had exchanged words. Nobody could put names to the descriptions he gave.

On the face of it, it was an open and shut case. Cope couldn't afford a fancy lawyer and was assigned a public defender. At his trial the jury found him guilty by majority verdict, with one juror dissenting.

Convicted of Murder One, Cope was sentenced to death by lethal injection. Barbara Lovelock took up his case and started the laborious appeals process. For five years, Cope remained on Death Row at San Quentin, while Lovelock worked her way up through the chain of courts. Then came the MacMahon Bill, and Cope drew the short straw.

When Mhairi had finished, she went to the window and parted the plastic curtains. The rain had turned to wet snow, the first of the winter. She watched it for a while, then let herself out into the corridor. Fender and Pilkinghorn had the rooms on each side. She put her face close to the door on the left.

'Harry, are you awake?' She tapped softly. 'Harry?'

A grunt was followed by shuffling steps. Fender, eyes gummy with sleep, blinked at her while trying to tie a dressing gown. 'Am now.'

His room was stale with tobacco fumes, but otherwise the atmosphere wasn't too offensive. He spoiled it by reflexively fumbling for his cigarettes.

'Do you have to?'

179

'I'd still be in eight-hour detox if you hadn't woken me up.' He parked himself on a table. 'You read up the case?' He took a drag. 'Satisfied?'

'Far from it.'

'Shit.'

Mhairi ignored the chair. 'First, the two accomplices who were never found.'

'Drifters, bums, following the work. Winter, they're wild-catting in Texas; spring they're gutting salmon off the Channel Isles; summer, they're dealing them off the elbow in Disney-land.'

'If Cope was part of a gang, why didn't he name them? It wasn't the kind of crime where honour's at stake.'

Fender shrugged. 'Snitching wouldn't have done him any good. The forensic evidence would still have got him turned off.'

'He never denied having consensual sex with the girl.'

'She was raped repeatedly and violently, and then she was strangled, knifed and shot.' Fender gave a tonsil-revealing yawn.

Mhairi did sentry go in the small room. 'Cope said he and Margot saw three people – two men and a woman – in the forest. They appeared high. They made suggestive comments. Suppose they followed Cope and Margot, saw them making love, then followed them back to the vacation cabin and waited for Cope to leave.'

'If Cope was Margot's boyfriend, why didn't anyone know about it?'

'It was just a vacation fling. She was on her own, and her parents weren't the kind of people who would have approved of Cope.' Mhairi stopped her pacing. 'Harry, I was the same age when I first got laid and I didn't tell anyone. He was an Italian fisherman.'

Fender brightened. 'Was it good for you?'

'So-so. Not so bad that it put me off. Not so earth-shattering that I rushed out to do it again. The point is, to this day, you're the only person I've told. If I'd been murdered an hour after the event, my first lover would have been the prime suspect.'

'Lucky guy,' Fender said. He studied the tip of his cigarette. 'If I'd been him, I'd have bragged. Cope, I mean. He would have told the guys he worked with.'

'He'd only been at the yard for a month. He didn't have any close friends. And that's another thing. Where did these so-called accomplices spring from?'

Fender unhitched himself from the table. 'Okay, John Cope was screwing the girl like you said. She was no Snow White. Lovelock proved that in court. She raised a shitstorm by putting up witnesses who testified Margot was a sexually adventurous risk-taker. The girl was two days from the end of her vacation when she was killed. I think what happened is, she told Cope she's going back to the city, thanks for the tingle and bye-bye. He's pissed at being treated like a stud, broods on the brush-off, calls up some buddies working down the road, tells them about this girl who's all take and no give, throws in the wealthy parents. They meet up, get drinking, start comparing notes about all the bitches who've done them wrong. They probably pop a few pills, and then suddenly they're in a pickup and it's gone ugly. Believe me, I've seen ugly.'

'Cope was sober when arrested, and there's nothing in the newspaper reports about him being a drugs user. The Earle's cabin had been robbed, all their valuables taken, yet none of their possessions was found on Cope. The gun used to shoot the parents was never recovered. Nor was the knife. Your theory stinks.'

Fender jammed his butt out. 'And what you've come up with is hard fact?'

'One of the jurors believed him.'

'There's always one. They see a good-looking kid acting earnest on the stand, they give him the benefit of the doubt. You got to ask yourself something, Mhairi. If you'd been in that courtroom, what would your verdict have been?'

'Not guilty. The only connection between Cope and Margot is his admitted sexual relationship. The rest isn't even circumstantial. If Lovelock had defended him at his original trial, he'd have been acquitted.'

'Just because she's got a good acquittal rate doesn't mean her clients were innocent. I worked homicide for nearly twenty years, and I've seen men I *know* were guilty walk free. I'm telling you, the prosecution gets it right more often than not.'

'What's that in percentage terms – ninety, seventy, more often right than wrong?'

Fender loosened up the skin on his skull. 'Calm down. You're fighting a case on newspaper evidence ten years old about a man you know fuck-all about.'

'I've got a damn sight clearer insight into his personality than any of those jurors or lawyers. John Cope is *not* a murderer.'

Fender scratched his eyelids. 'We're all capable of killing. A moment's madness – and bang! The night I told you about your parents, if that Fed bitch had come through your door, you'd have torn her throat out.'

'Innocent or guilty makes no difference. Zygote has no right to keep Cope.'

Fender walked to the window and stared out. Phlegm dragged in his throat. 'Okay, so what do you want me to do?'

'I'm not asking you to do anything. I just want to get it clear in my own mind.'

Fender fiddled with his lighter. 'Sam warned you off, huh?'

'He's quite right. You'll be leaving in a few days. Promise me one thing, though. Come and see me before you go. Let's try dinner again.'

At the door she leaned down to kiss his brow. 'Thank you, Harry.'

Fender examined himself in the mirror. 'Damn,' he said. 'Still a frog.'

24

Cope suddenly found himself the centre of attention. Men in white attended by men in grey began to call on him daily. The men in white had him perform all sorts of physical and mental routines. They wired him to machines and made him blow into bags and run on a treadmill. They took samples of his blood, sperm and skin. They put him in a centrifuge and spun him until he blacked out. They wired him to the couch he'd broken loose from and watched screens flickering like electronic pinball displays. They strapped him into the CybErotic harness and a middle-aged woman forced him to choose a partner for 3-D, wrap-around sex.

And after each session, the scientists looked at each other across his prone body and seemed to rub their hands in delight, while behind them the men in grey conferred with heads close together and hands cupped to their mouths.

In return for letting the scientists monkey with him, Grippe allowed Cope a measure of freedom. He could swim in the pool, work out in the gym and use the on-line sex service as much as he liked. They even let him make accompanied expeditions into the tundra.

All through these days, Cope knew he remained under a suspended death penalty – though from Grippe's pleased, almost fatherly attitude, he guessed that the means and timing of his execution had been changed.

He made friends with a guard – Dickey, black guy, former Ranger. One evening when they were playing chess, Parr, another of Zygote's bluecoat warriors burst in.

'Fellas,' he shouted, lunging for the TV remote. 'Big news!'

Up on the screen appeared a grave, prematurely grey man lavishly framed by huge windows that revealed slowly-falling snow.

'What's *he* selling?' Cope asked. 'Double-glazing?'

'He's the President, you dummy,' Dickey said, and then caught the glint in Cope's eye. 'Ah, hell, I never can tell what you know and what you don't.'

'Shh!' Parr hissed, eyes glued to the flatscreen..

The President had gone from the screen. In his place appeared three clean-cut young men – one black, one white, one oriental – joshing each other against models of Argo and Virginia Nova.

183

The President's voice remained.

'. . . these gallant volunteers,' he was saying, 'know they will be going on a journey from which they will not return. They will spend the rest of their lives – sixty or seventy years – on a voyage that will pave the way to the stars for generations yet to come.' The camera zoomed into medium close-up. 'The term hero is much abused in these times. But my fellow Americans, when I describe these volunteers as heroes, I use the word as the classical world understood it. To the Greeks, heroes were the children of gods and mortals, blessed with the gift of immortality. And it is in that sense that Duke Hoban, Lincoln McCrae and Lee Hammet are heroes. For though they will never set foot on Earth again, truly they will live forever in the hearts and minds of we who remain.'

When the broadcast had finished, both guards were bright-eyed, shy of meeting the other's gaze.

'Going on a one-way mission,' Parr said at last, his voice constricted into a piping treble. 'That's the bravest thing I ever heard.'

'Seem like damn fools to me.'

'Shut up, John. What do you know about self-sacrifice? Life's just five-star room service for you.'

'They're neither fools nor heroes,' a voice said behind them.

Paige was standing in the doorway.

'What the fuck are you saying?' Parr demanded.

'The astronaut called Duke,' Paige said, and lifted his chiselled jaw. He gave them a half-profile – first the left side, then the right. 'Notice anything familiar?'

Cope and his companions stared very hard at the screen.

Dickey's hands balled into fists. 'Are you saying they're robots?'

'You have to admit,' Paige said, 'the likeness is extraordinary. And notice how the cameras never show the eyes in close-up.'

Parr, glowering at Paige with real hatred, felt his way to his feet. 'You're a fucking liar! Those astronauts are as real as me. *Men*, you hear, not machines! Heroes, like the President said. Heroes, do you hear?' Lashing at the furniture, he stormed out.

Cope shook his head. 'You never know when to keep your mouth shut.'

'Truth shall make you free,' Paige told him, and coasted away.

'You think he's right?' Dickey asked eventually.

'Yeah,' Cope said. 'Those astronauts came from a machine shop.'

'Well,' Dickey said, 'there goes one more illusion.'

Cope's attention returned to the interrupted chess game. 'Here's another,' he said, moving his bishop to complete the pincer. 'Checkmate.'

Later that evening, Cope had another visitor. At first glance he didn't recognise her. It wasn't just that he hadn't expected to see Monica Scritti again; she looked a different person. She'd undergone a top-to-toe makeover – hair dyed auburn and styled in soft waves, mouth redder and fuller, clothes that made the most of her figure. Some subtler alteration, beneath the skin, completed the transformation.

Cope rose slowly. 'You look real pretty, Monica.'

She approached him with a spring in her step. 'You look good, too. Your hair's growing out. The convict look has gone.'

Cope rasped his hand over his scalp. 'Still locked up, though.'

'I hear you've been using the recreational facilities.' Scritti's eyes strayed to the closet, then firmly looked away. 'I hear you even go for walks on the tundra.'

'Yeah, but always with a couple of guards in tow.'

'They're being sensible. It's dangerous out there on your own. I've seen storms blow up from nowhere.' She lowered her eyes shyly. 'I've got to sort out my work schedule tomorrow, but maybe the day after I could come with you.'

Cope shrugged. Monica didn't strike him as an outdoor kind of girl. 'Sure? The guards think it's dead out there, but it's surprising what you see – foxes, snowy owls, all sorts.'

She kissed him. 'I'm sure.'

*

It was a raw, grey afternoon when Cope and Scritti took their walk. Parr and another guard mooched along a hundred yards behind, bored stiff. About a mile beyond the perimeter, Cope showed Monica where a gyrfalcon had killed a ptarmigan. A trail of feathers tapered from the point of the aerial strike to the carcass. He pointed out the tell-tale wedges sheared out of the breast keel.

But Monica was distracted, constantly looking around as if searching for bearings. Tundra fever, Cope assumed. Intimidated by the emptiness.

He indicated a scattered outcropping on a rise ahead. Monica lifted her dark glasses and squinted. Even though the snow glare was hurtful, the one-dimensional light made it hard to gauge scale or distance.

'Are those rocks?'

Cope smiled. 'Musk oxen.'

As he and Scritti approached, the herd gathered into a curved phalanx, the bulls flanking the calves and cows. Pressed shoulder to shoulder, their glossy guard coats brushing the ground, they resembled a fur-clad fortress. Their breath hung in a cloud above them.

Monica clung to Cope's arm. 'They'll charge.'

Cope left her and went on until the old herd bull in the centre pawed the snow and hooked the air with its double-curved horns. This close he could hear its breathing and see the stolid aggression in its bulging amber eyes. Fifteen yards apart, man and beast watched each other across a chasm of time.

'Please come back,' Monica begged.

The herd bull's slotted pupils moved sideways. It gave a soft snort and Cope just had time to retreat one step before the herd stampeded. But they weren't coming for him. They broke in the opposite direction, their skirts tossing like the hem of a Chinese festival dragon. On the next ridge they stopped to look back then, in one co-ordinated movement, they were gone.

Monica's face was white. 'They could have killed you.'

Cope sniffed the breeze. 'Wasn't me that scared them. Must have been wolves. I've seen a pack over the next ridge.'

He turned and saw Wellspring's domes glowing like a clutch of alien eggs against the forlorn sky. The hairs rose on his scalp and his heart beat faster.

One day when John was hunting buffalo on the prairie, he saw a light blazing from out the heavens.

He laughed in wonderment and turned in a circle. 'This is it.'

'What is?' Monica asked nervously.

'The place where they took me from.' Cope held his arms wide. 'The hunter on the plain. The space lights. This is where it started.'

She gave a despairing laugh and drooped, then stared at him, glanced over her shoulder at the guards and hooked her arm through his.

'You're right. This is where your journey begins. Keep walking. Don't look back.'

Now it was Cope's turn to be astonished.

'Hey!' one of the guards shouted.

'Ignore them.'

'What's going on?'

'There are people waiting out there for us. It's all arranged.'

Cope thought of the musk oxen and scoured the ground upwind. But if men had frightened the herd, where were they?

'Get the fuck back here,' Parr shouted.

They breasted a ridge and Cope looked out upon a vast emptiness.

'Monica, nobody's there.'

At that precise moment he heard a dull 'whomp' and turned to see Parr in the act of disappearing, the place where he'd been standing occupied by a cloud of red mist. The second guard was swinging his weapon up when he vaporised too, his body bursting in a welter of blood that hung in the air without moving and suddenly vanished.

'Holy shit!'

Shapes floated out of the snowscape, shimmering bipeds that resembled a denser version of the medium in which they moved.

'My God, they're fucking aliens!'

'No they're not,' Monica cried. 'They're soldiers, and they've

187

come to rescue us.' She gave a little skip and squeezed Cope's hand.

Some of the jellyfish men were mounted on vehicles like glass boats that skimmed the snow with a purr. Cope knuckled his eyes.

'Why can't I see them properly?'

'Smart polymers. Their suits contain photo-sensitive pigments that mimic their surroundings.'

One of the craft glided to a halt and settled on its skirts. Its occupants sprang out and one of them threw a snappy salute. Even from only a few feet away, Cope couldn't make him out clearly. He wore a helmet with a bronze-green visor faceted like a fly's eyes, each surface holding Cope's reflection. He hinged back the visor, exposing a grinning human face.

'Neat work, Dr Scritti. Nice to meet you, John. Climb aboard and let's blow.'

Weak with amazement, Cope allowed the soldiers to strap him into a seat in the craft's midsection. The commander and driver took their places in front, two more men in the stern. Looking around, Cope counted three craft in all, each holding a crew of four.

The harness bit into his chest and his head was forced against the backrest by a burst of groin-tightening acceleration. They were ground-flying, the wind flattening his scalp and scorching his lungs. Beside him, Scritti spread her arms and gave a jubilant howl that blew away in the slipstream. She sank her mouth into the nape of his neck and growled. 'I told you I'd get you out.'

'Who are these guys?'

Her first attempt to reply was suffocated by the wind. She masked her mouth. 'They work,' she shouted, fighting for each word, 'for my new employers. My knowledge for your freedom.'

As Cope's brain began to catch up, he remembered the slyness on Monica's face the night she'd asked to take a vacation. He remembered Grippe's speculative expression as she left.

'You should have told me,' he shouted.

'I couldn't take the risk.'

Cope was thinking quickly now. He shook her arm. 'Did Paige question you?'

'What?'

'When you came back from vacation, did . . . Paige . . . interrogate you?'

She swung her head violently and shouted something containing the word 'random'.

Random, my ass. 'Grippe's wise to you!'

She waved her hands, not so much responding to his statement as indicating that it was impossible to compete with the wind.

Cope shelved his misgivings. Too late now. The wind plucked tears from his eyes and blurred the horizon on both sides. Their speed was astonishing. They must have been planing at close to a hundred miles an hour, the vehicle smoothly riding a couple of feet above the contours. He looked back through the snow plume in their wake. Already, Wellspring had halved in size, withdrawing into the earth, and he could see no sign of pursuit.

He faced the buffeting again. Curiosity began to overcome his apprehension. The controls looked simple – an aircraft-style rudder and a cowled instrument panel, with illuminated readouts to the right of a yellow screen. A red blip crawling towards a black line marked their course.

The commander whacked him on the knee and pointed at poles pushed to drunken angles. A road. The driver veered to align their course with the flickering uprights. A minute later the commander elbowed Cope, jabbed a finger, then cocked a thumb in solemn triumph.

A much larger vehicle was approaching on an interception course, skimming so low that at first Cope thought it was a giant version of their own craft. Then he made out greater space between its belly and the ground, and saw stubby wings.

'Where are they taking us?' he shouted.

'New Mexico,' Scritti yelled.

He held her by the shoulders and put his mouth to her ear. 'I'm not going back in a cage. Never!'

Her teeth collided with his in a clumsy kiss. 'You won't, I promise. We'll live together.'

Their velocity decreased and Cope heard the whine of the plane's jets. They rose in pitch as the nacelles tilted to vertical and the plane stopped, the downthrust creating an explosion of snow.

Monica was rapt, her lips apart. At that moment, she was almost beautiful. Cope wondered about the implications of that 'together'.

In the corner of his eye a line of vapour streaked towards the plane and connected with its mid-section. It staggered. Poppy flames blossomed, shedding red and black petals. Another missile homed into a wing and disassembled it, lofting one of the engines in a smoking parabola. Before the debris had reached its zenith, the fuselage dumped onto the ground with a broken-backed crumpling.

The commander punched the release button on Cope's harness and swept him over the side. A blast of singeing flame boiled out from the carcass of the plane. He flattened himself, clutching at the snow, as shrapnel pattered around him. He kept his head down, listening to a myriad little sizzling sounds.

'You are surrounded and outnumbered,' a voice boomed. 'Lay down your weapons and give yourself up and you will not be harmed. Resist and you will be killed.'

The commander was lying half on top of him, trying to shield him. Cope thought of the Zygote guards vaporised in their boots and rolled violently out of his reach. He kept rolling until he found a hollow that offered illusory cover. The commander watched him through his one-way face mask, then slowly turned to face the invisible enemy. Cope couldn't pick out any of the other soldiers. Monica lay unmoving close to the snow glider, her hands clasped over the back of her head.

'I repeat,' the voice from the sky said, 'resist and you will be killed. We do not wish to inflict more casualties. Surrender with honour, hand over your hostages, and you will be returned to your company without harm.'

Snow had found its way down Cope's neck. He'd lost a glove.

190

He sucked on his fingers and cursed. The plane's skin was peeling away from its skeleton. Sticky black smoke billowed across the snow, fouling everything it touched.

'You have thirty seconds,' the voice said.

Ten seconds before the deadline, the commander drew his feet in, rose and hoisted his arms. Nine more of his men surrendered, leaving two elusive shapes humped in the snow. Cope remained prone. After a few seconds, another phantom army sprouted from behind the destroyed plane. Half of them knelt in firing position, covering the soldiers who advanced through the wreaths of smoke.

A group ran to Scritti and pulled her into a sitting position and put guns to her head. Cope charged at them.

'Leave her alone!'

Monica wore a remote smile. Her makeup had run. She picked at the top of her boot. 'It was all for nothing, really.'

Cope crouched beside her. 'It wasn't. We nearly made it.'

'I know you don't love me. You wouldn't have stayed with me if you'd been given a choice.'

Cope didn't know what to say. 'We're together now. I ain't scared of dying.'

She shook her head as though he had a lot to learn. 'You're not going to die, John.'

Her captors hauled her up and frog-marched her away.

'Why?' Cope shouted. 'What have they done to me?' Two of the Zygote men grabbed his hands and clipped them behind him. 'Monica!' he shouted.

She managed to twist her head for one last look before the soldiers hustled her on.

The plane was still burning fiercely. One of the Zygote guards draped a blanket over his shoulders. Another group had corralled the snatch squad. Cope saw a heliplane in Zygote livery approaching from the direction of Wellspring. It set down a hundred yards off and the passenger door opened. Steps lowered themselves.

Warren Grippe emerged and stood for a few seconds, surveying the scene. He wore a fur hat and an ankle-length coat trimmed

191

with sable that gave him the appearance of an old-time theatrical impresario. He descended and one of the Zygote soldiers saluted him. First he went to Scritti. Watching from forty yards away, Cope wasn't sure if he spoke to her. The cloud of breath that frosted around his head might have been a resigned sigh.

Hands clasped behind his back, he walked up to Cope. His expression wasn't unkindly.

'I don't hold you responsible, John.'

'What are you going to do to her?'

'I've terminated her contract. I think you'll agree there are sufficient grounds.'

'You harm her and I'll kill you.'

Grippe's expression was pained. 'John, Dr Scritti's a free agent now. She can take her talents wherever she pleases.'

Monica's escort had led her across the road. Cope took in the desolation on the other side. 'She won't last a day out there.'

'Frankly, that's *her* problem.'

'You knew she was planning something. Why did you let her get this far?'

'To send a warning to our competitors,' Grippe said. Anger engorged his face. 'What you have witnessed, John, is a gross act of commercial piracy.'

Cope lunged against his tether. 'What I seen is stark-staring craziness. You threw away the lives of your own men.'

'Now come on, John, you're cold and shocked. Let's get you back home.'

Cope fought his bonds. 'I'm not going. Turn me loose and I'll stay and die with her.'

Grippe smiled at his shoes. 'John, nobody's going to kill you.'

'I heard you, the night I woke. Put me back to sleep, you said. Put me back the way I was.'

'Ah,' Grippe said, 'that explains a lot. I admit, my first reaction was negative. I was worried that you'd remember too much. I foresaw trouble. Well, trouble there's been, but you're worth it. However, Wellspring isn't the place for you. In a few days you'll be leaving us, going below the Line.'

He signalled to a guard, and Cope was borne towards the

heliplane. He jammed himself against the door long enough to see that Monica was alone now, her guards returning to the plane. She was right, Cope thought. He didn't love her and never could have, but she'd sacrificed her life for him, and for that he owed her. He looked at Grippe and a sweet metallic taste filled his mouth.

The guard dumped him into a seat and the heliplane lifted off. It banked and made one pass over the wreck before heading for Wellspring. In the seat ahead of him, Grippe removed his hat, peeled off one glove and put his hand against the window, peering down. Cope had his last glimpse of Monica Scritti – a little hyphen on the whiteness.

'Admit it,' Grippe said. 'She wasn't your type.'

25

Next Tuesday evening, Trivers called Mhairi at her new home to prepare her for the bad news.

'We located your parents' address in BC, but they're no longer there and we haven't been able to find where they've gone. With no word of them for all these months, I have to say things aren't looking too hopeful.'

'It's what I expected.'

Silence gathered for a moment. 'Did you get your photo back?'

'Yesterday morning.'

'Well, if there's any news, you'll be the first to know.'

Mhairi replaced the phone gently and composed herself dry-eyed in a chair.

Some time later, she found herself outside on the balcony, watching the icebergs drifting beyond the Golden Gate. They were at the southern limits of their range here, and the warmer waters had eaten away at them, carving them into fantastic shapes. As she watched, one of the bergs slowly turned over, like a huge animal resignedly dying.

Shivering, she went back inside and got loaded on whisky. It suited her mood better than designer intoxicants. After drinking enough to deaden her senses, she passed out on a couch.

When she woke it was way past nine. She tried to get up, but cables seemed to have been attached to the back of her eyeballs. Finally up on her feet, the room swooped around her. She hadn't been hungover since student days and she felt like death. Her hand crept to the phone.

'Chantal,' she croaked. 'I'm sick.'

'Boy, you sound it. Shall I send someone round?'

'Migraine. Just a twenty-four hour migraine. I'll be over it by tomorrow.'

She made it to the bedroom, placed her palm over her eyes and sank into eddying nausea. Her mind was still a carousel when the door buzzed. It wouldn't stop. Mumbling weak oaths, she tottered across with little baby steps. On the way, her reflection ambushed her. Her lips curled in disgust. Raking her hand through her mussed hair, she opened up.

Fender stood there bearing a bunch of flowers. 'Your assistant told me you called in sick.' His eyes went shrewdly to the glass and bottle still on the floor by the couch.

'Self-inflicted,' she admitted.

Awkwardly, he thrust the bouquet at her. 'Doesn't make it feel any better.'

'Thank you. They're lovely. I'll put them in water.'

She got half way to the kitchen, then found she could get no further. She simply couldn't move. Her bottom lip quivered.

'Are you going to be sick?' Fender asked.

'Oh, Harry!' she cried, and threw her arms round him.

'Hey,' he murmured, his voice muffled by her breasts, shyly patting her between the shoulder-blades. 'Hey.' He disengaged and gently sat her on the couch. 'Tell Harry.'

'That woman Trivers called to soften me up for the death notice.'

Fender's lips rolled back in disgust. 'Jesus, that's fucking sick.' He sat heavily beside her.

Mhairi read his next question in the silence. 'I didn't let on.'

He held her hand. 'You're a brave woman.'

'No I'm not. If I had any courage, I would have screamed the roof down. If I had any guts, I would do something about John. I'm a doctor for Christ's sake. Simple-minded as it might sound, my job is to save life.' She wrapped her robe round herself. 'I've been twisting and turning for a solution. I thought of telling one of Zygote's competitors. That way, Grippe wouldn't know it came from me.'

'Without knowing what they've got him for, I doubt they'd give a shit. Besides, I bet all those outfits have got vats full of human bodies. No, we need to get the goodies on Zygote, find out how they got hold of John.'

She held him away at arm's length. 'Not you, Harry. We agreed.'

Fender ignored her. 'But before I go down that road, I need to know if Zygote's wise to Lovelock.'

Mhairi's eyes followed his to the phone. 'Now? But I'm in no state.'

'Go take a shower,' Fender told her. 'Straighten out your head.'

Five minutes under the spray, finishing with thirty seconds on cold, left Mhairi feeling semi-human. Fender was staring absently out of the window when she returned. Without speaking to him, she picked up the phone. She swallowed hard.

'This is Mhairi Magnusson. A few days ago, I spoke to Judge Lovelock about a patient of mine.'

'Oh, yes. She happens to be right here. One moment.'

Mhairi cast a rabbity glance at Fender.

'Dr Magnusson.' Lovelock said.

'That patient I called you about. I thought you'd like to know that we've cleared up the mystery – to an extent. It seems that John is confabulating, patching together a spurious identity. He suffers from the delusion that he's one of your former clients.'

'John Cope.'

It hit her like a hammer blow. Across the room, Fender was frantically mouthing questions. 'Oh,' she said, barely keeping her voice out of falsetto range, 'who told you that?'

Lovelock chuckled throatily. 'That's who came into my mind as soon as you described a good-looking young native American. Of course, I knew it couldn't be him.'

Mhairi waved Fender back. 'You remember him well, then?'

'Oh, yes. Failure lingers longer than success.'

'He didn't have a twin or a brother that you know of.'

'Cope was an only child. Never knew his father and I'm not sure his mother did. She was a dancer – a hooker, I guess. That boy was born under a bad sign.'

'I've been reading up the case. You believed he was innocent.'

'As a defence lawyer, I always tried to believe in my clients' innocence. As a judge, I never comment on cases. All I will say is that justice was done.' Lovelock's tone became executive. 'If you don't mind, Dr Magnusson, perhaps you'd tell me why your patient should identify with a murderer executed so long ago.'

'I have no idea. Perhaps the physical similarity. Did you attend the execution?'

'Yes. I also went to the funeral. Apart from myself and the prison chaplain, there were no other mourners.'

'Did anyone claim his body?'

It was one question too many. 'I fail to see the relevance of that question.'

'It's just that . . . just . . . No, it's irrelevant.'

'What clinic did you say your patient was in?'

'The Tuchmann Institute. Look . . .'

'Dr Magnusson, I think I'll bring this conversation to an end.'

Mhairi put down the phone and emptied the air from her lungs.

Fender fanned himself. 'Jeez, I nearly had a heart attack. She give you anything useful?'

'Nothing that contradicts the newspaper reports. She was there when he was executed. She saw him cremated.'

Fender sucked air through his teeth. 'I hate to say it, but it comes back to mistaken identity.'

Mhairi moved across the room as if following a faint beacon. 'Harry, do you know how lethal injection works?'

'A triple cocktail administered by IV. I'm not sure what they lace it with, but it's always done the trick in my experience.'

'Sodium pentathol to put the condemned man asleep; pancuronium to stop all muscle activity, including respiration; potassium chloride to paralyse the heart.'

'And it never goes wrong. It's failsafe. Mistakes don't happen.'

'They did the day John was executed. It was only a few hours after the meteor hit. Communications were down. When I tried to drive to town, the car wouldn't start. The engine management system had been knocked out by a massive electrical surge. That was nothing compared to what happened elsewhere. Airliners fell out of the sky; computers crashed, the entire infrastructure seized up. People thought there'd been a nuclear war, but even the ICBM guidance systems were disabled.'

'Yeah, but twelve witnesses, including your judge, saw Cope die. At least two doctors pronounced him dead.'

Mhairi moved carefully, as if she'd had a thought she didn't want to disturb. 'Suppose the electrical storm damaged the delivery system so that John received a dose of anaesthetic. No poison. Enough to stop his heart and indicate clinical signs of death. The doctors wouldn't have checked closely. The first blast waves were just reaching California. Outside, it was the twilight of the gods. People were fleeing from the anticipated earthquakes. They were expecting the end of the world. The last thing anyone was thinking about was a man who was already dead.'

Mhairi smacked her palm with a fist. 'But John *wasn't* dead, and later, someone found that out. Then what? The prison couldn't admit that one of their death row inmates had survived a lethal injection.'

'You're right,' Fender said. 'What the doc does is slip another needle into him.'

'Not if there were witnesses. After John was pronounced dead, his body would have been taken to the prison morgue. I think it was there that an orderly found a pulse or other vital sign. Maybe he told his colleagues and then called the doctor. Or maybe he had a better, more lucrative, way of disposing of John. There was a case about eight years ago where a biotech company was found guilty of buying the corpses of prisoners whose bodies weren't claimed by relatives. It was never proven, but the company was also alleged to have obtained terminally ill patients for experiments.'

Fender sniffed and took a notebook from his pocket.

'I'm ahead of you. Theo Salas was the doctor. He's retired, gone Mexico way. The morgue attendants on duty that night were Richard Morales and Robert Jackson. Morales is dead – drive-by shooting six weeks after Cope was turned off. Could be significant. The other attendant, Jackson, he's retired, too.' Fender snapped the notebook shut. 'He lives in Atwater, not more than an hour's drive.'

Excitement quickened Mhairi's blood. She tried to suppress it. 'I can't let you, Harry. I promised Sam.'

'It's not his call. I accepted the case, and once I get my teeth into something, I take it to the end.'

26

Next day, Mhairi returned from a ward round to find a strange man nosing around her desk. He didn't seem embarrassed. He had a hard face and a soft, expansive gut. Police.

'Lew Gallacher,' he said, flipping open a badge that identified him as a special investigator for the Sacramento State Court. 'I'd like to ask a few questions about the patient you discussed with Judge Barbara Lovelock.'

Mhairi's mouth went dry. 'All matters relating to my patients are confidential.'

'You discussed it with her honor.'

'Only because she was a possible source of information that might help me identify him.'

'His name isn't confidential. How about starting with that?'

'As I told the judge, we don't know who he is.'

'But he's presently a patient at the Tuchmann Institute in Santa Fe.'

Mhairi's hesitation incriminated her. 'That's correct.'

'No it's not. I spoke to the clinic this morning. They don't have a patient resembling the man you described. They do know you, but they told me you haven't visited in eighteen months. I've also spoken to Professor Newman. She informs me that the only consultancy work you've undertaken in the last few weeks has been for Zygote Investments.' Gallacher raised an eyebrow. 'Any connection there?'

'My work for Zygote is covered by a confidentiality agreement.'

Gallacher's scepticism was transparent. 'Seems like all your work is secret.'

'Have I broken any law?'

'Wasting a state court official's time is a misdemeanour at least. Judge Lovelock might take a lenient view if you explained why people are so wound up about a murderer who was executed ten years ago.'

Mhairi was trembling. She avoided his eye. 'I have nothing to add.'

Gallacher appraised her coolly before rising. 'I'll report your lack of co-operation to the judge. It's up to her to decide whether to take it further.'

As he walked to the door, Mhairi cast back over the conversation. Something was niggling her, something she'd missed.

'You said *people*?'

'Yesterday afternoon, Judge Lovelock took a call from a Justice Department official who claimed to have uncovered evidence that might shed fresh light on the Cope case. Mean anything to you?'

Mhairi's blood chilled. 'No.'

Gallacher touched an invisible hat brim and quietly let himself out.

After she'd closed the door, Mhairi squeezed her eyes tight shut, trying to hold back the terrors. 'Oh God,' she said, then again, louder, 'Oh God!' She ran for the phone. She was panting as if she'd run a mile. Her hands were all thumbs.

'I'm out,' Fender's voice said. 'Leave a message.'

The moment she put it down, it bleeped. 'Mhairi,' Professor Newman said, 'in my office immediately.'

Mhairi frantically dialled her apartment. There were two messages from builders, then a click and Fender's voice came on, choked by static.

'I'm outside the guy's house now. He's in. Should clear up here in an hour and be back in town around six. I'll come by afterwards. Eight suit you? Hey, let's finish that meal.'

Pilkinghorn. She had to call Sam. He'd given her his number. She emptied out her purse and combed through the contents. Not there. She must have left it at home.

She gagged, on the verge of throwing up. Her eyes darted madly around. She grabbed her coat and ran out, almost colliding with Professor Newman.

'I said immediately.'

Mhairi jostled her aside.

'Come back here at once!'

'I can't.'

'Dr Magnusson, you're suspended until I receive an explanation for this bizarre behaviour.'

The elevator was between floors. Mhairi took the stairs, her feet clattering on the steps. Second flight down, her ankle turned over – a starburst of pain followed by a wave of dizzying sickness. She kicked off her shoes and hopped on. Newman must have called security, because one of the guards made a half-hearted move to block her as she ran for the exit. She dodged him and raced for the gates in her stockinged feet, watched in bemusement by patients and visitors.

She reached the head of the cab rank and yanked an elderly lady away from the autobubble she was stooping to enter.

'Doctor! Emergency! The Valhalla. Please, someone's life depends on it.'

'Yeah, mine,' the cabbie said. 'You want to go downtown, hire a tank.'

Mhairi worked down the line, getting a similar response from each driver. Finally, one of them agreed to take her to a pirate rank at the far end of the East Bay bridge.

For half a week's salary, Mhairi persuaded a privateer driver to drop her near the Valhalla. Her ankle was beginning to swell. 'Hurry. Oh, please hurry.'

By daylight the downtown streets were emptier and meaner. The Valhalla sign was dead and the building appeared vacant. Mhairi hammered on the door. Finally, a cleaner opened up a chink.

'Closed.'

'I need to see Bobo.'

'No here. Sleep.'

Brute strength got Mhairi past. 'Wake him up. Tell him Harry Fender's in danger.'

She sat drumming her fingers on the table, looking at her watch every few seconds. Another cleaner mopped the floor around her. Oh, come on, she groaned.

Bobo appeared impassively behind the bar.

'Thank God! Sam Pilkinghorn, the man I was looking for the other night. I must find him. It's Harry Fender. He's in serious danger.'

With one slow eye movement, Bobo invited her to wait. He disappeared the way he had come.

Mhairi couldn't stay still. She twisted round at every imagined approach. If anything had happened to Fender, she wouldn't be able to live with herself. It was a mantra she must have repeated a thousand times before she heard a soft tread and saw Pilkinghorn weaving between the empty tables. The set of his face made her heart fall to her boots.

He stood above her. 'They on to you?'

'Yes.'

'Leave a trail?'

'No . . . Yes. The taxi rank at the hospital.'

Pilkinghorn deliberated a while.

'We're leaving,' he told Bobo. 'Expect some heavy company. Federal types. They could lean on you hard.'

From below the counter, Bobo took a weapon like a small artillery piece and laid it on the surface. 'Let the fuckers try.'

Mhairi followed Pilkinghorn, trying not to show she was crippled.

'I told you to let it go.' There was no censure in his voice. It was all in his eyes.

'I didn't force Harry. I tried to talk him out of it.'

'You didn't have to put a gun to his head. You know how he feels about you. One flutter of those green eyes and he'd cross hell for you.'

'I . . . you don't have to be so hateful.'

They were outside again, in an alley piled with barrels and garbage. A swarm of rats fled twittering. Pilkinghorn noticed Mhairi's bare feet for the first time. 'Tell me how bad it is.'

'It's nothing. Only a sprain.'

'I'm not talking about your ankle. What's Harry up against?'

Mhairi could have bawled like a child.

'Someone called the judge yesterday afternoon, asking about Cope. Even if she didn't give them my name, she must have told them they weren't the first.'

Pilkinghorn didn't speak again until they were in his car, rolling through the empty streets.

'And Harry's gone down to San Quentin to find out who was on morgue duty the night Cope was turned off.'

'How . . . ?'

Pilkinghorn produced the slimmest of smiles. 'You don't have to be a genius to figure out what his next move would be. How much start has he got?'

'He phoned about three, saying he was about to go in. He should be on his way back now. Can you warn him?'

Pilkinghorn was paying close attention to the mirror. 'I already tried. Nothing but white noise. The Feds must be jamming his phone.'

'What are we going to do?'

'Wait for him to call in, then pull him off.'

'He left a message saying he'd come round to my house at eight.'

'Then that's where we'll go.'

But when San Francisco Bay came in sight, Mhairi saw they were heading away from the bridge.

'This isn't the way.'

'I'm dropping you at the warehouse. I want you out of sight until the boat sails.'

'They're not going to shoot me in my own home.'

'They'll shoot you any place they like.'

Mhairi assimilated this. 'All my things are there. I need a pair of shoes.'

Pilkinghorn shook his head, marvelling at her sense of priorities, and turned the car round.

They waited at a standstill, Pilkinghorn on a chair beside the door, Mhairi at the window. Every time she heard a sound in the night, she looked at him, but he might have been asleep for all the reaction he showed.

Snow was seeding down, scratching against the glass like tiny fingernails. Mhairi watched it settle until the tarmac whited over. A car swished by, honked and went past slowly. She waited for it to come again, but it didn't. The flakes grew fatter. Mhairi tracked the crystals spinning down. The tyre tracks no longer showed.

The curtains stirred in a draught. Mhairi rubbed her arms.

Pilkinghorn rose decisively.

'Lock up and don't open to anyone. If I'm not back by midnight, take your passport and all the money you can lay hands on and get back to the Valhalla. Bobo will put you in touch with the man who booked our passage south. He'll make room for you.'

'If you're going to Harry's place, I'm coming with you.'

'No you're not. They'll probably be expecting me.'

'Then you stay and I'll go. Besides, if they come here, a locked door isn't going to keep them out.'

Pilkinghorn regarded her with vexation. 'Pack a bag. Essentials only – ID and valuables, winter clothes. You're not coming back.'

*

203

They took 3rd Street along the west side of the Bay. The lights grew fewer and eventually gave out in Bay View. They continued along the Point through streets that reminded Mhairi of war zone footage. The few people she saw were in groups.

They came to an open space where an entire block had been levelled. Pilkinghorn stopped by a group of black youths gathered around a bonfire. One of them slouched over and Pilkinghorn lowered his window a few inches. Words were murmured and money changed hands.

Mhairi watched the youths drift away across the rubble towards hulking apartment blocks built before she was born. When they'd disappeared, there was no life for two hundred yards. To the north, the Cyclops eye of the Science Tower peered from its monolith.

Ten minutes later, three of the youths came back. The one Pilkinghorn had given money to crouched by his window. As he spoke, his eyes were on Mhairi. More money crossed palms.

'What does he say?'

'If people have been around Fender's place, they ain't there now.'

'Did he say if Harry's home?'

Pilkinghorn turned and pressed a pistol into her hands. She pushed it back.

'I don't want it. I don't know how to use guns.'

'Point and squeeze.'

'I'd only muck it up, get us both killed.'

'I'm not asking you to cover me. You're staying here.' Pilkinghorn nodded at the youths silhouetted against the bonfire. 'It's for them, in case you have to go home by yourself.'

She was out of the door before he could stop her. 'You think I'd go home if you didn't come back?'

He scratched at his jaw and sighed. 'Okay, but from now on you do what I say, when I say it.'

They set off along the ruined roadway. Mhairi tried to disguise her limp, but couldn't avoid favouring her sprained ankle. Pilkinghorn took her arm without comment. In the dark, she glanced at him. He walked her towards a gaunt brick tenement that made her think of a prison ship. Inside, it smelt of poverty. Various deals were going down in dark corners.

They climbed echoing stairs and walked down a corridor lit by bald bulbs. Pilkinghorn stopped outside a blank door. A man stuck his head out of the adjoining apartment and pulled it back in when Pilkinghorn raised his gun in both hands.

Relief flooded Mhairi. 'Harry's in. I can hear music.'

Pilkinghorn tried the handle. Locked. He rocked back on one leg and kicked, splintering the hasp from its frame.

Fender was seated at a desk by the window, bent forward in a studious pose. An unpleasant smell tainted the freezing atmosphere. Fender didn't move when Mhairi uttered his name. The scorched smell came from the cigarette that had burned out in his fingers. His face had the cold oiliness of old cheese, and his sightless eyes were fixed on a photograph taken when he had more hair. He was grinning widely in the picture, holding firmly on to a woman who looked like she knew how to have a good time.

'I never even asked him if he had a family,' Mhairi whispered . . .

Pilkinghorn aimed his pistol at the music centre. 'Turn it off.'

Mhairi ejected an old-fashioned CD. *Gone*, it was called, *just like a train*.

Pilkinghorn peeled back Fender's jacket. 'No blood, no apparent injuries. Guess his heart went.'

'You mean it was natural?' Mhairi whispered.

Pilkinghorn's eyes raked around the room. 'Made to look that way. Harry wouldn't be sitting here without heat.'

Forcing herself to feel under his arms, Mhairi encountered a shocking reservoir of warmth. 'He hasn't been dead long – no more than a couple of hours.'

'Must have been waiting for him when he got home.'

Mhairi looked fearfully at the gaping door. 'They'll know we'd come looking for him.'

'No sense faking natural causes, then gunning us down beside him. Harry's a warning. If they do pick us up, they'll do it on the way back, or at your place.'

'Sam, you don't have to be part of this.'

'I got no choice now.'

27

'I was thinking about Harry having a last look at the sun.'

'Stop apologising. He was a cop on a job. He knew the risks.'

'There's no point trying to make me feel better.'

Pilkinghorn checked the mirrors again. 'Tell me one thing. This obsession with Cope. Is it personal?'

He meant sexual, she realised. 'In a way. He reminds me of my brother.'

Pilkinghorn glanced at her, a brief silent question, before returning his attention to the road.

'Charlie was two years younger than me. A wild boy. Some of the things he got up to scared me stupid. We had a holiday croft in Sutherland, and across the loch there was a crag where eagles nested. I'd always thought they nested on inaccessible ledges, but this eyrie was only a short scramble up a gully.'

In her mind's eye, Mhairi was back there.

'The last time we visited it, when Charlie was eighteen, it was March. The weather had been terrible – a two-day blizzard, followed by a thaw, then a freeze. The gully was sheet ice and the cloud was so low you could see only a few feet. I was worried that the eaglets had frozen to death, so I asked Charlie to climb up and check they were all right. It was a foolish dare, really. We'd been arguing – me telling him to get on with some coursework that was weeks overdue, him mocking me for being so conventional. I lost my temper. You know what I said? I said, "don't tell me you're scared."'

Mhairi laughed.

'Talk about a red rag to a bull. He was off – no equipment. Of course, the moment he was out of sight, I started shouting at him not to be such a fool. He didn't answer. Bits of ice were rattling down. I started screaming that he'd get himself killed. When he spoke, he didn't sound very far above me. He said, "Shut up, Mhairi. You're the one who got me into this." '

Mhairi was looking up.

'He never even cried out. I heard a slithering and a bump and then he came tumbling out of the fog and landed flat on his back in the snow. He lay there smiling, like he always smiled when some stunt had gone wrong, and I thought he was going to be all right. Then I saw fluid coming out of his ears and realised his pupils were different sizes.'

Her voice broke. 'Charlie went up that mountain the most alive person I've ever met, and he came down a vegetable.'

She tried to swallow the bitterness that would never go away.

'He spent a year in the Radcliffe before coming home. He couldn't do a thing for himself – eat, dress, use the lavatory. He could still speak, but most of what he said was obscene.'

She closed her eyes. 'Every time he leered at me, I felt he was reminding me of what I'd done to him. And what made it worse was wishing he'd been killed outright.'

They sat in the same room where Mhairi had first met Pilkinghorn. He'd lit a Coleman lamp and the eyes in the portraits seemed to be watching her.

'Do you have any other family?'

'No immediate kin. My parents were taken by cancer, one after the other, when I was at college. The twins – my older brothers – took over the ranch. That's how it worked. Eldest son inherited, younger ones made their own way, usually in the military. We were kind of Western feudal. The twins died when their Cessna iced up on a flight back from Missoula. I quit the army and came home. Sheriff's job came with the territory.'

'I don't see any pictures of your wife or daughter.'

'I keep them private.'

Mhairi looked towards the door. 'Tell me about them.'

'Anne was from the East, Baltimore. We met in Denver, in a

restaurant. She was looking out of the window. She seemed to be searching for something. I thought she was looking for me.'

'Were you mistaken?'

'Steadfast was a world away from what she knew. Don't get me wrong. We weren't grubbing a living. It was a big spread, more than 20,000 acres, but a hard place. Southern section was badlands, summers hotter than hell and in winter the mercury never got above freezing for weeks straight. Step out of the door and there was nothing higher than a fence-post for five miles. When Anne had a miscarriage, I thought that might be the end of things, but we hung in and a year later a daughter came along. Olivia put everything back in scale. Horizons looked a lot less empty.'

Years went by in Pilkinghorn's silence. 'Then the meteor hit.' He looked up at the portraits. 'My family came up on a drive from Texas in 1853. They fought the Sioux and they fought everything nature could throw at them – drought, grasshopper plagues, tornadoes.'

He pointed out a water-colour showing a spring issuing from a grove of trees. 'Sioux burial site. My great-great-great grand-father planted those cottonwoods, and every Pilkinghorn since then has been laid to rest there. Except for the ones who died on service overseas.'

He walked along the line of portraits. 'These faces stared down at me when I woke up and when I went to bed. It's hard admitting you're whipped with so many ghosts looking on. Then time came when it was too late to quit. We hung on, praying the climate would change. We ate caribou and snowshoe hares and wildfowl. We lived like Eskimos.'

He reached the end of the portraits. 'Anne and Olivia died within two days of each other. After I buried them, I loaded up, shut the door behind me and never looked back. Didn't get much past the county line before a road gang bushwhacked me. Left me with a blizzard coming and only the clothes I stood up in.' Pilkinghorn smiled oddly. 'I would have frozen that night, but a couple of miles down the road, I found where they'd thrown all the useless stuff overboard. Photos, paintings, diaries, books, accounts. I made a fire with them, kept myself alive by burning the family history.'

He noticed Mhairi's puzzlement. 'There was a lot of it. And I got some of the rest back when I caught up with the bandits in Rapid City.'

'Is that how you injured your leg?'

'No, that was this spring, bringing some Vags down from Spokane.'

'Is that why you became a tracer – because of your family?'

'It was the only way I could make a living.' He came over, the subject closed. 'You'd better let me look at that ankle.'

Mhairi pulled her feet in. 'It's only a sprain.'

'It still needs dressing.' He went into the next room and came back with a bandage.

Mhairi slid off her shoe. Her instep was puffed and mottled. Pilkinghorn knelt before her.

'You bruise easily.'

She watched him wind the bandage. It was a strange feeling to be nursed by a man like him. 'You've done this before.'

'Mostly on horses.'

When he'd pinned the bandage he didn't move. Nor did Mhairi. Head down, he felt for her knee. Mhairi laid a hand on his shoulder. He looked up and they read the sorrow in each other's eyes. He tried to smile.

'I guess nobody's got a monopoly on guilt or pain.'

She waited for him to take her in his arms. It was what she wanted – to be held. Nothing more.

He lifted her to her feet. 'You look exhausted. Bed's made up next door.'

'Where will you sleep?'

'Right here.'

Sleep eluded Mhairi. The room was huge and twitched with little noises. She listened in vain for some sound from next door. Eventually, she left her bed and crossed to the door. She rested one hand on the frame and spoke into pitch blackness.

209

'Sam, I'm scared.'

She waited until she heard the sound of him rising before returning to bed. A few seconds later, he entered the room and began undressing. He slid beneath the covers and for a moment leaned over her. Then he turned on his side.

Mhairi sank under and woke clear in her mind about what she was going to do. She waited, testing her resolve, telling herself that if she felt so determined at this low ebb of night, she'd have no difficulty going through with her plan. She touched Pilkinghorn.

'I have to make a call.'

Pilkinghorn stirred up. 'Who?'

She was glad he couldn't see her. 'It's about a patient who needs special treatment.'

After a few moments, he pulled pants on and launched off into the dark. Mhairi waited, listening to her heart, until he returned and put the phone in her hand. She used voice dial.

'Zygote Investments.'

Pilkinghorn grasped her around the wrist, but she was ready for it and tightened her grip.

'Get me Warren Grippe or Grover Byron. Yes, I know what time it is. Tell them it's Mhairi Magnusson. I'll call back in ten minutes.'

She lowered herself on to the pillows, her heart beat strong and uneven.

Pilkinghorn half rose above her. 'What are you playing at, Mhairi? You don't need this.'

'Yes I do. Now please don't interfere.'

They lay there invisible to each other until the ten minutes were up and she put the phone to her ear again.

It was Byron who answered.

'Mhairi? Where are you? We've been looking for you high and low.'

'You didn't look low enough. I've been to Hunter's Point, where the dead men are.'

'Huh? You're not making sense. Look, it's about John.'

'Is he okay?'

210

'Thriving. The guy's a miracle. The thing is, I told Grippe how unhappy you were with the way things worked out. Or didn't. He agrees with me that you're owed an explanation. Can you come up?'

'Of course.'

Pilkinghorn gasped and tried to wrench the phone from her.

'Who's that?' Byron asked after a pause. 'Is there someone with you?'

Mhairi's hand floated down Pilkinghorn's chest. 'My tall dark stranger.'

Byron's voice quivered. 'Tell us where you are. We'll send a car.'

'No, I'll come to the airport. What time?'

'Two o'clock,' he said at last. 'Thanks, Mhairi. Er, have you had word about your parents yet?'

'See you tomorrow,' she said, and broke the connection.

The only sounds in the room were her own and Pilkinghorn's breathing. She was scared he would yell at her, and she braced herself for the expected outburst. But he didn't speak. He lit the lamp and sat on the bedside, his back to her.

She stroked her hand across a belt of muscle. 'Go on, say it.'

'What's there to say? If you go up there, you're not coming back.'

'I got Harry killed. I walked out on my brother. I walked out on my parents. I'm not walking out on John.'

'But what's the point? They're not going to hand him over to you.'

'I want to know the truth about him. I want to confront Grippe about Harry, and I want to spit in Grover Byron's face.'

Pilkinghorn took a deep breath and let it go slowly. 'If I'd agreed to help you, none of this would have happened.'

She kissed his shoulder. 'Don't *you* start.'

Pilkinghorn muttered under his breath, then grabbed the lamp and strode into the next room. Mhairi followed and found him throwing papers around on the desk.

'Over here,' he said, spreading a map. 'Show me where Wellspring is.'

'I told you, I don't know.'

'You can do better than that. How long were you flying? Describe what you saw.'

'We went east, across the Sierra Nevada, and came out of the clouds east of Massacre Lake, not far from the Genesis wildlife reserve. After that – a high plateau with lakes, a chain of mountains to the west. One of them like a capsized ship. We landed soon after dark.'

Pilkinghorn's gaze went into the distance. 'Sounds like the Steens mountains. Give me more. Roads, towns.'

'There weren't any. Nothing for miles. Flat, empty.'

Pilkinghorn's finger traced a shrinking circle. 'Got to be the Alvord Desert. What's the layout like?'

'You're not following me up there. Don't even think about it. Wellspring has its own private army. Besides, it's unnecessary. I'll be back in two or three days.'

'If you're not, I'm going after Grippe and Byron.' His eyes left her in no doubt that he meant it. 'You tell them that from me.'

28

All the way uptown, Mhairi sensed Pilkinghorn working up to a final appeal. Scared that he'd undermine her resolution if she allowed him an opening, she kept her eyes firmly on the passing street scenes. Families were out and about, sorting through smoking heaps of trash. She saw some kids playing king of the castle and marvelled at their resilience – as resilient as cockroaches, and as adaptable.

Around a corner from the hospital gates, she asked Pilkinghorn to set her down near an autobubble rank. He pulled over and silence stretched between them.

'I'm asking one last time,' he said. 'Don't throw away your life for that man.'

Mhairi gathered her luggage. 'I don't think they intend doing

212

away with me. Odd as it sounds, I think Grippe has a soft spot for me.'

'At least let me take you to the airport.'

'No, too risky. You, they *might* kill.'

Once she was out on the sidewalk, she offered Pilkinghorn her hand. He didn't take it.

'Mhairi, will you come to South America with me?'

She'd been expecting it. 'That's a big move for people who hardly know each other.'

'I knew Anne was the woman I was going to marry before I'd spoken to her. Before I'd even seen her face.'

'Sam, that isn't the most romantic proposal that's come my way.' She patted his hand. 'Polish it a bit.'

'Call me tonight. Will you do that?'

'I promise,' she said, wondering if she'd be alive by this evening.

He started the engine. 'And remember what I said about going after them.'

A chill closed round Mhairi's heart. She walked to a cab, told the driver to start the meter, and loaded her luggage, saying she'd be back in thirty minutes. Then, no backward glance, she went round the corner, heading for the hospital gates. As she neared them, her breathing became rapid with nervous apprehension. If Newman had officially posted her as suspended, her mission would end in the next few yards.

One of the guards in the gatehouse nudged his partner and gave her a loose grin. 'Say, doc, what was all the rush about yesterday?'

'Emergency call,' she replied coolly, sweeping past.

All the way across the yard, she kept her head down in case Newman was watching out for her. Her path was diagonal, dictated by the arrows pointing towards the Microbiology Unit. The four-storey building was tucked away round the back of the complex, across fifty yards of slush-covered yard. Everything depended on whether Newman had revoked her security clearance and wiped her pass codes.

For the moment, she didn't have to test the possibility. As

soon as the guard saw her through the glass doors, his face lit up. Jack was an Irish ex-cop who treated her as an honorary Hibernian because of her red hair and Celtic eyes and the Highland lilt she'd never quite lost.

'Where have you been, girl? Haven't seen you for weeks.'

'Consultancies. This and that.' She signed the register and went on, feeling Jack's eyes admiring her butt.

'Slipped on ice, huh?'

She dealt him an off-the-shoulder smile. 'Yes, I'm the first casualty of winter.'

He rose in concern. 'Here, let me call the elevator for you.'

'No,' Mhairi said. She softened the refusal with a smile. 'Thanks, but I don't want it to stiffen up. I'm going to be on my feet a lot this week.'

She laboured up to the second floor, a Level 3 security zone manned by an unknown female guard who was trying to match her face to the photo on her ID tag before she'd even stopped.

'Level 3 Containment Facility,' she said, laying her security pass on the desk.

Rosa Spinelli was the name on the guard's tag. She took the pass in both hands and examined it carefully before feeding it into the processor. 'Didn't think I'd seen you over here before. Says here this is your first visit since May.'

'My clinical load doesn't leave much time for research these days. But you'll be seeing a lot more of me in the next few months . . . Rosa.'

Spinelli eyed her figure and twitched a smile. 'Look forward to it.' She pushed the register across and placed a swipe card on it. 'Autograph, please.'

Mhairi watched her fingers trace out the evidence that would guarantee her a life sentence. She picked up the card, walked to the door and waited for Spinelli to key in the electronic combination.

Once inside, she paused to gather her nerve. Until then, she hadn't been aware of how fast her pulse was racing. The atmosphere in here was secretive, harbouring tucked-away voices and the sinister rattle of a trolley. It was coming her way. She held back until it trundled past the junction at the end of the corridor. Somewhere else a door shut.

The room she wanted was third down on the left. She had the swipe card ready, but she overshot and stalked to the end of the corridor in time to glimpse the trolley-pusher's heels disappearing around the next right-angle. She walked back and hesitated long enough for all the warning voices in her head to raise a clamour.

So far, she'd committed no crime. If she went to Newman now, explained that she was in emotional freefall because of her parents' deaths, she'd be forgiven on the spot. Any questions about Zygote and the patient in Santa Fe could be deflected by dark hints about government arm-twisting and Byron's emotional blackmail. The more she thought about it, the more she wondered why she wasn't over there now, winning back her place in the system. Damn it, she'd worked hard to get where she was.

And if she went through that door, her career would be destroyed forever – all other doors closed to her.

The voices were pushing her away when the ghosts of Fender and Charlie and her parents assembled before her. And behind them, she saw Grippe's presence and knew that even if he allowed her to return from Wellspring, he'd exact punishment. *We ensure they don't prosper.*

Something she'd told him came back to her. *Just because you know what someone's feeling doesn't mean you can predict what they'll do.*

She swiped her card and the door jerked, hesitated, and gave way. In a step she was through, leaning against it to hold back her fears.

The room formed in front of her. Sterile and windowless, with shadowless lighting and white walls with curved skirtings. A faint hum of refrigeration units and extractor fans trembled in the air. Mhairi set off past armoured perspex isolation cabinets and an autoclave. At the far end of the room, a row of nitrogen tanks squatted on a plinth. After a backwards glance, Mhairi walked down them, checking the codes on their lids. Some of the tanks contained several different cultures. She must have wasted ten minutes before she located the one she was after: AQ731P/015.

Regulations demanded protective clothing, but she didn't have time for that. She took down a pair of elbow-length insulated gloves and opened the carboy. Nitrogen fumes shimmered. She raised one of the miniature ladles, checked the code again, and unclipped the tiny container from its mount. She slipped it into her pocket.

It was done, and the ease of it left her faint.

Back at the door, she listened for footsteps before stepping into the empty corridor. As the door locked behind her, round the corner came Zach Garber, a neuropathologist and just about the last man she wanted to see. He stopped, did a double take, took a single step towards her.

'Mhairi. What are you doing here?'

She forced herself into motion, exaggerating her limp. 'Checking on some cultures for an experiment I'm setting up with David Florida.'

'I meant,' Garber said, shifting uncomfortably, 'at the hospital.'

She back-stepped indignantly. 'Sorry?'

Garber writhed. 'It's just . . . well, I heard you'd been suspended.'

Mhairi rolled her eyes and clasped Garber's wrist. 'God, yes, it's so embarrassing. Lena and I had a falling out. Unfortunately, it involved Grover Byron, and you know how jealous Lena is.' Her eyes widened, inviting Garber to imagine sexual tensions. 'Anyway, I called Lena at home last night and we've made up. We're friends again.'

'Excellent,' Garber said, a bit distantly. His eyes kept drawing back to the freezer room. 'So,' he said, 'what are you and Dave working on?'

'Just kicking around some ideas on hetero-oligomeric channels.' Mhairi gave Garber's wrist a squeeze. 'Tell you more another time. Got a midday clinic.'

Three feet down the corridor, the knife went into her back.

'I had lunch with Dave last week. He told me his next project involved peptide precursors.'

Mhairi turned and back-pedalled gaily. 'I know, but I twisted his arm.'

All the way down the corridor, she strained to hear the sound of Garber moving from the spot, but she knew without looking that he was still watching as she rounded the corner. She cursed herself for spinning such a stupid and unnecessary tale. She speeded up, but she had to wait a minute for Spinelli to release her, and then more sand dribbled through the timer while she signed out.

'Find what you were looking for?'

'What? Oh, yes,' Mhairi said, grinning numbly at Garber, who'd appeared in ominous silence behind the security door.

Down the stairs, moving as fast as her ankle would allow. Her arrival at ground level brought another shine to Jack's face, and she remembered something Byron had once told her. 'They all love you to see you, Mhairi. You brighten up their day.'

Well, she thought with a sudden pitch into misery, they've seen the last of me around here.

'Come here, girl, and tell me what you've been up to.'

She made a tragic face. 'I can't, Jack. Got a clinic in ten minutes.' She winked. 'I'll be over tomorrow, though. We'll catch up on the crack then.'

The wink was as unnecessary as the lie. Those two deceits would be what Jack remembered her for, not the shared laughs and gossip.

His phone buzzed. Holding up his hand in salute, he picked it up, at the same time opening the doors for Mhairi. Outside, she checked the instinct to make off as fast as she could. She turned to give Jack one last smile.

Her stomach froze. He was staring at her in astonishment, trying to take in what the voice at the other end was telling him. Then his jowly features hardened and he lurched to his feet. Suddenly the yard looked as wide as a runway. Jack was twenty years older than her, sedentary as only an ex-patrolman can be. But Mhairi couldn't move faster than a walk.

In the time it took to think this, an electric cart pulled up on its garbage run. The driver trudged past without acknowledging her existence. She hopped down the steps and heard a flurry behind her as Jack and the porter collided. By the time they'd disentangled, Mhairi was in the cart, motor switched on, foot clapped to the floor.

Jack was hustling his bulk down the steps. The porter simply stood, expressionless, as though seeing some hotshot medic hijacking his cart was just one more downside of his lousy job. Mhairi's lead was less than ten yards by the time Jack reached the yard and hit his stride. Top speed of the cart couldn't have been faster than a brisk jog, and even Jack could work up to that in a short burst. Each backward glance showed him closing the gap, pounding nearer and nearer until his face congested with a final effort and he threw out his hand and grabbed one of the cart's frame uprights.

Mhairi spun the wheel so hard the truck lifted on to two wheels. Jack, hopping like a drunk trying to feed one foot into his pants, lost his balance and hit the ground with a thump. No longer looking where she was going, she waited for him to move. He lay unstirring in the slush.

'Oh, no!' she cried, hitting the brake. She hobbled back to find Jack's eyes fixed and staring. She gently rolled his head and saw a nasty graze on his temple. *Herniation of the temporal lobe over the free edge of the tentorial opening causes compression of the third cranial nerve, so a unilaterally dilated fixed pupil is indicative of the presence of a compressing mass lesion.*

She slapped his cheek and shook him until his jowls wobbled. 'Jack, speak to me!'

His eyes fluttered and went past her, then came back into focus all at once. He grabbed for her and she only just slipped from his grasp. As if frozen at a distance, she saw him paw for his radio. Her wits swooped back in a rush. An instant before he grabbed the radio, she ripped it off him and stepped back with a sharp gasp, almost a laugh of disbelief at herself. She backed to the cart and blindly felt for the door.

'Hold it there, Mhairi.'

Jack was sitting up, holding the pistol in a two-handed aim. Slowly he found his footing.

In that small slice of time, the universe had shrunk to the few feet between Mhairi and the muzzle of the pistol.

'Now, Jack, you wouldn't shoot me.'

'It's my job, girl. Get away from the cart.'

Mhairi's view broadened to include the imagined patients and medical staff holding their breaths behind windows as they waited for him to blow her away.

'No, Jack,' she said, and climbed aboard.

Under way again, she checked the wing mirror and saw Jack standing with the pistol hanging limp at his side. She wondered if he would have pulled the trigger if he'd known what was in her tunic. She remembered what he'd said about his job and realised he was telling her he'd lose it. It occurred to her she'd ruined the lives of everybody over whom she had emotional leverage.

By the time she'd driven across the yard, Jack had nearly made it back to the steps. Calculating that she had no more than twenty seconds before he hit the panic button, she kept going flat out at a sedate five or six miles an hour, aiming for the entrance.

The guards were facing the road, concentrating on incoming traffic. A car was being cleared through, the barrier going up. If the guards saw the cart coming, they thought nothing of it until it glided past, the barrier catching its flimsy roof and buckling it like tinfoil. She got a snapshot of the guards' pop-eyed faces. Yesterday, running through the snow in bare feet; today, buzzing along in a laundry cart. In other circumstances, it might almost have been funny.

A horn blasted her and she swerved out of the path of a car. It drew alongside and the driver furiously tapped his head. She grimaced an apology. If he thought she was an escaping mental patient, that was fine by her.

Around the corner from the cab rank, she dumped the cart, stripped off her whites and hobbled to her autobubble. The driver was asleep. She shook him violently, peering behind for signs of hue and cry. 'Drive,' she ordered. 'San Jose.'

The driver yawned. 'You keep me waiting forty minutes, then all of a sudden you got no time. My wife's just the same.'

One of the guards had come skidding round the corner. Mhairi slid down in her seat. 'Don't argue. Just go.'

He pulled out without haste. Mhairi kept her head down until they were a block clear. Her ankle throbbed sickeningly. She tried to estimate how much time she had. Jack would have raised the alarm by now, but the hospital wouldn't call the cops immediately. First, they'd instigate a search to find out what she'd removed. It would take them at least an hour to be sure, and even then, they'd be so shocked they'd double check and confer before shakily informing the police that one of their consultant neurologists was a suspected bio-terrorist.

The autobubble was on automatic, following a pre-determined course at a programmed speed. 'Can't you make this thing go any faster? I've got a plane to catch.'

'It's governed to fifty.'

It took an hour to reach San Jose. The departure hall wasn't crowded, and Mhairi was painfully conscious that her height and colouring made her conspicuous. A man seated outside the coffee shop was already eyeing her, but that wasn't unusual. The test was if he looked away when she frowned at him.

He didn't. She was the one who averted her hot face. She went over to the news-stand and pretended to look over some recreational software. She sensed a presence move up behind her.

'Dr Magnusson?'

She braced, expecting the man's next words to be 'Police' or 'FBI'.

'Zygote. Your plane is waiting.'

FOUR

29

Sergeant Murray was Mhairi's escort on the flight to Well-spring. She acted as though they'd never met before and sat one seat behind, reading beauty magazines. Mhairi watched the landscape as if it was a passing dream. Today the atmosphere beneath the ice shield was cloudless, the sky like watered silk, the plains and mountains and lakes washed with subtle tints of grey, lilac and lavender.

But across the Line, the pastel tones darkened and the heliplane followed a long finger of frozen inland water pointing towards a wall of charcoal cloud. In the daylight darkness, Wellspring was visible from thirty miles off, its electric blue domes clustered under a gunpowder sky crazed by lightning.

'Got some weather coming,' Murray said.

Mhairi went to the toilet and locked the door. She took a bottle from her purse and emptied two capsules into her shaking palm. Steadying her wrist with the other hand, she nuzzled the pills into her mouth and pushed them down with a finger.

She placed the tiny phial she'd stolen on the basin, then took from her purse a 1ml. syringe with a capped needle. Tongue in the corner of her mouth, she pierced the lid of the phial and inserted the needle. She sucked up the contents and withdrew the needle. A tiny droplet clung to the end. She shook it off and placed the syringe on a tissue.

Murray tapped on the door. 'We're beginning our descent.'

'One moment.'

Mhairi filled the empty containers with water, dropped them into the pan and flushed them out into the barrens. She removed her fake tortoiseshell hair-clip – a large double comb hinged at the top. Pressing it open, she laid the syringe inside the bar above the toothed jaws and secured it with thin strips of surgical adhesive. When the jaws hinged shut, she could see both ends of the syringe, but only if she looked hard. She brushed her hair and clamped the clip in place.

Murray rattled the handle. 'Resume your seat, please.'

Mhairi took a breath as if it was meant to last the rest of her life and went out.

They disembarked into a livid light. Thunder rolled between the distant ranges, a sonorous requiem. Only Murray's male colleague was waiting. On the walk to Module 1, the guards engaged each other in lame conversation about the coming storm, but once on the escalator they lapsed into purposeful silence, their attention fixed ahead. They guided Mhairi across the empty reception area towards the elevator.

They exited on Level 2 and led her down an empty corridor to an unmarked room. It was little more than a windowless cubicle, furnished with a bare table and a plastic-sheeted trolley.

'Lay your case and purse on the table,' Murray said.

She examined Mhairi's purse and her partner started on her overnight case. They examined her effects thoroughly, unscrewing lipstick barrels, toothpaste tubes and scent bottles, occasionally passing suspect objects between them. They replaced everything neatly, then Murray started on Mhairi's body, running her hands over her curves, first the outside, then the inside.

'Let down your hair, please.'

'This is outrageous,' Mhairi said, removing the clip.

Murray laid the clip aside, and combed her hands through Mhairi's hair as if searching for lice. At a nod from her, the man left.

'Remove all your clothes above the waist.'

'You're not . . .'

'Please do what I tell you.'

Mhairi tried to tell herself that the humiliation was no worse than what her patients suffered.

'Raise your arms. Turn around.'

Murray nodded at the discarded clothes. 'Put those back on and strip below the waist.'

Mhairi gave a little gasp. 'No, I refuse.'

'If you won't co-operate, I'll call for assistance.'

Mhairi undressed with wooden fingers. Her knees shook. The room clouded around her.

Sergeant Murray pulled on a pair of rubber gloves and disappeared behind her. 'Bend over.'

Mhairi closed her eyes.

'That's fine. Lie on the couch. Legs up and apart.'

Mhairi suffered the indignity with dulled anger. She knew who was responsible. This was Grippe's revenge, and Grippe would pay.

'Okay,' Murray said, discarding the gloves in a bin. 'Get dressed.' She faced the other way as if she respected Mhairi's privacy.

When Mhairi was clothed, she reached for her bags, but Murray stopped her. 'I'll take those.' She went to the door. 'Follow me, please.'

Another walk, another room. Paige, nattily suited and not a hair out of place, rose from behind a white table.

'Dr Magnusson, what a pleasure to see you again. Pleasant flight?' When Mhairi didn't answer, he pulled out a chair. 'Please be seated.' He waited for her to settle, then pulled his own chair close to the table. 'You know why you're here.' He smiled. 'When we first spoke, you said you weren't nervous of me.'

The drug hadn't taken. Mhairi was scared stiff. She desperately needed a pee.

'Give me your hands,' Paige said. 'Palms up, if you please. Shall I tell you who I credit with the invention of the polygraph? It was the playwright Richard Brinsley Sheridan, 1751–1816. "My valour is certainly going," he wrote in *The Rivals*. "It is sneaking off. I feel it oozing out as it were at the palms of my hands."'

Play for time, Mhairi thought. 'Don't you have any thoughts of your own, Mr Paige?'

'Everything that's worth saying has been said before.'

'Who said that?'

'I did, just this moment. Now then, you are Dr Mhairi Magnusson, a consultant neurophysiologist resident in San Francisco.'

'For heaven's sake.'

'Yes or no.'

'Yes.'

'You signed an agreement promising to keep confidential all matters pertaining to Wellspring's affairs. Have you broken that undertaking? Please answer yes or no.'

'Cha do bhris.'

Paige frowned. 'Repeat.'

'Cha do bhris.'

'I said yes or no, Dr Magnusson.'

'That *was* no – in Gaelic.'

'I don't speak Gaelic.'

'Oh, I thought you were a champion linguist.'

'I speak twelve languages fluently. Gaelic is not one of them. I'll ask you again, have you discussed your visit to Wellspring with anyone?'

'I can do Icelandic, if you prefer.'

Paige dilated his nostrils. 'Let's stick to English.'

Mhairi felt her muscles begin to loosen as the drug kicked in. A giggle bubbled up. 'You know, you're really very good, Paige. It seems such a shame to scrap you.'

'I beg your pardon?'

Mhairi put a finger to her mouth. 'Oh dear, hasn't Grover told you? You're to be replaced next spring. He can't wait to see the back of you.'

'I'm Zygote's property. They can do what they like with me.' He adjusted his seat, apparently finding it hard to get comfortable. 'Did you talk to anyone about John?'

Mhairi released a sigh. 'No.' She was coasting now.

'Have you spoken to Judge Barbara Lovelock?'

'Whoever she is, I've never spoken to her.'

'Do you know Harry Fender?'

226

'Who?'

'Yes or no'

'No.'

'Samuel Pilkinghorn?'

'No.'

Paige dropped her hands and raised his eyes. 'Session completed. The subject is telling the truth.'

'I'll be the judge of that,' Grippe's voice said. 'Bring her up.'

Byron greeted her with a palsied smile. Grippe applauded softly.

'I take my hat off to you. How did you fool Paige?'

'You told me he was foolproof. No wonder you're sending him to the breaker's yard.'

Grippe covered his mouth and tittered. 'Dr Magnusson, I assume you hope to make an ally of him.' He lowered his hand. 'Paige is incapable of harming anyone, no matter what the provocation. I could apply a blow-torch to him and the worst he would do is deliver a monologue on Wellspring's fire regulations.' Grippe smiled at the robot. 'It's quite true, Paige. In six months you are to be superseded by a new model.'

'Very good,' Paige said loftily. 'Mine not to reason why.'

'Please,' Grippe said, inviting Mhairi to sit. He took the seat opposite. Byron remained standing.

'I'm not sure I can contribute anything worthwhile to this discussion,' he said.

'Sit,' Grippe barked. 'You're the one who kicked the stone off the mountain top.'

With Byron in his place, Grippe was in no hurry to speak. He toyed with a sheet of paper. 'Your confidentiality agreement,' he said eventually, flicking it across the desk to Mhairi. 'I don't know how you cheated Paige, but it doesn't matter. We have proof that you hired a private investigator and spoke to Barbara Lovelock. We know that you've uncovered John's identity.'

'My word's not worth the paper it's written on,' Mhairi agreed. She picked up the document and tore it into shreds. 'Like your promise to rescue my parents.'

227

Byron twisted miserably. 'Mhairi . . .'

Grippe silenced him with a gesture. 'We didn't know they were dead. If they'd been alive, we would have kept our side of the agreement.'

Mhairi sighed, lifted up her hair as if its weight oppressed her, and took out the clip. 'Where's Dr Scritti?' she asked, her voice sunk low in her chest.

Grippe's face became as tragic as a bloodhound's. 'We had to let her go. You saw for yourself how unstable she was. Her attachment to John was unhealthy.'

'She loved him,' Mhairi said softly. 'The idiot.'

Neither man spoke. Byron looked down as though he wanted to grind something under his feet.

Mhairi stroked the syringe inside the clip. 'What have you done with her?'

'She's on sick leave in Hawaii. When she's recovered, she'll be assigned to new duties at our Arizona lab.'

'Does she know about John's past?'

Grippe's head shook sombrely. 'I don't think her infatuation would have survived that.'

Mhairi looked at Byron. 'Did you?'

'Not until this morning.'

Grippe steepled his hands under his chin. 'It must have been a terrible shock to discover that your patient is a murderer.'

'Devastating.'

'But at least you understand now why he can never be released.'

'Yes.'

'Good.' Grippe put the tips of his hands to his mouth and studied her. 'This has been a difficult time for you. At the least, you deserve an explanation about the nature of our research involving John Cope. However, I can only confide in you if you pledge to draw a line under this affair. Agree to forget John Cope, and I'll do more. I'll smooth over your difficulties with Professor Newman.'

Mhairi was on the far side now, responsive only to her own urges. 'That's why I came.'

Grippe stood with an admonishing wag of his finger. 'But please, no emotional outbursts.' He held out his hand. 'A very distinguished visitor is waiting to meet you.'

30

Two men occupied the conference chamber. One of them was a sharp-faced stranger, the other a white-haired man who rose in smiling welcome.

'I believe Professor Yrigoyen needs no introduction.'

The professor was tiny, almost doll-like. Under his Einstein-style mane he had the scrubbed pink features of a pug, snub nose and merry brown eyes. He bowed over Mhairi's hand with old-fashioned courtesy. 'We made passing acquaintance at the IAAS conference.'

'Lance Rocco of the Advanced Research Projects Agency,' Grippe said, off-handedly indicating the stranger.

Rocco remained seated, watching Mhairi with small-eyed suspicion.

'Can we fetch you anything?' Yrigoyen said, fussing around her. 'Coffee, something stronger?' He looked anxiously about as though searching for a waiter. 'No?'

'You can bring me John.'

Grippe flashed her a warning. 'Steady on, Dr Magnusson.'

'No, no,' Yrigoyen assured him. 'Her concern is understandable.' He spread his palms in a benign, almost priestly, gesture. 'Let us all sit.'

One by one they took their places. Yrigoyen beamed at Grippe. 'Begin, please.'

The lights dimmed momentarily as a discharge of lightning tripped the power supply.

'I suspect you've already guessed,' Grippe told Mhairi. 'Some of it, anyway.'

'Anti-ageing therapy has to be part of it,' she said. 'John doesn't look a day older than he did on the day of his execution.'

Grippe's eyes drifted to a point behind Mhairi's head. 'The search for immortality,' he said. 'We've known for decades that the life span of cells is governed by strips of DNA – telomeres – that protect the ends of the chromosomes. Each time the cell divides, these telomeres get a little shorter, until at last they erode away to the point where the genes on the chromosomes are exposed to wear and tear. The genes then malfunction, causing the cell to die or mutate into cancer cells. Arresting this process isn't difficult. By activating the gene that produces the enzyme telomerase, we can maintain the telomeres and ensure that the cells go on dividing indefinitely.'

'Fine for anti-wrinkle treatment,' Mhairi said, 'but telomere therapy doesn't arrest senescence. In fact, it's usually applied in reverse – starve cancer cells of telomerase and they age to death in a few weeks.'

'Not a magic bullet,' Grippe agreed. 'Telomeres are only one of the factors that regulate the biological clock. Cells are also damaged by free radicals, pathogens and copying errors in the DNA code. Many of these malfunctioning cells can be neutralised by search-and-destroy viruses. But that still leaves – well, as a neurologist, you don't need me to tell you the main problem.'

'Brain cells don't possess telomeres,' Mhairi said. 'Nor do heart tissue cells. They don't divide. Once gone, they're gone forever.'

Grippe nodded. 'The neurons we're born with are the ones we die with, minus the several hundred million that have died along the way. There's no attraction in having a 150-year-old body as smooth and firm as a twenty-year-old athlete's if it houses the brain of a drooling geriatric. Who wants to be a Struldbrugg?'

'A what?'

'Struldbruggs,' Grippe explained, 'were the race of immortals sought by Jonathan Swift's Gulliver, who believed they would pass on to him the knowledge that only great age can bring. But meeting these ancients turned out to be the most depressing experience of his life. They were immortal, certainly, but

230

whatever wisdom they had acquired had been eroded by senile decay. Their memories were so ruined, they couldn't even finish a sentence.' Grippe smiled. 'People don't want immortality; they want eternal youth.'

'And that's what Zygote is offering?'

'It was Dr Scritti who made the breakthrough. She discovered a method of introducing into brain tissues a gene that regenerates the neurons.'

Mhairi breathed out quietly, the circle closed. 'That's why John's brain scan revealed no damage. His brain's been repaired. The old cells have been replaced.'

'A new man,' Grippe said. 'A *tabula rasa*.'

Muffled thunder sounded through the roof. 'How long will he live?' Mhairi asked.

'Not forever. He's still mortal.'

'Subject to the slings and arrows of outrageous fortune,' Paige said. 'The heartache and the thousand natural shocks that flesh is heir to.'

'Spare us,' Grippe said. He bridged his hands. 'On a risk-assessment analysis, if John had remained comatose in his isolation chamber, he might have survived five hundred years. Now he's back in the real world, it depends on what sort of lifestyle he takes up. Even an everyday hazard like driving would reduce his life span to, say, three hundred years. Indulging in high-risk sports such as skiing or mountain climbing would carry a statistically greater risk of premature death. If he abused his body with drugs, he'd be lucky to reach his hundredth birthday – though he would make a lovely corpse.'

'How long?' Mhairi repeated.

'Our best projections, taking all clinical factors into account, suggest that John will live to see his second century.'

'I'd better put every cent I possess into Zygote stock.'

Grippe was tickled. 'I guarantee you won't be disappointed.' His prominent eyes shone. 'A one-stop treatment to double life span. How much do you think people would pay? One million? Five million? Ten?'

Mhairi looked at Rocco for the first time. His close-set eyes were level and trustless. 'Politicians will never license it for general use,' she said. 'I can see your client list now – ageing despots and dictators, a few billionaire tycoons. Instead of tyrannical regimes lasting for a few years or decades, they'll endure for centuries. One thing's for sure, your treatment won't be available at the neighbourhood beauty salon.'

Grippe laughed boisterously. 'Let the market decide.'

Yrigoyen coughed politely and stood. He was still for a moment, as if inviting applause, then he waved a dismissive hand at Grippe. 'The commercial and social implications are important but, to me, irrelevant.' He stared up through the domed roof. 'Many Americans believe Virginia Nova is an invention and Argo a fake – diversions from harsh reality.' He raised a silvery brow at Mhairi. 'Even some scientists are sceptical.'

'I believe Virginia Nova exists,' she told him. 'I believe Argo is real. I don't buy the story that it's carrying a human crew.'

He nodded distantly. 'You're correct. They're robots. The government decided that a manned mission to a new world would uplift humanity during the hard years that lie ahead. The crew's script has been written, characters assigned, story plotted. A soap opera, yes, but not an unworthy one.'

'Until it's found out.'

Yrigoyen smiled impishly. 'Mhairi, I could supply you with incontrovertible evidence of the hoax and the majority of the public would refuse to believe you. They need heroes. They need their illusions, and if those illusions are fed by TV images relayed from space, what earthly power could shatter them?'

'But ultimately, that's what they are – puppets.'

'You're right. There will be no happy ending.' Yrigoyen's brow ruffled. 'Do you enjoy science fiction?'

'No.'

'Nor I – all that drivel about warp drives and worm holes delivering people from one side of the universe to the other in literally no time at all. It's anti-science. We're bound by the laws of physics, and current technology remains closer to Newton's third law of motion than Einstein's theory of general relativity.

232

Even though anti-matter propulsion allows us to cruise at ten per cent of light speed, it is still too slow for interstellar travel. Too slow. A young male astronaut on Argo would be an old man by the time he reached Virginia Nova. His female counterpart would be past child-bearing age before she was half-way there.'

'Unless the astronaut was John Cope.'

'Yes, exactly.' His face shone. 'An astronaut with John's life expectancy could visit Virginia Nova, spend his working life there and still return to earth to enjoy a long retirement. In fact, at the speed Argo travels, he'd add another six months to his life as time is measured on Earth.'

Mhairi's hands trembled in her lap. 'So that's what you're going to do – send John to Virginia Nova.'

Yrigoyen spread his hands. 'The perfect payload.'

'Does he know?'

Yrigoyen was shocked. 'Tsk! Certainly not. Even if he volunteered, even if he could be trained, it isn't practicable. Imagine spending sixty years sealed into a capsule with only yourself for company. A nightmare! Imagine how much damage he might cause. He could sabotage the entire mission.'

'So you're going to put him back in a coma and keep him alive with the neurostimulators.'

Grippe stepped into the silence. 'Would that be such a terrible fate? Cope was condemned to death for appalling crimes. Technically, the sentence still stands. If we were to hand him over to the authorities, by law they would be compelled to carry out the order of the court. Instead, we've given him not only a lease on life, but also an opportunity to make amends for his crimes and give something back to society.'

'A glorious opportunity,' Yrigoyen murmured.

Mhairi uncapped the syringe needle. 'There must have been other guinea pigs.'

'The treatment was not universally successful,' Grippe admitted. 'In some cases it produced unfortunate reactions. We aren't inhumane. When the risks became apparent, we switched our trials to Grover's apes.'

'So John's the only one who made it.'

'The first,' Grippe said. 'But definitely not the last.'

Mhairi rose and raked her fingers through her hair as if she was struggling to reach a decision. She could understand Grippe's point of view, and Yrigoyen's. More than half a billion people had died as a result of the meteor strike. What was the life of one man – a convicted murderer – if it helped guarantee the survival of the human race?

The men turned to watch her pass behind them. Grippe had been her original target. He was the repository of everything vile about the new regime – a corporate hatchetman with a medieval mind-set. She walked past him.

Rocco, she ignored completely. An apparatchik, a government hireling, a dragon's tooth. Kill him, and a thousand more stood ready to take his place.

She returned Byron's mute appeal for forgiveness with a sad smile. He wasn't an evil man, just emotionally stunted and imbued with a sense of his own gorgeousness.

Her circuit brought her behind Yrigoyen. Father of Argo, begetter of the future, presidential hopeful. As she stopped, he reached for her hand and pressed it to his shoulder – an old man nourished by contact with young flesh. He probably made that gesture to his grandchildren at bedtime – the kids whose own children he hoped would one day tread the green and fertile surface of Virginia Nova.

When he let go, she didn't take her own hand away. She pressed harder and brought her other hand round to his neck.

At first her audience thought her gesture was respectful. When they saw her stance was too purposeful, puzzlement retarded their reactions. Yrigoyen tried to bring her hand into focus. 'Grover,' he said mildly, 'tell me what the young doctor is doing.'

Byron squeezed out an answer at his second attempt. 'I don't know. She's got something in her hand. It looks like a syringe.'

'That's impossible,' Grippe blurted. 'She was body-searched.'

Mhairi swirled her mane with slow deliberation and tossed her hair clip on to the table.

Byron closed his eyes. 'What's in the syringe?'

'One millilitre of encoded DNA linked to a herpes simplex retrovirus.'

Byron groaned. Yrigoyen chuckled. 'Even to my physicist's ear, I doubt if the doctor is threatening to inject me with shingles.'

'The virus is the vector,' Byron muttered. 'It's what the DNA is encoded for that matters.'

Yrigoyen smiled up at Mhairi. 'Encoded for what?'

'Neuronal functions,' she said. 'The virus is taken up at the synaptic terminals. From there it carries the DNA to the nuclei of neurons where it replicates and produces more infective particles that destroy the cells. It moves on, eating away the entire nervous system, eventually causing encephalitis and death. Before then it will have destroyed memory, thought and language. It's galloping Alzheimer's. In three months, Professor Yrigoyen won't be able to eat, dress, control his bladder or his bowels. He won't know who he is or recognise his grand-children. He'll be a Struldbrugg.'

Yrigoyen breathed in like a diver facing too high a plunge.

'Second childishness and mere oblivion,' Paige observed. 'Sans teeth, sans eyes, sans taste, sans everything.'

'Shut the fuck up,' Grippe shouted. His face was the colour of raw liver and veins stood out on his forehead. 'Grover, is she capable of it?'

Byron's throat bobbed against his collar. 'I don't know. I've never seen her like this.'

Grippe's eyes slitted. 'I don't think she is.'

'That,' Yrigoyen said mildly, 'is easy for you to say.'

'Grover's never seen me like this because I'm not in my right mind. That's how I fooled Paige. I've taken a drug that blocks the amygdala – the brain's fear centre. I'm in the same state as Viking berserkers, Shia suicide bombers, Kamikaze pilots. No fear, no inhibitions, no compunctions. At this moment I could kill the professor as carelessly as you'd swat a fly.'

'Shit's sake,' Byron hissed. 'You're talking about the most distinguished scientist of the age. Harming him would be a crime against humanity.'

235

'Humanity? What about the human guinea pigs who died so that you could come up with future-man? Do you lose sleep over them?' Mhairi speared Grippe with her eyes. 'I know it was you who had Harry Fender killed.'

'You'd better tell us what you want,' Rocco said. It was the first time he'd spoken.

'Guess,' Mhairi said.

Grippe's jaws grated. 'No.'

'It doesn't sound like much to ask,' Yrigoyen said, almost wheedling. 'A little visit to show how well John is.'

'Get him,' Rocco ordered.

Grippe's jaw tightened with a tremor. 'Go,' he told Paige

'If he alerts anyone . . .' Mhairi said, coiling a hank of Yrigoyen's hair around her fingers.

Halfway to the door, Paige suffered a moment of indecision and came back, stopped behind Byron, bent down and put his mouth to his ear like an unctuous bank manager telling a favoured customer that his account was overdrawn. Then he went on his way.

The room was very quiet for a while. During this phase, Mhairi saw Byron's face turn white. His lips worked silently, and when at last he spoke it was at the top of his voice.

'Warren, I want that fucking robot off the premises. Right now!'

Grippe was drumming his fingers on the desk. 'What the hell are you talking about?'

'He threatened me. The fucker threatened me!'

'For God's sake,' Grippe shouted, smashing a fist against the desk. 'Just for once, stop thinking about yourself!'

31

'Check,' Cope said, setting down his queen.

Dickey tugged at his collar and clicked his tongue. While he was dickering, Cope calculated his chances of taking the gun off him. Candy from a baby, but a weapon alone wouldn't take him far. He'd have to get through the security cordon, and then he'd need transport and time to get clear. He was working on the problem, though, stockpiling information. Dickey had already supplied a lot – how the hovercraft and suits worked, how far to the nearest road.

'You're beat,' Cope said. 'May as well resign.'

The guard wagged a finger. 'I'm thinking.'

Cope lazily looked up as Paige entered. 'You tell him.'

Paige assessed the state of play in a trice. 'John's correct. Checkmate in three moves.'

'How about if I take his rook with this pawn?'

'Then it's mate in two.'

Dickey toppled his king in a huff. 'Only one place a boy like you gets the time to learn them fancy moves – in the slammer.'

Cope began setting up the pieces again. 'Fancy your chances?' he asked Paige. A joke. He'd played three games with the robot and been trounced inside twenty moves each time.

'Another time, perhaps. Dr Magnusson's here. She requests your presence in Mr Grippe's suite.'

Electricity swarmed across Cope's skin. He studied Paige's face, but the robot was switched to receive only. Dickey was still replaying the game in his mind. Cope rose bit by bit.

'You're going on a journey,' Paige told him. 'May I suggest you pack outdoor clothes.'

Dickey forgot chess then. 'No one's going anywhere tonight, buddy. Take a look outside.'

He was right. Comet trails of snow streaked past the window. A man outside could lose himself and die between here and Module 1. Mind racing, Cope went to his closet and selected parka and pants, thermal boots and mitts. Grippe wasn't going to let him go – not after what he'd witnessed. They were using Mhairi's name to soften him up. But why the pretence? They could take him any time they pleased.

'Play another when you get back?' Dickey said.

Cope put finger-tip to thumb. 'For sure.'

The moment they were outside, Cope pinned Paige against

the wall. 'Dickey's right. Where's Mhairi gonna take me on a night like this?'

'I'm not sure she knows herself. She's in a very disturbed frame of mind. She's holding Mr Grippe, Dr Byron, Mr Rocco and Professor Yrigoyen hostage.'

Cope let go. 'You're shitting me.'

Paige rearranged the lie of his lapels. 'You know I cannot tell a lie. However, I must say I'm surprised. She struck me as such a kind lady.'

'Damn me,' Cope said, light-headed.

A couple of guards appeared round the curve. They nodded cool greetings and walked by in step. Adrenalin hit Cope's veins. Thoughts shot through each other, but by the time Paige ushered him into Grippe's private elevator, he still hadn't formed them into a coherent plan.

The elevator braked outside Grippe's suite. 'We'll miss you,' Paige said.

'Paige, I'd like to say the same to you, but I cannot tell a lie.'

'I know I'm not popular with my human colleagues. But they won't have to endure my presence much longer.' Paige raised his chin like a martyr. 'I, too, am leaving Wellspring. I'm being replaced.'

'How does that make you feel?'

'Tight, confused, unable to concentrate.'

'Sounds like anger, bud. You don't want to keep it bottled up. You'll blow a chip.'

The scene that met Cope's eyes had a delicate tension he was careful not to upset. Byron sat crumpled and still, all the swagger knocked out of him. Grippe, eyes moist with passion, showed his teeth in a tombstone smile. Next to him was a man with eyes like a shithouse rat who Cope recognised as one of the grey suits who'd looked on while the scientists were putting him through his paces. The calmest person in the room was the old guy Mhairi was standing over. One look at her grey, stark face told Cope she wasn't in control.

'Are you okay?' she asked shakily.

'Ain't decided,' Cope answered, assessing possible threats and narrowing them down to Rocco.

'Monica?'

'She's dead,' Cope said, still trying to work out the dynamics of the situation. 'She tried to spring me and Grippe left her on the prairie. Wasted a couple of Zygote guards, too. Blew up a plane and a whole load of troops.'

Byron's face fell to the table with a thump. Grippe eyed him with oblique contempt. 'Dr Scritti tried to sell John to our leading rival. What did you expect?'

A heavy silence.

'Where have we got to?' Cope asked Mhairi.

She stared blankly, no longer with it.

'What's the plan?' he demanded.

Her eyes blinked back into focus. 'We need a heliplane.'

Oh shit, Cope thought. 'Mhairi, it's blowing a shitstorm. The plane's grounded. There's no way out by air.'

She shuddered. Dark blotches circled her eyes. She was leaking away before his eyes.

Grippe battened on to her weakness. 'John, don't involve yourself in another disaster. Tell her you have no intention of leaving and let's bring this unpleasantness to an end.' He cracked his knuckles. 'Let's try acting like reasonable human beings.'

'Act away,' Cope said, making for Mhairi.

Whatever she held in her hand was the only thing keeping things together. Not for much longer, though. Her eyes looked as if they were about to roll up into her skull. Cope saw Rocco starting to coil down and grabbed for Mhairi's wrist.

'Give me that.'

'Watch out!' she cried. 'It's lethal.'

'Give it to me,' Cope yelled as Rocco came up out of his chair.

Syringe in one hand, he backhanded the Agency man with the other, sending him sprawling into the table. He stepped behind Grippe and locked an arm round his neck as Rocco scrambled up.

'Sit down.'

Rubbing his split lip, Rocco sidled back into his chair.

Cope levered Grippe's head back. 'Get me a gun.'

'John,' Grippe said in a strangled voice, 'nobody outside this room knows what's happening. If security's alerted, I can't answer for the consequences.'

Cope slid the syringe under his jaw. 'You got five seconds, then I'm terminating your contract.'

Grippe looked up at him, his eyes dark pools of panic. 'In my study,' he mumbled, trying not to move his mouth. 'Bottom drawer of my desk. Please, if that needle breaks my skin . . .'

Cope jerked his face at Mhairi. She backed off, tripping over her ankles, and stumbled into the next room. Grippe kept dabbing at the soft skin under his chin and inspecting his fingers for blood. A minute went by before Mhairi wobbled back holding a small automatic as if it was an object she'd retrieved from a latrine. She almost dropped it as she handed it over.

Cope tossed the syringe on to the table. It bounced with a tinkling sound that fascinated everyone but himself. Holding the pistol on the company, he backed to the window and looked at the slashing blizzard.

'Order up one of the magic sledges.'

'Don't be a fool,' Rocco said. 'It isn't only Zygote you're up against. Even if you succeeded in leaving Wellspring, you wouldn't get more than a few miles. All the resources of the Agency will be after you.'

Mhairi began gagging into her hand. Suddenly she wheeled to a corner and was explosively sick.

Rocco wafted the air in front of his nose. 'You see? You're in way over your head. Give it up, man.'

'Give what up? My life? What's the trade, pal? What are you offering?'

No one spoke. The air in the room seemed to have been replaced by some kind of unstable gas.

Cope swept the phone across the table. 'Now get me a hovercraft.'

Grippe's complexion was greenish. 'I'll have to clear it

through the commander of the guard. It will be out of my hands then.'

'It ain't in your hands now.'

Grippe inhaled through his nose, picked up the phone and cleared his throat. The voice at the other end brought a crippled smile to his face. 'No, things are far from good. As a result of your people's incompetence, my guests and I have been taken hostage. As I speak, John is pointing a pistol at my head . . . No, it's *my* gun . . . Dr Magnusson was allowed to walk into the facility with a deadly poison.' His voice shook. 'It's possible I've been contaminated.' He furiously crossed his legs. 'Shut up! Unless we agree to their demands, he's going to kill us.' Grippe smiled again, the smile not reaching his eyes. 'Oh, you think so. You think that a man who witnessed Dr Scritti's murder wouldn't have the nerve to pull the trigger.' Grippe's smile disintegrated. 'I'd rather you didn't look on it as a military challenge. Your career might survive *my* death, but I doubt if you'd advance far as the man who got Yrigoyen killed a few days before the Argo launch.'

He thrust the phone at Cope. 'Tell him.'

Cope sat on a corner of the desk. 'Me and Mhairi are checking out. We want a hovercraft, two camouflage suits with helmets and all the gizmos. Food, money, knife, maps, flashlights. Everything we need for a journey across the Line. Park the goods in Grippe's private bay. Make sure the sledge is tanked up and the helmets are charged. I'll know if they ain't. I don't want to see any blue uniforms when we get down there. Spook me and it's bye-bye Mr Grippe. Him and the other three are coming along part of the way. You'd better throw in suits and helmets for them, too.' Cope eyed Paige thoughtfully. 'Hold it. Make that seven suits – five large, one medium, one small.' He frowned. 'What do you mean, you don't have small?'

He listened long enough to get the gist of the commander's response. 'No, I don't want to discuss this with a trained negotiator. You've got ten minutes.'

He racked the phone and stood. Things would run their course now.

Grippe regarded Byron with resigned melancholy. 'I warned you. The night this monster woke, I told you we weren't dealing with a laboratory rat.'

'While we got a moment,' Cope said, 'why don't you tell me what we *are* dealing with. Like, who the hell am I and what have you done with me?'

Grippe shook with inward laughter, then his expression grew still and tragic. 'By a terrible irony, we've given you the gift of long life.'

Cope frowned at Mhairi. 'Huh?'

'You've been given anti-ageing therapy,' she whispered. 'Your life span's been extended.'

Cope turned it round in his mind and grinned. 'It has now.' He stopped grinning. 'Why?'

Nobody answered.

Cope ground the muzzle of the pistol into Grippe's temple. 'I asked a question.'

Mhairi began to sob. 'They were going to put you back into a coma and send you to Virginia Nova.'

While Cope was trying to digest that, Mhairi walked unsteadily to the table. 'I have to make a call below the Line.'

'Hold it,' Cope said, trapping her hand.

'It's my private line,' Grippe said tiredly. 'It's secure.'

Cope nodded permission for Mhairi to dial. She waited for someone to answer, her teeth sunk into her bottom lip, little tics breaking out on her skin. Her eyes faded. She was about to lay down the phone when her body straightened.

'Sam? Oh, thank God!'

She turned away. 'I'm here now, but not for much longer. John and I are about to leave. You were right; we're in the Alvord Desert. No, I don't know where. No, there's no time to explain.' Her voice broke. 'Look, I don't *know*. There's a terrible storm.' She listened, then felt for paper and pen. She wrote something down. 'Yes, I'll try. No. No. He's got a gun. Well then. Yes, I hope so, too. You don't have to say that.'

Tears spilled from her eyes as she put down the phone. Cope watched her, wondering what kind of ally she'd make. He was still wondering when the commander called in. He waited a few seconds before answering.

'You got it?'

'Everything you asked for. I need a guarantee that you won't harm your hostages.'

'You're it. Box me in and I'll shoot them. Give me space and I'll drop them once we're clear.' Cope handed the phone to Grippe. 'Convince him.'

Grippe's voice was husky. 'No pursuit until we're safe. That's an order.'

Cope snatched the phone back. 'Understand?'

'I understand.'

'Okay, we're coming down. Have the perimeter gates open.'

Cope marshalled the hostages outside the elevator and shielded himself with Grippe. The glass booth was empty. It was a tight squeeze and Byron put his hands against Paige's chest when the robot tried to join them.

'Not you.'

'Come right on in,' Cope told Paige. He put the pistol to Grippe's head. 'From now on, he takes his orders from me.'

'Paige, do what he says.'

'Very good.'

Rocco gave a curdled laugh. 'Warren, the Agency are going to sue the ass off Zygote. We are going to crucify you.'

Paige cleared his throat. 'Oh what a tangled . . .'

'Shut up!' Rocco shouted.

32

Dropping through the levels, Cope scanned the corridors radiating from the elevator shaft. A few scientists, but no blue uniforms. When the elevator reached bottom, he laid the pistol under Grippe's ear. The door opened.

For one heart-wrenching moment, he failed to see the hover-craft. But that was only because it was so well-camouflaged. It was by the door, the suits spread over the sides, everything present as demanded.

A voice crackled from an intercom. 'John, this is the commander. I understand you've picked up some basic knowledge about the snow gliders. In that case, you'll know their maximum range is thirty miles. Then what? You're more than a hundred miles from the Line.'

'Thirty miles sounds good to me,' Cope said. 'Now get off my back. If I've got something to say, I'll call you.'

He herded the hostages against one wall and went over to Mhairi. She was hanging back by the elevator, shaking. He didn't think she could cut it and for a moment he considered leaving her behind. 'You look like shit. What's wrong?'

'Sick. Awful.'

'You'll feel better once we're in fresh air.'

She pawed at him as he turned. 'We're never going to pull it off. I can't believe what I've done.'

He held her by the shoulders. 'This is as real as it gets, Mhairi.'

'But the commander's right. We won't survive out there. Where will we go?'

Cope ran his eyes across the walls. 'I ain't got time to explain, so just trust me when I say I know what I'm doing.' He looked into her eyes. 'Think you can manage that?'

After a moment, she gave a child-like nod.

Gently he led her to the craft and picked up one of the suits. It was lighter than he'd expected, but still quite a hefty garment. He handed it to Mhairi and raised his voice. 'The rest of you, put your suits on. Make it quick. You too, Paige.'

The arctic issue camouflage suits were three-piece outfits – boots with thick, cushioned soles; padded gauntlets; and overalls with a ribbed pack on the back that Dickey had told him stored and recycled surplus body heat. The material had been developed for the manned Mars mission and was 99.9 per cent heat-efficient, designed to insulate its wearers against the -80°C of a Martian spring day.

The helmets incorporated thermal-imaging units and

244

weighed more than twenty pounds with the built-in power-packs. Along the right side of the chin-guard were the radio and imaging controls – a green dial to enhance the thermal images and another that controlled the zoom facility. First thing Cope did was smash the mikes in five of the helmets with the butt of his pistol. He tossed them at the hostages. The remaining undamaged helmet he handed to Mhairi. 'Leave the red button alone,' he told her. 'It's the radio.'

Cope put on his own helmet, but left the visor up. He went to the door. 'Paige, you don't need a helmet to see in the dark.'

'Infra-red is my standard visual mode.'

'Then stick your head out and tell me what you see.'

'They might shoot me.'

'It won't hurt.' Using the wall switch, Cope opened the door a few inches. The moment the seal broke, the storm sucked air from the bay. The wind howled like a mad thing. A riot of snow cut visibility to a few feet. Paige craned out and rotated his head.

'All clear.'

Cope inched up behind him and pulled his visor down. Immediately, his perception turned topsy-turvy, the snow appearing an abnormally bright jade green. The faceted face-plate was set to wide-angle mode, and he fiddled with the zoom controls until the field of view narrowed. Through the blizzard's streaky luminescence, the perimeter and gatehouse lights showed as splashes of orange. The guards inside the gatehouse were dark red. The gates were open.

'Lower your visors,' he told the others.

By another piece of optical trickery, Cope could now see their faces behind the faceplates. It also threw the suits into sharp relief. The six figures resembled astronauts preparing to leave an air-lock for a space walk.

Cope settled himself at the snow glider's controls, trying to remember what he'd picked up about the craft's operating systems during his dash with Monica and his sessions with Dickey. It was equipped with radar and missile jamming devices, global positioning system – all sorts of bells and whistles. But for getting from A to B, Dickey claimed, it was simpler to pilot than a car. No gears, no clutch, everything taken care of by on-board computers. Just power up, point and squirt.

Power on/off was a big red switch with three settings. Position 1 illuminated the instrument display and computer screen. Cope checked fuel and electrical status. Fully charged.

'Paige, you know how to drive this thing?'

'Of course.'

Cope switched his head-set to transmit. 'Commander, you hearing this?'

'Go ahead.'

'I can't figure out how to work the snow glider, so Paige will be driving while I hold the gun at the prof's head.'

He ordered Byron into the front alongside Paige. Rocco and Grippe he put in the middle, while he and Mhairi sat in the stern with Yrigoyen between them.

'Start her up, Paige. Nice and easy.'

The robot switched on the engine. There was a faint turbine whine and the hovercraft levitated and began to creep forward.

Cope's heart knocked faster. 'Let's go.'

'Access,' Paige said.

The door opened full width. The craft glided into the weird underwater light and lined up for the perimeter gates.

'Cut loose,' Cope said.

Next moment he was pinned against the head-rest, his mouth stretched back in a stiff smile by the G-force. The gates flickered past and nothing lay ahead except the tundra. He widened his angle of vision for signs of pursuit. Behind them, Wellspring resembled a fiery palace on a spectral seabed. Looking up through the blizzard, he saw stars burning to infinity in the bottle-green coldness of deep space.

'What course shall I set?' Paige asked. His visor was up, but despite the rush of freezing air, his face was unruffled.

'West, towards the road.'

Mhairi was facing astern like an exile watching a retreating homeland. Cope reached across. 'Can you hear me?'

Her head came round.

'They can't see us. The suits and glider are insulated so they

246

leave no heat signature. The engine's a cold-combustion unit.' He grinned. 'We're cool.'

Her eyes behind the visor were more alert now. 'They're not fools. They'll have fitted a radio tag.'

Over the next few seconds, the possibility worked too deep to ignore. Cope switched to transmit. 'Commander, I've got a nasty feeling we're carrying a bug.'

'There's no bug.'

'Don't take me for a fool. I'd have tagged this thing, and so would you.'

'We didn't have time.'

'You've got even less now. Unless you tell me where the bleeper's hid, I'm gonna shoot your sonofabitch boss.'

He waited. 'Commander?'

'Under the stern seat.'

'Thank you.' Cope switched back to voice mode and told Mhairi where to look. She found the transmitter within seconds and tossed it into their wake.

'There might be another one,' she said.

'You're a comfort,' he told her. For a moment he considered re-opening communication, then decided the time for negotiations was gone. Ahead of him was space, behind him the wind. 'Paige, open it right up.'

When Wellspring had sunk to a small orange orb, he ordered Paige to throttle back to walking pace. He tapped Rocco's shoulder.

'Get lost.'

The Agency man baled out like a frogman and in a moment was hidden by the blizzard.

A mile further on, Cope told Paige to bring the craft to a stop and keep the motor running. His hand fell on Byron's shoulder.

Byron scrambled out. 'They'll kill you, Mhairi. You know they will. It's not too late. Stop this madness and come back with me.'

Mhairi didn't look at him.

Cope raised the pistol. 'Who said you were going back?'

Mhairi came alive. 'Don't you dare!'

'No,' Cope said, after a moment. 'Paige, this is where we say goodbye. Take care of Byron for me.'

As Paige unbuckled and stepped out, Byron began to back away. 'No.'

Paige walked towards him. 'There's no rush, Mr Byron. Hatred is by far the longest pleasure. Men love in haste, but they detest at leisure.'

'Keep away from me!'

Byron turned and floundered away, Paige treading unhurriedly in his footsteps.

When it was Yrigoyen's turn to disembark, Cope had to shake him to attract his attention. He'd spent the flight staring at the heavens, reciting the names of planets and constellations.

'Which one's Virginia Nova?' Cope asked.

'Oh, you can't see it. It's only a tiny planet, not much bigger than our own.' Yrigoyen pointed. 'There's her parent star, hidden against that bright cloud between Cassiopeia and Perseus.' His eyes twinkled. 'Imagine, in sixty years you would have been there, the first man to journey to the stars. It's not too late to change your mind.'

Cope looked at the broth of celestial matter. 'Who says I ain't already visited?' He buckled himself in to the driving seat. 'But when I go back, I'll buy my own ticket.'

He pushed the throttle forward until the digital read-out indicated they were doing eighty-five knots. The sense of endless forward motion was seductive, but the fuel gauge was already showing more than half empty. He turned the rudder.

Mhairi registered the change of direction. 'Why are we going north?'

'It's the last direction they'll expect us to take.'

'They'll comb the entire state. There are only a couple of roads, and Sam says there are patrols and checkpoints on each one.'

'Sam's the guy you called?'

She became more animated. 'He's a tracer. He gave me the name of a place on the Line – Antelope Falls. He's going to meet us there. We'll never get across without him.'

Cope placed a hand on her knee. 'I ain't got round to thanking you.'

She looked at his hand but didn't speak. Then she looked at Grippe. 'What about him?'

Cope checked the topographic display and saw they were within ten miles of the road. Wellspring's domes had disappeared, their position marked by a hazy thermal of dissipating heat. 'Yeah,' he said, lifting the pistol. 'It's time he went.'

'You mustn't!' Mhairi cried. 'You gave your word.'

'I ain't going to shoot him. He gets the same chance he gave Monica.' He nudged the pistol. 'Take the helmet off.'

Exposed to the frigid slipstream, the extremities of Grippe's face immediately chilled down to green. His teeth showed as a bilious glow. 'Why?' he asked Mhairi. 'A killer, a murderer.'

'For Monica,' Cope told him. 'Now get rid of the suit.'

Grippe hesitated, then began to unfasten the overalls.

'John!' Mhairi shouted, pointing ahead.

Cope turned and forgot Grippe. He twisted the rudder wildly, certain for a moment that the red splashes were an army lying in ambush. Then he laughed crazily. They'd come over a crest and run slap into a herd of caribou, heads down, rumps stoically presented to the storm. Startled chlorophyll eyes shied away as he zigzagged through the scattered mass of warm flesh.

The animals were ranged over a couple of miles and when he broke clear he spotted more red dots strung out in a line ahead. The screen confirmed that the hot spots were following the road. A column of vehicles, one of them way out in front, the rest trailing like the lanterns of nocturnal pilgrims.

Mhairi joined him in front. 'Zygote must have called in the military.'

Cope considered the possibility and rejected it. 'There isn't a garrison close enough.'

He remembered the unfinished business with Grippe. The

man's face was frozen, his eyes pale green sockets in a death mask. Cope decided he couldn't dump him alive so close to the road. He was going to have to shoot him.

'Keep your eye on him until I've checked out the vehicles.'

He steered to pass the lead one a mile out. Above it rose a curved column of snow like the tusk of some fabulous beast.

'Snow plough.'

It was about two miles ahead of the next vehicle – an armoured personnel carrier. Behind that came a rag-tag procession of trucks, cars, buses and some vehicles that were unclassifiable.

'Must be a Vag convoy.'

Another armoured wagon brought up the rear. Once he'd passed it, Cope spun round and headed back, slowing to the convoy's speed – less than ten miles an hour. He glided so close he could see the occupants of the vehicles. Not one of them so much as glanced his way. He fed in the power, holding the craft flat out until the convoy was well behind, then slowed and turned in towards the road.

As he lifted off, he caught movement behind him and glimpsed Grippe throw himself out backwards. He fired off balance, accidentally nudged the rudder and sent the craft veering the wrong way. By the time he'd straightened up, Grippe was nowhere to be seen.

'Where is he?' he yelled.

Mhairi was peering back into the blizzard. 'I don't know.'

'God damn it!' Cope yelled, and accelerated back the way they'd come.

'Leave him,' Mhairi pleaded. 'He's not worth it.'

Cope didn't answer. He tacked back and forth, straining to make out a heat trace in the blizzard. Nothing. Not even footprints.

Mhairi pulled at his arm. 'John, the best revenge is to let him live. You heard Rocco. Grippe's finished at Zygote.'

Cope shook her off. He searched for another five minutes, then stopped and stared around, sweating with rage and indecision.

'We're wasting time,' Mhairi said quietly. 'They'll be after us by now.'

He shot a barbed look at her, feeling she was somehow responsible for Grippe's escape, then wheeled the glider round and set course for the road. The thought of Grippe alive left a sour taste in his mouth. When he stopped, he didn't speak.

'Are we out of fuel?'

'Nearly.'

'So what now?'

Cope checked the lights of the oncoming convoy. 'Hitch a ride.'

33

Mhairi cast anxious glances at the column of lights bearing down on them.

'They're not going to pick us up – not dressed like this. They won't even see us.'

'You're right. Take your suit off.'

'Me! Why me?'

'Because you're a woman.' Cope pointed into the teeth of the storm. 'I'll be waiting out there. Soon as the plough stops, I'll jump it.'

'What happens if they *don't* stop?'

But Cope had lifted off her helmet and the wind obliterated his response. The snow assaulted her, gumming her eyes and nostrils. Cope unzipped her suit. Underneath, she was wearing indoor clothing. The wind fell on her, grabbing her bones.

'You have no idea what it's like out here,' she shouted, pounding Cope's back.

He stuffed a down jacket and pants into her hands. 'Put these on.'

While she was struggling into the clothes, he squatted and dug around in the sack. Suddenly Mhairi was isolated in a circle of crimson. A flare.

251

'John!' she shouted. 'John!'

He'd already gone. Everything he did was too fast for her. No sooner did he have a thought than he acted on it, leaving her wallowing in his wake. The cold was brutal. She hopped around the sputtering flame, trying to beat warmth into her body.

She stopped hopping and wiped her eyes. A shape, sensed rather than seen, had slid down to the road about twenty yards in front of her.

She took a cautious step towards it. 'John?'

Grippe's disembodied face, stained red by the flare, turned towards her. His mouth opened in a shout that was whisked away by the storm. For a moment they were eye to eye, then he turned back towards the convoy and she lost sight of him against the lights of the snowplough. The blizzard hurtled past the beams like feathers in a wind tunnel.

An orchestra of Klaxons blared. She could just make out Grippe's cryptic shape, his arms spread wide to welcome the convoy.

'Your suit,' she shouted. 'They can't see you!'

The horns bawled again, shivering her muscles to jelly. Behind the dazzle of lights she glimpsed a shadowy juggernaut – as big as a house, as big as a small office block. The impending mass glued her to the spot. She broke and threw herself face down on the verge just as the plough's iron beak sliced out of the whirling whiteness.

With a tremendous hiss and judder, the plough lurched to a halt right beside her. Music thudded her diaphragm. Abruptly, it turned off. She rolled over and brushed snow from her face. Twelve feet above her, a window opened and a man hanging on to a Stetson stuck his head out.

'Just what in hell's name do you suppose you're doing?'

She saw other blurred faces behind the glass. She sat up and searched around, but Grippe had vanished. The driver peered about, too, as if he'd caught a subliminal glimpse of Grippe before the plough sucked him in and blew him out in a fine red mist.

'You with someone?'

Mhairi shook her head. 'Any chance of a lift? My car got bogged in a drift.'

'We don't stop for no one, lady. Rules of the road. Truck pulled across us yesterday and we just kept on going. Cut that thing clean in two and never felt a bump. Every seat taken, too.' His mouth snapped into workmanlike lines. 'Now step aside, lady. Convoy's crawling up my ass. And don't you try throwing yourself on *their* mercy. Commander's been blasting off at shadows since we rolled out of Pendleton.' He blipped the throttle and the machine rocked under monumental torque.

'I'm a friend of Sam Pilkinghorn,' she shouted.

The huge engine dropped to a thumping idle. 'Say again.'

'Sam Pilkinghorn.' Mhairi was almost gibbering with cold.

This news was passed from mouth to mouth and finally reached the man at the other end of the cab. 'Sam's dead,' he called. 'Got killed by road pirates down on the Line last spring.'

'No he isn't,' Mhairi cried.

'Well by God, if Sam's still in business, and you're his friend, where is he?'

'He's . . . Look, I'm dying of cold. Please let me in.'

The door opened, dumping its accretion of snow. The cab deck was eight feet above ground and her injured ankle wouldn't carry her up the ladder. Rough hands hauled her aloft, passed her over knees and weapons until she was centred in the cab, three men to the left, two to the right. Wild faces boggled at her. She smiled inanely back, convulsed by paroxysms of shivering.

The plough revved up with a noise like a mighty spin-drier. The atmosphere settled into a semblance of calm. Feeling began to return to Mhairi's hands and feet. She sneaked a look at the driver's grizzled face.

'Name's Hollis,' he said. 'Where ya come from?'

'Winnipeg. I was with someone. We got separated. I . . .' Mhairi couldn't scale the necessary heights of deception. 'How far are you going?'

'Breaking at the next truckstop. Been driving since dawn.'

'Do you think I'll be able to get a lift with the convoy?'

'Not a prayer. Best bet is to find a friendly Tag.'

'Tag?'

Five faces homed in on her. 'Tailgaters. The people who trail behind the convoys. You telling us you come all the way from Winnipeg and don't know that?'

'Okay, Bernie, the lady's tired.'

Mhairi clutched her pack and stared miserably into the spinning whiteout. She must have nodded off because she found herself driving through a town before she saw it coming. The lights raked past Renee's beauty shop, a Black Bear hardware store, Daytona speedwash and filling station, Legion club, post office, general store and sheriff's office – all boarded up or smashed by storms and looters. Then Main Street was left behind. A mile or so on the other side, the beams reflected back from a sign swinging crazily in the storm.

Turk's Trucking Heaven.

Hollis turned in, the lights sliding across a double-cab pickup and a rig's tractor unit with a makeshift plough welded to the frame. He pulled up facing a row of dimly-lit windows and helped Mhairi down. She quaked in the wind.

'I wish I could repay you for your kindness.'

'Pass it on to the next person down the road.' He headed for the door. 'Tell Sam, Deke Hollis and his crew say hello.'

Before following, Mhairi checked on the snowplough, half-expecting to see Cope drop off it. She grimaced and hurried after Hollis.

At the entrance, a hand-scrawled sign said: *To avoid fatal misunderstandings, check firearms in before entering*. Inside the lobby, two nit-witted looking youths lounged in rockers, machine-guns across their laps. Chained to the wall beside defunct video games were enough weapons to start an insurrection.

The arms ban didn't apply to the plough crew. 'Howdy, Lester,' Hollis said, stamping snow from his boots. He raised his hand at the other youth. 'Hey, Doug.'

'Cruel night, Deke.'

'That's the honest truth.'

The boy leered at Mhairi. 'Least you got somethin' to keep you warm.'

Mhairi stuck close to Hollis as they entered the diner. Ancient tourist posters and centrefold pin-ups were just visible in the paltry light. Behind the counter stood a man in a chef's apron, topped by a bullet-proof vest slung with a fully-stocked bandoleer.

'Howdy, Turk,' Hollis said. 'Wagon train will be along in ten.'

Turk feasted baggy eyes on Mhairi. 'Where'd ya git her from?'

'Damnedest thing. She was standing in the road like she'd dropped from the sky.'

'No shit. Any more of you back there?'

Mhairi's mouth twitched in a feeble smile. She made to follow Hollis but he turned and blocked her.

'Parting of the ways, lady. I'm giving you the benefit of doubt about Sam, but everything else you told me is bullshit. You never come from Winnipeg. You didn't run into a drift. I don't know how you came to be on that road, but I'll tell you what I do know. Twenty miles from where we picked you up, the government's got themselves a research station where they're breeding aliens. I've seen them myself, scooting around on sledges.'

'Do I look like an alien?'

Hollis tilted his Stetson. 'You can't always tell.'

Abandoned and at a loss, Mhairi discovered that two other groups of wayfarers had sought shelter from the storm. In the darkest corner sat a trio of men. One glimpse and she looked elsewhere, but not before her mind had framed a picture of bandits from a bygone century – facial hair, cruel eyes, cartridge-belts and the remnants of uniform.

Cautiously she examined the couple in the opposite corner. A young woman with birch-blonde hair and a smooth white face, obviously pregnant, and a shock-haired boy with big hands and a small-town face. Harmless, Mhairi thought, but when she smiled in acknowledgement of shared hardship, they didn't move a muscle.

Their uninhibited stares herded her to the counter. Despite all the terrors, she was light-headed with hunger and desperately thirsty. She hadn't eaten for thirty-six hours and the drug had left her dehydrated. She guessed she had about seventy dollars on her.

'What can I fix you? Moose stew's good.'

Mhairi scanned the slate. 'Coffee and a caramel bun.'

Turk served up what resembled a fossilised turd and a mug of bark strainings. 'That'll be six-five.'

Relieved to have got off so cheaply, Mhairi counted out six bucks and fifty cents.

Turk stepped back as if to view the cash in a better light. '*Sixty*-five.'

'For coffee and a bun!'

'Down in Valley Falls, you wouldn't get change from eighty. Wouldn't be real coffee neither.'

'I don't have that kind of money.'

'I'll take trade goods – gold, medicines, passport, social security card, gas.'

'I haven't got anything to trade.'

Turk leaned conspiratorially. 'Well now, I wouldn't say that.' His eyes caressed her breasts, then flicked up towards the ceiling. 'Listen, we get a lot of passing trade this time of year. I can fix you up with a room. Bed and board, and you keep every second dollar. How about it?'

Mhairi turned and walked dismally to a booth.

'Them boys'll bleed you whiter'n a shroud,' one of the rednecks called.

Mhairi sank down, heavy with the weight of her predicament. Either Cope was dead or he'd ditched her. At best she could sit here until Zygote claimed her like a delinquent runaway. At worst . . . the image of the thugs in the corner supplied a premonition of what that might be. She forced herself not to look round. Minutes tolled by. The snowplough crew rose as a unit and walked out. At the door, Hollis spared her a nod.

Seconds later the smell of tallow and engine oil wafted across her. A tattooed hand plonked a mug down, then a belt-lapping gut strained between table and bench.

'They call me Sonny. Mind if I join you?'

Mhairi politely pushed the mug away. 'I'm with someone.'

Sonny looked all around the room. 'No you ain't.'

He had dirty blond hair and a pair of long ginger moustaches that made him look like a Dark Age Vandal. Frost-burn had blistered his cheeks and scabbed his lips. His milky blue eyes were blood-veined under colourless lashes. Dark patches on his uniform showed where he'd unstitched badges and insignia, but his tattoo – a compass with a lightning bolt pointing north – revealed his affiliation. True North, a white supremacist militia that blamed the ice age on land-grabbing Jews working in cahoots with the Wildlife Department and other federal agencies.

'I'd still prefer to be on my own.'

Sonny stirred the beverage with a thumb and sucked it. 'Good-looking woman like you will find that hard to manage. There ain't a lot of women between here and the Line and I bet there ain't one of them has your attainments.' He slurped the coffee and grimaced as if stricken with heartburn. 'We're about ready to haul out. You're welcome to come along. Cab's even got its own bed.'

His sidekicks were observing closely. One of them had a black beard down to his chest; the other a goatish lick of chin hair and a shaven skull. Mhairi felt a scream of panic rising.

'I'll wait for the convoy, thanks.'

Sonny twiddled the mug in his hands. 'If you think me and my buddies lack refinement, you ain't seen the other fellas.'

'John!' Mhairi shouted, leaping to her feet. 'Where have you *been*?'

Cope was sauntering towards her, distributing a devil-may-care smile. She'd never been so glad to see someone in all her life.

'Rearranging things,' he said, unslinging a tote bag. He nodded to Sonny. 'How goes it?'

'This is Sonny,' Mhairi said quickly. 'He thought I needed looking after.'

'Good of him,' Cope said. 'But now I'm back.'

Sonny blew on his coffee. 'Too late. Take a walk.'

Cope scratched his jaw, then stuck both hands into his back pockets. 'Suppose I say no?'

Sonny's tattoos seemed to bring back fond memories. As he began to rise, Mhairi saw Cope's smile grow aimless.

What she saw next occurred with the speed of a scene on flicker cards. Quicker than a lizard's tongue, a knife appeared in Cope's hand. She was still trying to work that one out when the knife flashed across Sonny's cheek. For a moment she thought Cope had missed, then a sheet of red ran down the militiaman's face like a flag unfurling. He touched his flayed cheek, stared at his bloody hand and crashed back, holding the flap together.

'The fuck.'

His buddies were charging over like characters erupting out of a comic-book frame. Cope pivoted on his toes.

A 'brrrp, brrp' brought the militiamen skidding to their heels. Chunks of ceiling plaster rained down on them. Turk slid out from around the counter, a wisp of smoke coiling from his machine gun. Mhairi darted a look behind and saw the youths in the lobby had their guns readied. The smell of cordite tickled her nostrils.

Turk rammed his gun into Cope's chest. 'Can't you fucking read?'

Mhairi found her voice. 'He was defending me.'

Turk swung on her. 'You're trouble, both of ya. Now hit the street. Git!'

Sonny, a bloody rag pressed to his cheek, was struggling to break out from his comrades' grip. Turk turned his gun on them. 'You boys are staying here until the convoy's left. You want to kill each other, I don't give a shit, but you do it outside town limits.'

When Turk's son returned Cope's pistol, Mhairi realised with horror that the rest of the arsenal must belong to the militia. The last thing she saw before Turk slammed the door on her was Sonny behind the glass, pointing two fingers at his temple.

She was still in ringing shock. Cope's actions had been

jailbird reflexes, the instinctual violence of a natural killer. Her shock expressed itself in anger.

'Picking a fight with the first man you meet. That was a real smart move.'

'If you had a smarter one, I'm still waiting to see it.' Cope went light-footed into the snow and sniffed the air.

A single word rose in Mhairi's mouth. 'Cope.'

After a moment, he turned. 'You speaking to me?' One side of his mouth was less mobile than the other and gave his grin an insolent twist. Mhairi wondered if that was the expression Margot Earle's aunt had seen the night the lethal needle was inserted into his arm.

'That's who you are,' she said lamely. 'John Cope.'

He stared at her, no light of recognition in his eyes, then snow eddied around him, and when the squall had passed, he was looking out to the road again. 'Save it till later. I believe the wagon train's about to hit town.'

34

Haloed headlights swam through the blizzard. The metallic clanking of a tracked vehicle set Mhairi's teeth on edge.

'How much money have we got?'

'About two grand.'

'Is that all? Up here that'll hardly buy you breakfast.'

Cope's teeth flashed. 'If it ain't worth nothing, we don't need it.'

Mhairi shut her eyes momentarily. 'What else?'

'Rations, flashlight, maps. Had to ditch one of the helmets. No room. Kept the suits, though.'

The flailing sound reached a crescendo. An armoured half-track trundled into the lot. Half a dozen people climbed out of it – women and children as well as men, every adult slung with weapons, and some of the kids, too. A tall, well-set man led the way towards the diner.

'Think it's worth a try?' Cope said.

'It doesn't hurt to ask,' Mhairi said. 'But leave it to me.'

The convoy master sprang on to the stoop, turned and spread his feet a nicely judged distance apart.

'Excuse me.' Mhairi said.

The man ignored her and went on talking to one of his lieutenants, lamenting the convoy's inability to keep in formation. The caravan began to pull in, overloaded vehicles disgorging clots of gaunt refugees. Some of the women carried sleeping babies. Very few old folk. The commander nodded them through like a shepherd counting his flock home.

When the last of them had passed, Mhairi made another approach. 'We're heading south, too. Do you think you could find space for us?'

The commander made a shooing motion with the back of his hand. Mhairi saw a light spark in Cope's eyes and remembered she'd seen that gleam in the moment before he drew his knife on Sonny. As she took a half-step towards him, the spark darkened or died.

'Hey, mister, where's your manners? The lady's speaking to you.'

The commander finally gave them the full weight of his attention. 'Crowded out.'

'I got a gun,' Cope said. 'I can fix things if they get broke. And Mhairi's a doctor.'

'We've got all the doctors and fighting men we need.'

'Won't do any harm to take along a couple extra,' Cope told him.

'How much you prepared to pay?' the lieutenant asked.

'How about a thousand bucks apiece.'

The lieutenant produced a weary guffaw.

'Then how about taking us along outta the spirit of kindness?'

Neither man could be bothered to reply.

Cope's jaw knotted tight. 'Floyd.'

The commander gave him a quick sideways look. 'My name's not Floyd.'

'Well, it oughta be. Every prick I ever met was called Floyd.'

As the lieutenant snapped his gun up, Mhairi grasped Cope by the collar. 'He's crazy. He's just got out of a clinic.'

The commander's jaw trembled. 'Run him out of my sight before I kill him.'

Mhairi hustled Cope away. 'What are you playing at?' she said through her teeth. 'That was our only chance.'

'Knock it off, Mhairi. He was never gonna take us.'

Another pair of lights forked into the yard. Two people got out, wrangling in French. Mother and daughter, both dark and chic, wearing expensive furs. Confronted by the commander, they stopped squabbling and hung their heads.

'How many times do I have to tell you? Stay ahead of the rearguard or lose our protection.'

The mother gestured eloquently. 'Something's not right with the car. The engine, I think the fuel is not good.'

'That's your problem. If you break down, nobody's coming back to help. Now get inside and grab something to eat.' He turned away. 'We leave in twenty minutes.'

As the women made to follow, Cope stepped into their path. 'You want, I'll take a look at that engine. I bet I could get her to run sweeter.'

The mother rolled her shoulder in a contemptuous Gallic shrug.

'Excuse me,' Mhairi said in French, 'are you from Quebec? I used to live in Montreal myself. I was a doctor there. We've lost our car and we're in a rather desperate situation.'

The mother gave her a don't-tell-me-your-troubles look and tried to step around them. Cope neatly blocked her.

'You look real beat. How about letting us share the driving?'

The woman stamped her foot and gabbled in French.

'What's she saying?'

'No space,' Mhairi said.

The girl eyed Cope with the beginnings of interest. Her fur hood framed a feline face – cute nose and wilful eyes. 'Mom, we could make room if we dumped some of that stuff.'

'That *stuff* is all we've got left in the world.'

'It won't be any use if we crash. You've gone off the road

twice already. I daren't fall asleep while you're driving. I haven't slept for days.'

The woman looked cornered. 'I'll take you,' she told Mhairi. 'Not him.'

Cope didn't need a translation. He grooved a line in the snow with his toe. 'Your decision,' he said. 'Don't you worry about me.'

The woman waited imperiously, chin raised.

'That's kind of you,' Mhairi said, 'but John and I have been through an awful lot and we're going to stick together.'

With a curt nod, the woman steered her daughter inside. All the way across the lobby, the girl kept smiling to see if Cope was smiling back at her. Aware of the chemistry, Mhairi felt her mouth stretch. Superimpose the image of Margot Earle on the girl's face and there wouldn't be much discrepancy. Mhairi looked at Cope and dug her nails into her palms. Down in San Francisco, at a safe distance, it had been easy to believe in his innocence. Now, having seen him in action, she was no longer sure. Not at all sure.

She half-raised her arms and let them flop. 'Got any ideas?'

Cope forgot about the girl. He unzipped his bag, threw Mhairi's suit at her and began climbing into his own. 'We're gonna have to grab some wheels,' he said, his eyes working the yard. 'Convoy vehicles are guarded and Sonny's rig's thief-proof.' His gaze alighted on the pickup. 'Looks like it'll have to be that old junker.'

Mhairi was still putting on her suit and Cope was starting across the lot before she realised what she was embarking on. 'We can't steal someone else's transport.'

'That's the only kind you *can* steal.'

Mhairi swore and hobbled after him. 'John, I'm telling you. This isn't right.'

'Keep a look out,' he ordered, doing something to the door.

'No,' Mhairi said. 'This must belong to the couple inside. The girl's pregnant.'

'Stick together, you said, and I appreciate the sentiment. But we're not going anywhere without wheels.'

'Then we'll just have to stay here until we can persuade someone to take us.'

Cope put his arms on the roof and rested his chin on them. 'Mhairi, in a minute Sonny and his boys are gonna come walking out of that door. When they do, our asses are dead.'

Fear dragged Mhairi's gaze towards the truckstop entrance.

'Now get in,' Cope said, opening the door.

Mhairi was tempted. Oh, how she was tempted.

'Keep your hands right there,' a voice said behind them.

Mhairi froze. Behind them the shock-haired boy came crabbing out of the snow. With extreme caution, he lifted Cope's pistol and knife. 'Okay, Dodie, I got them.'

The pregnant blonde girl appeared, walking with a stiff, processional gait.

'See that,' the boy said. 'Another minute and these guys would have been hightailing out of here.'

'I know it looks that way,' Cope said, 'but we were just planning to keep our heads down until the militia had cleared off.'

'And then you were gonna climb out and go your own sweet way.'

'Wrong. We were gonna stay right inside until we got the chance to explain things. I'll be straight with you. Mhairi and me are in a jam.'

The boy laughed and wiped a dewdrop from his nose. 'Ain't you just?'

'Let me in there,' Dodie said, pushing the boy aside. 'I'm about froze to death.' Wincing, she took her seat, pulling her swollen ankles inside one by one.

Despite the gun pointing at her, Mhairi's maternal instinct was engaged. 'When's the baby due?'

Dodie gave her a look of long suffering passively borne. 'Feels like I'm about to calve down any second.'

Cope brightened. 'Well ain't this your lucky day. It just so happens Mhairi's a doctor. You'll be damn glad to have her around when junior pops out.'

Dodie eyed Mhairi with mild curiosity. 'Are you really?'

'Yes I am. And John's right. You need proper medical care.'

'How about that?' Cope gloated. 'Your own personal physician.'

The boy's face was stern with the responsibility of impending fatherhood. 'Dodie?'

She shrugged. 'All right by me.'

Still holding them at gunpoint, the boy opened the rear door. 'Slide in.'

'Obliged,' Cope said. 'Name's John. Nice to meet you . . . ?'

'Dale.'

Mhairi held back. 'Aren't you going to wait for the convoy?'

'Safer to follow the plough,' Dale said. 'Bandits won't pester a piece of crap like this and warn the convoy they're up ahead. They wait for the Tailgaters. Easy pickings.'

It made grim sense to Mhairi. She wedged up against Cope on a seat crammed with chattels. Dale started up.

'How far you come?' he asked when they were clear of the truckstop.

'Not far. Upstate. You?'

'Lightning, North Dakota. Drive through and it's gone in a flash.'

Mhairi smiled dutifully.

'It's at the dead centre of the continent of North America,' Dodie said.

'An asshole,' Dale added, 'geographically speaking.'

Cope said something back, but Mhairi wasn't listening. Exhaustion had hit her like a cosh. For a while she was fixated on the white tunnel ahead, then her eyes fluttered shut, and though she willed them open, she was unable to stop them closing again.

Something hard was pressing into her forehead. She moaned and raised her hand to remove the annoyance. It goaded harder and she spluttered awake to find Dodie had her pinned on the cold bore of Cope's pistol. She rotated her eyes and saw Cope skewered on the muzzle of Dale's shotgun. The truck had come

264

to a halt between embankments of snow. The wind shoved at the vehicle like the hands of a mob.

Dale nudged the shotgun sideways. 'Leave the bag and ease out.'

Mhairi had to put all her weight behind the door to open it. The gale nearly blew her legs from under her. Dale began to frisk her while Dodie ransacked the pack.

'What do you call this?' she demanded.

'A flying helmet,' Cope said.

She tossed it aside. Dale unzipped Mhairi's parka. He blinked at the suit underneath. 'What's that you're wearing?'

'A survival suit.'

He unfastened it from neck to crotch and the cold rushed in. He stripped her of ID and cash, removed her watch and ripped off her gold necklace. Quickly he moved on to Cope.

'Where's your ID?'

'Ain't got any.'

The boy shoved the gun under his nose, lifting him on tiptoes.

'You ain't gonna use that,' Cope said.

'Be crazy if I didn't.'

Cope's eye met Mhairi's. 'You gonna shoot her, too? Some daddy you're gonna be.'

Dale gave her a quick look. She could see he wasn't too bright.

'Hurry it up,' Dodie said. 'The convoy's coming.'

'What do you say, honeypie? Think it's safe to let 'em go? You seen how he sliced that militiaman.'

Dodie shrugged indifferently. 'Oh, leave 'em. Personally, I took real satisfaction in seeing that pig's flubbery old face hanging off of him.'

Dale chewed it over, then took a quick backward step. Holding a bead on them until the last possible moment, he slid around the pickup, lowered himself inside and took off.

Teeth rattling, Mhairi sealed her suit and watched until the snow had closed round the tail lights. 'They might as well have shot us,' she said bitterly. 'They'd have been doing us a favour.'

'That Dale's a damn fool,' Cope said. 'I guarantee we'll come out of this ahead of him. He'd just better start praying I don't see him when I go past.'

Mhairi choked back tears. 'How far have we come?'

'Too far to go back.' Cope faced the ghostly coronas of the convoy. 'Maybe that Canadian girl's got her ma to change her mind.'

The convoy swept past like an instrument of war, tyre chains ripping at the snow. The French-Canadian couple brought up the rear, only yards ahead of the armoured wagon. The mother pretended not to see Cope's cocked thumb. The girl mouthed an apology which he acknowledged with a rueful wave.

'There's another set of fools,' he said.

Half a mile behind came the Tag's convoy, headed by the militiamen. Lying on her belly in the snow, Mhairi glimpsed Sonny's wrathful eyes burning above his swaddled face.

When the last vehicle had gone and the wind was all she could hear, the awfulness of their situation hit her. Stranded way above the Line, no food or money or weapons, every man's hand against them.

'We're not going to get out of this,' she yelled.

'Sure we will. We've still got our suits. We'll find a place to sit out the storm.' Cope tugged at her. 'Come on.'

The sky had cleared, but the wind had grown fiercer, blowing the snowfall across the road in scudding waves so thick Mhairi couldn't see her feet moving beneath her. Already it had laid tongues across the trail carved by the convoy, and in places they fought through drifts up to their knees.

They trudged between the frozen embankments. On and on, nothing to aim for. Mhairi's walking became mechanical, each step a repetition of the one that had gone before. She had no idea how far they'd gone when Cope cried out and darted to one side. She followed stupidly and stared uncomprehendingly at an iced-over pillar.

'Mail box,' Cope shouted, pointing downwind. 'Got to be a house.'

Mhairi draped her arms over his shoulders like an exhausted boxer hanging on in a clinch. 'It'll probably be burnt down or wrecked.'

'It's our only shot.'

With the gale directly behind them, Mhairi had to lean back to stay upright. Every few seconds a stronger gust sent her staggering out of control. Sometimes the blasts were so sustained they had to stop and crouch and hold on to each other to prevent themselves from being bowled away.

All they had for guidance were the nub-ends of fenceposts and the banshee shriek of the wind in broken telephone wires. Mhairi's life-force began to weaken without her being aware of it. The blood thickened in her head and her mind grew sluggish, wandered off on strange detours. She'd stopped worrying about the course they were following. She no longer cared about the pain of her ankle.

A gust upended her and she made no attempt to get up. An enormous physical indifference claimed her. When Cope's snow-plastered face leaned down and he began pulling her to her feet, she fought to stay where she was. Warm, comfortable.

He dragged her on and the wind began to ease. The snow got deeper until she was floundering thigh-deep, her hands waving for balance.

'Nearly there,' Cope yelled.

Something more solid than darkness massed before her. All of a sudden, the snow released her and she plunged face first. Dimly she was aware of something slamming up ahead. Brute reflex pushed her into a crawl. She encountered a step and pulled herself up it. The banging sound guided her to the door. Inside, darkness wrapped around her and the wind dropped an octave. They were in a porch or hallway. She slumped against a wall and curled up over her knees. Cope was opposite, panting invisibly. He gave a sudden laugh, rose and moved away.

'Anyone at home?'

She lost track of him. When he spoke again, his voice came from a distance.

'This way.'

Mhairi groped down a passage. At the end she encountered a banister. Cope's hands found her wrist and encouraged her up a staircase. She moved blindly on. Her knees hit something and her hands patted fabric – a bed, a mattress. She toppled onto it and Cope fell alongside her. The house creaked and groaned around them. Downstairs, the door banged back and forth.

Returning circulation inflamed raw nerves in the back of her head. The pain was excruciating. She must have cried out because she found Cope massaging her neck. She pushed him away. 'Don't.'

He laughed. 'Hey, I'm not making a move on you.'

She lay on her back, melted snow wet on her face. She felt remote from herself, gone into the distance. Her last thought was that this was as far as they'd get. By morning, the way back to the road would be blocked. They'd remain trapped here until one of them died and ate the other, gnawing on a fingerbone while gangrene blackened and split their feet.

FIVE

35

Mhairi awoke with a sense of foreboding. Her dreams had incorporated the rampaging wind and the demented banging of the door. Now there was absolute silence. A feeble greyness diffused through the window. She lifted herself on to her elbows.

'John?'

He'd gone. She stood up, and in the next moment her head seemed to float off her shoulders. She felt for the bed and sat down until the faintness passed. Nearly two days without food. Her tongue was swollen and she yelped with pain when she rotated her ankle. She looked at it and shivered.

The bedroom was partially furnished. She used a chair as a walking frame to reach the window. The floor sloped alarmingly. She parted curtains rigid with frost, but even scraping away the ice from the glass didn't make the light any brighter. Snowed under. That's why it was so quiet. With geriatric slowness, she made it to the stairs and hopped down one step at a time.

Down in the passage, she turned left, into the kitchen. Stalactites hung from the ceiling, and the work surfaces and appliances had been transformed into a surreal ice sculpture by repeated freezing and melting of burst pipes. Three sets of plates and cutlery were laid out on the table. The household had eaten, downed forks and left without doing the washing up. An agricultural insurance calendar confirmed that they'd pulled out four years ago, during the big stampede.

Mhairi went clumsily along the passage. The light grew brighter towards the other end. She opened the door and threw up her hand.

'Good Lord!'

Dazzling sunlight blackened her vision. She took one step and stopped in wonder at the sight of her shadow.

271

A ragged blue hole had been torn in the space smog, and right at its centre stood the blazing sun. Mhairi blinked around the sugar-icing scene. The house was in a draw, drifted up to its eaves on the windward side. The lopsided structure had divided the snow downwind into two deep crescents. Those were the hip-high drifts they'd waded through last night, the furrows smoothed over now.

A fresh path led down the hollow towards a flattened barn and a breezeblock outbuilding. The shelter belt beyond had been stripped to spindly skeletons. A pair of ravens launched into ragged flight from one of the dead branches and flew barking through the crystalline stillness.

'Cleared up fine.'

Cope was standing less than fifteen yards from her, his breath frosting the air. It was uncanny. The suit really did make him part of the background.

Mhairi shielded her eyes against the glare. 'This is my first proper sight of the sun in ten years.' Her eyes pricked. She smiled at Cope through her tears. 'I keep forgetting you missed the meteor. To you, this is just another day.'

He extended a supporting arm. 'See what I found.'

He helped her down to the outbuilding, a garage-cum-workshop occupied by a vehicle draped in a dust-cover. He pulled it back with a flourish to reveal a vintage auto covered with decals: Firestone, Crane, Edelbrock, RAM.

'Ain't she a classic? Plymouth Fury, modded for Super Stock.'

Mhairi could have wept for disappointment. The sun had lit hopes of miracles. 'It's a museum piece. It's older than my parents. They stopped producing the fuel for these things years ago.'

Cope rocked the car, producing a fat sloshing. 'Still gas in the tank and air in the tyres.' He sprung the hood. 'And take a look at that.'

A primitive lump of industrial-age cast iron.

'Mopar 426 hemi. Dual Carter Thermoquads, Rat Roaster intake manifold.' He unscrewed the radiator cap, dipped a finger in and let the liquid drain off as if it was a precious elixir. 'Pure anti-freeze. Someone loved this baby. Boy, I bet it broke his heart to walk away from her.'

Mhairi kicked a tyre. 'It'll never start. It's been standing for years. The engine will be seized. The battery will be flat. We don't even have the keys.'

Cope gave her a reproving look. 'Hey.' He jammed a rusty screwdriver through the window frame and levered it open half an inch. He took a length of stiff, plastic webbing, formed a loop with it, slid it into the gap, held his tongue delicately between his teeth, fed the loop over the door button and pulled it up. He opened the door, slid behind the wheel, leaned over and trawled through the glove compartment. It yielded a box of matches, some burger-house tokens and a pair of 20th-century sunglasses. He folded down the sun visors and a key slipped winking into his palm. 'Someone's looking out for us,' he said, and slotted the key into the ignition.

A parched click, nothing more.

'Tell me if the lights work.'

Any faint hope Mhairi may have harboured faded as quickly as the headlamp filaments. 'Hardly a glimmer.'

Cope was hard to see behind the dusty windshield. Mhairi jumped back as a tinny din filled the workshop.

Cope emerged and dusted his hands. 'That's rock'n'roll. Battery can't be flat as all that.'

Mhairi crossed and uncrossed her arms, grudging every minute Cope wasted on the car. The sun, longed for over so many years, was their worst enemy. By now Zygote's search would be in full swing. Each time she scanned the sky, she expected to locate the fat bee shapes of heliplanes. She patrolled a little beat, muttering to herself, and when the anticipation of Zygote's arrival became unbearable, she stormed into the workshop and glared at Cope's back bent lovingly over the car's innards.

'While you're fiddling with that piece of crap, Zygote's closing in.'

Cope didn't lift his head. 'I'm open to suggestions.'

'Even if you get it started, it'll never reach the road. The snow's three feet deep on the slope and the sun's turning it to mush.'

'Weather holds clear, it'll be hard as glass tonight. If necessary, I'll put runners under the wheels and man-haul it to the road.' He raised his head, inviting her to say different.

Mhairi slapped a fender and went back to waiting. Meltwater splattered from the roof and fat droplets fell from the icicles. She cupped her hands and gathered enough drips to salve her parched lips. She held her face to the sun and absorbed its nourishment. It filled her head with a bright placenta red. Her stomach growled. She tried to rub it into submission, but it kept on complaining.

Cope ran past, knocking her elbow. He crouched and listened intently.

'Company! Hide!'

'Hide where?'

But he was off, sprinting splay-legged up past the house.

Mhairi's stomach yawed. It had to be Zygote. Vags hadn't been up here since the owners had left. They must be searching every property along the road. She looked about in panic.

Cope, an elusive outline on the ridge, shouted something she didn't catch. He raced back and disappeared into the house. Seconds later he rushed out with their packs. 'Militia,' he gasped. 'Sonny must have caught Dale and Dodie. We'll head on to the prairie.'

It was happening again – Cope taking over a situation she hadn't even begun to comprehend. 'You know I can hardly walk,' she cried.

Cope tensed, then twisted towards the car. 'Shit, damn,' he said. He ran to the rear, applied his shoulder and heaved. 'Lend a hand.' His face contorted with effort. 'C'mon!'

Mhairi added her weight without knowing what purpose it would serve. With a squeaking of metal unbinding, the car rolled forward, revealing a rectangle of oil-stained planks.

Cope dropped to his knees. 'Should have known there'd be a pit.'

Mhairi recoiled. 'I'm not going in there. It's the first place they'll look.'

'Not if the Fury's on top.'

'If you thought of it, so will they.'

'Our tracks from last night are gone,' Cope said, pulling up the planking. 'When those guys see my trail heading out, they'll think I'm on my own.'

Mhairi shelved her counter-arguments as the pit was exposed. Auto components and tools filled it to within two feet of the top. Cope dived his hand into the junk and pulled out what Mhairi took to be a car jack wrapped in oilcloth. Feverishly he unwrapped it and kissed the oiled blue barrel of a rifle that even to Mhairi's uninformed eye looked antique. He worked the lever. 'Quick,' he said, scrabbling through the junk, 'there's got to be shells.'

Both of them began scrabbling like dogs digging for a bone. Mhairi gave up as the noise of the approaching vehicle swelled. She scuttled to the door to see an exhaust stack belch smoke into the flawless sky. Her guts contracted as the blunt snout of the tractor barged over the crest, sunlight flaring off a corner of the windshield, the makeshift plough jutting like a battle axe. The vehicle stopped while the militia-men conned the homestead, then another spurt of smoke ejected from the stack and, with a clashing of gears, the vehicle tilted into its descent.

Cope was still rooting for ammunition. 'Forget that!' Mhairi shouted.

'They'll search the house first.'

She dragged him away. 'Our tracks lead straight to the door. They could be here any second.'

Cope wiped his hands on his thighs. 'Okay. In you get.'

The pit gaped like a grave. Mhairi locked eyes with Cope. 'No.'

'It's the only chance,' he said, and manhandled her down.

No room to kneel or crouch. She had to lie flat, forcing her body into unnatural accommodation with unyielding angles. Before she could shift things for a less painful arrangement,

Cope was laying the planks back in place. As the last one came down, Mhairi saw the outcome with hideous clarity.

'If anything happens to you, I won't be able to get out.'

'Nothing's gonna happen to me.'

The last plank slotted in. Mhairi could still make out hairline glimmers where the boards didn't meet true, then she heard the rubbery crawl of tyres and the darkness was total. In the few seconds she reckoned were left before the militiamen arrived, she tried to shift some of the instruments of torture, but moving one torment only exposed her to another and made too much racket. She gave up and whimpered. Oh what a way to die!

Her breathing, at first very loud, stopped dead as brakes squealed. Doors slammed, one after the other, and feet scrunched on the snow. A few seconds of silence, then fingers drummed on the car's bodywork. Staring up, Mhairi thought this was how denned animals must feel, alone with their terrified heartbeats, waiting for the rush of light that heralds eyes and final darkness. She clamped her teeth on a knuckle. What a fucking awful way to die!

Snatches of speech penetrated the hole.

'. . . they was in here, though . . . go out onto the prairie.'

Then a faint, distant shout.

'You hear that?'

'. . . he ain't armed.'

A few seconds later the truck started up. Silence crept back, but Mhairi didn't dare stir. For all she could tell, one of the men might have been left to stand guard. Her thoughts spiralled into evermore dreary speculation. Even if John evaded the militia, they would know he'd been tinkering with the car and would immobilise it before they left. They'd burn it. She imagined screaming and beating at the chassis as strings of burning rubber dropped into her hair.

How, she wondered, did I get into such a terrible mess?

She guessed she was incarcerated for more than a hour – not much short of eternity – before a half-heard sound froze her back into spastic immobility.

'Mhairi, you still there?'

Wheel bearings rumbled and a plank lifted. Cope's face, burnished by fresh air and triumph, grinned down.

'They quit. I led them back to the road and they lost my trail there. The plough came back after it stopped snowing. Sonny and his boys took off south.'

Mhairi raised one arm pathetically. 'I can't move. I'm in agony.'

Cope stepped into the pit, straddling her, and hooked her under her arms. 'My,' he said, 'you're a big woman.' He steadied her on her feet. 'Everything in the right place, though.'

Mhairi was too far gone to take offence. Her left leg was dead. Grease smeared her suit and face. Her hair stank of mineral oil. She chafed her seized knees.

Cope looked wistfully at the door. 'Damn, I could have shot any one of them a dozen times if I'd had slugs.'

Mhairi kicked viciously at a box that had been grinding into her kidneys. 'Try looking in there.'

36

Points, plugs, HT leads, LT leads, oil, coolant, alternator belt. Cope inspected each component, emerying all electrical contacts and demoisturising them with an aerosol of water repellent he'd found on the workbench. It was a boost to be working.

Mhairi was silhouetted in the dooway, the sunlight filling her hair. He couldn't pretend *she* was warming to the adventure. It wasn't just hunger or fear. She'd turned off to him. Sometimes he caught her looking at him as if she was viewing him from behind a barrier.

He unclamped the battery and removed it. 'So who's John Cope?'

She turned and cupped her hands at her waist. 'You were born in Winthrop, Washington State. Your mother was called Susan. I don't know anything about your father. You were brought up in a home in Ellensburg. After that . . . the trail grows cold. There's a big gap missing.'

He grinned. 'I bet stealing cars comes into it.'

She didn't smile back.

He looked away.

'Well, I guess I never amounted to much.'

She gave him another one of her guarded inspections. 'Does any of what I just told you mean anything? Do you have any memories of childhood?'

Cope rubbed his forehead. 'I get flashes. Places, faces.' He pinched the flesh on his brow. 'There's a woman, blonde-haired. She's sitting on the steps of a trailer, laughing.'

Mhairi fingered her throat. 'Your mother was blonde,' she said eventually. 'Anything else?'

He wiped his fingers on a rag and squinted. 'It's real hard to pin down. It's like trying to catch a fish with your hands. You see it clearly, but when you grab, it's not where you think it is, and then it's gone.'

Mhairi nodded gravely, but didn't say anything. Her shadowed face was hard to read against the backlight. He had the feeling there was a lot more she could tell him, and guessed that what she knew was what put the distance between them. He rolled the car away from the pit. 'How did you find out my name?'

'A private investigator. It was quite a business.' She stepped forward and changed the subject. 'What are you doing?'

'Gonna heat through the engine and battery.' He began to lift the planks, his mood thoughtful. 'Everyone told me I was in a coma for three years, but this morning you said I missed the meteor.' He looked up. 'That happened ten years ago.'

Her mouth moved before any words came. 'John, this is going to take a bit of getting used to. Zygote lied to you. You went into a coma the night the meteor struck. When you were twenty-four.'

Cope began removing the junk from the pit. It was a while before he processed what Mhairi had told him.

She was ready for him. 'That's right, John. You're about the same age as me.' She tried to smile. 'I'd better book myself in for some of Zygote's anti-ageing treatment.'

'You mean I won't ever get old?'

'No, it'll just take longer.'

'How much longer?'

Her tone was light. 'Oh, I couldn't say – eighty, ninety years.'

She was lying, Cope knew, scared to tell him the truth. There was pity in her eyes, as if long life was not a gift but a curse. It reminded him of the question that had burned through his waking moments since he'd woken. He pretended to adjust the carb settings so that he wouldn't have to see her face.

'You know when you die, your soul's supposed to leave your body?'

'Ye-es.'

He gripped metalwork with both hands. 'Well, what if the soul checks out before the body's dead?'

Behind him there was stone-cold silence.

'The soul's gonna head off somewhere, but sooner or later it's gonna realise it's made a mistake and come back.'

Mhairi's hands clasped him from behind. 'This is about Sun Dog, isn't it?' She turned him round. 'That's one thing you *can* forget. He's just a voice you heard when you were in a confused and suggestible state. For a time, what he said was the only thing in your head. It's as if you'd been hypnotised. Do you understand?'

'Yeah, I guess.'

Mhairi let go. 'Good.'

'Only . . .'

'Yes?'

'Sun Dog said to expect a man called John. That's *my* name. He said John's an Indian and *I'm* part Indian. He said John had been away from Earth for ten years, and – well – that's how long I was out of things.'

Mhairi stared at him and slowly lifted a hand. 'Give me some of the matches. I'll see if I can find something to eat or drink.'

Cope didn't blame her. Even his own mind was split. He didn't feel like he was anyone's saviour. The only way to settle

279

the mystery was to get down to Mustang and ask Sun Dog direct.

With that resolution filed away, he went back to work. He made a fire in the pit with scrap timber and tar paper, laid the battery alongside and rolled the Plymouth forward so the flames licked its oil pan.

While the engine was heating, he removed the plugs and turned the crankshaft with a bar and socket, easing the pistons in their bores, loosening things generally. After jacking the car and fitting snow chains, the engine was still cold. He found a knife on the bench, ground the blade on a sharpening wheel and spent ten minutes putting an edge on it with an oilstone. He held it up to catch the light and saw a shape in it.

Mhairi was standing in the doorway. He had the feeling she'd been there for some time.

Silently, at arm's length, she handed him a pickle jar of tepid water. They drank and watched the sun slant down towards the smoking edge of the ice-shield.

'Time we were on our way.'

The engine block and manifold were warmed through. He rolled the car back, dropped into the pit and retrieved the battery. It was almost too hot to handle. Lucky it hadn't exploded. Quickly he refitted it and tightened the terminals. Then he took off the air cleaners and made sure the choke linkage and butterflies moved freely. He handed Mhairi the aerosol.

'Soon as the engine cranks, spray this into the carbs.'

He got in and inserted the key. He turned the ignition to position one and the fuel pump chattered. When it stopped ticking, he primed the carbs with three pumps of the throttle, kept the pedal pressed a third down and reached for the key.

The starter motor engaged and the engine spun lustily for a second, but gave up before the mixture ignited.

The plastic steering wheel had turned clammy in his hands. He gave the battery a minute to recover before twisting the key again. At the very moment when the starter began to groan, fuel spat out of the carbs with a flash. Puffs of soot shot from the tail pipes and the V8 barked into life.

Cope stepped out. Mhairi's face was a treat – a mixture of incredulity and awe.

'John, I'll never doubt your word again.'

Then she kissed him, a real smacker that arrived before he could open his lips to receive it. He worked them free and found her tongue. It wasn't really the time or place, but kissing Mhairi wouldn't have been a stretch in any circumstances. Mouth open, tongue exploring, he searched for the zip to her suit. He found her breast.

She mewed and pushed him away. 'No,' she said. 'Not that!' She was flushed and dishevelled. She put her hand to her forehead. 'No.'

Cope ran a hand over his scalp. 'Mhairi, I can't read you. Hot one minute, cold the next.'

She laughed shakily. 'John, you're an attractive man, but I didn't come back to Wellspring out of uncontrollable passion for you. Besides, you're too young for me. I'll be an old crone before you've reached middle age.'

'Why did you come back?'

Mhairi scored a nail back and forth across her palm. 'What Zygote was doing was terribly wrong, and . . . I had a younger brother I loved very much and he died because of something I did. You remind me of him and I couldn't bear the idea of you ending up . . .' Mhairi's breath escaped in a long sigh. 'Oh, I don't know. Why *do* people do the things they do?'

'My theory is they got no choice. Like, it's fate. Like, Sonny coming down here and clearing the track for us. You were right; we'd never have made it to the road.'

While Mhairi was trying to absorb that, Cope turned his attention back to the car. The engine had settled into a contented burbling. He climbed in.

'Tank says less than a quarter full, and this beast's a guzzler. We'll be lucky to make twenty miles.'

'Then let's make the most of it.'

Cope shifted to Drive and the Torque-Flite took up. Holding it on the brakes to stall the converter and heat through the transmission fluid, he revved hard. The car leapt forward and only a frantic haul on the handbrake reined it in before it smashed into the wall.

'Brake pistons rusted in their bores.'

'How will we stop?'

She looked so anxious, he had to laugh. 'We ain't stopping. We ride till we crash.' He opened the door and patted the passenger seat. 'Let's hit it.'

Even fitted with chains, the tyres struggled for traction in the truck's path. At the top of the rise, Cope let momentum die, awed by the sight of a snowy plain that spread flat and shining towards a glycerine smear of mountains.

'Five good looks would take us clear to China.'

He slipped the old sunglasses on and slotted a rock 'n' roll tape into the ancient sound system. The raw music made them burst out laughing. They looked at each other and both of them stopped laughing at the same time. Cope turned the volume down. He put his arm round her and they rested head to head.

'I know you're holding back something,' he said. 'But I ain't bothered about the past. It's what I am now that counts.'

She kissed him on the cheek. 'Yes,' she said. 'It is.'

He brought the sound back up. 'Ready to move it?'

'Ready.'

'Ready to groove it?'

'Really, *really* ready.'

'Then let's shake it,' he said, and went fish-tailing down the track.

It was rough going. The militiamen's truck hadn't cleared down to the gravel and on some sections they scraped along on the floor pan. Twice the snow dragged them to a stop and they had to dig their way out. By the time they reached the road, the sky had faded to mauve, dotted with flamingo-pink clouds. Half a day's labour had earned them only a few miles.

The plough had carved a fresh path through last night's drifts, but years of frost heave had lifted the blacktop into floes that battered the car's suspension. Vehicles abandoned long past bulged under the snow. Cope watched the fuel gauge needle sink towards the stop. The sun dropped into the pall and the light returned to the gloom of partial eclipse. In the clear patch of sky the bellies of the clouds had turned black.

They drove past a cluster of wrecks – an accident black-spot, it seemed, though the road was straight and revealed no natural hazards. The most recent casualty had nose-dived into a gully, its rear wheels clear of the ground. Cope lifted off and adjusted the rearview.

'Why are we stopping?'

'That's the Canadians' car.'

Mhairi looked back for only a moment. 'Someone will have picked them up. Keep going.'

'You heard Floyd. Fall behind and you're on your own.' Cope shifted into reverse and slalomed back. He climbed out and approached the crashed car with the Winchester held ready.

'Empty.'

'I'm telling you, they've been rescued by the convoy.'

Cope inspected the rear of the cabin. No blood, no luggage. He opened the trunk. 'Cleaned out,' he called, and surveyed the road down to its vanishing point. 'You reckon Floyd would stop the convoy just so those ladies could shift their knickknacks? You think the other Vags would make room for a load of someone else's stuff?'

Mhairi hadn't moved from the Plymouth. Water vapour steamed up from the tailpipes. 'I don't know. And frankly, I don't care. We're wasting fuel.'

Cope sprang onto the embankment and read the story from the tracks straight-lining towards the south-west. Looked like four snowmobiles and a tracked vehicle. Quite a party, judging by the footprints. He spotted one set leading away from the melee. Nothing moved in that direction, but the land was only generally flat. Blue shadows revealed dips and swells that could have hidden a battalion.

'Where are you going?' Mhairi called. 'John, come back here!'

Holding the Winchester at half aim, Cope followed the prints. They led to a wind ridge that might once have been a field boundary. He looked over the scalloped edge and let the rifle hang limp.

'We need a doctor.'

It was the daughter, wrapped in a silvered survival blanket, her face blotched and grey. She held up her hands in pathetic supplication.

'They took mom!'

'Okay,' Mhairi said, rushing past. She inspected the girl's eyes, felt her hands, measured her pulse. 'Hypothermia. Help me get her into the car.'

Once they'd carried her to shelter, Cope turned the heater to full and dropped to his haunches in front of her. 'Was it the guys in the rig?'

A tremor ran through her. 'Indians.'

Cope exchanged a frown with Mhairi. 'When?'

'Skidded off the road last night. Waited for someone to come back, but they didn't. Spent night in the car. When it got light walked up the road to look for help. Saw them on way back.' She pointed. 'Out there.' Another spasm shook her.

'How many?'

'Lots – fifteen, twenty.'

'How do you know they were Indians?'

The girl scratched at her face. 'Painted faces and some wore helmets. Howling and shooting. I was so scared I just hid. Afterwards, I went back to the car and my mother was gone.' The girl cried some more. 'The plough came through, but it wouldn't stop. Then a truck. Went past both ways. I was too scared to show myself.' She gulped and looked up wildly. 'There are such terrible people. That's why mom wouldn't take you. I asked her. In the diner and when we went past.'

Cope brushed her cheek. 'What's your name?'

Her long lashes were spiky with tears. Even distraught and swollen-eyed, she was real pretty. 'Danielle.'

'Okay, Danielle.'

Cope straightened and went up and held his rifle like a yoke across the back of his neck. The clearing in the sky had darkened to purple and a couple of planets winked near the border of the

284

ice cloud. Cope's gaze settled for a while on the horizon where the tracks led. He jumped down, reached in and switched the engine off.

'Don't worry,' he said. 'We'll get your mom back.'

Mhairi grimaced at him behind Danielle's back and went to stand behind the car. Cope, prepared for ructions, joined her.

'Are you mad? What can you do against more than a dozen armed men? I know it's tragic for Danielle, but if you go looking for her mother, you'll get yourself killed and probably us, too. Be thankful for the life you've saved.'

'I don't reckon Danielle's gonna give thanks if we drive off without her ma.'

Mhairi's voice dropped to a choked mutter. 'That woman refused to give you a lift. A *lift* for Christ's sake. She drove past us knowing we would perish.'

'She was scared.'

'What do you think I am? Two people have died trying to help you. You don't know how much I've sacrificed for you. And for what? The moment a pretty young girl bats her eyes, you forget about me.' Her voice, about to break completely, steadied. 'You owe me, John. You *owe* me.'

'Okay,' Cope said. 'You tell her.'

Mhairi flared her nostrils. 'Right.' She took a deep breath and began to stride to the car. She got as far as the trunk and faltered. She leaned on it with both hands.

Cope waited.

'While you're playing cowboys and Indians, what about us?' Mhairi looked back at him. 'What if someone comes?'

More stars had appeared. 'I doubt anyone will be driving through after dark. I'll start out now. Give me till midnight. After that . . .' Cope dropped the Fury's keys into Mhairi's hand.

37

A half moon swollen by refraction slid clear of the overcast and glided through a lake of stars. Pale boreal fire encircled the hole in the sky and this seemed to be the source of the faint crackling Cope could hear – like distant banners snapping in a wind.

He estimated he'd walked three miles by the time he found the Indians' base. The cold air trapped woodsmoke and transmitted a bass beat from the darkened farmhouse. He hunkered down in the lunar chill. Far away, coyotes maddened by the giddy moon kept up a constant yipping.

After a few minutes with no answering bark or whimper, he closed up until he made out orange light leaking through one of the blacked-out windows. He could hear the music behind the beat and voices on top of that. The vehicle tracks led to a corrugated barn set at right angles to the house and projecting in front of it. He crawled to the double doors and squinted through the jamb. Four snowmobiles and a white Sno-Cat were drawn up behind. The rest of the barn was stacked with crates and furniture. An alley leading into the repository contained the suggestion of a light. Subdued voices, too. Cope worked left until he found a bolthole that framed two figures hunched around a pot-bellied stove.

He dropped to his knees and discovered the doors were chained inside. A smaller door was set into one of the pair. Teeth together, he pulled and met solid resistance.

He settled in for opportunity or inspiration to strike. He reckoned it was about ten now, and the sounds from the house told him not much sleeping would be done that night.

The clearing in the sky began to congeal. The stars dimmed and the moon shrank like an eye withdrawing down a tunnel. Cope tried not to worry about Mhairi and Danielle. About the woman in the house, he refused to think at all. The Indians had caught her more than twelve hours ago. Whatever they'd done to her, they'd done.

A couple of times, men came out of the house to piss in the cosy bar of light that fell from the porch. Cope, without emotion, knew he could have killed both of them without anyone inside being immediately the wiser. Killing wasn't part of his strategy, though. With only seven slugs in the magazine, he had no intention of starting a firefight.

He was dozing on his feet when the barn door bolts scraped back. One man came out. Cope didn't have to consult his brain before reacting. As the man turned to drop the latch, Cope stepped up behind him and placed the rifle's rim between his vertebrae. The man sucked in his breath as if an ice cube had dropped down his neck, but didn't move again.

'Turn round.'

Hands half-raised, the man obeyed. He was wearing a ski mask under a pair of eyeglasses with one lens missing. The effect was more goofy than sinister. He was dressed in an overcoat crudely tailored from what looked like soundproofing felt.

'What they call you?'

The man made a sticky sound far back on his palate. 'Carl.'

'Who's the other fella?'

'Tom.'

'Call him out here. Tell him there's a weird light in the sky – like a spaceship.'

The way Carl's defective eyes kept moving between Cope's solid head and the ghostly outline below suggested he was already half convinced he'd been captured by an alien. Cope prodded him towards the door.

'Hey, Tom.' Carl said feebly. 'You gotta see this. It's like a spaceship or something.'

Cope swung him round by the elbow and crooked his chin up with the barrel. 'Soon as Tom steps out, say "look at that".'

Carl stared miserably at the sky. 'Hey, take a look at that.'

Tom emerged, jaws chewing, head searching. 'What?'

'This.'

Tom couldn't have been meeker if the chariot of the lord had set down beside him. He put his hands up unasked, showing the pistol at his waist. Cope took it off him and chivvied them inside. 'Take those masks off.'

Carl was black and geeky in his one-lensed specs. Tom was collegiate in appearance. Both cut wretched figures, twenty-year-old starvelings.

'Damn funny-looking Indians,' Cope said.

'We're not . . .' Tom began, but couldn't take it any further.

'We're students,' Carl said. 'From Tacoma. They caught us six months ago. We've been here ever since. We're . . .' He couldn't go on.

'Slaves,' Tom finished miserably.

'Slaves with guns?'

'Just that pistol and a shotgun. You should see what stuff they've got in there.'

'What kind of Indians are they?'

Carl looked embarrassed. 'They aren't. They're students, too. At least some of them were.'

Cope panned around the mountain of boxes. 'They take all this off Vags?'

Carl nodded. 'They've been here a year now. At least, Miles has.'

Cope's inspection ended at the vehicles. 'Why don't you skedaddle?'

'Miles keeps the keys,' Carl said. He anticipated Cope's reaction. 'There's no point escaping. Ten, twenty miles south, we'd run into another bunch of road pirates. There's a gang at every cross-roads. At least here we get fed.'

'Miles is the chief?'

Carl uttered a bitter laugh. 'Miles is crazy. I mean, real psycho, homicidal crazy.'

All this could wait, Cope decided. 'What's the set-up over there?'

Neither man answered.

'They'll kill us if we help you,' Tom said.

'Miles will kill us anyway,' Carl told him.

'There are eleven of them,' Tom said. 'Eight men, three women. Four rooms downstairs – two each side of the passage

288

and a kitchen straight through. The stairs lead off the hall. Two bedrooms upstairs. Miles has one. The other one he uses as his treasure chamber.'

'Is the Canadian woman with him?'

'Yes. Miles always has the first night. After the others have had their turn, he never touches them again.'

Cope was forming a mental picture of Miles. He took a closer look at the vehicles. 'Where does Miles keep the keys?'

'On him.'

'Any food in here?'

'No, they bring it out to us.'

'What about fuel?'

Carl nodded to a drum in the corner. 'We've got most things.'

Cope marched them to their fireside. Beside it was a nest formed from crates and pallets. He pondered. The survival suit was designed to bamboozle the enemy in battlefield conditions. It didn't make him invisible and would be a real draw inside the house. 'Take your coat off,' he told Carl.

He pulled it on over his suit. 'Do the Indians ever call up or come over at night?'

'Most nights they do.'

'How would you like to get out of this place?'

They both squirmed, embarrassed by the impossibility of the proposition.

'I can kill you or I can tie you up, but if one of them pays a call, we're all dead. Here's the deal. Get things ready for when we come out, and I'll take you with me. Gas up the tractor and load everything we need for a run to the Line – blankets, sleeping bags, tents, lamps. Fix the skidoos. Drain the tanks, pack snow into them, whatever it takes. You think you can manage that?'

They shifted from foot to foot, rolling dice in their minds. 'Okay,' Carl said.

Cope pulled on the boy's ski mask and unhooked his spectacles. 'Come with me.'

At the door, he issued his last instruction. 'It may be a while before I go in, and I might not be out in a hurry. Stay cool. Anyone comes over, act like nothing's happened.'

Carl followed him to the corner. 'Listen, one of the women . . . Patty. I don't care what happens to the rest, but Patty . . .'

Cope was ready to go. 'She black, too?'

Carl nodded.

Cope waited behind a water butt at the windowless gable end. Three more men and a white woman came out before the black girl emerged. She stepped away from the light, seeking privacy. She walked past Cope and went another five yards until no one inside the house could have seen her. She peeled down her breeches and squatted with a luxurious sigh.

Cope remained leaning against the house. 'Patty.'

The trickling abruptly stopped. She turned, her face like a swarm of angry bees. 'Carl, what are you doing? You know what Miles will do if he catches you sneaking around up here.'

'I ain't Carl, so keep your voice down.'

She stayed squatting. 'Who the hell are you?'

'My business.'

'What are you doing in Carl's clothes?'

'More of my business.'

'In that case, why don't you let me go ahead with mine?'

Cope grinned. 'I ain't stopping you, but I tell you what. Five bucks says you can't squeeze another drop.'

Patty's face set in concentration. 'Damn,' she said, and pulled her breeches tight up.

'Step over,' Cope told her.

She joined him in the shadows. 'Have you killed them?'

'Nope.'

'What are you after?'

'The Canadian woman.'

Patty's eyes roamed the darkness. 'How many of you are there?'

'Just me.'

She took a step back. 'You're crazy. They'll hang you and skin you and set fire to your balls.'

'Well, I'm not leaving without the woman, so you'd better decide where that leaves you.'

Patty had a mobile face. She gave it a workout before reaching a decision. 'She's with Miles, upstairs in the back.'

'Where are the others? What are they doing?'

'All over, drinking and screwing.'

'What's the light like? Think I'd pass for Carl?'

Patty studied him. 'Not up close.'

'You're going to make sure that doesn't happen.'

'Like hell,' she said, backing away.

Cope reeled her in. 'Carl and the other fella have already signed up for the ride out. You're invited, too. Your choice, but if I were you, I wouldn't want to be here about an hour from now.'

Curiosity competed with fear. 'What do I have to do?'

Cope nodded down the veranda. 'Check the hallway's clear. I'll come in behind you. If anyone asks, tell 'em you've brung Carl to see Miles.'

'You're crazy.'

'You already said that.'

'That was before I knew you.'

38

At Patty's signal, Cope ghosted down the veranda. The hall, stairway and kitchen were empty. The party was still going full-swing – gang-banging behind the closed door to the left, music and drinking through the open door on the right. There was probably frequent traffic between the two, so Cope didn't hang back. A guttering candle lit the hall. He pinched it out, prodded Patty ahead of him and crossed past the open door. Carl's single lens gave him a blurred glimpse of three or four men with their backs turned to him. A hog pen reek reached him, then he was on the first tread of the stairs.

'Who's that?'

Mouthing at Patty to get below him, Cope rushed halfway up the stairs and turned as a man wearing battledress and war-paint appeared in the hall. Cope fingered the pistol in his pocket.

'Who do you think?' Patty said.

The man half-aimed a gun at Cope and squinched his eyes for a better look. 'What the fuck's he doing up there?'

'Miles sent for him. Problem with one of the skidoos.'

Another voice spoke and the man in the hall, still loosely aiming at Cope, turned his head right round and laughed. Cope began to slide the pistol out as the man turned again. He waved his gun dangerously.

'Hey, if Miles is through with the Canuck bitch, bring her on down.'

Patty nodded grimly and started up again. Her eyes signalled Cope to get going. The man was still standing there, but his eyes had gone blank, as if he couldn't remember what he was doing. Cope reversed up the stairs. Around the corner, he flattened against the wall, pulled Patty past him, slid the rifle from under his coat and held his knife to his lips. After a few seconds, he heard the man mutter and reel back into the sitting room.

'Are they all that loaded?' he whispered.

Patty was biting the tip of her thumb. 'Miles isn't. He never touches alcohol or drugs.'

Cope jabbed a finger at the far door and Patty nodded. Cope tiptoed to it and listened hard. No sound. He crouched and applied his eye to the keyhole. No light. He put his face so close to Patty's they were breathing each other's air.

'I really do need that pee now,' she whispered.

Cope stopped her with a hand against her chest. 'Stay here till I call. If anyone comes, tell 'em you're waiting for Miles to finish with Carl.'

Patty breathed deep, like a dental patient watching the drill approach. 'Boy, you don't ask for much.'

'Where's the bed?'

Patty's chin indicated it was to the left.

Cope faced the door. *Bless this house* said a china plaque, bordered by flowers and butterflies.

The handle rotated noiselessly. Cope slipped through the gap into darkness, the only light the dim bar under the door. He didn't move until he could distinguish the bedstead and two mounded shapes on it. Rifle in his left hand, knife in his right, he zoned in on the breathing.

His heart jumped into his windpipe. The few available grains of light were gathered in a pair of eyes looking right back at him. His finger tightened on the curve of the trigger. Seconds went by and the eyes didn't move. Cope's heart gradually settled back on its mounts. It had to be the woman. He took another step and put a finger to his lips.

She misinterpreted his intentions and shied. The other half of the bed reared up and Cope only just figured where Miles' head was in time to get the knife to the throat.

'Make a peep and it'll come out of a hole in your neck.'

Unquiet silence, Miles trying to figure things out. He'd lunged to the right and the side of his eye was looking the same way. Very slowly, not taking his gaze from the highlight in the man's eye or the knife from his throat, Cope felt with the barrel of his rifle, running it down the man's forearm, wrist, hand, outstretched fingers. They were empty. Cope stirred the muzzle further right and made metal-to-metal contact inches from Miles' grasp. Carefully, he poked the gun out of reach.

He released his breath. 'Patty.'

He had to whisper twice more before the door cracked open. 'Is he dead?'

'Get in here and shut the door.'

She edged up behind him in the dark. 'Is he dead?'

'There's rope in my pocket. Lash his hands to the bed rail.'

'I'm telling you, you'd best finish him.'

'Tie him good.'

The tiny pane of light in Miles' eye hadn't wavered. Cope never altered the pressure on his throat while Patty fiddled and cursed. At last she gasped and moved back.

'Here,' Cope ordered, feeling for her hand. 'Give us a light.'

She broke three matches before one caught. Cope checked Miles' bonds before seeing what kind of creature he'd caught.

With the picture of the militiamen fresh in his mind, he'd been expecting a hairy barbarian with a blood-rimmed mouth. But Miles was as clean-cut as a yearbook portrait. Only his eyes hinted at the venom distilled within.

Patty sucked in her breath as the match scorched her fingers. Cope took the box off her and lit the hurricane lamp on Miles' bedside table. Neatly folded over an inlaid chair was a suit of ribbed body armour and a horned helmet like a Japanese warlord's headpiece. The room was furnished with antiques – a glossy walnut desk and brocades and oil paintings. On the table next to Miles lay a leather-bound Bible open at well-thumbed pages – *Revelations*, many passages excitedly underlined in red.

> And the fifth angel sounded, and I saw a star fall from heaven unto the earth: and to him was given the key of the bottomless pit. And he opened the bottomless pit; and there arose a smoke out of the pit, as the smoke of a great furnace; and the sun and the air were darkened by reason of the smoke of the pit.

Miles smiled.
Cope turned the pages.

> And the woman was arrayed in purple and scarlet colour, and decked with gold and precious stones and pearls, having a golden cup in her hand full of abominations and filthiness of her fornication: And upon her forehead was written, Mystery, Babylon The Great, The Mother Of Harlots And Abominations Of The Earth.

Cope looked at the woman's garishly painted face. He looked down at Miles and his mouth puckered. 'Bad all the way through.'
Miles smiled some more.
'Where's your keys?'
'I dreamed you were coming,' Miles whispered. 'I've been waiting for you.'
Cope raised the Winchester like a tamping rod and drove it into Miles' stomach. His eyes bulged up in their sockets. While he was wondering if his first breath would ever come, Cope gagged him with a strip of pillowcase. It took no time at all to

locate the keys on a ring clipped to his belt. Cope lobbed them at Patty. 'Leave through the kitchen and lock the door behind you. If you can, lock the front door, too. Soon as the woman reaches you, start the tractor and hit the gas. Head left.'

'How are *you* going to get out?'

'Through the window.'

Patty stared at Miles' face as if committing it to memory, then spat in it. He blinked once, slowly, and returned his stare to Cope.

'If it was me,' Patty said from the door, 'I'd kill him.'

'Wait up. Can you lay your hands on some food? Me and Mhairi are kind of hungry.'

Patty stuck out her hip and propped a hand on it. 'You sure you don't want me to run you a bath?' She went out, then popped her head back. 'Who's Mhairi?'

'She's a doctor. You'll like her.'

When Patty had gone, Cope gave his attention to the woman for the first time. She hadn't shifted since her first start of fright. She was backed up against the wall as if she'd been nailed there.

'Are you okay?' He couldn't think of any other way of asking.

She searched blindly for his voice. 'Am I okay? Am I . . . ?'

'Can you walk is what I'm saying?' Cope squeezed her by her cheeks and shook her face until the pupils came back into whack. 'We ain't got a lot of time. I had to leave Danielle on the road.'

That stirred a reflex. 'I can walk.'

While she was dressing, Cope stood sentry at the door. He could feel Miles' stare drilling him and the brain behind it planning all the things he'd do once he was free. It had been so simple up to now that Cope was sure he must have missed something.

When the sounds behind him ceased, he figured it was okay to look. She'd scrubbed off most of the whoreish make-up, and in her fur coat and boots, she looked like a respectable, attractive middle-aged woman about to go out for the evening.

'Watch the stairs,' Cope told her, making for the window.

He turned out the lamp and cut away the blackout. That's when he hit the first snag. The window was warped and frozen in its frame and no amount of prising with the knife was going to budge it. He considered their chances of making it out through the house and decided they were poor to suicidal. He scooped a pillow from the bed, flattened it against the bottom pane and struck it with the butt of the Winchester. The glass fractured with the muffled sound of pond ice breaking, but though most of the pieces buried themselves soundlessly into the snow, a few splintered with nerve-wincing clarity.

No outcry from below. Cope removed shards from the frame and measured the drop. Ten feet, reduced to seven by a drift. He brought the woman over. 'Head round the back of the barn, then make for the doors. They're expecting you.'

He picked her up around the waist. She was light and small-boned, and he had an image of her dark-eyed daughter. As he raised her, she tensed and paddled at the sill with her feet.

'Shit's sake,' Cope hissed.

Her eyes in the dark weren't looking at him. She was staring in the direction of the bed. 'We don't have time for that,' Cope said, trying for a fresh grip on the woman.

She patted at his clothes and jabbered in French on a rising note that Cope knew would crack into hysterics any second. He smothered her mouth with his palm, but she continued to kick.

'Okay,' he said. 'Okay.'

She stopped struggling. Her hand traced his arm until it found the knife. Cope gave it up. Even though he couldn't see, he turned his back and stared at the wall, projecting himself away from what was happening behind him. Miles gave a gagged cry that became a choked whistle as the knife severed his windpipe. Cope's whole body jumped. He wasn't sure if the splash he heard was real or in his mind. He still hadn't turned when the woman put the knife back in his hand. Hers was slippery and shockingly hot.

Cope lifted her through the window feet first. She'd just have to take her chances with the glass. She thumped into the drift like a sack of kapok, and Cope prayed anyone downstairs would think it was snow sliding off the roof. She made more commotion fighting free of the drift. Cope decided to let her get into the thinner stuff before baling out himself.

He felt his way round the bed, uncapped the oil lamp reservoir and sprinkled the fuel over the bedspread and furniture. He stroked a match against the box.

'Miles,' a discreet voice said, 'you awake?'

Cope frantically waved the match out. He ran to the window, raised one foot to the sill, then thought what a damn fool he'd look if he was shot halfway through.

He faced the door and aimed chest high. Drip, drip went Miles' lifeblood on the carpet. His corpse made a faint crepitation, like a piece of scrunched-up paper relaxing.

'Miles,' the voice said, growing bolder. 'Patty said you told her to fix a meal, but she's not in the kitchen. She's gone out and locked the doors from outside. What the fuck's she playing at?' There was a foot-shuffling hiatus. 'Say, Miles, why are you in the dark?'

Cope had already let the silence stretch too long. In the interval, the man outside had either readied his own weapon or crept downstairs to warn his comrades. Praying it was the former, Cope glided to the left.

The door opened cautiously and a flashlight probed at the bed. Cope shot at the shape behind the light and a swathe of bullets told him he'd missed. He swung the rifle left, racked off two shots through the wall, swung the other way, and loosed another couple. The flashlight bounced on the floor and a man stepped past the doorway holding out a gun as if it was too long and limber to straighten. He made a wheezing sound, missed his footing and lurched up the corridor. Cope levered another bullet into the chamber, ran into the corridor, grabbed the flashlight, saw the man folded over his knees, wrenched the machine pistol from his hand and emptied half the clip into the empty stairway. He ran back into the bedroom and sprang into the air as splinters of flooring leapt up at him. He flung himself flat along Miles' body, stretched one arm out and fired the remainder of the magazine into the room below. He threw the gun away and grabbed Miles' weapon. Still lying on the corpse, he felt for the matches, struck half a dozen and dropped them onto the bed, igniting the kerosene as he rolled off.

Diving head-first through the window, the image Cope carried away with him was Miles' double grin and his horned helmet sitting like an idol on the chair behind the dancing flames.

He rolled as he hit the snow. *Flump*. He was three feet down, blinking out of a hole as tight as a shoe. Getting out was like one of those nightmares where you fight invisible tethers while enemies rush in on all sides. But when his head surfaced, the people inside were still firing blind through the blackout. Cope was back on his feet by the time they'd ripped away the curtains. He divided the remaining contents of Miles' gun between each window. Someone inside was screaming incessantly and the music was still playing.

Sighting on the barn, he was dismayed to see the woman still working her way along the rear wall. He was wrestling Carl's coat off when instinct told him his lead time was up. He jinked and dived a split second before heavy-calibre gunnery punched holes in the corrugated iron above his head. He got free from the coat, whirled it away and rolled against the base of the barn. Something plucked at the coat and he heard a triumphant cry. The woman was either hit or had got round the corner. He bellied forward. The firing was coming from both sides of the house now.

Not a sound from the barn. Those chickenshit slaves were cowering down waiting to see which side came out on top. Rage powered him on. He reached the corner and saw the woman ahead. As he rose to his feet, he distinguished small-bore popping from the area of the barn entrance. Either it was one of the slaves returning fire, or an Indian had made it to the front and he was dead.

He caught up with the woman and dragged her on. Still no activity inside. He'd almost reached the corner when the tractor engine spluttered and caught. From inside the barn came a splintering and scraping, and then right in front of him the corrugated panels bulged and split open and the tractor came chugging out, pushing crates that spewed domestic bric-a-brac.

Patty was driving the tractor. They'd hitched a trailer to it and Carl was in the back with the shotgun. Cope waved Patty onward. As the trailer came past, he picked up the woman and threw her over the side. He caught the tailgate by his fingertips and Carl grappled him on board. He fell on to his back and began feeding shells into the Winchester. By the time he'd loaded, the figures milling around the house were too distant to bother wasting ammo on.

He turned and saw that the slaves had managed to load a snowmobile and a drum of fuel.

'Did you fix the other sledges?'

'Patty ran over them.'

Cope subsided on to his back and laughed, the laughter hurting his chest. He stopped laughing and felt wasted. Carl meekly leaned over him.

'I don't suppose you've got my specs.'

Cope pawed at his suit, but his fingers had lost their usefulness and Carl had to retrieve the eyeglasses himself. He helped Cope into a sitting position. The buildings were alight, the house well ablaze, cherry-red sparks spiralling on the updraught. Even as he watched, a puffball of fire rose out of the barn roof, illuminating termite figures scurrying on the pink snow. Cope watched the conflagration until it was just a reflection on the clouds, then turned towards the road, praying he hadn't left it too late.

39

Mhairi scraped at the glaze of condensation on the windshield. It made no difference. The moon and stars had gone behind the overcast sky and the night was as dark as it could be.

Danielle was asleep beside her. They'd exhausted conversation hours ago. It turned out that Danielle and her mother,

Sylvie, had lived within half a mile of Mhairi in Montreal. The neighbourhood, already three-quarters abandoned when she left, had gone to the wolves. Polar bears overturned garbage cans and dug for corpses where ladies in Paris fashions had once shopped for patisserie and perfumes. Danielle's father had died last winter – gone foraging one morning and never returned.

Mhairi jammed her hands into her armpits and waggled her toes. She'd swapped her survival suit for Danielle's furs and her wasted body wasn't generating enough warmth. The girl had given her a few squares of chocolate which she'd gobbled like an animal. It wasn't enough. Her mind kept floating and she was seeing double.

She lifted Danielle's wrist and worked out that Cope's deadline had expired nearly two hours ago. Only the girl's tears had persuaded her to extend the waiting time this long. Well, John certainly had what it took to play on the old heartstrings. Monica had succumbed, so had she, and now sweet, sexy Danielle was smitten. The girl hadn't wasted any time establishing whether Mhairi and Cope were lovers.

Too cold to settle, Mhairi let herself out and climbed up the bank. Not a light to be seen in the whole world. The thought that the man she'd rescued had abandoned her and was almost certainly dead prompted a spiky laugh. All for nothing. Career gone, no sanctuary even if she managed to cross the Line. Grippe's disappearance and presumed death wouldn't be considered an accident – on top of everything else, she had a murder charge hanging over her.

She looked south. Sam Pilkinghorn was waiting down there for her. She remembered his sure-handed touch as he bandaged her, the feel of his back against hers. She knew that she'd go with him to South America if she made it back across the Line. If.

She took a slow, open-mouthed breath, her mind made up.

When she returned to the car, Danielle was awake. She watched wide-eyed as Mhairi reached for the ignition.

'Just another half-hour.'

'He's not coming back. If they've got him, they'll soon be after us.'

Mhairi twisted the key. The engine grunted – like a hibernating beast kicked in the ribs. She switched off, her stomach tight and empty, and let a few prayer-filled seconds elapse before trying again.

Click.

Danielle chewed her nails, too frightened to speak.

Mhairi lifted her head from the steering wheel and squeezed the tension knots in her neck. 'Try and get some sleep. I'll keep watch.'

A thought drifted into her head and floated out the other side.

Engine.

She jerked awake and held her breath. Only Danielle's purring snores. She twisted to get comfortable again, but her mind had more tricks in store. Now moonlight seemed to be filling the windshield.

She stumbled out and fear took up all the play in her muscles. No illusion. A wash of light was spreading from the west and she could hear a rhythmic chuffing.

She turned and Danielle's fear collided with hers. She pulled her gaze away and climbed the bank. Headlights were approaching, pointing towards them.

Danielle emitted a husky sob. 'It's the Indians, isn't it?'

Mhairi crouched down like an animal, wondering what to do. Every other car on the road was smothered in snow. The hot-rod stood out like a whore in a vestry. She looked back up the road, past Danielle's wrecked car.

She hurried back to the girl and pushed her into motion. 'Run! I'll catch you up.'

She removed the ignition key, and hurried to the trunk. She splintered her nails before she managed to open it. She found a wheelbrace among the tools Cope had stowed. The light was getting stronger. She raised the brace and struck the windshield. It crazed, but didn't break. She put all her strength into the next blow and the sheet collapsed in a thousand pieces. She did the same to one of the sidescreens, then ferreted in the trunk again, took out a shovel, whacked the rear screen ineffectually and set off after Danielle. The girl had only gone as far as her own car before stopping.

'Keep going,' Mhairi panted. 'Here, take my arm.'

In her borrowed boots, she could move at little more than walking pace. Tonight's freeze after yesterday's thaw had turned the surface to glass. The noise of the tractor nagged at her back. Any second she expected to be pinned by a pencil of light.

'Where are we going?' Danielle gasped.

'You'll see.'

Mhairi was aiming for the graveyard of vehicles further up the road. How much further she couldn't say – quarter of a mile, she guessed.

In fact, they must have stumbled twice that distance before she spotted the unnatural hummocks. Her hopes were focused on one of those irrelevant details registered in passing. She couldn't find the bloody thing and the lights had grown strong enough to cast pale shadows. She was at the point of giving up when she saw it – a car shunted into the nearside verge, almost completely drifted over, only part of one rear door visible. A wave of wet snow pushed against its side by the tractor had frozen solid. Mhairi attacked it with the shovel, sobbing with fear and frustration.

'They're nearly at the road.'

Mhairi wiped sweat from her eyes and saw solid beams finger the night above the Fury. She continued wielding the shovel until she'd more or less exposed the door. Expecting it to be locked, she catapulted back when it opened at the first tug. Her feet shot from under her and she sprawled back, banging her head on the ice.

Pain inflamed her anger when she saw Danielle dithering. 'What are you waiting for?'

Danielle was aghast. 'There are people inside.'

'What?' Mhairi slithered across and pushed the girl aside. Two corpses, frozen in the attitude of giant foetuses, occupied the front

302

seats. 'They're not going to bother us,' she gasped, shoving Danielle inside so roughly that she banged her head on the frame.

Two feet of snow covered the roof and windshield. The sidescreens exposed to the road were only frosted, but there was no way of lowering them. Mhairi opened the door and saw the lights dip as the vehicle nosed onto the road. They halted at the Plymouth and engine and lights shut down. Shouts jolted Mhairi. A torch beam cast in all directions. Go away, she muttered. There's no one here.

Danielle was sobbing quietly into her hands. Mhairi put an arm around her. 'They won't find us. They'll see the smashed windshield and assume someone else got to us.'

She risked another look. The flashlight was bobbing down the road, flicking from side to side. At the Canadians' car, it stopped, disappeared briefly, then stabbed round again. Mhairi held her breath, waiting for it to turn back.

Instead, it shone rock-steady at her. She pulled in her head, not sure if she'd been seen. Danielle's terrified stare overwhelmed her own fear. Her heart swelled with pity. She folded the girl in her arms.

'I won't let them hurt you.'

She tried to think rationally about what the Indians would do to them. Women, as she'd already discovered, were in short supply above the Line, and she had never subscribed to the view that rape was a fate worse than death.

She waited with her mouth open, listening. The corpses must have died recently, but even in the sub-zero temperature the stench of decay thickened the air.

In the approaching glow of the torch, they seemed to slowly turn. Feet creaked in the snow and halted. The flashlight dazzled against the rimed windows. Everything inside Mhairi shook. She could feel Danielle battling her own hysteria.

Without warning, the shape of a hand rubbed against the sidelight, leaving a pink smear. The outline of a face pressed against the glass.

Danielle shrieked as the door opened. Mhairi swung the shovel and a figure skipped back.

'You!' she shouted. 'Where the fucking hell have you been?'

Cope looked as frightened as she was. 'Oh, Jesus!' he gasped. 'I saw the Fury smashed up and thought you were . . .'

'Dead? Well, what a surprise that would have been! You leave two women alone on a road infested with killers, and when you come swanning back six hours later, you're surprised the little ladies aren't swapping recipes and makeup tips.' All her resentment came to a spitting boil. 'Bastard!' she cried, hitting him with the flat of the shovel.

Cope made only a token attempt to roll with the blow. 'I'm sorry. Things took longer than I expected.'

She threw the shovel down. 'Screw sorry! Screw you!'

'I don't blame you,' Cope said. Giving her a wide berth and keeping her within vision, he leaned in towards Danielle. 'Your mother's all right. She's waiting for you.'

Danielle gabbled in French and clambered out. She saw the figures around the tractor, flung herself at Cope and smothered his face with kisses. She broke away and took off up the road. Mhairi watched as two of the shapes merged into one. Her anger went still.

'Who are the others?'

'Slaves.'

Mhairi saw that his suit was stained with blood. 'How many did you kill this time?'

'One for sure, but I guess there were a couple of others. Don't shed any tears.' He noticed Mhairi's stare and brushed at the stain. 'That wasn't me.'

'Are we expecting the rest to come after us?'

'No, they're finished.'

That silenced her. Cope was quiet, too.

'Thanks for waiting.'

'The only reason we're still here is because I couldn't get the car started.'

'I'll fix it. We've got a spare battery. Who smashed the glass?'

Mhairi was dismayed to find she couldn't keep her fury on the boil. 'I did.'

'Good save, but boy was I anxious.'

Good save indeed! Another flow of rage welled up but never reached the surface. Her legs turned rubbery and she folded down on to the car's sill.

'What would you have done if you'd found us dead?'

He lowered himself beside her. His face sank almost to his knees. He flicked the torch on and off. 'I had to take the chance. In a few miles we'd have used up the gas. Now we've got a vehicle that can go off-road and enough fuel to drive to the Line. We've got some food, too.' He stood wearily, raised her up and took her face in his hands. 'I won't leave you again, I promise.'

Cope followed the tractor in the Plymouth. Beside him, Mhairi's teeth ached in the icy draught blowing through the smashed windshield. Danielle and her mother were in the back, silent and withdrawn. Sylvie had refused to let Mhairi examine her, but she didn't seem to be injured – not physically. The blood freckling her face wasn't hers, apparently, and Cope's expression had warned her off asking.

'We have to get off the road,' Mhairi murmured. 'It's a death trap.'

'Carl says there's a deserted motel a few miles on. We'll take a break there and work out a route. It'll be light in a couple of hours.'

The thought of another sleepless night nearly gone made Mhairi's eyes close.

Only a moment seemed to pass before Cope was shaking her again. Her fuddled brain registered a grid of bungalows lit by their headlamps. Most of the buildings were razed and all of them were storm-damaged.

'See that?' Cope said, pointing at the rear section of a pickup poking from behind one of the cabins. 'Our friends from Lightning.'

Mhairi was fully conscious in an instant. 'Oh, no! Please, not again.'

'If it was them who put Sonny on to us, they're probably

dead.' Cope let himself out. 'Take Danielle and her mother up to the trailer. Here.'

Mhairi found herself holding a pistol. Bent to avoid sniper fire, she hurried Danielle and Sylvie to the trailer. All its occupants were lying on their stomachs except for Patty, the black girl. She and Mhairi exchanged beleaguered smiles. An immediate rapport.

A minute or two passed. When the shot came, Mhairi convulsed once, then remained absolutely still. There was no more firing. One shot was ominously final.

'Mhairi,' Cope called. 'Over here.'

Relief flipped to concern. She hurried forward and found him standing by the pickup. 'Are you hurt?'

'I'm fine,' Cope said. He flashed the torch at the cab. Dale was in the driving seat, his head a strange shape.

'Did you . . . ?'

'No, he's been dead all day. Sonny and his boys.'

Mhairi snagged a finger on her teeth. 'My God, you mean Dodie . . .'

'In there,' Cope said, jerking his head at one of the cabins. 'She's alive, but I guess she's hurt. She's the one who fired. I don't think she's got a lot of time for men right now.'

Mhairi followed him. Inside, he led her cautiously down the passage and shone his light on a splintered door panel. He spread himself against the wall to one side.

'Dodie, I ain't mad at you for taking a shot at me. I brought the doctor like I said.' He nodded at Mhairi to speak.

She swallowed. 'We're not angry with you, Dodie. It's terrible about Dale. If you're injured, we want to help you.'

After a minute's silence, Cope frowned a question at her and lifted the rifle. She shook her head emphatically.

'Dodie, you've got to think about your baby.'

She talked herself hoarse without getting a response. Finally, she handed the pistol back to Cope, quashing his protest with a fierce look.

'I'm going to come in now, Dodie. I'm not armed. Please don't shoot.'

Heart quailing away from the anticipated blast, she pushed open the door.

'Dodie?'

She slowly raised the torch and saw her lodged in a corner under a blanket. In her right hand was the shotgun, aimed at Mhairi's chest. As the light caught her, Mhairi heard a mewing, grizzling sound that made her bones melt with relief.

'Oh thank God.'

'You all right in there?'

'Fine. Emergency over. I'll call if I need you.' She knelt down by Dodie. 'Right then, let's have a look at the two of you.'

Gently she pulled back the blanket, revealing the new-born baby clamped to Dodie's breast. Neither of them appeared to be hurt. Dodie's eyes stayed staring straight ahead, one hand stroking the baby's back. Mhairi smiled at its wizened little face.

'Does he have a name?'

'Dale,' Dodie said dreamily. 'After his daddy.'

'Of course.'

When Mhairi emerged a few minutes later, she found Cope had lit the passage with a kerosene lamp. He was standing face to face with Danielle, not exactly holding hands, but getting on that way. He stepped smartly back. 'How is she?'

'Both doing well. No complications. I'll need some hot water and Dodie could use a drink.'

'I'll go,' the girl said, finally getting the message. Cope made to leave with her.

'John.'

He stopped sheepishly.

'Treat her properly.'

'You don't mind? I mean, you're not jealous? I know you didn't like it when I came on to you, but then other times . . . well, you're hard to figure.'

Mhairi's laugh came from the far side of exhaustion. 'No, I'm not jealous. I'm only concerned for Danielle's welfare.'

'Me too. For all of you,' he added quickly. After a moment,

307

he walked away. At the end of the passage, he stopped again. 'When I got back, you asked how many did I kill *this* time. Like I'd done some killing before.'

Goose pimples rose on Mhairi's skin. 'I don't remember what I said.'

He turned. 'If there's something I've done, something bad, I ain't scared to hear it.'

But Mhairi knew she would never tell him now. Not ever. Even if he had committed that terrible crime, he'd served his sentence.

'No, John, I don't know if there's anything bad in your past. And as you said, it's what you are now that counts.'

40

Cope caught an hour's sleep and rose without disturbing Mhairi. The Vags were sacked out around the walls of the reception area. As he tiptoed past, he noticed Sylvie's eyes following him. He squatted in front of her. 'Let Mhairi sleep in,' he whispered.

Sylvie's hand found his arm. 'John?'

'Go ahead.'

Her hand squeezed. Tears welled. 'You are a good man. So brave.'

'Mhairi's the brave one. I ain't got nothing to lose.'

Cope left the cabin and filled his lungs with cold air. On the off-chance that the militia hadn't stripped the pickup, he searched the cab. Part of Dale's brain was frozen on the headrest and the rear screen was rusty with his blood. In the footwell, Cope found the thermal imaging helmet. He tested it and found it was still in working order. The bar gauge showed a few hours' power remaining.

He left the motel complex through what had once been a kids' play area and walked a short way out on the prairie. Gusting wind kicked up little snow-twisters. Daylight was beginning to fill the sky, the sun rising bloodshot through clouds that threatened more snow. All around him the tundra lay bleeding.

As the dawn began to fade to grey, he spotted something darker than cloud fouling the horizon to the south. He focused Carl's binoculars on two coils of smoke a few miles down the road.

He put on the helmet and turned the gain dial. The smoke columns wavered dark red against the aquarium-green background. On the ground, three bugs crawled around the fires.

Cope ran back to the motel and climbed on to the roof of the tractor. The extra seven feet and the strengthening light revealed a column of vehicles, the lead vehicle skewed like a derailed locomotive.

He jumped down and hurried into the reception area. Patty and Sylvie were up, heating breakfast on a couple of propane stoves.

'Wake the others. We have to leave.'

Before they could react, he was in Mhairi's room. She was still fast asleep, her lips parted. His heart filled. Gently he squeezed her shoulder.

'Mhairi, there's some heavy activity down the road. We gotta clear out.'

She sighed liked a tired horse and reached blindly for her things.

Back in reception, he found the Vags waiting with expressions of dependence and dread. He realised he was meant to have a plan.

'Okay, there's a road-block a few miles south. Too far to see who it is, but I think it's the military. Mhairi and me are on the run. From the government. The reasons needn't bother you, but the fallout might.'

Their faces remained as blank as if he'd been addressing them in Tibetan.

'What I'm saying is, we're bad company. You can come along and share the risks or give yourselves up to the soldiers. It's your choice.'

Danielle put her hand up like an eager student. 'I'm coming with you.'

Patty took Carl's arm. 'Us too. If we give ourselves up, they'll just throw us in a camp.'

The decision was unanimous. It was the response Cope had been expecting. He didn't know if it was the one he wanted. 'Patty, get the tractor started.'

Mhairi came through the doorway, lines of tiredness drawn around her mouth. Cope led her out. One of the smoke columns had disappeared and the other had thinned to a stylus.

'It's the convoy,' he told her.

Her jaw dropped. 'But they had tanks. They had . . .'

'It wasn't Sonny or road bandits. It was the military. They're still down there. They must have tried to flag Floyd down and he started shooting. That's his armoured car you can see burning.'

'They must have been looking for us.' Mhairi covered her mouth with her hands. 'People are dead because of *us*.'

'The other vehicles aren't damaged. I reckon the troopers have taken the Vags away. They'll be in camp by now.'

Mhairi's troubled eyes shifted toward their companions.

'They know the score,' Cope told her. 'If we get across the Line, they get across. It's as simple as that.'

'That's a big "if".'

'Not to me. The one thing I know is I'm gonna be at Mustang the night Argo launches.'

Mhairi scratched her eyes. 'Just because you believe something doesn't make it true.' She touched him and turned away.

Cope watched her climb into the trailer. He lavished a last look on the Plymouth before joining her. The Sno-Cat was steered by an unfamiliar arrangement of levers and he was happy to let Patty do the driving.

'Which way?' she asked.

'North a couple of miles. There's a junction.'

'Where are we aiming for?' Carl asked.

'Depends where we're starting from.'

'Well,' Tom said, rattling a map. 'Right here, on US 95, between Burns and McDermitt. About forty miles north of the Line.'

Cope looked over his shoulder and saw the map showed only main highways. 'We've got to keep to back roads and farm trails. Anyone familiar with the country round here?'

They stuck out their lower lips and slowly shook their heads. All except for Tom. 'I heard Miles say you could leave by the back door and drive cross-country all the way to Denio.'

'That's right on the Line,' Patty explained.

'Which means it'll be heaving with patrols,' Carl added.

'We have to go to Antelope Falls,' Mhairi insisted. 'Sam will be waiting for us there. He's crossed the Line a dozen times. He's helped dozens of Vags escape.'

'Then that's where we're headed,' Cope agreed. 'Where is it?'

They searched long and hard, but finally had to admit that Antelope Falls wasn't shown on their map.

The junction was unsigned, its narrow western arm dwindling over a series of crests until it was just a hairline on a distant snowy apron. Cope nodded at Patty to take it.

They passed a few derelict farms and then the landscape emptied of habitation. Under the heavy overcast, the scenery was roughly sketched – a few pencil lines and grey shadings on a white sheet. The Sno-Cat tracked along at a steady ten to twelve miles an hour. The road undulated and in the flat light it was hard to tell where the horizons lay.

Tom slung together a breakfast of canned soup and biscuits. They ate on the move, huddled in sleeping bags and blankets.

'How are we off for food?' Cope asked.

'That's pretty much it.'

'Don't worry,' Cope said, wondering where the next meal would come from.

The road led on. Though it generally inclined upwards, the snow cover thinned to reveal slopes of shattered basalt. The Vags' pinched faces and hunched postures showed how cold they were, and though none of them complained, Cope knew they wouldn't be able to stand more than a day of this without hot food and shelter.

311

Patty's cry cut through the collective numbness. Cope vaulted over the side and ran forward.

She'd halted on a watershed – a broad, dished shoulder above a wide lake that bent around a headland to the left. The lake was frozen inshore, a margin of frost vapour separating the shelf from lacquer-black water dotted with panes of ice.

'Which way's south?'

Tom consulted a compass. 'Left. Straight down the lake.'

'I didn't see any lake on the map.'

'That's because the map's out of date. We're in the Great Basin. All the rivers drain inland.' Carl made a broad gesture. 'In the last ice age, most of this was inland sea.'

'You think the lake leads into Nevada?'

'Right direction, but I doubt it'll take us all the way.'

Even if it did, the ice wasn't thick enough to support a vehicle. Cope surveyed the terrain. North, the lake ended in a basin scattered with bluffs and cut by coulees. No way through round there. South, beyond the turn in the lake, folded hills climbed towards a gap like a missing tooth in a worn-down jaw. Small buttes and shadowed defiles lay in the way, but Cope reckoned that the Sno-Cat might be able to negotiate a passage.

While he was prospecting a route, Tom produced a camera and asked them to group for a portrait. Smiling at the lens, Cope spotted a slow drift of movement on the slope to the north. A herd of caribou grazing in front of the wind about a mile off.

He hitched the Winchester over his shoulder. 'Wait for me down at the lake. I'll try to get us our supper.'

The caribou were upwind. Secure in his camouflage, Cope approached within easy range before a clumsy step alerted a cow on the flanks of the herd. It raised its head and pricked its ears, looking straight at him, but when it failed to locate danger it started foraging again. Cope lowered himself on to one knee and selected a yearling bull about sixty yards off. Not sure how true the rifle aimed, he made it a chest shot. The young buck ran fifteen yards and dropped. The rest of the herd bounded away, not knowing what they were running from, and when Cope reached the fallen animal, they'd already resumed feeding.

He paunched the deer and took a minute's rest. From up here, the Sno-Cat was very small and the people around it insignificant. His God's-eye view oppressed him. Eight lives in his keeping, and one of them a baby less than a day old.

Snow squalls bustling in from the east stirred him to his feet. He slung the carcass over his shoulders and started his descent. He'd covered quarter of the distance when a movement snagged the tail of his eye. Somewhere on the track, hidden now by a fast-moving veil of snow. He let the carcass slip from his back and brought the binoculars up.

In the eye of the squall he caught a wicked glint of metal. He kept the glasses on the spot and in a few seconds a vehicle came out of the snow front. Its superstructure was tall and boxy, and the light glancing off a steel blade told him that Sonny had picked up their trail.

There was no time to get within shouting distance of the group below. They wouldn't see the truck until it came over the watershed, and by then it would be too late. Even if they started running now, they wouldn't get clear on foot.

He fired two warning shots and waited for the reports to carry. Pinpoint faces turned. He semaphored wildly and then remembered they couldn't see him. He stripped off his suit and danced in the snow until someone's raised arm showed he'd been spotted. He pointed south, leaning his whole body into the gesture. Get going! Down the lake!

Even at this distance, he could see them milling indecisively. He fired the rest of the clip over their heads and again swept his hand towards the south. The truck's gruff engine note reached him faintly, but the sound wouldn't carry over the hill. He crammed seven more shells into the rifle and shot them one after another at the truck – not with any hope of hitting it, but to show the Vags where the danger was coming from.

A scurry of movement. Good, they were unloading the snowmobile. That would get three of them clear – four including Dodie's baby.

Three figures had already gone on to the lake on foot, heading south down the ice shelf. Pulling back the distance with the binoculars, Cope identified Carl, Tom, and a woman – probably Danielle. That meant Mhairi was going to be on the snowmobile. They'd finally lifted it off the trailer and were scrambling on to it.

The roar of the truck burst through an invisible barrier. It breasted the crest, slowed almost to a stop, then accelerated downhill with a gout of exhaust smoke. Carl and the other figures on the ice hadn't covered a hundred yards and the snowmobile had just started moving.

Cope reloaded with all the shells that came to hand, adjusted the sight for maximum range and shot with slow deliberation at the cab. An impossible target. He had no idea if any of the bullets hit or whether the occupants registered the fact they were under fire. If they did, it didn't slow them. Cope felt in his pocket for more shells. None there. He fumbled in the other pocket.

Empty. He couldn't believe it until he did some simple arithmetic. He'd shot nearly three clips off. The remaining ammunition was in his pack on the trailer.

He swore quietly, muted by the action below beginning to race towards its inevitable conclusion.

The truck had less than half a mile to go, and Carl's party looked as if they were only a stone's throw from their starting point. The snowmobile overtook them and headed on. Half a mile beyond them, with the truck less than half that distance from the lake, the snowmobile dropped its passengers and circled tightly back, aiming to ferry the others to safety before the truck reached the shore. But from his vantage, Cope could see that the truck would reach the lake at the same moment the returning snowmobile reached the stragglers.

He jumped up. 'Well kiss my ass!'

Only a couple of hundred yards from the lake, the truck had skidded off the track. A wave of snow broke over it, and when the commotion cleared, Cope knew from the rig's ungainly stance that it wasn't going to drive out under its own power.

If Sonny had baled out then, he could still have caught Carl's party. Instead, he wasted a minute thrashing through the gears and gunning the engine. The whine of spinning tyres carried to Cope. When the truck had dug itself in to its axles, the militia spilled out and set off running.

Down on the lake, the snowmobile had stopped to pick up Carl and the other two Vags. It skidded round, and by the time the militia reached the waterside and opened up with their weapons, it was more than half a mile off. Above the clatter of machine guns, Cope heard twanging detonations. Fountains of ice erupted fifty yards from the snowmobile. A grenade gun, not designed to be fired from the hand. Another salvo burst a little closer, but the sledge kept going. Unless the militia got flukier than they deserved, the Vags would make it.

They did. The snowmobile reached the first set of passengers and kept going. The militia wasted hundreds of rounds. When they ceased fire, Cope punched the air.

The militia bolted to the Sno–Cat and he assumed they were going to give chase down the lake shore. But after a couple of minutes, they jumped out and hustled back up to the truck.

The urgency of their movements told Cope they hadn't given up. One of them passed out what looked like jackets. Over these they pulled arctic camouflage overalls and back-packs, then hurried down to the lakeside and straight on to the ice. They were going to pursue the Vags on foot. Cope considered showing himself, leading them a dance into the hills, but he suspected they wouldn't be tempted. Better to hold back and see how things panned out.

Pretty well, he calculated. Already the snowmobile had dropped Carl's party ahead of the original passengers and had now returned to pick them up.

Cope realised he was freezing. He put his suit back on, went back to the caribou, and sliced several pounds of meat from the haunches.

He jogged down the slope. The militia were still tramping away down the ice shelf and never once looked back. Their relentlessness cast a shadow over Cope's optimism. Running a shuttle service would cut the range of the snowmobile by half. He pushed the doubts away. The Vags had several hours of daylight left. Assuming they established only a ten- to twelve-mile lead by the time night fell or the tank ran dry, they would be half a day's slog ahead of the militia. On their own, with at least two days' journey-time to the Line, that still wasn't a safe margin, but Cope was determined to eliminate the militia before they could close the gap. He wondered if Mhairi had rescued his ammunition.

Before starting the chase, he made for the truck, hoping to pick up a weapon. No luck. The ignition was still on, and the glowing fuel warning light showed why the militia had dumped the vehicle. When Cope reached the lake shore, the Vags were almost lost in the grain of distance, the militia grey scribbles in the frost smoke.

He pulled himself into the Sno-Cat. Patty or some other quick-thinking person had broken off the key in the ignition and torn out part of the wiring loom. Wondering if it was restorable, Cope stretched out on the seat and peered under the dash.

'John.'

Rearing up, he banged his head on the steering lever. 'Mhairi! What the hell are you doing here? I thought you were on the snowmobile.'

'There wasn't room and on foot I'd have slowed everyone down.' She lifted his pack. 'Also, I thought you'd need this.'

Cope rubbed his bruised head, not sure if he was relieved or dismayed. 'You remembered the shells?'

'That's the first thing I thought of.'

41

Within an hour of setting out, the militia had doubled their lead. Mhairi knew it was her fault. Cope was having to adjust his pace to her hobble.

Worse, they'd found pink stains and splashes of fuel in the snowmobile's tracks.

After a mile or so, the bloodstains petered out and so did the spilt fuel. When neither a body nor the vehicle showed in the next half hour, Mhairi's anxiety began to recede. The militia were now little more than tremors that came and went between the snow squalls.

Around the headland, Mhairi spotted a shape on the ice. The snowmobile.

A grenade fragment had punctured the tank. Mhairi didn't need Cope to tell her that the advantage had tilted back in the militiamen's favour. The Vags would have a lead of two or three miles at most. With the baby to carry and one of the party injured, it wouldn't take Sonny and company long to eat into that.

Cope glassed the long reach of the lake. On this side of the headland, it stretched south-west for as far as he could make out.

'See anything?'

He didn't answer immediately and then shook his head.

'You'd better go ahead,' she said.

He scratched his cheek and squinted at the darkening sky. 'We'll keep going.'

Half an hour later, the tracks were blurring under the snow.

'We're falling further and further behind,' Mhairi said. 'You have to get after them.'

For the first time since they'd made their break, Cope was in a frenzy of indecision. 'I said I wouldn't leave you.'

'Patty and the others agreed to come with us because they thought you'd be there to protect them. And the only reason Sonny's chasing them is because he thinks you're with them. So that's where you're needed. Now go *on*.' She made her tone light. 'I'll just keep plugging along until I catch up.'

Cope studied the leaden sky again. The wind had dropped to nothing. 'We're in for some heavy stuff,' he said. 'Stick to the tracks. When the snow comes, get on to land. If the tracks leave the lake, don't try and follow. Lose them in the mountains and you could stay lost. Stay by the shore until I come back for you. The suit will keep you warm. Have you got food?'

'Carl put the spare stove in your pack. There's a flashlight, too.'

Cope removed them. 'You take them. Here's your supper.'

Mhairi gingerly accepted a slice of raw, bloody caribou steak.

'You'd better have this,' he said, handing her the pistol. 'It holds nine bullets and the clip's full. This is the safety. Down is off. That's all you need to know.'

Impatient to see him get started, she stuffed the pistol into her pocket.

Cope shouldered his pack. 'When I finish things with Sonny, I'll signal. Three flashes means it's safe to come up. Give me the same signal if you hit trouble.'

'Good luck.'

He got five yards before stopping. 'Mhairi . . .'

'Get. Just get.'

He broke into a lope and disappeared into the gloaming.

The heavy snow began to fall soon after he'd left. Mhairi made a mistake. Instead of making for the shore when visibility shortened, she continued along the tracks until she was forced to admit she'd lost them, as John had said she would. By then she couldn't see the lakeside. She was sure it was to her left, no more than a hundred yards away. Facing in that direction, she began to count off the steps. At a hundred and twenty, she still hadn't reached land. She went on step by step, her count slowing as she approached two hundred.

Beyond that she didn't dare continue. Was it conceivable that a moment's carelessness had sent her out towards open water? Turning a circle on herself, she realised it was all too likely. Her orientation had gone completely. The torch beam showed only falling snow. None of her senses was the slightest use to her. All she knew was that she was somewhere on an ice shelf that narrowed in places to less than two hundred yards before petering out in floating sludge.

Stay where you are until the snow stops, she commanded herself.

It was a long standstill. The snow deepened around her. Every so often, she raised her hand and made a wiping motion.

Deprived of sensory data, her mind began to construct a primitive reality of its own. She imagined shapes creeping up on her. She cringed away from them and shouted at them to leave her alone.

At last the snow began to lift and a mountainside formed under a ceiling of cloud. She forced her cramped legs straight and saw why she'd failed to find the shore. The lake forked and she had wandered into the left arm.

The question was: which direction had the Vags taken? She forced her tired mind to work logically. This arm of the lake looked as if it ended less than a mile off, under a steep hill. She doubted if the Vags would have gone down a dead end. They must have steered right, continuing up the main lake. That conclusion brought its own dilemma. To get back on course, she would have to head straight across this inlet. It was at least half a mile wide, and the night was so dark she couldn't see if it was frozen over completely.

Patty knew the militia were hunting them, she reasoned, and would have taken the shortest route. She'd do the same.

She was about halfway across when she realised that the springiness underfoot was not her balance going, but the ice giving under her weight. She took another step and the ice bowed and produced a groaning sound. Her chest squeezed out a throttled sob. She was on young ice, only a few inches thick, and pliant.

This must be a salt lake saturated with minerals deposited in the ten thousand years since the last ice age. Saltwater ice was more plastic than its freshwater equivalent, but did that make it stronger?

Go back, she told herself. Retrace her steps and take the long way round. But that would lose her hours and she was already deep in the danger zone. The shore ahead was so close, and surely the ice must thicken soon.

One foot at a time, not lifting her boots from the ice, she shuffled forward. The layer deformed each time her weight came down. Often she stopped in a paralysis of terror until the thought of her weight bearing down on the same spot, melting the ice by pressure alone, sent her on again.

She rejected the impulse to signal for help. She was one life set against seven.

Finally, only fifty yards offshore, the ice stiffened. She skated clumsily to land, and when she reached it she threw herself down like a shipwrecked mariner.

What happened next happened all at once and without warning. Up into the sky at the far end of the lake rose a flare. Explosions sounded, their flashes pulsing dull red against the clouds.

Cope had found the militia. All her qualms about killing vanished. The thought of Sonny dead filled her with a visceral joy.

Darkness settled again. She watched it hungrily for the signal she knew would come. Minutes passed, and though her exultation faded, her certainty never wavered. Cope wasn't dead. He couldn't be. He was indestructible. He had a rendezvous he wouldn't miss. At that moment, half mad with stress and exhaustion, Mhairi believed everything he'd told her.

And her faith was justified. Far away, a light winked – once, twice, three times. A pause, and again – three flashes. Then once more.

She laughed and hurried towards it, talking to herself.

Her flashlight began to fail and she decided to wait where she was and let Cope come to her. Every minute or so, she switched on her torch and got his flash in return.

Much sooner than she'd expected, she heard his footsteps, dragging as if he was very tired. He was breathing far back in his throat. Her wits were in disarray and she switched on the torch without thought. Its fading beam failed to pick him up. She played it from side to side.

'John, is that you?'

Hundreds of yards away, a light flickered three times.

'No, bitch, it's me.'

She whirled.

Sonny was standing twenty yards behind her – a walking corpse, a shining visitant from the far side. He'd fallen through the ice and the water had frozen into an icy shroud. Frost glittered on his overalls. His hair and moustaches were stiff and hoary.

He lurched towards her.

'Get away from me.'

He kept coming.

'I'm warning you.'

The pistol was shaking in her hand like a dowsing wand. Sonny stopped. He lowered his head and laughed with despair and rage, as though everything up till now had gone terribly wrong and killing her would be the consolation he'd take to his grave. He raised his face and his eyes filled with purpose.

Keeping the fading beam on him, Mhairi tried to steady her aim. Sonny was only yards away, his burning eyes ringed by shadow.

She fired as if she'd done it before in a dream. And just like in a dream, the bullets had no effect. Six or seven times she pulled the trigger, and though nearly every concussion shoved Sonny back a short step, he recovered and kept coming.

'Die!' she screamed. 'Die, you bastard!'

He stopped and put his hands to his chest and ripped apart his overalls, baring the bullet-proof vest underneath. He patted his chest and came on.

Mhairi dropped the torch and took three steps backwards. For a couple of moments, she couldn't see Sonny, then his shape parted the night. She aimed at it with both hands, and when it filled her vision, she raised the pistol towards the pale disc of his face and fired the remaining bullets.

Sonny ran back with mincing little steps and sat down on his butt like a toddler who'd abruptly lost his balance. His head sagged towards his knees and then stopped. It was such an incomplete movement that Mhairi held her breath, waiting for him to complete it, but he remained slumped over in the posture of an abandoned doll. Her torch was glowing on the ice. She grabbed it and shone its dying light on him. The back of his head gleamed stickily.

Mhairi's legs folded like cardboard. She slumped down, still holding the pistol on Sonny.

They were both in the same positions when she heard her name called. She didn't answer. A light approached, but she didn't dare take her eyes off Sonny in case he put his hands to the ice and wearily pushed himself up.

A pair of legs appeared in the beam of the flashlight. They stopped at Sonny. One of them lifted and the sole of a boot nudged him, toppling him on to his side. The legs came on and bent at the knees. A hand lifted her face. She looked up with haggard astonishment.

'Sam . . . ?'

42

Cope had been using the thermal imaging facility sparingly, and he was in the dark when the starshell burst, fixing the militiamen like photographic images. Tracer shells sketched flat curves across the lake. The pyrotechnics lasted a very short time before darkness and silence descended. Cope switched on the imager and located two bundles of warmth on the ice.

Before he could locate the third, a red silhouette emanated from the shore and began to walk towards the dead militiamen. Cradled in his arms was the bulkiest firearm Cope had ever seen. The man stopped briefly at the first corpse and walked on to the next. After examining him, he raised something to his eyes – night glasses – and scanned the ice shelf in his direction. Even though Cope knew he was invisible, the chilling economy of the man's movements made him lie still. Whoever he was, this guy was in a different league from Sonny and his goons.

'Mhairi!'

Cope's hands bunched on the ice. The man had to be one of Zygote's agents.

'Cope!' the man yelled. He began to walk down the lake. 'John Cope!'

Cope had to keep telling himself the man couldn't see him. He brought the rifle to his eye but couldn't align the sights through the faceplate. The man came on. Cope commanded his nerve to hold until the target was unmissable. At a range of fifty yards he took up pressure on the trigger.

Forty yards away, the man stopped. An easy shot. Cope's finger hesitated at squeeze point. If this man was a Zygote agent, why was he on his own? Why wasn't he wearing uniform or camouflage gear?

The questions filled the space between them.

'I'm Cope,' he called, 'and I'm staring at you down the barrel of a gun. Who the hell are *you*?'

The man swung the unwieldy weapon in his direction. 'Sam Pilkinghorn. Where's Mhairi?'

Cope rose in relief. 'Down the lake. We figured with Sonny right on the Vags' heels, I'd better get on up here and finish him off.'

He'd forgotten he was semi-invisible and the tracer shied when he materialised out of the dark in one step. He lifted off his helmet and removed a gauntlet. 'Pleased to meet you.'

Pilkinghorn looked at his hand as if it was leprous and walked past. 'Go join the rest of your crew.'

Cope took a few steps after him before the message sank home. The tracer was pissed at him for leaving Mhairi.

'Three flashes is the signal,' he shouted.

Pilkinghorn didn't answer.

'Hey, where's the third man?'

Pilkinghorn indicated the water. After searching the ice margin and failing to pick up any trace of a body, Cope swore wearily and joined the Vags.

Tom was the injured party. A piece of shrapnel had torn his arm, leaving a ragged flesh wound that Pilkinghorn had dressed. The Vags had pitched two tents and were preparing food the tracer had left. Cope had just accepted a hot drink from Sylvie when he heard distant shots. Six popping sounds, a long pause, then another three reports.

'Shit!'

Throwing away his drink, Cope sprinted down the lake. He must have run a mile before he spotted two shapes returning, one supporting the other. He didn't stop until he was sure that the ravaged figure propped against Pilkinghorn was Mhairi.

'Is she hurt?' he gasped.

Pilkinghorn spurned his helping hand. 'She ran into one of the militia. It's damn lucky he didn't get her.'

'You're the one who said he was in the water.'

'You shouldn't have left her.'

Cope spat a laugh. 'You try riding herd on this lot.'

Anger beat behind Pilkinghorn's eyes. 'Mhairi's the only reason you're alive. You've got a damn peculiar sense of priorities, but I guess with your record, I shouldn't be surprised.'

'What record? What the hell are you talking about?'

Pilkinghorn went on without answering.

Cope stopped, rooted to the spot by the injustice of the accusations. 'Piss on you, too.'

He trudged back to camp, frozen out. The tracer had taken Mhairi into one of the tents. When Danielle came over and asked him to join the others inside, Cope tetchily told her he was happy with his own company. She left in tears.

The tracer's hostility continued to rankle. You bust your balls saving people's asses and got cold contempt for thanks.

Only four days to the Argo launch. He studied the broken-toothed gap in the mountain wall and an urge rose in him. Go. Mhairi didn't need him any more. The tracer would look after her and the others.

He heard footsteps behind him. Pilkinghorn stepped in front and held out a dish of stew. 'There ain't much. I wasn't expecting such a big party.'

'Save it,' Cope told him, and patted the frozen caribou steak in his pack. 'I got my own.'

Pilkinghorn hunkered down and dribbled snow through his fingers. 'Mhairi says I've judged you wrong. Looks like I owe you a debt of gratitude. I spoke hasty out of worry for her. You want an apology, you got it.'

324

'Too late, mister. Soon as morning comes, I'm on my way. Soon as I've said goodbye to Mhairi.'

Pilkinghorn shook his head with controlled impatience. 'You won't make it. The feds and the troopers have closed every road. They're offering reward money for turning you in. If I figured out where to pick you up, so can they.'

'You didn't pick me up,' Cope reminded him. He patted his suit. 'They could put a million men across these mountains and I'd walk by under their noses. Just point me in the right direction.'

Pilkinghorn stood. 'I came up here for Mhairi. The others aren't my responsibility. You're the one who offered to lead them to the promised land.'

Cope's eyes narrowed. 'You're saying you'd let them make their own way?'

Pilkinghorn half shrugged. 'No. If you ship out, I'd have to try finishing what you started. Can't say it makes me happy, but I don't think Mhairi would have it any other way.' He looked down. 'Do you?'

Cope found himself avoiding the tracer's eye. 'Well, you've crossed the Line enough times. Mhairi says you've brought dozens out.'

'Lost a lot, too. Last trip I started out with seven and ended up with none. And that bunch didn't include a mother and new-born infant and all the other lost souls you've accumulated.'

Pilkinghorn hadn't raised his voice, but his eyes were slivers of bitter experience.

'Shit,' Cope said, feeling time beginning to speed up. 'I gotta be at Mustang before Argo blasts off.'

Pilkinghorn sank back on his haunches. 'We've got time.'

Cope studied the quilted mountainside. 'How many days to the Line?'

'Forget days. We have to get across before the cloud breaks. It's the only thing saving us.' He eyed Cope's helmet thoughtfully. 'How far does that thing let you see in dark and fog.'

'As far as I like, but there ain't much power left.'

'Then save it till we need it.' Pilkinghorn nodded at the plate. 'Your stew's getting cold.'

Cope began to attack it with his fingers. 'How did you know where to find us?'

'Deke Hollis got a message down to one of my contacts. The rest was luck.'

'That weapon you used. What the hell you call that?'

'Electro-magnetic rifle. Fires explosive shells. You'd better upgrade your own piece.' Pilkinghorn pointed at one of the bodies on the ice. 'Guy there's got a nice machine gun.'

Cope looked at the corpse and sniffed. 'Didn't do him much good. I believe this old Winchester suits me fine.'

They set off in another grey dawn, starting a journey that only baby Dale wouldn't remember to his dying day. Cope and Pilkinghorn took turns carrying him in a papoose fashioned from a down jacket.

Within minutes of breaking camp they were in clouds, and that's the way it stayed. Most of the time they were walking in a pocket of black and white only a few yards across. For Cope, bringing up the rear, it took an effort of concentration just to keep in sight of Danielle directly ahead. Somewhere in front, Pilkinghorn was calculating the route by means of a global positioning device, compass and large-scale map.

For the first time since leaving Wellspring, Cope knew what it was to be cold. He'd given up his suit and boots to Dodie, supplementing his clothing with gear stripped from one of the dead militiamen. The Vags had also taken food and sleeping bags from the corpses. Cope reckoned he was humping at least sixty pounds in his back-pack – and that didn't include his stints with the baby.

All morning they laboured upwards. The afternoon found them in a fastness of rock, winding through defiles and scrambling over fans of scree. Cope's borrowed boots pinched, and by the time he reeled into some arbitrary bivouac of Pilkinghorn's choosing, his feet were so numb he felt as if he was pegging along on the stumps of his ankle-bones. He slept in one of the tents with Tom and Dodie. Despite his exhaustion, the baby's crying kept him awake most of the night.

At dawn they were on their way again. Soon they began descending, dropping through deep pockets of snow. The mist thickened, frosting everything it touched. They entered a dead pine forest and came upon a sombre convocation of boreal owls perched on fractured branches. The owls had no fear of them, taking it in turns to glide soundlessly down and flop with muffled talons on prey hidden in the snow. Their unblinking citron eyes watched the fugitives from pale round heads like shamans' masks.

Below the forest the slope relented and finally levelled into sagebrush flats. The pilgrims threaded their way through bushes that collapsed into powdered ice at a touch. They had long since stopped talking among themselves or paying attention to anything other than the next place to put their feet. When Cope barged into Danielle and found everyone at a stop, he assumed they had simply reached their limits of endurance.

Then he heard a sizzling sound he couldn't place.

Pilkinghorn raised his eyes from the screen of his GPS.

'This is where the journey gets serious.' He strode into the fog. 'Follow me.'

The first thing Cope saw was a rust-blotched pickup riddled with bullet holes. Forty yards past it a blurred white rectangle hung in the air – a sign on a fence. With great effort, his tired eyes tracked the message.

DANGER OF DEATH
TOTAL EXCLUSION ZONE. DO NOT CROSS PERIMETER.
ARMED RANGERS PATROLLING. ALL TRESPASSERS WILL BE SHOT
Genesis Ranching Corporation

Pilkinghorn turned to him. 'Tell us what you can see.'

Cope isolated several heat signatures in the green cast. 'Big glow a long way to the east. Could be a settlement.'

'It's a research centre. About eight miles away. Anything else?'

'Some animals. Most likely caribou.'

'Any vehicles?'

Cope did a slow scan. 'No vehicles.'

Pilkinghorn raised his voice. 'Listen up. Ten miles south of here, we'll be across the Line. Someone's waiting for us there. We have to move fast. That means not stopping – not stopping for anything. We stay in a real tight bunch, within touching distance.' He smiled at the nervous faces. 'One last push and we're home free.'

'Er, that sounds like 40,000 volts,' Carl said, eyeing the wires fizzing in the saturated air.

Pilkinghorn tossed a collapsible shovel at him. 'We go under. Watch out for the stock fence the other side. It'll knock you cold.'

He took Cope aside. 'Genesis has infra-red microsensors all along the fence. The guy who's going to meet us has knocked out the ones on this section. There are more inside, but by sticking close together, I'm hoping the rangers will think we're part of the menagerie. If they make us out, they'll come at us from the research centre. You're going to have to be our eyes.'

Cope knew that with the women and walking wounded, the crossing would take at least four hours. 'The power won't hold out. Isn't there some other route?'

'Nope. The rangers can't get to us in less than ten minutes. Take a peek every six or seven.'

'What happens if they do come?'

Pilkinghorn was already going away to supervise the digging. He slapped his rifle.

Cope shrugged and went to help excavate the hole. From the grim looks Pilkinghorn kept casting at the pickup, it was clear he'd come this route before and it hadn't left him with pleasant memories.

43

They held on to each other's sleeves as they shuffled on. It wasn't just that they were obeying Pilkinghorn's order to stay tight. Conditions were a true whiteout, the light diffusing from all directions with equal dim intensity. There were no shadows, no depth of field, no horizon. Cope could hardly tell which way was up and kept missing his footing and tripping into his neighbours.

They had been walking for two hours when a mournful descant behind them made his skin grab. Everyone jostled closer.

'What the hell was that?'

Pilkinghorn didn't look round. 'Dire wolves. They won't bother us.'

'What's a dire wolf?'

'What it sounds like.'

Automatically, they increased pace. The howling grew louder, reaching a pitch of excitement before suddenly stopping.

'Any activity around the centre?' Pilkinghorn asked.

Cope had been rationing his inspections. He switched on and his jaw dropped.

'What?' Pilkinghorn demanded. 'Where?'

'Animals. Big animals. Enormous. About a mile ahead, to our left. Moving this way. Moving slowly.'

Pilkinghorn sighted through his 'scope. 'Got them.' He shouldered his gun. 'Keep going.'

After an interchange of baffled glances, they hurried on. A few minutes later, Cope took another look at the massive glowing shapes. He cleared his throat. 'If we keep walking, we'll cut right through them.'

Pilkinghorn gave a vexed sigh. 'Okay, everyone down until they get clear.'

They squatted.

'How's it looking?' Pilkinghorn asked after a few minutes.

'Coming right at us.'

Danielle jumped up. 'Let's get away from here!'

Pilkinghorn pulled her back down. 'Run and someone will get lost. Now sit still. They'll sheer off once they scent us.'

Cope watched the tiny droplets of moisture floating past, moving from left to right, carrying their scent away from the approaching animals. Dale the baby set up a thin wailing. Everybody glared at it. Dodie grimaced and unfastened the top of her suit. For a little while, the only sound was the baby's greedy sucking.

'Ain't you the lucky one?' Cope murmured

The faintest of breezes stirred the fog, moving it through the clumps of sagebrush in huge billows. Cope heard a papery rustling, then a heavy shuffling and the cushioned tread of giant feet. All his short hairs stiffened. With one hand he raised the rifle, with the other he felt for Danielle's arm.

Out of the mist at the limits of his vision loomed a shaggy behemoth with tusks curved almost into a figure of eight.

'Holy cow,' he breathed. 'A mammoth!'

It filed past, dispersing into the mist. Another took its place, then another, the herd swinging past like a scene from a prehistoric pageant. Self-absorbed, impassive, they moved towards some destiny known only to them. Above the tramp of their feet, Cope heard their slow respiration and the complicated gurgling of their digestive systems. They made no other sound until the last member of the caravan loomed by. It looked straight at them with tiny bloodshot eyes, rolled back its trunk and emitted a blaring squeal that reverberated down to the soles of Cope's feet. It backed away after the rest of the herd, shaking its ears, defying them to follow.

It was gone as if swallowed by time itself.

Cope let his breath go. Nobody moved.

'Fog's beginning to lift,' Pilkinghorn said at last.

'Thank God,' Patty sighed.

'That's our safety blanket. Let's move it before we lose it. Not far now.'

The prospect of reaching their goal put temporary vigour into legs pushed almost to collapse. The formation stretched and grew ragged. Cope made it his business to keep an eye on Danielle and Sylvie, but there were passages of blankness when he was conscious of nothing except lifting one foot, putting it down, lifting the other . . .

'Anyone behind you?'

Startled, Cope found Pilkinghorn at his side. He turned and blinked into the cold clamminess. 'Guess not.'

'Whoa!'

They stopped dull-eyed in their tracks. Cope eased his pack off and massaged his aching shoulders.

'Where's Tom?' Pilkinghorn demanded.

Mouths slackened.

'Dodie, he was next to you. When did you last see him?'

'I don't know.' She looked to her side. 'I thought he was right there.'

'Someone must know when he fell out. Come on. Anyone.'

Nobody could say for sure when they'd last seen him.

Pilkinghorn shut his eyes briefly. 'Cope, lighten our darkness.'

The bar gauge showed only a hairline of power remaining. Cope scanned for the signature of a single upright figure. Instead, he found a group of hot tints circling in a weird dance.

'All I'm picking up is animals. Reckon it's those wolves. 'Bout a mile to the east. Damn! The image is going dark. Gone.'

Worry worked behind Pilkinghorn's eyes. 'Did Tom have a gun?'

'No,' Carl said. 'His arm. He couldn't . . .'

Pilkinghorn breathed hard at the ground, then brought his fierce eyes to bear. 'I can't go back and risk losing all of you.'

Mhairi took a step towards him. 'Sam, we can't . . .'

'You think I like it any better than you do? I have to play the odds, and I make them nine to one. In a few minutes the fog'll be gone and we'll be in clear sight.'

Cope could see they were all poised to take the one step that would condemn Tom.

'I'll go,' Carl said.

The idea of gentle, half-blind Carl riding to Tom's rescue was so preposterous that Cope slid the Winchester off his shoulder.

Pilkinghorn blocked him. 'Don't be a fool. The wolves will have got him by now.'

'You said they weren't dangerous.'

'Not to an armed party. But an injured man without a weapon and carrying a fresh wound.' Pilkinghorn turned. 'Listen to that. They're probably fighting over the scraps.'

Ravenous babbling rose and fell in the mist.

'What the hell,' Cope said, and broke into a run.

'We can't wait on you,' the tracer called after him.

The helmet was no good to him now, but he didn't need it. The sounds led him. The fog was lifting in patches and his shadow fleeted on it like a phantom. The cries of the dire wolves grew louder and more frenzied.

He burst into pearly sunlight stretching across the flats to a pale porcelain rim of mountains. The wolves were a quarter mile ahead, very black in the brightness, attacking something in the side of a gravel bench. Cope loosed a shot, knowing he was too late. The pack shifted and went on with their work. He ran full tilt, firing from the hip, working the lever as he charged. The wolves began to scatter, lolloping with a humped and furtive gallop that suggested they were repellent even to themselves. But three of them were too excited by what they'd got to give it up. Broken-winded, Cope kept firing and saw one of the wolves spin and sink its teeth into its thigh.

They were gone. All except for the injured beast. It whirled round itself, tearing chunks of flesh from its haunches, spraying the snow with its blood. A set of jaws with a digestive system attached.

Cope shot it dead and came to a heaving, sweating halt. He caught his breath, prepared to be sickened by the sight of a few shreds of flesh and clothing. His breath burst in a gasp when he didn't see them. The wolves had been digging under a rock plugged into the bank.

'Tom?'

From behind it came a muffled cry.

Cope rolled it away and peered into Tom's terrified face. He was in a tunnel – an old coyote den – wedged so tight that Cope had to exert full strength to drag him out. Only the desperation of mortal terror could have squeezed him into such a tight spot. His hands were lacerated from holding the rock jammed in the entrance. The hollow dug underneath showed how close the wolves had come to getting their next meal. Another couple of minutes, and they'd have started eating Tom from the fingertips down.

He was gibbering with shock, tears and snot running down his face. No time to let him pull himself together. The Genesis research centre, unnoticed at first, was in plain view to the east. Even if they hadn't been spotted, the rangers must have heard the shots.

'I'm sorry,' Tom wailed.

Cope lifted him by his bloody hands. 'No time for that. We're in someone's back yard and they don't like visitors.'

He pushed the Vag in front of him. The fog was rolling back on itself and by the time they reached the spot where he'd dropped his pack, the edge of the bank was still far ahead. He was trying to muster enough energy to pick up the load when his peripheral vision caught a glimmer to his left. He focused his binoculars and followed the gleam into the murk.

He let the binoculars drop and slapped Tom on the back. 'See that? The Line!'

Tom shifted as if he was desperate to relieve himself.

Cope swung round to see what was agitating him. He kicked his pack.

'Aw no!'

Two vehicles were cutting across the flats with a malign swiftness that immediately ruled out flight on foot. Cope pushed Tom down and flattened out alongside him. He reloaded the Winchester and placed the rest of the box to hand. He wasn't going to win a shoot-out, and for the first time he regretted ignoring Pilkinghorn's suggestion to trade in the rifle for something with a little more punch.

'All we've done is trespass,' Tom whimpered. 'I mean, they're not going to shoot us for taking a short cut.'

That's exactly what the notices said they'd do. But even if the rangers took them alive, Cope was in a no-win situation. Once they discovered who he was, they'd ship him back to Wellspring, and that was the one fate he would never accept.

Tom began to cry softly. 'This is all my fault. If you hadn't come back, you'd be across the Line now.'

'Wouldn't have been the same without you.'

In less than a minute, it would be all over. Why wait? Cope thought. Pull the plug now. Swallow the barrel and suck down a slug. Dead before he heard the bang.

'John.'

'Uh-huh.'

'Behind us.'

Cope squirmed round and blinked. Projected on the retreating fog bank was the giant figure of a man. He knuckled his eyes. 'Is it my imagination, or is that who I think it is?'

'It's Sam all right. The cold air on the ground's acting as a magnifying lens.'

'How far off is he?'

'Further than it looks. At least a mile.'

The vehicles were now close enough to see their crews with the naked eye. 'Well,' Cope said, 'he may as well be a mirage for all the help he can give us.'

A sound like arcing electricity crackled above them and a tongue of flame licked from one of the vehicles. It veered violently to a halt and three figures spilled out and disappeared. Seconds later, the other vehicle took a hit and boiled up spectacularly. This time, nobody emerged.

'Well, I'll be darned!' Cope said. He was back on his feet, dragging Tom upright. 'Run like shit!'

They jinked jack-rabbit fashion towards the apparition on the fog screen. It seemed to retreat as they approached, getting smaller and smaller until suddenly it was man-sized and solid.

'Don't lift off,' Pilkinghorn ordered, not raising his eyes from the sights. 'The rangers are still after you. Follow the tracks.'

'How much further?' Cope gasped.

'Far enough for Genesis to get a plane in the air.'

Far enough became further than any distance Cope had run in his life. His heart was at bursting point when the fence appeared out of the mist. They scrambled under and ran on, Cope harrying Tom ahead of him. Behind them came steady concussions. Out of the mist jumped an all-terrain vehicle in winter camouflage. From behind it stepped a man with a face like an Easter Island statue. He opened a door and waiting hands pulled Cope and Tom through.

The firing at their backs stopped. A minute later, Pilkinghorn dived in.

'Okay, Bobo, when you're ready.'

44

If it had been a normal day, Zygote could still have caught them. But this was the day before the Argo launch, and an estimated two million people were pouring into northern Nevada, converging on the Black Rock Desert to join the seven million spectators already gathered around the site.

Maybe Zygote had set up road blocks, but the Vags weren't following the highways. Nor was anyone else. Most of the old routes had been drowned by years of heavy rains that had turned the playa flats into a vast frozen lake.

'Not a stoplight between here and Hawthorne,' Pilkinghorn said.

For the first few miles, they had the lake to themselves and he maintained vigilance. At a signal from him, Bobo altered course to avoid a distant speck trembling in frost shimmers. He changed tack again as another mirage appeared, miles away. Then it became impossible to avoid traffic. It gathered from all directions – a scattered swarm that steadily grew denser until within a few miles, the lake was clogged to the horizons with cars and coaches, all heading south.

At dusk Bobo pulled in at a motel where Pilkinghorn was known. The Vags were too exhausted to celebrate their escape, too wasted even to eat. When Cope saw the waiting bed, he took three faltering steps, fell face-down on the covers and went sling-shotting into darkness.

Waking past midnight, he was still in the same position and had difficulty remembering where he was. He rolled upright with a groan and set off for the shower, peeling off his clothes as he went. He spent half an hour sluicing away the days of accumulated grime.

He returned naked and stopped in the door. Danielle was sitting back against the pillows, her breasts luminous in the soft lamplight.

He slid in beside her. He put his arm around her and that was about the only move he felt capable of.

'It's real sweet of you, Danielle, but I'm whipped.'

She settled into the crook of his shoulder. 'I just wanted to be close. I might not see you after tomorrow.'

He shut his eyes, but couldn't relax with that warm, yielding pressure against his back. His skin seemed to have grown three times as many nerve endings as normal. His prick began to swell. He cleared his throat and shifted slightly.

Danielle, as alert as a cat, piloted her tongue down his neck. 'Changed your mind?'

'Ain't so sure as I was a few minutes ago.'

She slid over him, her breasts suspended above his face. His lips closed on one rosy nipple. She raised herself up on her arms, looked down into his eyes with bruised intensity, and very slowly began to move.

When the flash bulbs popped behind his eyes, it wasn't Danielle's face he saw. Nor was it her name that rose trembling to his lips. Afterwards, he mouthed it silently, chasing the echo through the empty rooms of his mind. He saw a wood, a woman

336

running through it naked, eyes watching from among the trees. He gave a start and was wide awake. There were doors in there he was scared to open.

Easing out from under Danielle's arm, he crossed to the window. Deep in the night, traffic was still moving, thousands of tail lights drifting towards a brilliant spire of light. He was looking at the Argo launch site, the rocket itself crouched below the curve of the earth.

Danielle stirred in her sleep. Looking at her shape in the dark, Cope suddenly felt profoundly lonely. For the first time, the implications of what Zygote had done to him sank home. It wasn't the fact that he had no friends or home to go to. It was what Mhairi had said about being too old for him. She'd said it jokingly, but there'd been a warning, too – the implication that he was different from everyone else.

He picked up his discarded clothes, put the helmet on charge, and went back to staring at the pyramid of light until sleep overtook him.

Daylight assaulted his eyes. Danielle had left. He stumbled to the window and saw shreds of denim blue among the mother-of-pearl clouds. Down on the lake the armada of sightseers kept coming. He surfed the TV. Argo filled every channel.

Launch minus seven hours and counting.

Gone midday. He'd come close to missing the blast-off.

As he was throwing on his clothes, he caught an item about Sun Dog. He was watching it when Mhairi came in with a tray, her skin aglow, her hair brushed and shining.

'Sleep well?' she asked.

'Patchy. *You* look like you had a relaxing night.'

Her eyes dropped and her mouth twitched in a secret smile. She set down the tray. 'Everyone else has eaten. We've been discussing plans. Sam's going to help the Vags with ID and work until they find their feet. That's what I want to talk to you about.'

She sat down on the foot of the bed. 'Sam's asked me to go to

337

Ecuador with him.' She blushed slightly. 'I've agreed. We're leaving the day after tomorrow. All a bit sudden, but it's not safe for me to stay in this country. Nor for you. I want you to come with us.'

Cope knew without a moment's thought that he couldn't accept. 'That's real kind of you. Let's talk about it after we've seen Argo on its way. Can't miss the greatest event of the century.'

Mhairi winced. 'Is that wise? Zygote will still be looking for you.'

'With nine million people around the site, it's the safest place to be. In any case, the roads are so jammed, we wouldn't make it back to California today.'

Mhairi began to rise. 'I'll speak to Sam.'

'I don't need his permission.' Cope told her. 'I'm going.'

Mhairi flopped back. 'Not to Mustang. Zygote knows about . . . your obsession. That's where they'll concentrate their search.'

'I heard that Sun Dog's rigged up a video screen and is preaching to the crowd.' Cope knelt in front of Mhairi. 'I know you think he's just a figment of my imagination, but if he ain't . . . Maybe if I see him, the missing bits will come back.'

Mhairi's gaze cast about desperately. 'I don't know, John. I'm scared you'll do something silly.'

Cope waited until she was forced to meet his eye. 'You don't want me to remember.'

'Of course I do, but Sun Dog's not going to help.'

'I can see it in the way you look at me. Sam, too. You know something you don't want me to find out.'

Mhairi jumped up. 'That's not true.'

'Then answer me this.'

She stopped, her back braced.

'Who's Margot?'

She remained as rigid as a stone. 'I don't know any Margot.' She smiled unhappily. 'John, we agreed that your past doesn't matter.'

'That was up there. That was in limbo. I'm back in the real

world now, and if I don't catch up on my life, sooner or later it's gonna catch up on *me*.'

Twenty five miles from the launch site, Argo's upper section was a glacial white monument brooding in clouds of gas. By this time the Vags were trapped in a tide of traffic so sluggish that it took two hours of stop-go driving to get within a mile of Mustang.

The ghost town was on an outlying extension of the Granite Range. Silver miners had struck it rich here in the 1870s, but most of the metal was on the surface, and within five years the prospectors had pulled out, leaving the town to rattlesnakes and coyotes. Now, only half a dozen buildings remained.

Argo was still seventeen miles away, but Cope could watch the countdown preparations in close-up, courtesy of giant screens that duplicated images of the rocket all the way to the horizon.

He climbed out into a scene pitched between a fundamentalist rally, a county fair and the world's biggest car boot sale. Many of the spectators had dressed up in party best – ballgowns and tuxes beneath furs. Some were in fancy dress themed to the Argo mission, with a lot of imaginative attempts to emulate the flora and fauna of Virginia Nova. Others had come as skeletons, grim reapers, pale horsemen. Barbecue fumes hazed the air. Fast food vendors and souvenir hawkers were doing brisk business. Even if this was the day of judgement, people still had to eat.

Cope stepped up on the sill of the car and swept the view with his binoculars. Gauzy blue lights marked the military barricade around Mustang. In the shadowy island where the settlement lay, a gaunt, shadowy face jerked on a glowing screen.

Mhairi was looking on anxiously. 'Do you recognise him?'

Cope shook his head. He needed to get closer.

Launch minus two hours and twenty minutes.

The crowd stirred as if a wind had passed across them. From Argo's base, a tiny capsule had begun to ascend the service tower. Up and up it crawled like a bead of mercury until, at a height of more than two thousand feet, it stopped.

Three tiny figures in silver suits emerged into the floodlit glare and walked with clumsy deliberation across a fifty-yard bridge to the command module that would be their home for the next sixty years. Before they climbed in, they turned, looked down on the sea of lights and raised their hands.

Nine million people waved back and leaned on their car horns. Many of them had tears streaming down their faces.

Mhairi took Cope's arm. Her eyes were misty.

'Remember they're only robots,' he told her.

'I was thinking that could have been you.'

'Personally, I think I'd make a pretty good astronaut.'

She squeezed tight. 'You would, too.'

He returned his attention to the launch. Clouds of vapour spewed from the fuel tanks of the first-stage rockets and second-stage booster. He'd absorbed the technical details during his TV-watching stints at Wellspring. Each first-stage rocket produced more than ten million pounds of thrust. That was firecracker stuff compared to the stored energy of the final-stage anti-matter rocket. But for safety's sake, the designers had decided to use no-frills cryogenic propellants to shove Argo out of the planet's gravitational field. Only when the ship had broken its bonds with Earth would the anti-matter rocket light up to carry it the billions of miles to Virginia Nova.

Cope checked on Mhairi. She was engrossed, and it was the act of a moment to step back into the crowd.

He headed for the blue lights. The crowd thinned as he approached them. Through the hubbub, he heard Sun Dog's voice – snatched phrases about plagues and firestorms and cosmic signals. Then:

He is coming, my friends. He is close. Perhaps he's out there at this very moment. But I tell you this. At the appointed time, he will make himself known. I want you to close your eyes now and focus on him.

Sections of the nearby crowd jeered.

Cope raised his binoculars and steadied them on Sun Dog's

face. It was thin and harrowed, the expression that of a man who'd organised a huge party and was worried the main guest wasn't going to turn up. Cope felt a stirring in his chest. 'I seen you before,' he murmured.

He carried on. The crowd petered out and he found himself facing the military cordon across a fifty-yard gap. Mustang lay another half mile behind it, across dead ground, surrounded by a high fence. The security line appeared impregnable – tanks and armoured wagons drawn up in close formation, the gaps blocked by soldiers.

Except for a space about two hundred yards to the left. An APC came out of it and cruised down the corridor, scanners whizzing.

Cope sized things up, then made his way back.

Mhairi fell on him. 'Where the hell have you been?'

'Where do you think?'

She stepped back and swallowed. 'Do you recognise him?'

'Nah. You're right. He's just a crazy.'

Her relief was palpable. 'I was sick with worry. Promise you won't try anything like that again. Zygote will have circulated your description. All it would take is for one trooper to recognise you.'

'I didn't come this far to get sent back to Wellspring.'

She shook her head, deeply mistrustful, but it wasn't long before her attention was drawn back to the countdown.

At launch minus two minutes and thirty seconds, the access bridge swung away. The three astronauts lay strapped inside the command module. Swarms of heliplanes criss-crossed the sky on cones of light.

Launch minus sixty seconds.

The car horns and chanting fell away. In the immense silence, Sun Dog's voice continued quacking.

Nine, eight, seven, six . . .

The crowd was rapt, lips moving in unison. Cope felt remote from them. He looked at Mhairi, thinking how much he'd miss her. He looked at Danielle. Another fond memory.

. . . Ignition!

On dozens of screens, flame and smoke boiled out from the launch pad. Almost simultaneously, a flash erupted on the horizon and huge shadows leapt. For long suspended seconds, while the jets built up to maximum thrust, Argo remained earthbound in a boiling sea of golden-white fire.

Lift-off!

Hoses and clamps fell away. Released from their grip, Argo began to climb the tower. It rose so uncertainly, so agonisingly slowly, that people moaned in dread that when it struggled free it would simply topple over – a damp squib stuffed with enough energy to blow them all to kingdom come. Some of the spectators punched the air, willing the rocket on in its battle with gravity. Others stooped and cocked their elbows in pathetic defence against the anticipated fireball. A little girl close to Cope put her hands over her ears and shut her eyes very tight.

Argo, you're clear.

Up into the night rose a fiery yellow column, ascending in uncanny silence.

Cope slipped his coat off and took his helmet from the car. The little girl frowned at his strange suit and tugged her father's arm. Cope put a finger to his mouth, winked, and backed into the crowd.

Looking good, Argo.

45

Somehow, Mhairi sensed Cope's presence withdraw. Her eyes found him as he was about to disappear, but her shout was meaningless in the cacophony of car horns and firecrackers and waves of cheering. He raised a hand and mouthed an apology, then he was gone.

'John!' she yelled, plunging after him.

She fought her way through the crowd. Everyone's face was tilted back, eyes fixed on the soaring plume of flame. On the screens, the astronauts lay pinned in their couches by massive gravitational force.

Argo, your trajectory and guidance are Go.

All Mhairi had for guidance was Sun Dog's face on the screen. That's where John would be headed. She ploughed on, shoving spectators out of her path.

A hand seized her. Pilkinghorn dragged her round, shouting to make himself heard. 'You'll never find him. He could be anywhere.'

'He's trying to get into Mustang. I know he is.'

'He doesn't have a chance.'

'That's why we have to stop him. Now let go!'

'Mhairi, if they catch him, they'll throw a net round this whole area. We've got to leave. Now!'

'Not without John.'

Pilkinghorn shook her. 'What is it between you two?'

'Don't be so childish. We're wasting time. Help me find him.'

One minute and thirty-eight seconds after Ignition, Argo's sonic boom swept past with a roar that doubled the crowd over.

Mhairi struggled on as if she was fighting through a dream. Some people were already beginning to leave, hoping to beat the rush home and simply adding to the chaos. At last she burst out into the corridor between the crowd and the military cordon. It stretched for miles. She looked around wildly.

'John!' she shouted. 'John!'

Pilkinghorn pulled her back. 'Not so loud.'

Troopers opposite had tensed and were fingering their weapons. A searchlight blinded her.

'Stand away there.'

Mhairi searched frantically up and down the line. She turned circles on herself and folded over with her hands on her knees. 'Where is he?' she screamed.

Unseen by her, Argo's tail of fire fanned out as the rocket entered the rarefied upper atmosphere.

'We've got to get back,' Pilkinghorn told her. 'If the others come looking for us, we'll end up scattered across the lake.'

'I *know* he's here. He's got to be.'

'Mhairi, our boat leaves in two days. Please give this up. Please!'

'Not until I know what's happened to him.'

Pilkinghorn grabbed her. 'No, I'm not going to risk losing you again.'

She shook him away and went still, staring at Sun Dog's face.

'John's inside.'

'That's impossible. A mouse couldn't sneak through that cordon.'

Mhairi laughed manically. 'You don't know John.'

Pilkinghorn dragged his hand across his mouth, stifling a curse. The rumble of Argo's rockets was growing fainter. Across the lake, millions of people were partying. Fireworks screeched and gyrated.

Ten seconds to final stage, Argo.

The rocket had punched through the ice shield and was transmitting pictures of the Earth's curvature – a blinding white arc against a deep black backdrop.

Sections of the crowd had begun to taunt the cult members. 'We want apocalypse. When do we want it? We want it now!'

Mhairi's concentration was riveted on Sun Dog. She saw him break off in mid-sentence and turn aside with a frown. He stooped almost out of camera shot, then straightened and stared into the night, his brows knitted.

Abruptly, the screen emptied.

'Something's happening,' Mhairi said, blindly feeling for Pilkinghorn.

'Damn right. The troops are taking up new positions. For the last time, let's get the hell out of here.'

Nearly two hundred miles above Earth, Argo's anti-matter rocket kicked in with a splash of energy that was absorbed by the ice shield.

That went like clockwork, Argo. Next stop Virginia Nova. Stay in touch.

Will do. Thanks for the send-off.

*

Nobody inside Mustang had seen Cope approach. Like the soldiers, Sun Dog's disciples only had eyes for the rocket, and he was halfway up the fence before someone spotted his fuzzy outline and raised the alarm. As he reached the top, he saw a movement of armed men pushing towards him. One of them raised a gun and he jumped, winding himself. Semi-stunned, he lay on his back, blinking into an empty sky.

Next moment, a boot smashed into his side. Another glanced off his cheek. He curled into a ball, soaking up the punishment. Something crushed his right hand and the pain blacked him out.

The assault stopped. Cope slowly uncurled. A black man stood astride him, pinning his throat with a gun.

'Who sent you? What are they planning?'

A bubble of blood popped on Cope's lips. 'I thought I was invited.'

'The hell you are. You're a spy. A Trojan horse.'

Cope could see the man was primed to kill him. 'Tell Sun Dog I'm here. John Cope. Tell him.'

Someone else spoke and pulled the black man off him. Hands grabbed him. As they hauled him upright, something grated in his side and he knew at least one of his ribs was broken. His right hand was a useless throbbing appendage. His captors ran him forwards through a sea of frightened faces. They hurled him through a door and he sprawled in a circle of pointed weapons and rabid paranoia.

While he waited for his fate to be decided, pain caught up with him. Each breath he took was like a knife going into his lungs. His right hand throbbed agonisingly and felt as large as a football.

'Sun Dog says bring him down.'

Cope's captors hoisted him and swung him round. A trap door had opened in the floor. A ladder led into a shaft about twenty feet deep. Cope descended with difficulty, attempting to hold his ribs together with his broken hand. At the bottom, ancient rails vanished into a tunnel to the left. The men led him the other way, to a metal door in a concrete wall. One of them knocked and a young woman opened up. Eyes as hard as pebbles stared out from a face painted with arcane symbols.

'The rest of you stay outside,' a voice said behind her.

The door banged shut behind Cope and bars dropped across it. The siege mentality went all the way to the top. He found himself in a compartment about twenty feet long. The sweet stink of a chemical latrine choked him.

Sun Dog stood beside a video camera, behind a pointed assault rifle. He was a big man but emaciated, jaundiced flesh hanging loose on his bones, his eyes pits of fever or madness. Cope saw empty booze and pill bottles on a rough table. Sun Dog closed to within rifle length and stared as if peering through a pinhole. His body shook in a spasm of passion.

'He's the one.'

The woman sidled in front of Cope with tight-coiled hostility. 'You said his coming would be made manifest. You promised signs and wonders.'

Sun Dog didn't take his eyes off Cope. 'There's no sign more manifest than a man returning from the dead.'

'You know who he is?'

Sun Dog ignored her. His hand reached towards Cope's face and stopped just short. 'You're not a day older.'

'You don't grow old where I've been.'

Sun Dog nodded solemnly. 'I wasn't expecting it to be you.'

Cope drew painful breath. 'It's me you got.'

'But for what purpose? To punish or to save?'

Cope noticed another door on the other side of the chamber. 'To fulfil the prophecy.'

The woman didn't like being left out of things. She thrust herself between them. 'What's going on? Who the hell is he?'

'He's who he says he is. He's John Cope.'

'So what?' she said. 'What makes him so special?'

'John Cope died years ago.' Sun Dog smiled dully. 'You could say I'm the one who killed him.'

'Don't tell *her*,' Cope said. He pointed at the camera. 'Tell them.'

*

My friends. My friends.

Mhairi saw Sun Dog's eyes pan in slow triumph.

He's here. John is here. How do I know he is the one? My friends, I know because this man left our world ten years ago.

'Oh, no,' Mhairi whispered.

Cope appeared beside Sun Dog, his face bruised and bloody. Pilkinghorn scratched his head. 'How the hell did he get in there?'

Mhairi's mood veered between despair and triumph. 'I told you he'd do it.'

'The clever part's getting out.'

Around them, puzzled faces had begun to turn towards the figures on the screen. There was some derisive heckling.

Sun Dog raised his hands.

John Cope. Does that name mean anything to you? John Cope?

The name ran through the crowd amid a shaking of heads.

John Cope died ten years ago, executed for murder. Executed for a murder he didn't commit. How do I know that? My friends, I'll tell you.

A chill closed on Mhairi's heart.

I have not always lived in the light. My friends, my past life was a thing of shame, a pit of vice. Before I found the path, I lived in abomination, a slave to drugs and carnal desires.

An ironic cheer went up from the mockers.

My friends, I was the one who committed the murders for which John Cope was executed. My companions and I slew the Earle family.

'Oh my God,' Mhairi whispered.

John's half-shadowed face showed not a flicker of emotion.

Mhairi's heart swelled with pity. 'I told you he was innocent. All those years in jail. All those years in a coma. And now, when he's free . . .'

But he's forgiven me, forgiven us all. He's come to redeem us, my friends. Come to lead us into the light. Come to carry us into the great Rapture. To a world where there will be no more pain, no more suffering.

Sun Dog's voice broke.

347

Tell us John. Show us the way.

Cope shifted awkwardly under the lens. 'Hi there.' He squinted. 'Can you hear me?' He looked at Sun Dog. 'Can they hear me?'

They can hear you, John. The whole world can hear you.

Cope scratched his jaw and winced. 'Well,' he said. 'Lookit.'

Mhairi smiled because she recognised the body language. It gave her hope. He would say something so down to earth that the crowd would laugh and everybody could go home.

Pilkinghorn seized her and stabbed at the sky beyond Mustang. 'Heliplanes,' he shouted. 'They're going in.'

He got her in a grip she couldn't break and ran her into the crowd. As he hustled her along, she craned back and saw Cope still talking.

Whatever he was saying was drowned by a barrage of stun shells that dropped into Mustang. Flares bloomed, lighting the scene brighter than day. Someone screamed and the panic was swiftly taken up. The first gunshots sent everyone running, the crowd transformed into a mob with only one brain between them.

Pilkinghorn pushed Mhairi down behind a truck as bullets whizzed overhead. The mob surged past and she saw a man go down under trampling feet. An amplified voice told the crowd not to panic.

Heliplanes hovered on lights above the screen where Cope was speaking. He took no notice as ropes unravelled from their bellies and soldiers slid down them.

'Why doesn't he get out?' Mhairi shouted.

'He doesn't know what's happening. He must be underground.'

The first wave of soldiers hit the deck. One of the heliplanes followed them down.

At last word got through to Cope. His head turned and for a moment his eyes seemed to look straight at Mhairi.

He disappeared. Waves of interference looped across the screen, settling into a single flat line that thinned and suddenly broke.

Mhairi was slow to find her wits. In the distance, the party was still going full swing, but around her the lake was nearly deserted. A few figures lay prone on the ice and some were groaning. The shooting from within Mustang had become sporadic. The amplified voice insisted there was nothing, repeat nothing, to be alarmed about. The situation was under control, all hostile positions secured.

'Come away,' Pilkinghorn said. 'There's nothing we can do. He's gone.'

Mhairi was laughing and crying at the same time. 'Where? Where do you think he's gone?'

Pilkinghorn laid her face against his chest and held it there.

In the bunker, the assault registered as a subterranean tremor that set the lamps gently swaying. Sun Dog ignored the disciples pounding outside. His febrile eyes remained locked on Cope.

'It's time,' Cope told him.

Sun Dog's gaze roamed upwards. 'How?'

'Not from down here. We gotta get into the light.'

As the woman glanced at the bolt-hole in the opposite wall, Sun Dog gestured towards the clamour at the other door. 'What about them?'

Cope touched his battered face. 'They're not ready. True disciples would have recognised me.'

The woman watched him with her mean eyes and whispered fiercely in Sun Dog's ear. Turmoil gathered in his face. He turned his head away.

'Doubts?' Cope asked.

Sun Dog appeared embarrassed. 'She's scared it's a set-up. She thinks you might have soldiers waiting.'

Cope smiled. 'What do *you* believe?'

The cloud lifted from Sun Dog's face. 'I believe you're the one. What more proof could I ask for?'

'Then let's get started. The window's open for only a short time.'

Sun Dog took one of the oil lamps and headed for the door.

He realised he was carrying the rifle and shamefacedly made to lay it down. 'Shall I . . . ?'

'Take it if it makes you feel better.'

Sun Dog unlocked the door and stepped through. As the woman began to follow, Cope put his arm across the aperture. 'Not her.'

'But she's . . .'

'You heard her,' Cope said. 'There's no room for doubters. That's the way it is.'

'You mean it's just me?'

'The two of us.'

When the woman realised she was being left behind, she became hysterical, a wildcat. It took all Sun Dog's strength to force her back into the chamber and lock the door on her. Her screams faded into silence. Sun Dog led the way, setting a pace Cope found hard to match. He stooped painfully under sagging roof joists. In places they had to crawl over cave-ins. Cope picked up a rock in his left hand.

They must have walked and crawled half a mile before reaching a fall that choked the passage. Sun Dog scrabbled up it and began to claw at the spoil. He laid his rifle down and attacked the debris with both hands. Cope began to reach for the rifle, then stopped.

Sun Dog rolled aside a boulder and gasped in a draught of cold night air. He wormed through the hole and pulled Cope clear. There was no sign of the launch site and the crowd was a distant murmur. Cope saw lights bobbing on the ridge behind him. They must have come out on the far side of the causeway.

Sun Dog searched all about. 'There's nothing here,' he said in a voice stricken with disappointment.

Cope pointed at the diaphanous folds of light weaving between the clouds. 'What do you think that is?'

'The Rapture. But how are we going to get there?'

'The same way I did.'

'Yes, but . . .' Sun Dog cast a bewildered look around. 'No, I don't understand.'

'You do,' Cope told him, and reached out and touched his arm. 'It's a journey of the soul. That's why you brought this.'

Sun Dog looked down at his gun and licked his lips.

'You don't have to come,' Cope told him. 'Walk away if you want. But I'm leaving now, and I'm not coming back.'

Sun Dog fell against the rock and stared at the sky. 'Tell me what it's like. Is it how I imagined?'

'Better,' Cope answered. 'But you have to see it to believe it – and you have to believe it before you can see it.'

Sun Dog had closed his eyes to listen. He gave a whispered sigh. 'I believe it.'

'I know you do. You've got a whole universe in your head.'

When Sun Dog opened his eyes, there was a faraway look in them. He raised the gun in both hands and held it out apologetically. 'John, will you do it for me?'

Cope shook his head gravely. 'You've got to do it yourself. Faith's the ticket that'll take you all the way.'

'Yes,' Sun Dog murmured. 'Yes,' he said again, louder. Slowly he put the muzzle between his clenched teeth. At Cope's nod of approval, he lifted his enraptured eyes to the heavens and pulled the trigger.

Cope summoned the strength to rise. Clutching his battered body, he set off across the lake and eventually he encountered knots of people. Nobody paid him any attention. Their faces floated past him. He came around the headland and saw images from space flashing on the screens.

Argo was now forty-eight minutes into mission-elapsed time, already so far from Earth that to its crew the planet was a complete sphere, dazzling white, with here and there blue and green windows where the ice shield had melted. Second by second, the planet was shrinking.

The view switched ahead, to a swirling infinity of stars.

So long, world. So long.

Cope lifted a hand and went on walking.

EPILOGUE

On her drive back from the hospital in Esmeraldas, Mhairi slowed to feast her eyes on the chequered greens of the coastal hills and the deep welling blues of the Pacific. After living for so long in a world of monotones, she still had an insatiable hunger for colour and warmth.

By the time she reached home it was late afternoon, the shutters on the seaward side of the bungalow closed against the slanted sun. An unfamiliar car was parked in the yard. She climbed out and stepped cautiously around it. Even after all these years, a strange car or face close to home made her heart beat a little faster.

When she saw the local hire firm sticker, she relaxed. She ran on to the veranda, smiling in anticipation.

'Harry, Julia, I'm home.'

Cool, shadowy silence. Nuria had probably taken the children down to the beach. Mhairi went into their room and groaned, taken aback by the chaos that had accumulated since morning. The television was on, tuned to the Argo channel. The kids never missed the regular round-up of the astronauts' adventures. By now the craft was so deep in space that messages took six months to travel back to Earth.

Mhairi switched off the TV and stooped to collect the scattered toys. Among them were Argo astronaut dolls and comics. Mhairi hadn't told the kids that Duke, Lincoln and Lee were robots. At their age, that would have been like telling them Father Christmas was make-believe.

The irony was that Argo was already obsolete. In three months, Argo 2 would launch off from moon orbit, and because it would travel at nearly one-sixth the speed of light, its crew of three men and three women would arrive on Virginia Nova eight years ahead of the pioneer craft. This time the crew would be

352

flesh and blood, the first acknowledged recipients of Zygote's anti-ageing therapy. As Mhairi had foreseen, the treatment wasn't available to the general public, but there were rumours that certain politicians and Hollywood stars had shelled out fortunes to hold back the clock.

Mhairi saw a photograph lying face down among the clutter. Frowning, she picked it up and turned it over. It was the photo Tom had snapped all those years ago by the lakeside. She clicked her tongue in exasperation. Harry must have taken the picture from the desk in her study.

She went into the bedroom and propped the photo on her dressing table. She studied it as she brushed her hair. In the picture, only Cope's face was clear, smiling distractedly, his attention fixed on something beyond the lens – the caribou.

Though his name hadn't appeared on the list of Mustang casualties, she had long since given him up for dead – one of the hundred or so fatalities of the assault. Public anger at the loss of life had been offset by the discovery that the dead cult leader was in reality Burl Terry, a bad guy who'd spent most of his adult life incarcerated for crimes of rape, pandering and armed robbery.

Mhairi examined her reflection in the mirror. She wore her hair shorter now that silver was replacing the gold and copper. By this time next year, she would have to seriously consider tinting it.

She went outside and the feel of the sun on her face banished thoughts of mortality. She walked down through a grove of pine trees and came out on to the beach. The sky was lemon and turquoise, the sun making its last descent behind a dark raft of clouds. She kicked off her shoes, relishing the sensation of soft warm sand between her toes. Nuria and the children were playing by the water's edge, the kids stick-insect thin against the golden ocean. Harry was four and a half, Julia nearly three, but their temperaments cancelled out the age difference. Julia kicked water over her brother, who squealed and hunched up his bony arms. The sea was far too cold for swimming. Though the veil of diamond dust had melted, it would take centuries for the oceans to warm up again. In the high latitudes the glaciers were still advancing, beginning to coalesce into ice sheets that within five thousand years would grind through Chicago and Edinburgh.

The children spotted her, charged up the beach and flung themselves at her like missiles.

'A man came,' Harry shouted.

Julia lashed out at him. '*I* wanted to tell her. I saw him first.'

Mhairi caught them one in each arm, and swung them up. 'All right, all right.' She waited for Nuria, placidly following in the kids' wake. 'What man?'

The nanny shrugged. 'Didn't tell me his name. He say he is an old friend.'

Mhairi controlled her impatience. Nuria's passive good nature, ideal for coping with fractious toddlers, could be maddening in other circumstances. 'What did he look like?'

A slow smile animated Nuria's face. 'Muy bello.'

'Dark or fair? Brown-eyed, grey-eyed, blue-eyed? Tall, fat, thin?'

Nuria brought the weight of her thought to bear. 'Blue,' she said at last, and put a finger on each side of her eyes, elongating them slightly.

A charge went off in Mhairi's chest. No, she thought. Impossible. 'How old was he?' She almost snapped the question.

'Oh, young,' Nuria said, and sighed. 'Too young for us.'

Mhairi looked towards the house. 'Where is he? Where did he go?'

'There,' Nuria said, pointing to a tiny figure up the beach. 'I tell him you not return for an hour.'

Heart pounding, Mhairi let Harry and Julia slide from her grasp. 'Take the children inside, will you?'

'Ah, mom,' Julia complained.

Harry gave her an evil look. '*I* know who he is.'

Mhairi dropped to her knees. 'Who?'

But Harry wrapped his arms round himself and swivelled away in a sulk.

'I'll be back in time to give you your bath,' Mhairi promised. She set off up the beach, resisting the urge to break into a run.

The man saw her from quarter of a mile off and began to walk towards her. It *couldn't* be him. Closer and closer until, at a distance of ten yards, there was no doubt.

'It really is you. It really is!'

She managed to stop herself saying you haven't changed a bit. It would have sounded so facetious. Besides, it wasn't true. Cope's features may not have changed, but he'd acquired an air of maturity, a poise, which had nothing to do with age.

He in turn made no comment about her appearance. 'Hello, Mhairi,' is all he said before taking her in his arms. For a long minute, neither of them spoke.

Mhairi smiled at the sunset through a prism of tears. 'Why didn't you tell Nuria who you were? Why have you waited so long?'

'I'm not supposed to be here.'

She stepped out of his arms and looked both ways along the darkening beach.

He smiled reassurance. 'No one's after me. I'm on the side of the angels now.' He put his arm through hers and began to walk her back. 'Tell me how you are. How's Sam?'

'We're very well. Very happy.' She laughed and squeezed his arm. 'I'm very happy, thank you.'

'You ever see the rest of the gang?'

'Bobo comes by for a meal every once in a while. He's bought a bar in Esmeraldas. He's a big hit with the children. I keep in touch with Patty. She's a journalist in Phoenix. She and Carl split up a couple of years ago. He's still living in California, and we exchange the occasional e-mail. Tom and Dodie got married and Dale has two sisters.'

Cope grinned. 'You don't say.'

Mhairi found she was prattling. 'I've lost track of Sylvie and Danielle. I believe they settled in French Guiana.'

She thought Danielle's name would raise a nostalgic smile, but Cope didn't react. 'You hear about Grover Byron?'

'His Nobel? Sure. Good luck to him.'

'I meant his accident.'

It wasn't a matter Mhairi liked to think about. 'All I know is that Genghis got out of his enclosure and badly mauled him. Thank God the surgeons were able to save his arm.'

'It was Paige,' Cope said. 'Genghis couldn't have got out of an electronically-locked cage by himself, and computer data ruled out a mistake on the part of the technicians. Paige was the only other employee with access.'

Though there was nothing gloating in Cope's tone, his casual knowingness was unsettling. 'John, I don't want to talk about Grover Byron. I want to hear about *you*. What have you been doing all these years? Why didn't you get in touch?'

'The first bit doesn't take much telling. After I got out of Mustang, I went east, fetched up in Oklahoma. Found steady work, even got serious about a woman. But things didn't work out.'

Mhairi looked at the sand. 'Did you tell her?'

'About what Zygote had done to me?' Cope stopped. 'How could I tell the woman I was thinking of spending my life with that I'd watch her grow old while I stayed the same as the day she met me? That our kids would die of old age before my hair had turned grey?' Cope shook his head. 'I'm a race apart, Mhairi.'

She reached for him. 'Oh, John.'

'Nobody likes to be an outsider. There were times when I even thought of taking things in my own hands. But then . . .' He stared into the sky and began to smile. 'Remember the night we escaped from Wellspring? Yrigoyen telling me what a glorious opportunity I'd missed?'

'He's mad. No wonder the President wiped the floor with him.'

'I know,' Cope said, and smiled crookedly. 'But one night, when I was real low, getting drunk in a bar with some woman fifteen years younger than me, I heard on the TV that NASA was selecting a crew for the Argo 2 mission, and that this time they'd be humans. I thought about the last thing Yrigoyen said to me. If I ever changed my mind . . .'

Mhairi stared at him.

'So I put a call through to him.'

'You're crazy.'

'He was thrilled, welcomed me back like the prodigal son. Of course, the other mission planners weren't enthusiastic about taking a high school drop-out who'd done jail time. But Yrigoyen wielded his clout, and after I'd passed the aptitude tests and physicals, they packed me off to Cal Tech to learn a little rocket science. I graduated last year.'

'You mean . . .'

'That's right. I'm an astronaut. I've crewed on a couple of lunar shuttles, and now I'm counting down to the big one.'

Mhairi looked up at the first evening stars. 'Not you? Not Argo 2?'

Cope laughed. 'There aren't a lot of people with my special qualities, and you did once tell me I'd make a good spaceman.'

'Yes, but locked in a capsule for nearly forty years.'

'Less than a fifth of my life. Anyway, I'm used to confined spaces, and I won't be alone.'

'You'll go mad. You'll fight over women. You'll kill each other.'

'Most of the time we'll be in induced sleep. And when we're not, our every move is monitored and controlled. To be honest, while we're aboard Argo, we'll be little more than robots.'

You, a robot? is what she wanted to say. 'But why? After having been deprived of so much of your life, how can you bear to give up all this to go to some God-forsaken planet halfway across the Milky Way?'

Cope looked around at the hills and ocean. 'Oh, there's a lot I'll miss. This ain't a bad old world. A bit dinged, a bit beat-up, but nothing a decoke and valve job wouldn't fix.'

Mhairi smiled, recognising the voice of the Cope she knew of old.

'Trouble is,' he continued, 'until everyone gets the Zygote treatment, I'll never be able to feel part of it.' He took Mhairi by the shoulders. 'Most important of all, I *want* to go. I want to be the first to the stars.'

She felt numb, sick.

He let go. 'In a month's time, we're leaving for the lunar

357

launch site. There'll be a lot of publicity. I didn't want you to see me climbing into that rocket and think I'd left without saying goodbye.'

It hit her then. She'd given him up for dead twice and now, having found him again, she was losing him for good. When – if – he reached Virginia Nova, she'd be nearly eighty, her children grown up with kids of their own. By the time he came back, her grandchildren would be dust.

'So this is it – the last goodbye.' She couldn't keep bitterness from her voice.

He slipped something into her hand – a carving. 'It's mammoth ivory, one of a pair. Every time you see me holding the other one, I'll be speaking to you. Knowing I'm in touch will mean a lot to me.'

It had got dark without Mhairi being aware of it. Headlights were coming down the hill. Unable to comprehend the enormity of what Cope had told her, she took refuge in the mundane. 'That'll be Sam. You'll stay tonight.'

'I can't, Mhairi. I've got a flight to catch. I have to be back at base by noon tomorrow.'

'Supper then.' She tugged at his arm. 'Come on, John. You can't miss Sam, and the kids are dying to meet you.'